Also by Ray Bradbury

Something Wicked This Way Comes

Ray Bradbury

Simon and Schuster Paperbacks
New York London Toronto Sydney New Delhi

Simon & Schuster Paperbacks
An Imprint of Simon & Schuster, Inc.
1230 Avenue of the Americas
New York, NY 10020

First Simon & Schuster trade paperback edition October 2017

SIMON & SCHUSTER PAPERBACKS and colophon are registered trademarks of Simon & Schuster, Inc.

For information about special discounts for bulk purchases, please contact Simon & Schuster Special Sales at 1-866-506-1949 or business@simonandschuster.com.

The Simon & Schuster Speakers Bureau can bring authors to your live event. For more information or to book an event contact the Simon & Schuster Speakers Bureau at 1-866-248-3049 or visit our website at www.simonspeakers.com.

Interior design by Lewelin Polanco

Manufactured in Italy

15 17 19 20 18 16 14

Library of Congress Cataloging-in-Publication Data is available.

ISBN 978-1-5011-6771-3

Text and image permissions can be found on page 336

With love
to the memory of
GENE KELLY,
whose performances
influenced and
changed my life

contents

Man is in love, and loves what vanishes.

—W. B. YEATS

They sleep not, except they have done mischief;
And their sleep is taken away, unless they cause some to fall.
For they eat the bread of wickedness,
And drink the wine of violence.

—Proverbs 4:16–17

I know not all that may be coming, but be it what it will, I'll
go to it laughing.

—STUBB in *Moby Dick*

SOMETHING WICKED THIS WAY COMES

prologue

First of all, it was October, a rare month for boys. Not that all months aren't rare. But there be bad and good, as the pirates say. Take September, a bad month: school begins. Consider August, a good month: school hasn't begun yet. July, well, July's really fine: there's no chance in the world for school. June, no doubting it, June's best of all, for the school doors spring wide and September's a billion years away.

But you take October, now. School's been on a month and you're riding easier in the reins, jogging along. You got time to think of the garbage you'll dump on old man Prickett's porch, or the hairy-ape costume you'll wear to the YMCA the last night of the month. And if it's around October twentieth and everything smoky-smelling and the sky orange and ash gray at twilight, it seems Halloween will never come in a fall of broomsticks and a soft flap of bed-sheets around corners.

But one strange wild dark long year, Halloween came early.

One year Halloween came on October 24, three hours after midnight.

At that time, James Nightshade of 97 Oak Street was thirteen years, eleven months, twenty-three days old. Next door, William

Halloway was thirteen years, eleven months and twenty-*four* days old. Both touched toward fourteen; it almost trembled in their hands.

And that was the October week when they grew up overnight, and were never so young anymore. . . .

Arrivals

chapter one

The seller of lightning rods arrived just ahead of the storm. He came along the street of Green Town, Illinois, in the late cloudy October day, sneaking glances over his shoulder. Somewhere not so far back, vast lightnings stomped the earth. Somewhere, a storm like a great beast with terrible teeth could not be denied.

So the salesman jangled and clanged his huge leather kit in which oversized puzzles of ironmongery lay unseen but which his tongue conjured from door to door until he came at last to a lawn which was cut all wrong.

No, not the grass. The salesman lifted his gaze. But two boys, far up the gentle slope, lying *on* the grass. Of a like size and general shape, the boys sat carving twig whistles, talking of olden or future times, content with having left their fingerprints on every movable object in Green Town during summer past and their footprints on every open path between here and the lake and there and the river since school began.

"Howdy, boys!" called the man all dressed in storm-colored clothes. "Folks home?"

The boys shook their heads.

"Got any money, yourselves?"

The boys shook their heads.

"Well—" The salesman walked about three feet, stopped and hunched his shoulders. Suddenly he seemed aware of house windows or the cold sky staring at his neck. He turned slowly, sniffing the air. Wind rattled the empty trees. Sunlight, breaking through a small rift in the clouds, minted a last few oak leaves all gold. But the sun vanished, the coins were spent, the air blew gray; the salesman shook himself from the spell.

The salesman edged slowly up the lawn.

"Boy," he said. "What's your name?"

And the first boy, with hair as blond-white as milk thistle, shut up one eye, tilted his head, and looked at the salesman with a single eye as open, bright and clear as a drop of summer rain.

"Will," he said. "William Halloway."

The storm gentleman turned. "And *you?*"

The second boy did not move, but lay stomach down on the autumn grass, debating as if he might make up a name. His hair was wild, thick, and the glossy color of waxed chestnuts. His eyes, fixed to some distant point within himself, were mint rock-crystal green. At last he put a blade of dry grass in his casual mouth.

"Jim Nightshade," he said.

The storm salesman nodded as if he had known it all along.

"Nightshade. That's quite a name."

"And only fitting," said Will Halloway. "I was born one minute *before* midnight, October thirtieth. Jim was born one minute *after* midnight, which makes it October thirty-first."

"Halloween," said Jim.

By their voices, the boys had told the tale all their lives, proud of their mothers, living house next to house, running for the hospital together, bringing sons into the world seconds apart; one light, one dark. There was a history of mutual celebration behind them. Each year Will lit the candles on a single cake at one minute to midnight. Jim, at one minute after, with the last day of the month begun, blew them out.

So much Will said, excitedly. So much Jim agreed to, silently.

So much the salesman, running before the storm, but poised here uncertainly, heard looking from face to face.

"Halloway. Nightshade. No money, you say?"

The man, grieved by his own conscientiousness, rummaged in his leathery bag and seized forth an iron contraption.

"Take this, free! Why? One of those houses will be struck by lightning! Without this rod, bang! Fire and ash, roast pork and cinders! Grab!"

The salesman released the rod. Jim did not move. But Will caught the iron and gasped.

"Boy, it's heavy! And funny-looking. Never seen a lightning rod like this. Look, Jim!"

And Jim, at last, stretched like a cat, and turned his head. His green eyes got big and then very narrow.

The metal thing was hammered and shaped half-crescent, half-cross. Around the rim of the main rod little curlicues and doohingies had been soldered on, later. The entire surface of the rod was finely scratched and etched with strange languages, names that could tie the tongue or break the jaw, numerals that added to incomprehensible sums, pictographs of insect-animals all bristle, chaff, and claw.

"That's Egyptian." Jim pointed his nose at a bug soldered to the iron. "Scarab beetle."

"So it is, boy!"

Jim squinted. "And those there—Phoenician hen tracks."

"Right!"

"Why?" asked Jim.

"Why?" said the man. "Why the Egyptian, Arabic, Abyssinian, Choctaw? Well, what tongue does the wind talk? What nationality is a storm? What country do rains come from? What color is lightning? Where does thunder go when it dies? Boys, you got to be ready in every dialect with every shape and form to hex the St. Elmo's fires, the balls of blue light that prowl the earth like sizzling cats. I got the only lightning rods in the world that hear, feel, know, and sass back any storm, no matter what tongue, voice, or sign. No foreign thunder so loud this rod can't soft-talk it!"

But Will was staring beyond the man now.

"Which," he said. "Which house will it strike?"

"Which? Hold on. Wait." The salesman searched deep in their faces. "Some folks draw lightning, suck it like cats suck babies' breath. Some folks' polarities are negative, some positive. Some glow in the dark. Some snuff out. You now, the two of you . . . I—"

"What makes you so sure lightning will strike anywhere around here?" said Jim suddenly, his eyes bright.

The salesman almost flinched. "Why, I got a nose, an eye, an ear. Both those houses, their timbers! Listen!"

They listened. Maybe their houses leaned under the cool afternoon wind. Maybe not.

"Lightning needs channels, like rivers, to run in. One of those attics is a dry river bottom, itching to let lightning pour through! Tonight!"

"Tonight?" Jim sat up, happily.

"No ordinary storm!" said the salesman. "Tom Fury tells you. Fury, ain't that a fine name for one who sells lightning rods? Did I *take* the name? No! Did the name fire *me* to my occupations? Yes! Grown up, I saw cloudy fires jumping the world, making men hop and hide. Thought: I'll chart hurricanes, map storms, then run ahead shaking my iron cudgels, my miraculous defenders, in my fists! I've shielded and made snug-safe one hundred thousand, count 'em, God-fearing homes. So when I tell you, boys, you're in dire need, listen! Climb that roof, nail this rod high, ground it in the good earth before nightfall!"

"But which house, which!" asked Will.

The salesman reared off, blew his nose in a great kerchief, then walked slowly across the lawn as if approaching a huge time bomb that ticked silently there.

He touched Will's front porch newels, ran his hand over a post, a floorboard, then shut his eyes and leaned against the house to let its bones speak to him.

Then, hesitant, he made his cautious way to Jim's house next door.

Jim stood up to watch.

The salesman put his hand out to touch, to stroke, to quiver his fingertips on the old paint.

"This," he said at last, "is the one."

Jim looked proud.

Without looking back, the salesman said, "Jim Nightshade, this your place?"

"Mine," said Jim.

"I should've known," said the man.

"Hey, what about *me?*" said Will.

The salesman snuffed again at Will's house. "No, no. Oh, a few sparks'll jump on your rainspouts. But the real show's next door here, at the Nightshades'! Well!"

The salesman hurried back across the lawn to seize his huge leather bag.

"I'm on my way. Storm's coming. Don't wait, Jim boy. Otherwise—bamm! You'll be found, your nickels, dimes and Indianheads fused by electroplating. Abe Lincolns melted into Miss Columbias, eagles plucked raw on the backs of quarters, all run to quicksilver in your jeans. More! Any boy hit by lightning, lift his lid and there on his eyeball, pretty as the Lord's Prayer on a pin, find the last scene the boy ever saw! A box-Brownie photo, by God, of that fire climbing down the sky to blow you like a penny whistle, suck your soul back up along the bright stair! Git, boy! Hammer it high or you're dead come dawn!"

And jangling his case full of iron rods, the salesman wheeled about and charged down the walk, blinking wildly at the sky, the roof, the trees, at last closing his eyes, moving, sniffing, muttering. "Yes, bad, here it comes, feel it, way off now, but running fast. . . ."

And the man in the storm-dark clothes was gone, his cloud-colored hat pulled down over his eyes, and the trees rustled and the sky seemed very old suddenly and Jim and Will stood testing the wind to see if they could smell electricity, the lightning rod fallen between them.

"Jim," said Will. "Don't stand there. *Your* house, he said. You going to nail up the rod or ain't you?"

"No," smiled Jim. "Why spoil the fun?"

"Fun! You *crazy?* I'll get the ladder! You the hammer, some nails and wire!"

But Jim did not move. Will broke and ran. He came back with the ladder.

"Jim. Think of your mom. You want *her* burnt?"

Will climbed the side of the house, alone, and looked down. Slowly, Jim moved to the ladder below and started up.

Thunder sounded far off in the cloud-shadowed hills.

The air smelled fresh and raw, on top of Jim Nightshade's roof.

Even Jim admitted that.

chapter two

There's nothing in the living world like books on water cures, deaths-of-a-thousand-slices, or pouring white-hot lava off castle walls on drolls and mountebanks.

So said Jim Nightshade, that's all he read. If it wasn't how to burgle the First National, it was how to build catapults, or shape black bumbershoots into lurking bat costumes for Cabbage Night.

Jim breathed it out all fine.

And Will, he breathed it in.

With the lightning rod nailed to Jim's roof, Will proud, and Jim ashamed of what he considered mutual cowardice, it was late in the day. Supper over, it was time for their weekly jog to the library.

Like all boys, they never walked anywhere, but named a goal and lit for it, scissors and elbows. Nobody won. Nobody wanted to win. It was in their friendship they just wanted to run forever, shadow and shadow. Their hands slapped library door handles together, their chests broke track tapes together, their tennis shoes beat parallel pony tracks over lawns, trimmed bushes, squirreled trees, no one losing, both winning, thus saving their friendship for other times of loss.

So it was on this night that blew warm, then cool, as they let the wind take them downtown at eight o'clock. They felt the wings on their fingers and elbows flying, then, suddenly plunged in new sweeps of air, the clear autumn river flung them headlong where they must go.

Up steps, three, six, nine, twelve! Slap! Their palms hit the library door.

Jim and Will grinned at each other. It was all so good, these blowing quiet October nights and the library waiting inside now with its green-shaded lamps and papyrus dust.

Jim listened. "What's *that?*"

"What, the wind?"

"Like music . . ." Jim squinted at the horizon.

"Don't hear no music."

Jim shook his head. "Gone. Or it wasn't even there. Come on!"

They opened the door and stepped in.

They stopped.

The library deeps lay waiting for them.

Out in the world, not much happened. But here in the special night, a land bricked with paper and leather, anything might happen, always did. Listen! and you heard ten thousand people screaming so high only dogs feathered their ears. A million folk ran toting cannons, sharpening guillotines; Chinese, four abreast, marched on forever. Invisible, silent, yes, but Jim and Will had the gift of ears and noses as well as the gift of tongues. This was a factory of spices from far countries. Here alien deserts slumbered. Up front was the desk where the nice old lady, Miss Watriss, purple-stamped your books, but down off away were Tibet and Antarctica, the Congo. There went Miss Wills, the other librarian, through Outer Mongolia, calmly toting fragments of Peiping and Yokohama and the Celebes. Way down the third book corridor, an oldish man whispered his broom along in the dark, mounding the fallen spices. . . .

Will stared.

It was always a surprise—that old man, his work, his name.

That's Charles William Halloway, thought Will, not grand-father, not far-wandering, ancient uncle, as some might think, but . . . *my father.*

So, looking back down the corridor, was Dad shocked to see he owned a son who visited this separate 20,000-fathoms-deep world? Dad always seemed stunned when Will rose up before him, as if they had met a lifetime ago and one had grown old while the other stayed young, and this fact stood between. . . .

Far off, the old man smiled.

They approached each other, carefully.

"Is that you, Will? Grown an inch since this morning." Charles Halloway shifted his gaze. "Jim? Eyes darker, cheeks paler; you burn yourself at both ends, Jim?"

"Heck," said Jim.

"No such place as Heck. But hell's right here under 'A' for Alighieri."

"Allegory's beyond me," said Jim.

"How stupid of me," Dad laughed. "I mean Dante. Look at this. Pictures by Mister Doré, showing all the aspects. Hell never looked better. Here's souls sunk to their gills in slime. There's someone upside down, wrongside out."

"Boy howdy!" Jim eyed the pages two different ways and thumbed on. "Got any dinosaur pictures?"

Dad shook his head. "That's over in the next aisle." He strolled them around and reached out. "Here we are: *Pterodactyl, Kite of Destruction!* Or what about *Drums of Doom: The Saga of the Thunder Lizards!* Pep you up, Jim?"

"I'm pepped!"

Dad winked at Will. Will winked back. They stood now, a boy with corn-colored hair and a man with moon-white hair, a boy with a summer-apple, a man with a winter-apple face. Dad, Dad, thought Will, why, why, he looks . . . like *me* in a smashed mirror!

And suddenly Will remembered nights rising at two in the morning to go to the bathroom and spying across town to see that one single light in the high library window and know Dad had lingered on late murmuring and reading alone under these green jungle lamps. It made Will sad and funny to see that light, to know the old man—he stopped to change the word—his father, was here in all this shadow.

"Will," said the old man who was also a janitor who happened to be his father, "what about you?"

"Huh?" Will shook himself.

"You need a white-hat or a black-hat book?"

"Hats?" said Will.

"Well, Jim—" they perambulated, Dad running his fingers along the book spines—"he wears the black ten-gallon hats and reads books to fit. Middle name's Moriarty, right, Jim? Any day now he'll move up from Fu Manchu to Machiavelli here—medium-size dark fedora. Or over along to Dr. Faustus—extra large black Stetson. That leaves the white-hat boys to you, Will. Here's Gandhi. Next door is St. Thomas. And on the next level, well . . . Buddha."

"You don't mind," said Will, "I'll settle for *The Mysterious Island*."

"What," asked Jim, scowling, "is all this talk about white and black hats?"

"Why—" Dad handed Jules Verne to Will—"it's just, a long time ago, I had to decide, myself, which color I'd wear."

"So," said Jim, "which *did* you pick?"

Dad looked surprised. Then he laughed, uneasily.

"Since you need to ask, Jim, you make me wonder. Will, tell Mom I'll be home soon. Get out of here, both of you. Miss Watriss!" he called softly to the librarian at the desk. "Dinosaurs and mysterious islands, coming up!"

The door slammed.

Outside, a weather of stars ran clear in an ocean sky.

"Heck." Jim sniffed north, Jim sniffed south. "Where's the storm? That darn salesman promised. I just *got* to watch that lightning fizz down my drainpipes!"

Will let the wind ruffle and refit his clothes, his skin, his hair. Then he said, faintly, "It'll be here. By morning."

"Who says?"

"The huckleberries all down my arms. *They* say."

"Great!"

The wind flew Jim away.

A similar kite, Will swooped to follow.

chapter three

Watching the boys vanish away, Charles Halloway suppressed a sudden urge to run with them, make the pack. He knew what the wind was doing to them, where it was taking them, to all the secret places that were never so secret again in life. Somewhere in him, a shadow turned mournfully over. You had to run with a night like this, so the sadness could not hurt.

Look! he thought. Will runs because running is its own excuse. Jim runs because something's up ahead of him.

Yet, strangely, they *do* run together.

What's the answer, he wondered, walking through the library, putting out the lights, putting out the lights, putting out the lights, is it all in the whorls on our thumbs and fingers? Why are some people all grasshopper fiddlings, scrapings, all antennae shivering, one big ganglion eternally knotting, slip-knotting, square-knotting themselves? They stoke a furnace all their lives, sweat their lips, shine their eyes and start it all in the crib. Caesar's lean and hungry friends. They eat the dark, who only stand and breathe.

That's Jim, all bramblehair and itchweed.

And Will? Why, he's the last peach, high on a summer tree.

Some boys walk by and you cry, seeing them. They feel good, they look good, they are good. Oh, they're not above peeing off a bridge, or stealing an occasional dime-store pencil sharpener; it's not that. It's just, you know, seeing them pass, that's how they'll be all their life; they'll get hit, hurt, cut, bruised, and always wonder why, why does it happen? how can it happen to *them?*

But Jim, now, he knows it happens, he watches for it happening, he sees it start, he sees it finish, he licks the wound he expected, and never asks why: he *knows.* He *always* knew. Someone knew before him, a long time ago, someone who had wolves for pets and lions for night conversants. Hell, Jim doesn't know with his mind. But his body knows. And while Will's putting a bandage on his latest scratch, Jim's ducking, weaving, bouncing away from the knockout blow which must inevitably come.

So there they go, Jim running slower to stay with Will, Will running faster to stay with Jim, Jim breaking two windows in a haunted house because Will's along, Will breaking one window instead of none, because Jim's watching. God, how we get our fingers in each other's clay. That's friendship, each playing the potter to see what shapes we can make of the other.

Jim, Will, he thought, strangers. Go on. I'll catch up, some day. . . .

The library door gasped open, slammed.

Five minutes later, he turned into the corner saloon for his nightly one-and-only drink, in time to hear a man say:

" . . . I read when alcohol was invented, the Italians thought it was the big thing they'd been looking for for centuries. The Elixir of Life! Did you know that?"

"No." The bartender's back was turned.

"Sure," the man went on. "Distilled wine. Ninth, tenth century. Looked like water. But it burnt. I mean, it not only burnt the mouth and stomach, but you could set it on fire. So they thought they'd mixed water and fire. Fire-water, the Elixir Vitae, By God. Maybe they weren't so far wrong thinking it was the Cure-all, the thing that worked miracles. Have a drink!?"

"I don't need it," said Halloway. "But someone inside me does."

"Who?"

The boy I once was, thought Halloway, who runs like the leaves down the sidewalk autumn nights.

But he couldn't say that.

So he drank, eyes shut, listening to hear if that thing inside turned over again, rustling in the deep bons that were stacked for burning but never burned.

chapter four

W ill stopped. Will looked at the Friday night town.

It seemed when the first stroke of nine banged from the big courthouse clock all the lights were on and business humming in the shops. But by the time the last stroke of nine shook everyone's fillings in his teeth, the barbers had yanked off the sheets, powdered the customers, trotted them forth; the druggist's fount had stopped fizzing like a nest of snakes, the insect neons everywhere had ceased buzzing, and the vast glittering acreage of the dime store with its ten billion metal, glass and paper oddments waiting to be fished over, suddenly blacked out. Shades slithered, doors boomed, keys rattled their bones in locks, people fled with hordes of torn newspaper mice nibbling their heels.

Bang! they were gone!

"Boy!" yelled Will. "Folks run like they thought the storm was here!"

"It is!" shouted Jim. "*Us!*"

They stomp-pound-thundered over iron grates, steel trapdoors, past a dozen unlit shops, a dozen half-lit, a dozen dying dark. The city was dead as they rounded the United Cigar Store corner to see a wooden Cherokee glide in darkness, by himself.

"Hey!"

Mr. Tetley, the proprietor, peered over the Indian's shoulder. "Scare you, boys?"

"Naw!"

But Will shivered, feeling cold tidal waves of strange rain moving down the prairie as on a deserted shore. When the lightning nailed the town, he wanted to be layered under sixteen blankets and a pillow.

"Mr. Tetley?" said Will, quietly.

For now there were two wooden Indians upright in ripe tobacco darkness. Mr. Tetley, amidst his jest, had frozen, mouth open, listening.

"Mr. Tetley?"

He heard something far away on the wind, but couldn't say what it was.

The boys backed off.

He did not see them. He did not move. He only listened.

They left him. They ran.

In the fourth empty block from the library, the boys came upon a third wooden Indian.

Mr. Crosetti, in front of his barber shop, his door key in his trembling fingers, did not see them stop.

What had stopped them?

A teardrop.

It moved shining down Mr. Crosetti's left cheek. He breathed heavily.

"Crosetti, you fool! *Something* happens, *nothing* happens, you cry like a baby!"

Mr. Crosetti took a trembling breath, snuffing. "Don't you *smell* it?"

Jim and Will sniffed.

"Licorice!"

"Heck, no. Cotton candy!"

"I haven't smelled that in years," said Mr. Crosetti.

Jim snorted. "It's around."

"Yes, but who notices? When? Now, my nose tells me, breathe! And I'm crying. Why? Because I remember how a long time ago, boys ate that stuff. Why haven't I stopped to think and smell the last thirty years?"

"You're busy, Mr. Crosetti," Will said. "You haven't got time."

"Time, time." Mr. Crosetti wiped his eyes. "Where does that smell come from? There's no place in town sells cotton candy. Only circuses."

"Hey," said Will. "That's right!"

"Well, Crosetti is done crying." The barber blew his nose and turned to lock his shop door. As he did this, Will watched the barber pole whirl its red serpentine up out of nothing, leading his gaze around, rising to vanish into more nothing. On countless noons Will had stood here trying to unravel that ribbon, watch it come, go, end without ending.

Mr. Crosetti put his hand to the light switch under the spinning pole.

"Don't," said Will. Then, murmuring, "Don't turn it off."

Mr. Crosetti looked at the pole, as if freshly aware of its miraculous properties. He nodded, gently, his eyes soft. "Where does it come from, where does it go, eh? Who knows? Not you, not him, not me. Oh, the mysteries, by God. So. We'll leave it on!"

It's good to know, thought Will, it'll be running until dawn, winding up from nothing, winding away to nothing, while we sleep.

"Good night!"

"Good night."

And they left him behind in a wind that very faintly smelled of licorice and cotton candy.

chapter five

Charles Halloway put his hand to the saloon's double swing doors, hesitant, as if the gray hairs on the back of his hand, like antennae, had felt something beyond slide by in the October night. Perhaps great fires burned somewhere and their furnace blasts warned him not to step forth. Or another Ice Age had loomed across the land, its freezing bulk might already have laid waste a billion people in the hour. Perhaps Time itself was draining off down an immense glass, with powdered darkness falling after to bury all.

Or maybe it was only that man in a dark suit, seen through the saloon window, across the street. Great paper rolls under one arm, a brush and bucket in his free hand, the man was whistling a tune, very far away.

It was a tune from another season, one that never ceased making Charles Halloway sad when he heard it. The song was incongruous for October, but immensely moving, overwhelming, no matter what day or what month it was sung:

I heard the bells on Christmas Day
Their old, familiar carols play.
And wild and sweet

Their words repeat
Of peace on earth, good will to men!

Charles Halloway shivered. Suddenly there was the old sense of terrified elation, of wanting to laugh and cry together when he saw the innocents of the earth wandering the snowy streets the day before Christmas among all the tired men and women whose faces were dirty with guilt, unwashed of sin, and smashed like small windows by life that hit without warning, ran, hid, came back and hit again.

Then pealed the bells more loud and deep:
"God is not dead, nor doth He sleep!
The Wrong shall fail,
The Right prevail,
With peace on earth, good will to men!"

The whistling died.

Charles Halloway stepped out. Far up ahead, the man who had whistled the tune was motioning his arms by a telegraph pole, silently working. Now he vanished into the open door of a shop.

Charles Halloway, not knowing why, crossed the street to watch the man pasting up one of the posters inside the unrented and empty store.

Now the man stepped out the door with his brush, his paste bucket, his rolled papers. His eyes, a fierce and lustful shine, fixed on Charles Halloway. Smiling, he gestured an open hand.

Halloway stared.

The palm of that hand was covered with fine black silken hair. It looked like—

The hand clenched, tight. It waved. The man swept around the corner. Charles Halloway, stunned, flushed with sudden summer heat, swayed, then turned to gaze into the empty shop.

Two sawhorses stood parallel to each other under a single spotlight.

Placed over these two sawhorses like a funeral of snow and crystal was a block of ice six feet long. It shone dimly with its own effulgence, and its color was light green-blue. It was a great cool gem resting there in the dark.

On a little white placard at one side near the window the following calligraphic message could be read by lamplight:

Cooger & Dark's Pandemonium Shadow Show—
Fantoccini, Marionette Circus, and Your
Plain Meadow Carnival. Arriving
Immediately! Here on Display, one of
our many attractions:

THE MOST BEAUTIFUL WOMAN IN THE WORLD!

Halloway's eyes leaped to the poster on the inside of the window.

THE MOST BEAUTIFUL WOMAN IN THE WORLD!

And back to the cold long block of ice.

It was such a block of ice as he remembered from traveling magician's shows when he was a boy, when the local ice company contributed a chunk of winter in which, for 12 hours on end, frost maidens lay embedded, on display while people watched and comedies toppled down the raw white screen and coming attractions came and went and at last the pale ladies slid forth all rimed, chipped free by perspiring sorcerers to be led off smiling into the dark behind the curtains.

THE MOST BEAUTIFUL WOMAN IN THE WORLD!

And yet this vast chunk of wintry glass held nothing but frozen river water.

No. Not quite empty.

Halloway felt his heart pound one special time.

Within the huge winter gem was there not a special vacuum? a voluptuous hollow, a prolonged emptiness which undulated from tip to toe of the ice? and wasn't this vacuum, this emptiness waiting to be filled with summer flesh, was it not shaped somewhat like a . . . woman?

Yes.

The ice. And the lovely hollows, the horizontal flow of emptiness within the ice. The lovely nothingness. The exquisite flow of an invisible mermaid daring the ice to capture it.

The ice was cold.

The emptiness within the ice was warm.

He wanted to go away from here.

But Charles Halloway stood in the strange night for a long time looking in at the empty shop and the two sawhorses and the cold waiting arctic coffin set there like a vast Star of India in the dark. . . .

chapter six

Jim Nightshade stopped at the corner of Hickory and Main, breathing easily, his eyes fixed tenderly on the leafy darkness of Hickory Street.

"Will . . . ?"

"No!" Will stopped, surprised at his own violence.

"It's just there. The fifth house. Just *one* minute, Will," Jim pleaded, softly.

"Minute . . . ?" Will glanced down the street.

Which was the street of the Theater.

Until this summer it had been an ordinary street where they stole peaches, plums and apricots, each in its day. But late in August, while they were monkey-climbing for the sourest apples, the "thing" happened which changed the houses, the taste of the fruit, and the very air within the gossiping trees.

"Will! It's waiting. Maybe something's *happening!*" hissed Jim.

Maybe something is. Will swallowed hard, and felt Jim's hand pinch his arm.

For it was no longer the street of the apples or plums or apricots, it was the one house with a window at the side and this window, Jim said, was a stage, with a curtain—the shade, that is—up. And in that room, on that strange stage, were the actors, who spoke mysteries, mouthed wild things, laughed, sighed, murmured so much; so *much* of it was whispers Will did not understand.

"Just one last time, Will."

"You know it won't be last!"

Jim's face was flushed, his cheeks blazing, his eyes green-glass fire. He thought of that night, them picking the apples, Jim suddenly crying softly, "Oh, there!"

And Will, hanging to the limbs of the tree, tight-pressed, terribly excited, staring in at the Theater, that peculiar stage where people, all unknowing, flourished shirts above their heads, let fall clothes to the rug, stood raw and animal-crazy, naked, like shivering horses, hands out to touch each other.

What're they *doing!* thought Will. Why are they laughing? What's wrong with them, what's *wrong!?*

He wished the light would go out.

But he hung tight to the suddenly slippery tree and watched the bright window Theater, heard the laughing, and numb at last let go, slid, fell, lay dazed, then stood in dark gazing up at Jim, who still clung to his high limb. Jim's face, hearth-flushed, cheeks fire-fuzzed, lips parted, stared in. "Jim, Jim, come down!" But Jim did not hear. "Jim!" And when Jim looked down at last he saw Will as a stranger below with some silly request to give off living and come down to earth. So Will ran off, alone, thinking too much, thinking nothing at all, not knowing what to think.

"Will, please . . ."

Will looked at Jim now, with the library books in his hands.

"We been to the library. Ain't that enough?"

Jim shook his head. "Carry these for me."

He handed Will his books and trotted softly off under the hissing whispering trees. Three houses down he called back: "Will? Know what you *are?* A darn old dimwit Episcopal Baptist!"

Then Jim was gone.

Will seized the books tight to his chest. They were wet from his hands.

Don't look back! he thought.

I won't! I won't!

And looking only toward home, he walked that way. Quickly.

chapter seven

Halfway home, Will felt a shadow breathing hard behind him.

"Theater closed?" said Will, not looking back.

Jim walked in silence beside him for a long while and then said, "Nobody home."

"Swell!"

Jim spat. "Darn Baptist preacher, you!"

And around the corner a tumbleweed slithered, a great cotton ball of pale paper which bounced, then clung shivering to Jim's legs.

Will grabbed the paper, laughing, pulled it off, let it fly! He stopped laughing.

The boys, watching the pale throwaway rattle and flit through the trees, were suddenly cold.

"Wait a minute . . ." said Jim, slowly.

All of a sudden they were yelling, running, leaping. "Don't tear it! Careful!"

The paper fluttered like a snare drum in their hands.

"COMING, OCTOBER TWENTY-FOURTH!"

Their lips moved, shadowing the words set in rococo type.

"Cooger and Dark's . . ."

"Carnival!"

"October twenty-fourth! That's tomorrow!"

"It can't be," said Will. "All carnivals stop after Labor Day—"

"Who cares? A thousand and one wonders! See! MEPHIS-TOPHELE, THE LAVA DRINKER! MR. ELECTRICO! THE MONSTER MONTGOLFIER?"

"Balloon," said Will. "A Montgolfier is a balloon."

"MADEMOISELLE TAROT!" read Jim. "THE DANGLING MAN. THE DEMON GUILLOTINE! THE ILLUSTRATED MAN! Hey!"

"That's just an old guy with tattoos."

"No." Jim breathed warm on the paper. "He's *illustrated*. Special. See! Covered with monsters! A menagerie!" Jim's eyes jumped, "SEE! THE SKELETON! Ain't that fine, Will? Not Thin Man, no, but SKELETON! SEE! THE DUST WITCH! What's a Dust Witch, Will?"

"Dirty old Gypsy—"

"No." Jim squinted off, seeing things. "A Gypsy that was born in the Dust, raised in the Dust, and some day winds up *back* in the Dust. Here's more: EGYPTIAN MIRROR MAZE! SEE YOUR-SELF TEN THOUSAND TIMES! SAINT ANTHONY'S TEMPLE OF TEMPTATION!"

"THE MOST BEAUTIFUL—" read Will.

"—WOMAN IN THE WORLD," finished Jim.

They looked at each other.

"*Can* a carnival have the Most Beautiful Woman on Earth in its side show, Will?"

"You ever *seen* carnival ladies, Jim?"

"Grizzly bears. But how come this handbill claims—"

"Oh, shut up!"

"You mad at me, Will?"

"No, it's just—get it!"

The wind had torn the paper from their hands.

The handbill blew over the trees and away in an idiot caper, gone.

"It's not true, anyway," Will gasped. "Carnivals don't come this late in the year. Silly darn-sounding thing. Who'd *go* to it?"

"Me." Jim stood quiet in the dark.

Me, thought Will, seeing the guillotine flash, the Egyptian mirrors unfold accordions of light, and the sulphur-skinned devil-man sipping lava, like gunpowder tea.

"That music . . ." Jim murmured. "Calliope. Must be coming *tonight!*"

"Carnivals come at sunrise."

"Yeah, but what about the licorice and cotton candy we smelled, close?"

And Will thought of the smells and the sounds flowing on the river of wind from beyond the darkening houses, Mr. Tetley listening by his wooden Indian friend, Mr. Crosetti with the single tear shining down his cheek, and the barber pole sliding its red tongue up and around forever out of nowhere and away to eternity.

Will's teeth chattered.

"Let's go home."

"We *are* home!" cried Jim, surprised.

For, not knowing it, they had reached their separate houses and now moved up separate walks.

On his porch, Jim leaned over and called softly.

"Will. You're not mad?"

"Heck, no."

"We won't go by that street, that house, the Theater, again for a month. A *year!* I swear."

"Sure, Jim, sure."

They stood with their hands on the doorknobs of their houses, and Will looked up at Jim's roof where the lightning rod glittered against the cold stars.

The storm was coming. The storm *wasn't* coming.

No matter which, he was glad Jim had that grand contraption up there.

"Night!"

"Night."

Their separate doors slammed.

chapter eight

Will opened the door and shut it again. Quietly, this time.

"That's better," said his mother's voice.

Framed through the hall door Will saw the only theater he cared for now, the familiar stage where sat his father (home already! he and Jim *must* have run the long way round!) holding a book but reading the empty spaces. In a chair by the fire mother knitted and hummed like a tea-kettle.

He wanted to be near and not near them, he saw them close, he saw them far. Suddenly they were awfully small in too large a room in too big a town and much too huge a world. In this unlocked place they seemed at the mercy of anything that might break in from the night.

Including me, Will thought. Including me.

Suddenly he loved them more for their smallness than he ever had when they seemed tall.

His mother's fingers twitched, her mouth counted, the happiest woman he had ever seen. He remembered a greenhouse on a winter day, pushing aside thick jungle leaves to find a creamy pink hothouse rose poised alone in the wilderness. That was mother, smelling like fresh milk, happy, to herself, in this room.

Happy? But how and why? Here, a few feet off, was the janitor, the library man, the stranger, his uniform gone, but his face still the face of a man happier at night alone in the deep marble vaults, whispering his broom in the drafty corridors.

Will watched, wondering why this woman was so happy and this man so sad.

His father stared deep in the fire, one hand relaxed. Half cupped in that hand lay a crumpled paper ball.

Will blinked.

He remembered the wind blowing the pale handbill skittering in the trees. Now the same color paper lay crushed, its rococo type hidden, in his father's fingers.

"Hey!"

Will stepped into the parlor.

Immediately Mom opened a smile that was like lighting a second fire.

Dad, stricken, looked dismayed, as if caught in a criminal act.

Will wanted to say, "Hey, what'd you think of the handbill . . . ?"

But Dad was cramming the handbill deep in the chair upholstery.

And mother was leafing the library books.

"Oh, these are fine, Willy!"

So Will just stood with Cooger and Dark on his tongue and said:

"Boy, the wind really *flew* us home. Streets full of *paper* blowing."

Dad did not flinch at this.

"Anything new, Dad?"

Dad's hand still lay tucked in the side of the chair. He lifted a gray, slightly worried, very tired gaze to his son:

"Stone lion blew off the library steps. Prowling the town now, looking for Christians. Won't find any. Got the only one in captivity here, and she's a good cook."

"Bosh," said Mom.

Walking upstairs, Will heard what he half expected to hear.

A soft fluming sigh as something fresh was tossed on the fire. In his mind, he saw Dad standing at the hearth looking down as the paper crinkled to ash:

"... COOGER ... DARK ... CARNIVAL ... WITCH ... WONDERS ..."

He wanted to go back down and stand with Dad, hands out, to be warmed by the fire.

Instead he went slowly up to shut the door of his room.

Some nights, abed, Will put his ear to the wall to listen, and if his folks talked things that were right, he stayed, and if not right he turned away. If it was about time and passing years or himself or town or just the general inconclusive way God ran the world, he listened warmly, comfortably, secretly, for it was usually Dad talking. He could not often speak with Dad anywhere in the world, inside or out, but this was different. There was a thing in Dad's voice, up, over, down, easy as a hand winging soft in the air like a white bird describing flight patterns, made the ear want to follow and the mind's eye to see.

And the odd thing in Dad's voice was the sound truth makes being said. The sound of truth, in a wild roving land of city or plain country lies, will spell any boy. Many nights Will drowsed this way, his senses like stopped clocks long before that half-singing voice was still. Dad's voice was a midnight school, teaching deep fathom hours, and the subject was life.

So it was this night, Will's eyes shut, head leaned to the cool plaster. At first Dad's voice, a Congo drum, boomed softly, horizons away. Mother's voice, she used her water-bright soprano in the Baptist choir, did not sing, yet sang back replies. Will imagined Dad sprawled talking to the empty ceiling:

"... Will ... makes me feel so *old* ... a man should play baseball with his son. ..."

"Not necessary," said the woman's voice, kindly. "You're a good man."

"—in a bad season. Hell, I was forty when he was *born!* And *you.* Who's your *daughter?* people say. God, when you lie down your thoughts turn to mush. Hell!"

Will heard the shift of weight as Dad sat up in the dark. A match was being struck, a pipe was being smoked. The wind rattled the windows.

" . . . man with posters under his arm . . ."

" . . . carnival . . ." said his mother's voice, " . . . *this* late in the year??"

Will wanted to turn away, but couldn't.

" . . . most beautiful . . . woman . . . in the world," Dad's voice murmured.

Mother laughed softly. "You know I'm not."

No! thought Will, that's from the handbill! Why doesn't Dad *tell!!?*

Because, Will answered himself. Something's going on. Oh, something *is* going on!

Will saw that paper frolicked in the trees, its words THE MOST BEAUTIFUL WOMAN, and fever prickled his cheeks. He thought: Jim, the street of the Theater, the naked people in the stage of that Theater window, crazy as Chinese opera, darn odd crazy as old Chinese opera, judo, jujitsu, Indian puzzles, and now his father's voice, dreaming off, sad, sadder, saddest, much too much to understand. And suddenly he was scared because Dad wouldn't talk about the handbill he had secretly burned. Will gazed out the window. There! Like a milkweed plume! White paper danced in the air.

"No," he whispered, "no carnival's coming *this* late. It can't!" He hid under the covers, switched on his flashlight, opened a book. The first picture he saw was a prehistoric reptile trap-drumming a night sky a million years lost.

Heck, he thought, in the rush I got Jim's book, he's got one of mine.

But it was a pretty fine reptile.

And flying toward sleep, he thought he heard his father, restless, below. The front door shut. His father was going back to work late, for no reason, with brooms, or books, downtown, away . . . away. . . .

And mother asleep, content, not knowing he had gone.

chapter nine

No one else in the world had a name came so well off the tongue.

"Jim Nightshade. That's me."

Jim stood tall and now lay long in bed, strung together by marsh-grass, his bones easy in his flesh, his flesh easy on his bones. The library books lay unopened by his relaxed right hand.

Waiting, his eyes were dark as twilight, with shadows under the eyes from the time, his mother said, he had almost died when he was three and still remembered. His hair was dark autumn chestnut and the veins in his temples and brow and in his neck and ticking in his wrists and on the backs of his slender hands, all these were dark blue. He was marbled with dark, was Jim Nightshade, a boy who talked less and smiled less as the years increased.

The trouble with Jim was he looked at the world and could not look away. And when you never look away all your life, by the time you are thirteen you have done *twenty* years taking in the laundry of the world.

Will Halloway, it was in him young to always look just beyond, over or to one side. So at thirteen he had saved up only six years of staring.

Jim knew every centimeter of his shadow, could have cut it out of tar paper, furled it, and run it up a flagpole—his banner.

Will, he was occasionally surprised to see his shadow following him somewhere, but that was that.

"Jim? You awake?"

"Hi, Mom."

A door opened and now shut. He felt her weight on the bed.

"Why, Jim, your hands are ice. You shouldn't have the window so high. Mind your health."

"Sure."

"Don't say 'sure' that way. You don't know until you've had three children and lost all but one."

"Never going to have any," said Jim.

"You just say that."

"I *know* it. I know everything."

She waited a moment. "What do you know?"

"No use making more people. People die."

His voice was very calm and quiet and almost sad.

"That's everything."

"Almost everything. *You're* here, Jim. If you weren't, I'd given up long ago."

"Mom." A long silence. "Can you remember Dad's face? Do I look like him?"

"The day you go away is the day he leaves forever."

"Who's going away?"

"Why, just lying there, Jim, you run so fast. I never saw anyone move so much, just sleeping. Promise me, Jim. Wherever you go and come back, bring lots of kids. Let them run wild. Let me spoil them, some day."

"I'm never going to own anything can hurt me."

"You going to collect rocks, Jim? No, some day, you've got to be hurt."

"No, I don't."

He looked at her. Her face had been hit a long time ago. The bruises had never gone from around her eyes.

"You'll live and get hurt," she said, in the dark. "But when it's time, tell me. Say goodbye. Otherwise, I might not let you go. Wouldn't that be terrible, to just grab ahold?"

She rose up suddenly and went to put the window down.

"Why do boys want their windows open wide?"

"Warm blood."

"Warm blood." She stood alone. "That's the story of all our sorrows. And don't ask why."

The door shut.

Jim, alone, raised the window, and leaned into the absolutely clear night.

Storm, he thought, you *there?*

Yes.

Feel . . . away to the west . . . a real humdinger, rushing along!

The shadow of the lightning rod lay on the drive below.

He sucked in cold air, gave out a vast exhilaration of heat.

Why, he thought, why don't I climb up, knock that lightning rod loose, throw it away?

And then see what happens?

Yes.

And *then* see what happens!

chapter ten

J ust after midnight.

Shuffling footsteps.

Along the empty street came the lightning-rod salesman, his leather valise swung almost empty in his baseball-mitt hand, his face at ease. He turned a corner and stopped.

Paper-soft white moths tapped at an empty store window, looking in.

And in the window, like a great coffin boat of star-colored glass, beached on two sawhorses lay a chunk of Alaska Snow Company ice chopped to a size great enough to flash in a giant's ring.

And sealed in this ice was the most beautiful woman in the world.

The lightning-rod salesman's smile faded.

In the dreaming coldness of ice like someone fallen and slept in snow avalanches a thousand years, forever young, was this woman.

She was as fair as this morning and fresh as tomorrow's flowers and lovely as any maid when a man shuts up his eyes and traps her, in cameo perfection, on the shell of his eyelids.

The lightning-rod salesman remembered to breathe.

Once, long ago, traveling among the marbles of Rome and Florence, he had seen women like this, kept in stone instead of ice. Once, wandering in the Louvre, he had found women like this, washed in summer color and kept in paint. Once, as a boy, sneaking the cool grottos behind a motion picture theater screen, on his way to a free seat, he had glanced up and there towering and flooding the haunted dark seen a woman's face as he had never seen it since, of such size and beauty built of milk-bone and moon-flesh as to freeze him there alone behind the stage, shadowed by the motion of her lips, the bird-wing flicker of her eyes, the snow-pale-death-shimmering illumination from her cheeks.

So from other years there jumped forth images which flowed and found new substance here within the ice.

What color was her hair? It was blond to whiteness and might take any color, once set free of cold.

How tall was she?

The prism of the ice might well multiply her size or diminish her as you moved this way or that before the empty store, the window, the night-soft rap-tapping ever-fingering, gently probing moths.

Not important.

Far above all—the lightning-rod salesman shivered—he knew the most extraordinary thing.

If by some miracle her eyelids should open within that sapphire and she should look at him, he knew what color her eyes would be.

He knew what color her eyes would be.

If one were to enter this lonely night shop—

If one were to put forth one's hand, the warmth of that hand would ... what?

Melt the ice.

The lightning-rod salesman stood there for a long moment, his eyes quickened shut.

He let his breath out.

It was warm as summer on his teeth.

His hand touched the shop door. It swung open. Cold arctic air blew out around him. He stepped in.

The door shut.

The white snowflake moths tapped at the window.

chapter eleven

Midnight then and the town clocks chiming on toward one and two and then three in the deep morning and the peals of the great clocks shaking dust off old toys in high attics and shedding silver off old mirrors in yet higher attics and stirring up dreams about clocks in all the beds where children slept.

Will heard it.

Muffled away in the prairie lands, the chuffing of an engine, the slow-following dragon-glide of a train.

Will sat up in bed.

Across the way, like a mirror image, Jim sat up, too.

A calliope began to play oh so softly, grieving to itself, a million miles away.

In one single motion, Will leaned from his window, as did Jim. Without a word they gazed over the trembling surf of trees.

Their rooms were high, as boys' rooms should be. From these gaunt windows they could rifle-fire their gaze artillery distances past library, city hall, depot, cow barns, farmlands to empty prairie!

There, on the world's rim, the lovely snail-gleam of the railway tracks ran, flinging wild gesticulations of lemon or cherry-colored semaphore to the stars.

There, on the precipice of earth, a small steam feather uprose like the first of a storm cloud yet to come.

The train itself appeared, link by link, engine, coal-car, and numerous and numbered all-asleep-and-slumbering-dreamfilled cars that followed the firefly-sparked churn, chant, drowsy autumn hearthfire roar. Hellfires flushed the stunned hills. Even at this remote view, one imagined men with buffalo-haunched arms shoveling black meteor falls of coal into the open boilers of the engine.

The engine!

Both boys vanished, came back to lift binoculars.

"The engine!"

"Civil War! No other stack like that since 1900!"

"The rest of the train, *all* of it's old!"

"The flags! The cages! It's the carnival!"

They listened. At first Will thought he heard the air whistling fast in his nostrils. But no—it was the train, and the calliope sighing, weeping, on that train.

"Sounds like church music!"

"Hell. Why would a carnival play church music?"

"Don't say hell," hissed Will.

"Hell." Jim ferociously leaned out. "I've saved up all day. Everyone's asleep so—hell!"

The music drifted by their windows. Goose pimples rose big as boils on Will's arms.

"That *is* church music. Changed."

"For cri-yi, I'm froze, let's go watch them set up!"

"At three A.M.?"

"At three A.M.!"

Jim vanished.

For a moment, Will watched Jim dance around over there, shirt uplifted, pants going on, while off in night country, panting, churning was this funeral train all black plumed cars, licorice-colored cages, and a sooty calliope clamoring, banging three different hymns mixed and lost, maybe not there at all.

"Here goes nothing!"

Jim slid down the drainpipe on his house, toward the sleeping lawns.

"Jim! Wait!"

Will thrashed into his clothes.

"Jim, don't go *alone!*"

And followed after.

chapter twelve

Sometimes you see a kite so high, so wise it almost knows the wind. It travels, then chooses to land in one spot and no other and no matter how you yank, run this way or that, it will simply break its cord, seek its resting place and bring you, blood-mouthed, running.

"Jim! Wait for me!"

So now Jim was the kite, the wild twine cut, and whatever wisdom was his taking him away from Will who could only run, earthbound, after one so high and dark silent and suddenly strange.

"Jim, here I come!"

And running, Will thought, Boy, it's the same old thing. I talk. Jim runs. I tilt stones, Jim grabs the cold junk under the stones and—lickety-split! I climb hills. Jim yells off church steeples. I got a bank account. Jim's got the hair on his head, the yell in his mouth, the shirt on his back and the tennis shoes on his feet. How come I think *he's* richer? Because, Will thought, I sit on a rock in the sun and old Jim, he prickles his arm-hairs by moonlight and dances with hoptoads. I tend cows. Jim tames Gila monsters. Fool! I yell at Jim. Coward! he yells back. And here we—*go!*

And they ran from town, across fields and both froze under a rail bridge with the moon ready beyond the hills and the meadows trembling with a fur of dew.

WHAM!

The carnival train thundered the bridge. The calliope wailed.

"There's no one playing it!" Jim stared up.

"Jim, no jokes!"

"Mother's honor, look!"

Going away, away, the calliope pipes shimmered with star explosions, but no one sat at the high keyboard. The wind, sluicing ice-water air in the pipes, made the music.

The boys ran. The train curved away, gonging its undersea funeral bell, sunk, rusted, green-mossed, tolling, tolling. Then the engine whistle blew a great steam whiff and Will broke out in pearls of ice.

Way late at night Will had heard—how often?—train whistles jetting steam along the rim of sleep, forlorn, alone and far, no matter how near they came. Sometimes he woke to find tears on his cheek, asked why, lay back, listened and thought, Yes! *they* make me cry, going east, going west, the trains so far gone in country deeps they drown in tides of sleep that escape the towns.

Those trains and their grieving sounds were lost forever between stations, not remembering where they had been, not guessing where they might go, exhaling their last pale breaths over the horizon, gone. So it was with all trains, ever.

Yet *this* train's whistle!

The wails of a lifetime were gathered in it from other nights in other slumbering years; the howl of moon-dreamed dogs, the seep of river-cold winds through January porch screens which stopped the blood, a thousand fire sirens weeping, or worse! the outgone shreds of breath, the protests of a billion people dead or dying, not wanting to be dead, their groans, their sighs, burst over the earth!

Tears jumped to Will's eyes. He lurched. He knelt. He pretended to lace one shoe.

But then he saw Jim's hands clap *his* ears, his eyes wet, too. The whistle screamed. Jim screamed against the scream. The whistle shrieked. Will shrieked against the shriek.

Then the billion voices ceased, instantly, as if the train had plunged in a fire storm off the earth.

The train skimmed on softly, slithering, black pennants fluttering, black confetti lost on its own sick-sweet candy wind, down the hill, with the boys pursuing, the air so cold they ate ice cream with each breath.

They climbed a last rise to look down.

"Boy," whispered Jim.

The train had pulled off into Rolfe's moon meadow, so-called because town couples came out to see the moon rise here over a land so wide, so long, it was like an inland sea, filled with grass in spring, or hay in late summer or snow in winter, it was fine walking here along its crisp shore with the moon coming up to tremble in its tides.

Well, the carnival train was crouched there now in the autumn grass on the old rail spur near the woods, and the boys crept and lay down under a bush, waiting.

"It's so quiet," whispered Will.

The train just stood in the middle of the dry autumn field, no one in the locomotive, no one in the tender, no one in any of the cars behind, all black under the moon, and just the small sounds of its metal cooling, ticking on the rails.

"Ssst," said Jim. "I *feel* them *moving* in there."

Will felt the cat fuzz on his body bramble up by the thousands.

"You think they *mind* us watching?"

"Maybe," said Jim, happily.

"Then why the noisy calliope?"

"When I figure that," Jim smiled, "I'll tell you. Look!"

Whisper.

As if exhaling itself straight down from the sky, a vast moss-green balloon touched at the moon.

It hovered two hundred yards above and away, quietly riding the wind.

"The basket under the balloon, someone *in* it!"

But then a tall man stepped down from the train caboose platform like a captain assaying the tidal weathers of this inland sea. All dark suit, shadow-faced, he waded to the center of the meadow, his shirt as black as the gloved hands he now stretched to the sky.

He gestured, once.

And the train came to life.

At first a head lifted in one window, then an arm, then another head like a puppet in a marionette theater. Suddenly two men in black were carrying a dark tent pole out across the hissing grass.

It was the silence that made Will pull back, even as Jim leaned forward, eyes moon-bright.

A carnival should be all growls, roars like timberlands stacked, bundled, rolled and crashed, great explosions of lion dust, men ablaze with working anger, pop bottles jangling, horse buckles shivering, engines and elephants in full stampede through rains of sweat while zebras neighed and trembled like cage trapped in cage.

But this was like old movies, the silent theater haunted with black-and-white ghosts, silvery mouths opening to let moonlight smoke out, gestures made in silence so hushed you could hear the wind fizz the hair on your cheeks.

More shadows rustled from the train, passing the animal cages where darkness prowled with unlit eyes and the calliope stood mute save for the faintest idiot tune the breeze piped wandering up the flues.

The ringmaster stood in the middle of the land. The balloon like a vast moldy green cheese stood fixed to the sky. Then— darkness came.

The last thing Will saw was the balloon swooping down, as clouds covered the moon.

In the night he felt the men rush to unseen tasks. He sensed the balloon, like a great fat spider, fiddling with the lines and poles, rearing a tapestry in the sky.

The clouds arose. The balloon sifted up.

In the meadow stood the skeleton main poles and wires of the main tent, waiting for its canvas skin.

More clouds poured over the white moon. Shadowed, Will shivered. He heard Jim crawling forward, seized his ankle, felt him stiffen.

"Wait!" said Will. "They're bringing out the canvas!"

"No," said Jim. "Oh, no . . ."

For somehow instead, they both knew, the wires high-flung on the poles were catching swift clouds, ripping them free from the wind in streamers which, stitched and sewn by some great monster shadow, made canvas and more canvas as the tent took shape. At last there was the clear-water sound of vast flags blowing.

The motion stopped. The darkness within darkness was still.

Will lay, eyes shut, hearing the beat of great oil-black wings as if a huge, ancient bird had drummed down to live, to breathe, to survive in the night meadow.

The clouds blew away.

The balloon was gone.

The men were gone.

The tents rippled like black rain on their poles.

Suddenly it seemed a long way to town.

Instinctively, Will glanced behind himself.

Nothing but grass and whispers.

Slowly he looked back at the silent, dark, seemingly empty tents.

"I don't like it," he said.

Jim could not tear his eyes away.

"Yeah," he whispered. "Yeah."

Will stood up. Jim lay on the earth.

"Jim!" said Will.

Jim jerked his head as if slapped. He was on his knees, he swayed up. His body turned, but his eyes were fastened to those black flags, the great side-show signs swarming with unguessed wings, horns, and demon smiles.

A bird screamed.

Jim jumped. Jim gasped.

Cloud shadows panicked them over the hills to the edge of town.

From there, the two boys ran alone.

chapter thirteen

The air was cold blowing in through the wide-open library window.

Charles Halloway had stood there for a long time.

Now, he quickened.

Along the street below fled two shadows, two boys above them matching shadow stride for stride. They softly printed the night air with treads.

"Jim!" cried the old man. "Will!"

But not aloud.

The boys went away toward home.

Charles Halloway looked out into the country.

Wandering alone in the library, letting his broom tell him things no one else could hear, he had heard the whistle and the disjointed calliope hymns.

"Three," he now said, half-aloud. "Three in the morning . . ."

In the meadow, the tents, the carnival waited. Waited for someone, anyone to wade along the grassy surf. The great tents filled like bellows. They softly issued forth exhalations of air that smelled like ancient yellow beasts.

But only the moon looked in at the hollow dark, the deep

caverns. Outside, night beasts hung in midgallop on a carousel. Beyond lay fathoms of Mirror Maze which housed a multifold series of empty vanities one wave on another, still, serene, silvered with age, white with time. Any shadow, at the entrance, might stir reverberations the color of fright, unravel deep-buried moons.

If a man stood here would he see himself unfolded away a billion times to eternity? Would a billion images look back, each face and the face after and the face after that old, older, oldest? Would he find himself lost in a fine dust away off deep down there, not fifty but sixty, not sixty but seventy, not seventy but eighty, ninety, ninety-nine years old?

The maze did not ask.

The maze did not tell.

It simply stood and waited like a great arctic floe.

"Three o'clock..."

Charles Halloway was cold. His skin was suddenly a lizard's skin. His stomach filled with blood turned to rust. His mouth tasted of night damps.

Yet he could not turn from the library window.

Far off, something glittered in the meadow.

It was moonlight, flashing on a great glass.

Perhaps the light said something, perhaps it spoke in code.

I'll *go* there, thought Charles Halloway, I *won't* go there.

I *like* it, he thought, I *don't* like it.

A moment later the library door slammed.

Going home, he passed the empty store window.

Inside stood two abandoned sawhorses.

Between lay a pool of water. In the water floated a few shards of ice. In the ice were a few long strands of hair.

Charles Halloway saw but chose not to see. He turned and was gone. The street was soon as empty as the hardware-store window.

Far away, in the meadow, shadows flickered in the Mirror

Maze, as if parts of someone's life, yet unborn, were trapped there, waiting to be lived.

So the maze waited, its cold gaze ready, for so much as a bird to come look, see, and fly away shrieking.

But no bird came.

chapter fourteen

T hree," a voice said.

Will listened, cold but warming, glad to be in with a roof above, floor below, wall and door between too much exposure, too much freedom, too much night.

"Three..."

Dad's voice, home now, moving down the hall, speaking to itself.

"Three..."

Why, thought Will, that's when the train came. Had Dad seen, heard, followed?

No, he *mustn't!* Will hunched himself. Why not? He trembled. What did he fear?

The carnival rushing in like a black stampede of storm waves on the shore out beyond? Of him and Jim and Dad knowing, of the town asleep, not knowing, was *that* it?

Yes. Will buried himself, deep. Yes...

"Three..."

Three in the morning, thought Charles Halloway, seated on the edge of his bed. Why did the train come at that hour?

For, he thought, it's a special hour. Women never wake then, do they? They sleep the sleep of babes and children. But men in middle age? They know that hour well. Oh God, midnight's not bad, you wake and go back to sleep, one or two's not bad, you toss but sleep again. Five or six in the morning, there's hope, for dawn's just under the horizon. But three, now, Christ, three A.M.! Doctors say the body's at low tide then. The soul is out. The blood moves slow. You're the nearest to dead you'll ever be save dying. Sleep is a patch of death, but three in the morn, full wide-eyed staring, is living death! You dream with your eyes open. God, if you had strength to rouse up, you'd slaughter your half-dreams with buckshot! But no, you lie pinned to a deep well-bottom that's burned dry. The moon rolls by to look at you down there, with its idiot face. It's a long way back to sunset, a far way on to dawn, so you summon all the fool things of your life, the stupid lovely things done with people known so very well who are now so very dead—And wasn't it true, had he read it some-where, more people in hospitals die at 3 A.M. than at any other time . . . ?

Stop! he cried silently.

"Charlie?" his wife said in her sleep.

Slowly, he took off the other shoe.

His wife smiled in her sleep.

Why?

She's immortal. She has a son.

Your son, too!

But what father ever really believes it? He carries no burden, he feels no pain. What man, like woman, lies down in darkness and gets up with child? The gentle, smiling ones own the good secret. Oh, what strange wonderful clocks women are. They nest in Time. They make the flesh that holds fast and binds eternity. They live inside the gift, know power, accept, and need not mention it. Why speak of Time when you *are* Time, and shape the universal moments, as they pass, into warmth and action? How men envy and often hate these warm clocks, these wives, who know they will live forever. So what do we do? We men turn terribly mean, because we can't hold to the world or ourselves or anything. We are blind to continuity, all breaks down, falls, melts, stops, rots, or runs away. So, since we cannot shape Time, where does that leave men? Sleepless. Staring.

Three A.M. That's our reward. Three in the morn. The soul's midnight. The tide goes out, the soul ebbs. And a train arrives at an hour of despair. . . . *Why?*

"Charlie . . . ?"

His wife's hand moved to his.

"You . . . *all right* . . . Charlie?"

She drowsed.

He did not answer.

He could not tell her how he was.

chapter fifteen

The sun rose yellow as a lemon.

   The sky was round and blue.

   The birds looped clear water songs in the air.

Will and Jim leaned from their windows.

Nothing had changed.

Except the look in Jim's eyes.

"Last night . . ." said Will. "Did or didn't it happen?"

They both gazed toward the far meadows.

The air was sweet as syrup. They could find no shadows, anywhere, even under trees.

"Six minutes!" cried Jim.

"Five!"

Four minutes later, corn flakes lurching in their stomachs,
they frisked the leaves to a fine red dust going out of town.

With a wild flutter of breath, they raised their eyes from the
earth they had been treading.

And the carnival was there.

"Hey . . ."

For the tents were lemon like the sun, brass like wheat fields
a few weeks ago. Flags and banners bright as blue-birds snapped
above lion-colored canvas. From booths painted cotton-candy

colors, fine Saturday smells of bacon and eggs, hot dogs and pancakes swam the wind. Everywhere ran boys. Everywhere, sleepy fathers followed.

"It's just a plain old carnival," said Will.

"Like heck," said Jim. "We weren't blind last night. Come on!"

They marched one hundred yards straight on and deep into the midway. And the deeper they went, the more obvious it became they would find no night men cat-treading balloon shadow while strange tents plumed like thunder clouds. Instead, close up, the carnival was mildewed rope, moth-eaten canvas, rain-worn, sun-bleached tinsel. The side show paintings, hung like sad albatrosses on their poles, flapped and let fall flakes of ancient paint, shivering and at the same time revealing the unwondrous wonders of a thin man, fat man, needle-head, tattooed man, hula dancer. . . .

They prowled on but found no mysterious midnight spheres of evil gas tied by mysterious Oriental knots to daggers plunged in dark earth, no maniac ticket takers bent on terrible revenges. The calliope by the ticket booth neither screamed deaths nor hummed idiot songs to itself. The train? Pulled off on a spur in the warming grass, it was old, yes, and welded tight with rust, but it looked like a titanic magnet that had collected to itself, from locomotive boneyards across three continents, drive shafts, flywheels, smoke stacks, and hand-me-down second-rate nightmares. It did not cut a black and mortuary silhouette. It asked permission but to lie dead in autumn strewings, so much tired steam and iron gunpowder blowing away.

"Jim! Will!"

Here came Miss Foley, their seventh-grade schoolteacher, along the midway, all smiles.

"Boys," she said, "what's wrong? You look as if you lost something."

"Well," said Will, "last night, did you hear that calliope—"

"Calliope? No—"

"Then why're you out here so early, Miss Foley?" asked Jim.

"I love carnivals," said Miss Foley, a little woman lost somewhere in her gray fifties, beaming around. "I'll buy hot dogs and
you eat while I look for my fool nephew. You *seen* him?"

"Nephew?"

"Robert. Staying with me a few weeks. Father's dead, mother's sick in Wisconsin. I took him in. He ran out here early today.
Said he'd meet me. But you know boys! My, you look glum." She
shoved food at them. "Eat! Cheer up! Rides'll open in ten minutes. Meantime, I think I'll spy through that Mirror Maze and—"

"No," said Will.

"No what?" asked Miss Foley.

"No Mirror Maze." Will swallowed. He stared at fathoms of
reflections. You could never strike bottom there. It was like winter standing tall, waiting to kill you with a glance. "Miss Foley,"
he said at last, and wondered to hear his mouth say it, "don't go
in there."

"Why not?"

Jim peered, fascinated, into Will's face. "Yeah, tell us. Why
not?"

"People get lost," said Will, lamely.

"All the more reason. Robert might be wandering, loose, and
not find his way out if I don't grab his ear—"

"Never can tell—" Will could not take his eyes off the millions of miles of blind glass—"what might be swimming around
in there. . . ."

"Swimming!" Miss Foley laughed. "What a lovely mind you
have, Willy. Well, yes, but I'm an old fish. So . . ."

"Miss Foley!"

Miss Foley waved, poised, took a step, and vanished into the
mirror ocean. They watched as she settled, wandered, sank deep,
deep, and was finally dissolved, gray among silver.

Jim grabbed Will. "What was all *that?*"

"Gosh, Jim, it's the mirrors! They're the only things I don't
like. I mean, they're the only things *like* last night."

"Boy, boy, you been out in the sun," snorted Jim. "That maze there is . . ." His voice trailed off. He sniffed the cold air blowing out as from an ice house between the tall reflections.

"Jim? You were saying?"

But Jim said nothing. After a long time he clapped his hand to the back of his neck. "It really *does!*" he cried, in soft amaze.

"What does?"

"Hair! I read it all my life. In scary stories, it stands on end! Mine's doing it—now!"

"Gosh, Jim. So's mine!"

They stood entranced with the delicious cold bumps on their necks and the suddenly stiffened small hairs quilled up over their scalps.

There was a flourish of light and shadow.

Bumping out through the Mirror Maze they saw two, four, a dozen Miss Foleys.

They didn't know which one was real, so they waved to all of them.

But none of the Miss Foleys saw or waved back. Blind, she walked. Blind, she tacked her nails to cold glass.

"Miss Foley!"

Her eyes, flexed wide as from blasts of photographic powder, were skinned white like a statue's. Deep under the glass, she spoke. She murmured. She whimpered. Now she cried. Now she shouted. Now she yelled. She knocked glass with her head, her elbows, tilted drunken as a light-blind moth, raised her hands in claws. "Oh God! Help!" she wailed. "Help, oh God!"

Jim and Will saw their own faces, pale, their own eyes, wide, in the mirrors as they plunged.

"Miss Foley, here!" Jim cracked his brow.

"*This* way!" But Will found only cold glass.

A hand flew from empty space. An old woman's hand, sinking for the last time. It seized anything to save itself. The anything was Will. She pulled him under.

"Will!"

"Jim! Jim!"

And Jim held him and he held her and pulled her free of the silently rushing mirrors coming in coming in from the desolate seas.

They stepped into sunlight.

Miss Foley, one hand to her bruised cheek, bleated, muttered, then laughed quickly, then gasped, and wiped her eyes.

"Thank you, Will, Jim, oh thank you, I'd of drowned! I mean . . . oh, Will you were *right!* My God, did you *see* her, she's lost, drowned in there, poor girl, oh the poor lost sweet . . . save her, oh, we must *save* her!"

"Miss Foley, boy, you're hurting." Will firmly removed her fists from clenching the flesh of his arm. "There's no one in there."

"I saw her! Please! Look! Save her!"

Will jumped to the maze entrance and stopped. The ticket taker gave him an idle glance of contempt. Will backed away to Miss Foley.

"I swear, no one went in ahead or after you, ma'am. It's my fault, I joked about the water, you must've got mixed up, lost, and scared. . . ."

But if she heard, she went on biting the back of her hand, her voice the voice of someone come out of the sea after no air, a long dread time deep, no hope of life and now set free.

"Gone? She's at the bottom! Poor girl. I knew her. 'I *know* you!' I said when I first saw her a minute ago. I waved, she waved. 'Hello!' I ran!—bang! I fell. *She* fell. A dozen, a thousand of her fell. 'Wait!' I said. Oh, she looked so fine, so lovely, so young. But it scared me. 'What're you doing *here?*' I said. 'Why,' I think she said, '*I'm* real. You're *not!*' she laughed, way under water. She ran off in the maze. We *must* find her! before—"

Miss Foley, Will's arm around her, took a last trembling breath and grew strangely quiet.

Jim was staring deep into those cold mirrors, looking for sharks that could not be seen.

"Miss Foley," he said, "what did *she* look like?"

Miss Foley's voice was pale but calm.

"The fact is . . . she looked like myself, many, many years ago.

"I'll go home now," she said.

"Miss Foley, we'll—"

"No. Stay. I'm just fine. Have fun, boys. Enjoy."

And she walked slowly away, alone, down the midway.

Somewhere a vast animal made water. Ammonia made the wind turn ancient as it passed.

"I'm leaving!" said Will.

"Will," said Jim. "We're staying until sundown, boy, dark sundown, and figure it *all*. You chicken?"

"No," murmured Will. "But . . . anybody want to dive back in that maze?"

Jim gazed fiercely deep into the bottomless sea, where now only the pure light glanced back at itself, held up emptiness upon emptiness beyond emptiness before their eyes.

"Nobody." Jim let his heart beat twice. " . . . I guess."

chapter sixteen

A bad thing happened at sunset.

Jim vanished.

Through noon and after noon, they had screamed up half the rides, knocked over dirty milk-bottles, smashed kewpie-doll winning plates, smelling, listening, looking their way through the autumn crowd trampling the leafy sawdust.

And then quite suddenly Jim was gone.

And Will, not asking anyone but himself, absolutely silent certain-sure, walked steadily through the late crowd as the sky was turning plum colored until he came to the maze and paid his dime and stepped up inside and called softly just one time:

" . . . Jim . . . ?"

And Jim was there, half in, half out of the cold glass tides like someone abandoned on a seashore when a close friend has gone far out, and there is wonder if he will ever come back. Jim stood as if he had not moved so much as an eyelash in five minutes, staring, his mouth half-open, waiting for the next wave to come in and show him more.

"Jim! Get outa there!"

"Will . . ." Jim sighed faintly. "Let me be."

"Like heck!" With one leap, Will grabbed Jim's belt and hauled. Shuffling backward, Jim did not seem to know he was being dragged from the maze, for he kept protesting in awe at some unseen wonder: "Oh, Will, oh, Willy, Will, oh, Willy . . ."

"Jim, you nut, I'm taking you home!"

"What? What? What?"

They were in the cold air. The sky was darker than plums now, with a few clouds burning late sun-fire above. The sun-fire flamed on Jim's feverish cheeks, his open lips, his wide and terribly rich green shining eyes.

"Jim, what'd you see in there? The same as Miss Foley?"

"What, what?"

"I'm gonna bust your nose! Come on!" He hustled, pulled, shoved, half carried this fever, this elation, this unstruggling friend.

"Can't tell you, Will, wouldn't believe, can't tell you, in there, oh, in there, in there . . ."

"Shut up!" Will socked his arm. "Scare heck outa me, just like *she* scared us. Bugs! It's almost suppertime. Folks'll think we're dead and buried!"

They were striding now, slashing the autumn grass with their shoes, beyond the tents in the hay-smelling, leaf-mold fields, Will glaring at town, Jim staring back at the high now-darkening banners as the last of the sun hid under the earth.

"Will, we got to come back. Tonight—"

"Okay, come back alone."

Jim stopped.

"You wouldn't let me come alone. You're always going to be around, aren't you, Will? To protect me?"

"Look who needs protection." Will laughed and then did not laugh again, for Jim was looking at him, the last wild light dying in his mouth and caught in the thin hollows of his nostrils and in his suddenly deep-set eyes.

"You'll always be with me, huh, Will?"

Jim simply breathed warm upon him and his blood stirred with the old, the familiar answers: yes, yes, you know it, yes, yes.

And turning together, they stumbled over a clanking dark mound of leather bag.

chapter seventeen

T hey stood for a long moment over the huge leather bag. Almost secretively, Will kicked it. It made a sound of iron indigestion.

"Why," said Will, "that belongs to the lightning-rod salesman!"

Jim slipped his hand through the leather mouth and hefted forth a metal shaft clustered with chimeras, Chinese dragons all fang, eyeball and moss-green armor, all cross and crescent; every symbol around the world that made men safe, or seemed to, clung here, greaving the boys' hands with odd weight and meaning.

"Storm never came. But he *went*."

"*Where?* And why did he leave his bag?"

They both looked to the carnival where dusk colored the canvas billows. Shadows ran coolly out to engulf them. People in cars honked home in tired commotions. Boys on skeleton bikes whistled dogs after. Soon night would own the midway, while shadows rode the ferris wheel up to cloud the stars.

"People," said Jim, "don't leave their whole life lying around. This is everything that old man owned. Something important—" Jim breathed soft fire—"made him forget. So he just walked off and left this here."

"What? What's so important you forget *everything*?"

"Why—" Jim examined his friend, curiously, twilight in his face—"no one can tell you. You find out yourself. Mysteries and mysteries. Storm salesman. Storm salesman's bag. If we don't look now, we might never know."

"Jim, in ten minutes—"

"Sure! Midway'll be dark. Everyone home for dinner. Just us alone. But won't it feel great? Just *us!* And here we go, back in!"

Passing the Mirror Maze, they saw two armies—a billion Jims, a billion Wills—collide, melt, vanish. And like those armies, so vanished the real army of people.

The boys stood alone among the encampments of dusk thinking of all the boys in town sitting down to warm food in bright rooms.

chapter eighteen

The red-lettered sign said: OUT OF ORDER! KEEP OFF! "Sign's been up all day. I don't believe signs," said Jim.

They peered in at the merry-go-round which lay under a dry rattle and roar of wind-tumbled oak trees. Its horses, goats, antelopes, zebras, speared through their spines with brass javelins, hung contorted as in a death rictus, asking mercy with their fright-colored eyes, seeking revenge with their panic-colored teeth.

"Don't look broke to me."

Jim ambled across the clanking chain, leaped to a turntable surface vast as the moon, among the frantic but forever spelled beasts.

"Jim!"

"Will, this is the only ride we haven't *looked* at. So . . ."

Jim swayed. The lunatic carousel world stirred atilt with his lean bulk. He strolled through brass forests amidst animal rousts. He swung astride a plum-dusk stallion.

"Ho, boy, *git!*"

A man rose from machinery darkness.

"Jim!"

Reaching out from the shadows among the calliope tubes

and moon-skinned drums the man hoisted Jim yelling out on
the air.

"Help, Will, help!"

Will leaped through the animals.

The man smiled easily, welcomed him handily, swung him
high beside Jim. They stared down at bright flame-red hair, bright
flame-blue eyes, and rippling biceps.

"Out of order," said the man. "Can't you read?"

"Put them down," said a gentle voice.

Hung high, Jim and Will glanced over at a second man standing tall beyond the chains.

"Down," he said again.

And they were carried through the brass forest of wild but
uncomplaining brutes and set in the dust.

"We were—" said Will.

"Curious?" This second man was tall as a lamp post. His pale
face, lunar pockmarks denting it, cast light on those who stood
below. His vest was the color of fresh blood. His eyebrows, his
hair, his suit were licorice black, and the sun-yellow gem which
stared from the tie pin thrust in his cravat was the same unblink-
ing shade and bright crystal as his eyes. But in this instant, swiftly,
and with utter clearness, it was the suit which fascinated Will.
For it seemed woven of boar-bramble, clock-spring hair, bristle,
and a sort of ever-trembling, ever-glistening dark hemp. The suit
caught light and stirred like a bed of black tweed-thorns, inter-
minably itching, covering the man's long body with motion so it
seemed he should excruciate, cry out, and tear the clothes free.
Yet here he stood, moon-calm, inhabiting his itchweed suit and
watching Jim's mouth with his yellow eyes. He never looked once
at Will.

"The name is Dark."

He flourished a white calling card. It turned blue.

Whisper. Red.

Whisk. A green man dangled from a tree stamped on the card.

Flit. Shh.

"Dark. And my friend with the red hair there is Mr. Cooger. Of Cooger and Dark's . . ."

Flip-flick-shhh.

Names appeared, disappeared on the white square:

" . . . Combined Shadow Shows . . ."

Tick-wash.

A mushroom-witch stirred moldering herb pots.

" . . . and cross-continental Pandemonium Theater Company . . ."

He handed the card to Jim. It now read:

Our specialty: to examine, oil, polish, and repair Death-Watch Beetles.

Calmly, Jim read it. Calmly, Jim put a fist into his copious and richly treasured pockets, rummaged, and held out his hand.

On his palm lay a dead brown insect.

"Here," Jim said. "Fix *this.*"

Mr. Dark exploded his laugh. "Superb! I will!" He extended his hand. His shirt sleeve pulled up.

Bright purple, black, green and lightning-blue eels, worms, and Latin scrolls slid to view on his wrist.

"Boy!" cried Will. "You must be the Tattooed Man!"

"No." Jim studied the stranger. "The Illustrated Man. There's a difference."

Mr. Dark nodded, pleased. "What's your name, boy?"

Don't tell him! thought Will, and stopped. Why not? he wondered, why?

Jim's lips hardly twitched.

"Simon," he said.

He smiled to show it was a lie.

Mr. Dark smiled to show he knew it.

"Want to see more, 'Simon'?"

Jim would not give him the satisfaction of a nod.

Slowly, with great mouth-working pleasure, Mr. Dark pushed his sleeve high to his elbow.

Jim stared. The arm was like a cobra weaving, bobbing, swaying to strike. Mr. Dark clenched his fist, wriggled his fingers. The muscles danced.

Will wanted to run around and see, but could only watch, thinking Jim, oh, Jim!

For there stood Jim and there was this tall man, each examining the other as if he were a reflection in a shop window late at night. The tall man's brambled suit, shadowed out now to color Jim's cheeks and storm over his wide and drinking eyes with a look of rain instead of the sharp cat-green they always were. Jim stood like a runner who has come a long way, fever in his mouth, hands open to receive any gift. And right now it was a gift of pictures twitched in pantomime, as Mr. Dark made his illustrations jerk cold-skinned over his warm-pulsed wrist as the stars came out above and Jim stared and Will could not see and a long way off the last of the town people went away toward town in their warm cars, and Jim said, faintly, "Gosh . . ." and Mr. Dark rolled down his sleeve.

"Show's over. Suppertime. Carnival's shut up until seven. Everyone out. Come back, 'Simon,' and ride the merry-go-round, when it's fixed. Take this card. Free ride."

Jim stared at the hidden wrist and put the card in his pocket.

"So long!"

Jim ran. Will ran.

Jim whirled, glanced back, leaped, and for the second time in the hour, vanished.

Will looked up into the tree where Jim squirmed on a limb, hidden. He looked back. Mr. Dark and Mr. Cooger were turned away, busy with the merry-go-round.

"Quick, Will!"

"Jim . . . ?"

"They'll *see* you. Jump!"

Will jumped. Jim hauled him up. The great tree shook. A wind roared by in the sky. Jim helped him cling, gasping, among the branches.

"Jim, we don't belong here!"

"Shut up! Look!" whispered Jim.

Somewhere in the carousel machinery there were taps and brass knockings, a faint squeal and whistle of calliope steam.

"What was on his arm, Jim?"

"A picture."

"Yeah, but what kind?"

"It was—" Jim shut his eyes. "It was—a picture of a . . . snake . . . that's it . . . snake." But when he opened his eyes, he would not look at Will.

"Okay, if you don't want to tell me."

"I told you, Will, a snake. I'll get him to show it to you, later, you want that?"

No, thought Will, I don't want that.

He looked down at the billion footprints left in the sawdust on the empty midway and suddenly it was a lot closer to midnight than to noon.

"I'm going home. . . ."

"Sure, Will, go on. Mirror mazes, old teacher-ladies, lost lightning-rod bags, lightning-rod salesmen disappear, snake pictures dancing, unbroken merry-go-rounds, and you want to go home!? Sure, old friend Will, so long."

"I . . ." Will started down the tree, and froze.

"All clear?" cried a voice below.

"Clear!" someone shouted at the far end of the midway.

Mr. Dark moved, not fifty feet away, to a red control box near the merry-go-round ticket booth. He glared in all directions. He glared into the tree.

Will hugged, Jim hugged the limb, tightened into smallness.

"Start up!"

With a pop, a bang, a jangle of reins, a lift and downfall, a rise and descent of brass, the carousel moved.

But, thought Will, it's broke, out of order!

He flicked a glance at Jim, who pointed wildly down.

The merry-go-round was running, yes, but . . .

It was running *backward*.

The small calliope inside the carousel machinery rattle-snapped its nervous-stallion shivering drums, clashed its harvest-moon cymbals, toothed its castanets, and throatily choked and sobbed its reeds, whistles, and baroque flutes.

The music, Will thought, it's backwards, *too*!

Mr. Dark jerked about, glanced up, as if he had heard Will's thought. A wind shook the trees in black tumults. Mr. Dark shrugged and looked away.

The carousel wheeled faster, shrieking, plunging, going roundabout-back!

Now Mr. Cooger, with his flaming red hair and fire-blue eyes, was pacing the midway, making a last check. He stood under their tree. Will could have let spit down on him. Then the calliope gave a particularly violent cry of foul murder which made dogs howl in far countries, and Mr. Cooger, spinning, ran and leaped on the back-whirling universe of animals who, tail first, head last, pursued an endless circling night toward unfound and never to be discovered destinations. Hand-slapping brass poles, he flung himself into a seat where with his bristly red hair, pink face, and incredible sharp blue eyes he sat silent, going back around, back around, the music squealing swift back with him like insucked breath.

The music, thought Will, what is it? And how do I know it's backside first? He hugged the limb, tried to catch the tune, then hum it forward in his head. But the brass bells, the drums, hammered his chest, revved his heart so he felt his pulse reverse, his blood turn back in perverse thrusts through all his flesh, so he was nearly shaken free to fall, so all he did was clutch, hang pale, and drink the sight of the backward-turning machine and Mr. Dark, alert at the controls, on the sidelines.

It was Jim who first noticed the new thing happening, for he kicked Will, once, Will looked over, and Jim nodded frantically at the man in the machine as he came around the next time.

Mr. Cooger's face was melting like pink wax.

His hands were becoming doll's hands.

His bones sank away beneath his clothes; his clothes then shrank down to fit his dwindling frame.

His face flickered going, and each time around he melted more.

Will saw Jim's head shift, circling.

The carousel wheeled, a great back-drifting lunar dream, the horses thrusting, the music in-gasped after, while Mr. Cooger, as simple as shadows, as simple as light, as simple as time, got younger. And younger. And younger.

Each time he wheeled to view he sat alone with his bones, which shaped like warm candles burning away to tender years. He gazed serenely at the fiery constellations, the children-inhabited trees, which went away from him as he removed himself from them and his nose diminished and his sweet wax ears reshaped themselves to small pink roses.

Now no longer forty where he had begun his back-spiraled journey, Mr. Cooger was nineteen.

Around went the reverse parade of horse, pole, music, man become young man, young man fast rendered down to boy....

Mr. Cooger was seventeen, sixteen....

Another and another time around under the sky and trees and Will whispering, Jim counting the times around, around, while the night air warmed to summer heat by friction of sun-metal brass, the passionate backturned flight of beasts, wore the wax doll down and down and washed him clean with still stranger musics until all ceased, all died away to stillness, the calliope shut up its brassworks, the ironmongery machines hissed off, and with a last faint whine like desert sands blown back up Arabian hourglasses, the carousel rocked on seaweed waters and stood still.

The figure seated in the carved white wooden sleigh chair was very small.

Mr. Cooger was twelve years old.

No. Will's mouth shaped the word. No. Jim's did the same.

The small shape stepped down from the silent world, its face in shadow, but its hands, newborn wrinkled pink, held out in raw carnival lamplight.

The strange man-boy shot his gaze up, down, smelling fright somewhere, terror and awe in the vicinity. Will balled himself tight and shut his eyes. He felt the terrible gaze shoot through the leaves like blown needle-darts, pass on. Then, rabbit-running, the small shape lit off down the empty midway.

Jim was first to stir the leaves aside.

Mr. Dark was gone, too, in the evening hush.

It seemed to take Jim forever to fall down to earth. Will fell after and they both stood, clamorous with alarms, shaken by concussions of silent pantomime, blasted by events all the more numbing because they ran off into night and unknown. And it was Jim who spoke from their mutual confusion and trembling as each held to the other's arm, seeing the small shadow rush, luring them across the meadow.

"Oh, Will, I wish we could go home, I wish we could eat. But it's too late, we saw! We got to see more! *Don't* we?"

"Lord," said Will, miserably. "I guess we do."

And they ran together, following they didn't know what on out and away to who could possibly guess where.

chapter nineteen

Out on the highway the last faint water colors of the sun were gone beyond the hills and whatever they were chasing was so far ahead as to be only a swift fleck now shown in lamplight now set free, running, into dark.

"Twenty-eight!" gasped Jim. "Twenty-eight times!"

"The merry-go-round, sure!" Will jerked his head. "Twenty-eight times I counted, it went around back!"

Up ahead, the small shape stopped and looked back.

Jim and Will ducked in by a tree and let it move on.

"It," thought Will. Why do I think "it"? He's a boy, he's a man . . . no . . . *it* is something that has changed, that's what *it* is.

They reached and passed the city limits, and swiftly jogging, Will said, "Jim, there must've been *two* people on that ride, Mr. Cooger *and* this boy and—"

"No. I never took my eyes off him!"

They ran by the barber shop. Will saw but did not see a sign in the window. He read but did not read. He remembered, he forgot. He plunged on.

"Hey! He's turned on Culpepper Street! Quick!"

They rounded a corner.

"He's gone!"

The street lay long and empty in the lamplight.

Leaves blew on the hopscotch-chalked sidewalks.

"Will, Miss Foley lives on this street."

"Sure, fourth house, but—"

Jim strolled, casually whistling, hands in pockets, Will with him. At Miss Foley's house, they glanced up.

In one of the softly lit front windows, someone stood looking out.

A boy, no more and no less than twelve years old.

"Will!" cried Jim, softly. "That boy—"

"Her nephew . . . ?"

"Nephew, heck! Keep your head away. Maybe he can read lips. Walk slow. To the corner and back. You see his face? The eyes, Will! That's one part of people don't change, young, old, six or sixty! Boy's face, sure, but the eyes were the eyes of Mr. Cooger!"

"No!"

"Yes!"

They both stopped to enjoy the swift pound of each other's heart.

"Keep moving." They moved. Jim held Will's arm tight, leading him. "You did see Mr. Cooger's eyes, huh? When he held us up fit to crack our heads together? You did see the boy, just off the ride? He looked right up near me, hid in the tree, and boy! it was like opening the door of a furnace! I'll never forget those eyes! And there they are now, in the window. Turn around. Now, let's walk back easy and nice and slow. . . . We got to warn Miss Foley what's hiding in her house, don't we?"

"Jim, look, you don't give a darn about Miss Foley or what's in her house!"

Jim said nothing. Walking arm in arm with Will he just looked over at his friend and blinked once, let the lids come down over his shiny green eyes and go up.

And again Will had the feeling about Jim that he had always had about an old almost forgotten dog. Some time every year that dog, good for many months, just ran on out into the world and didn't come back for days and finally did limp back all burred and scrawny and odorous of swamps and dumps; he had rolled in the dirty mangers and foul dropping places of the world, simply to turn home with a funny little smile pinned to his muzzle. Dad had named the dog Plato, the wilderness philosopher, for you saw by his eyes there was nothing he didn't know. Returned, the dog would live in innocence again, tread patterns of grace, for months, then vanish, and the whole thing start over. Now, walking here he thought he heard Jim whimper under his breath. He could feel the bristles stiffen all over Jim. He felt Jim's ears flatten, saw him sniff the new dark. Jim smelled smells that no one knew, heard ticks from clocks that told another time. Even his tongue was strange now, moving along his lower, and now his upper lip as they stopped in front of Miss Foley's house again.

The front window was empty.

"Going to walk up and ring the bell," said Jim.

"What, meet him face to face?!"

"My aunt's eyebrows, Will. We got to check, don't we? Shake his paw, stare him in his good eye or some such, and if it *is* him—"

"We don't warn Miss Foley right in front of him, *do* we?"

"We'll phone her, later, dumb. Up we go!"

Will sighed and let himself be walked up the steps wanting but not wanting to know if the boy in this house had Mr. Cooger hid but showing like a firefly between his eyelashes.

Jim rang the bell.

"What if *he* answers?" Will demanded. "Boy, I'm so scared I could sprinkle dust. Jim, why aren't you scared, why?"

Jim examined both of his untrembled hands. "I'll be darned," he gasped. "You're right! I'm *not!*"

The door swung wide.

Miss Foley beamed out at them.

"Jim! Will! How nice."

"Miss Foley," blurted Will. "You *okay?*"

Jim glared at him. Miss Foley laughed.

"Why shouldn't I be?"

Will flushed. "All those darn carnival mirrors—"

"Nonsense, I've forgotten all about it. Well, boys, are you coming in?"

She held the door wide.

Will shuffled a foot and stopped.

Beyond Miss Foley, a beaded curtain hung like a dark blue thunder shower across the parlor entry.

Where the colored rain touched the floor, a pair of dusty small shoes poked out. Just beyond the downpour the evil boy loitered.

Evil? Will blinked. Why evil? Because. "Because" was reason enough. A boy, yes, and evil.

"Robert?" Miss Foley turned, calling through the dark blue always-falling beads of rain. She took Will's hand and gently pulled him inside. "Come meet two of my students."

The rain poured aside. A fresh candy-pink hand broke through, all by itself, as if testing the weather in the hall.

Good grief, thought Will, he'll look me in the eye! see the merry-go-round and himself on it moving back, back. I *know* it's printed on my eyeball like I been struck by lightning!

"Miss Foley!" said Will.

Now a pink face stuck out through the dim frozen necklaces of storm.

"We got to tell you a terrible thing."

Jim struck Will's elbow, hard, to shut him.

Now the body came out through the dark watery flow of beads. The rain shushed behind the small boy.

Miss Foley leaned toward him, expectant. Jim gripped his elbow, fiercely. He stammered, flushed, then spat it out:

"Mr. Crosetti!"

Quite suddenly, clearly, he saw the sign in the barber's window. The sign seen but not seen as they ran by:

CLOSED ON ACCOUNT OF ILLNESS.

"Mr. Crosetti!" he repeated, and added, swiftly, "He's . . . dead!"

"What . . . the barber?"

"The barber?" echoed Jim.

"See this haircut?" Will turned, trembling, his hand to his head. "He did it. And we just walked by there and the sign was up and people told us—"

"What a shame." Miss Foley was reaching out to fetch the strange boy forward. "I'm so sorry. Boys, this is Robert, my nephew from Wisconsin."

Jim stuck out his hand. Robert the Nephew examined it, curiously. "What are you *looking* at?" he asked.

"You look familiar," said Jim.

Jim! Will yelled to himself.

"Like an uncle of mine," said Jim, all sweet and calm.

The nephew flicked his eyes to Will, who looked only at the floor, afraid the boy would see his eyeballs whirl with the remembered carousel. Crazily, he wanted to hum the backward music.

Now, he thought, face him!

He looked up straight at the boy.

And it was wild and crazy and the floor sank away beneath for there was the pink shiny Halloween mask of a small pretty boy's face, but almost as if holes were cut where the eyes of Mr. Cooger shone out, old, old, eyes as bright as sharp blue stars and the light from those stars taking a million years to get here. And through the little nostrils cut in the shiny wax mask, Mr. Cooger's breath went in steam came out ice. And the Valentine candy tongue moved small behind those trim white candy-kernel teeth.

Mr. Cooger, somewhere behind the eye slits, went *blink-click* with his insect-Kodak pupils. The lenses exploded like suns, then burnt chilly and serene again.

He swiveled his glance to Jim. *Blink-click.* He had Jim flexed, focussed, shot, developed, dried, filed away in dark. *Blink-click.*

Yet this was only a boy standing in a hall with two other boys and a woman. . . .

And all the while Jim gazed steadily back, feathers unruffled, taking his own pictures of Robert.

"Have you boys had supper?" asked Miss Foley. "We're just sitting down—"

"We got to go!"

Everyone looked at Will as if amazed he didn't want to stick here forever.

"Jim—" he stammered. "Your mom's home alone—"

"Oh, sure," Jim said, reluctantly.

"I know what." The nephew paused for their attention. When their faces turned, Mr. Cooger inside the nephew went silently *blink-click, blink-click,* listening through the toy ears, watching through the toy-charm eyes, whetting the doll's mouth with a Pekingese tongue. "Join us later for dessert, huh?"

"Dessert?"

"I'm taking Aunt Willa to the carnival." The boy stroked Miss Foley's arm until she laughed nervously.

"Carnival?" cried Will, and lowered his voice. "Miss Foley, you said—"

"I said I was foolish and scared myself," said Miss Foley. "It's Saturday night, the best night for tent shows and showing my nephew the sights."

"Join us?" asked Robert, holding Miss Foley's hand. "Later?"

"Great!" said Jim.

"Jim," said Will. "We been out all day. Your mom's sick."

"I forgot." Jim flashed him a look filled with purest snake poison.

Flick. The nephew made an X-ray of both, showing them, no doubt, as cold bones trembling in warm flesh. He stuck out his hand.

"Tomorrow, then. Meet you by the side shows."

"Swell!" Jim grabbed the small hand.

"So long!" Will jumped out the door, then turned with a last agonized appeal to the teacher.

"Miss Foley . . . ?"

"Yes, Will?"

Don't go with that boy, he thought. Don't go near the shows. Stay home, oh, please! But then he said:

"Mr. Crosetti's dead."

She nodded, touched, waiting for his tears. And while she waited, he dragged Jim outside and the door swung shut on Miss Foley and the pink small face with the lenses in it going *blink-click,* snapshotting two incoherent boys, and them fumbling down the steps in October dark, while the merry-go-round started again in Will's head, rushing while the leaves in the trees above cracked and fried with wind. Aside, Will spluttered, "Jim, you shook hands with him! Mr. Cooger! You're not going to *meet* him!?"

"It's Mr. Cooger, all right. Boy, those eyes. If I met him tonight, we'd solve the whole shooting match. What's eating you, Will?"

"Eating *me!*" At the bottom of the steps now, they tussled in fierce and frantic whispers, glancing up at the empty windows where, now and again, a shadow passed. Will stopped. The music turned in his head. Stunned, he squinched his eyes. "Jim, the music that the calliope played when Mr. Cooger got younger—"

"Yeah?"

"It was the 'Funeral March'! Played *backwards!*"

"*Which* 'Funeral March'?"

"Which! Jim, Chopin only wrote one tune! *The* 'Funeral March'!"

"But why played backward?"

"Mr. Cooger was marching *away* from the grave, not toward it, wasn't he, getting younger, smaller, instead of older and dropping dead?"

"Willy, you're terrific!"

"Sure, but—" Will stiffened. "He's there. The window, again. Wave at him. So long! Now, walk and whistle something. *Not* Chopin, for gosh sakes—"

Jim waved. Will waved. Both whistled, "Oh, Susanna."

The shadow gestured small in the high window.

The boys hurried off down the street.

chapter twenty

Two suppers were waiting in two houses.

One parent yelled at Jim, two parents yelled at Will.

Both were sent hungry upstairs.

It started at seven o'clock. It was done by seven-three.

Doors slammed. Locks clacked.

Clocks ticked.

Will stood by the door. The telephone was locked away outside. And even if he called, Miss Foley wouldn't answer. By now she'd be gone beyond town . . . good grief! Anyway, what could he say? Miss Foley, that nephew's no nephew? That boy's no boy? Wouldn't she laugh? She would. For the nephew was a nephew, the boy was a boy, or seemed such.

He turned to the window. Jim, across the way, stood facing the same dilemma, in his room. Both struggled. It was too early to raise the windows and stage-whisper to each other. Parents below were busy growing crystal-radio peach fuzz in their ears, alert.

The boys threw themselves on their separate beds in their separate houses, probed mattresses for chocolate chunks put away against the lean years, and ate moodily.

Clocks ticked.

Nine. Nine-thirty. Ten.

The knob rattled, softly, as Dad unlocked the door.

Dad! thought Will. Come in! We got to talk!

But Dad chewed his breath in the hall. Only his confusion, his always puzzled, half-bewildered face could be felt beyond the door.

He won't come in, thought Will. Walk around, talk around, back off from a thing, yes. But come sit, listen? When had he, when *would* he, ever?

"Will . . . ?"

Will quickened.

"Will . . ." said Dad, " . . . be careful."

"Careful?" cried mother, coming along the hall. "Is *that* all you're going to say?"

"What else?" Dad was going downstairs now. "He jumps, I creep. How can you get two people together like that? He's too young, I'm too old. God, sometimes I wish we'd never . . ."

The door shut. Dad was walking away on the sidewalk.

Will wanted to fling up the window and call. Suddenly, Dad was so lost in the night. Not me, don't worry about me, Dad, he thought, you, Dad, stay in! It's not safe! Don't go!

But he didn't shout. And when he softly raised the window at last, the street was empty, and he knew it would be just a matter of time before that light went on in the library across town. When rivers flooded, when fire fell from the sky, what a fine place the library was, the many rooms, the books. With luck, no one found you. How could they!—when you were off to Tanganyika in '98, Cairo in 1812, Florence in 1492!?

" . . . careful . . ."

What did Dad mean? Did he smell the panic, had he heard the music, had he prowled near the tents? No. Not Dad ever.

Will tossed a marble over at Jim's window.

Tap. Silence.

He imagined Jim seated alone in the dark, his breath like phosphorus on the air, ticking away to himself.

Tap. Silence.

This wasn't like Jim. Always before, the window slid up, Jim's head popped out, ripe with yells, secret hissings, giggles, riots and rebel charges.

"Jim, I know you're there!"

Tap.

Silence.

Dad's out in the town. Miss Foley's with you-know-who! he thought. Good gosh, Jim, we got to do something! Tonight!

He threw a last small marble.

... tap ...

It fell to the hushed grass below.

Jim did not come to the window.

Tonight, thought Will. He bit his knuckles. He lay back cold straight stiff on his bed.

chapter twenty-one

I n the alley behind the house was a huge old-fashioned pine-
plank boardwalk. It had been there ever since Will remembered, since civilization unthinkingly poured forth the dull
hard unresisting cement sidewalks. His grandfather, a man of
strong sentiment and wild impulse, who let nothing go without
a roar, had flexed his muscles in favor of this vanishing landmark,
and with a dozen handymen had toted a good forty feet of the
walk into the alley where it had lain like the skeleton of some in-
definable monster through the years, baked by sun, lushly rotted
by rains.

The town clock struck ten.

Lying abed, Will realized he had been thinking about Grand-
father's vast gift from another time. He was waiting to hear the
boardwalk speak. In what language? Well . . .

Boys have never been known to go straight up to houses to
ring bells to summon forth friends. They prefer to chunk dirt at
clapboards, hurl acorns down roof shingles, or leave mysterious
notes flapping from kites stranded on attic window sills.

So it was with Jim and Will.

Late nights, if there were gravestones to be leapfrogged
or dead cats to be hurled down sour people's chimneys, one

or the other of the boys would prowl out under the moon and xylophone-dance on that old hollow-echoing musical boardwalk.

Over the years, they had *tuned* the walk, prying up an *A* board and nailing it here, lifting up an *F* board and pounding it back down there until the walk was as near onto being melodious as weather and two entrepreneurs could fashion it.

By the tune treaded out, you could tell the night's venture. If Will heard Jim tromping hard on seven or eight notes of "Way Down Upon the Swanee River," he scrambled out knowing it was moon-trail time on the creek leading to the river caves. If Jim heard Will out leaping about like a scalded airedale on the timbers and the tune remotely suggested "Marching Through Georgia," it meant plums, peaches, or apples were ripe enough to get sick on out beyond town.

So this night Will held his breath waiting for some tune to call him forth.

What kind of tune would Jim play to represent the carnival, Miss Foley, Mr. Cooger, and/or the evil nephew?

Ten-fifteen. Ten-thirty.

No music.

Will did not like Jim sitting in his room thinking *what?* Of the Mirror Maze? What *had* he seen there? And, seeing, what did he plan?

Will stirred, restively.

Especially he did not like to think of Jim with no father between him and the tent shows and all that lay dark in the meadows. And a mother who wanted him around so very much, he just *had* to get away, get out, breathe free night air, know free night waters running toward bigger freer seas.

Jim! he thought. Let's have the music!

And at ten-thirty-five, it came.

He heard, or thought he heard, Jim out in the starlight leaping way up and coming flat down like a spring tomcat on the vast xylophone. And the tune! Was or wasn't it like the funeral dirge played backwards by the old carousel calliope?!!

Will started to raise his window to be sure. But suddenly, Jim's window slid quietly up.

He hadn't been down on the boards! It was just Will's wild wish that made the tune! Will started to whisper, but stopped.

For Jim, without a word, scuttled down the drainpipe.

Jim! Will thought.

Jim, on the lawn, stiffened as if hearing his name.

You're not going without me, Jim?

Jim glanced swiftly up.

If he saw Will, he made no sign.

Jim, Will thought, we're still pals, smell things nobody else smells, hear things no one else hears, got the same blood, run the same way. Now, this first time ever, you're sneaking out! Ditching me!

But the driveway was empty.

A salamander flicking the hedge, there went Jim.

Will was out the window, down the trellis, and over the hedge, before he thought: *I'm* alone. If I lose Jim, it's the first ever I'll be out alone at night, too. And where am I going? Wherever Jim goes.

Lord, let me keep up!

Jim skimmed like a dark owl after a mouse. Will loped like a weaponless hunter after the owl. They sailed their shadows over October lawns.

And when they stopped . . .

There was Miss Foley's house.

chapter twenty-two

Jim glanced back.

Will became a bush behind a bush, a shadow among shadows, with two starlight rounds of glass, his eyes, holding the image of Jim calling up in a whisper toward the second-floor windows.

"Hey there . . . hey . . ."

Good grief, thought Will, he wants to be slit and stuffed with broken Mirror Maze glass.

"Hey!" called Jim, softly. "You . . . !"

A shadow uprose on a dim-lit shade, above. A small shadow. The nephew had brought Miss Foley home, they were in their separate rooms or—Oh Lord, thought Will, I *hope* she's safe home. Maybe, like the lightning-rod salesman, she—

"Hey . . . !"

Jim gazed up with that funny warm look of breathless anticipation he often had nights in summer at the shadow-show window Theater in that house a few streets over. Looking up with love, with devotion, like a cat Jim waited for some special dark mouse to run forth. Crouched, now slowly he seemed to grow taller, as if his bones were pulled by the thing in the window above, which now suddenly vanished.

Will ground his teeth.

He felt the shadow sift down through the house like a cold breath. He could wait no longer. He leaped forth.

"Jim!"

He seized Jim's arm.

"Will, what *you* doing here?!"

"Jim, don't talk to *him!* Get out of here. My gosh, he'll chew and spit out your bones!"

Jim writhed himself free.

"Will, go home! You'll spoil everything!"

"He scares me, Jim, what you *want* from him!? This afternoon . . . in the maze, did you *see* something!!?"

" . . . Yes . . ."

"For gosh sakes, *what!*"

Will grabbed Jim's shirt front, felt his heart bang under the chest bones. "Jim—"

"Let go." Jim was terribly quiet. "If he knows you're here, he won't come out. Willy, if you don't let go, I'll remember when—"

"When *what!*"

"When I'm older, darn it, *older!*"

Jim spat.

As if he was struck by lightning, Will jumped back.

He looked at his empty hands and put one up to wipe the spittle off his cheek.

"Oh, Jim," he mourned.

And he heard the merry-go-round motioning, gliding on black night waters around, around, and Jim on a black stallion riding off and about, circling in tree-shadow and he wanted to cry out, Look! the merry-go-round! you want it to go forward, don't you, Jim? forward instead of back! and you on it, around once and you're fifteen, circling and you're sixteen, three times more and nineteen! music! and you're twenty and off, standing tall! not Jim any more, still thirteen, almost fourteen on the empty midway, with me small, me young, me scared!

Will hauled off and hit Jim, hard, on the nose.

Then he jumped Jim, wrapped him tight, and toppled him rolling down, yelling, in the bushes. He slapped Jim's mouth, stuffed it, mashed it full of fingers to snap and bite at, suffocating the angry grunts and yells.

The front door opened.

Will crushed the air out of Jim, lay heavy on him, fisting his mouth tight.

Something stood on the porch. A tiny shadow scanned the town, searching for but not finding Jim.

But it was just the boy Robert, the friendly nephew, come almost casually forth, hands in pockets, whistling under his breath, to breathe the night air as boys do, curious for adventures that they themselves must make, that rarely happen by. Threshed tight, mortally locked and bound to Jim, staring up, Will was all the more shaken to see the normal boy, the airy glance, the unassuming poise, the small, the easy self in which no man at all was revealed by street light.

At any moment, Robert, in full cry, might leap to play with them, tangle legs, lock arms, bark-snap like pups in May, the whole thing end with them strewn in laughing tears on the lawn, the terror spent, the fear melted off in dew, a dream of nothings quickly gone as such dreams go when the eye snaps wide. For there indeed stood the nephew, his face round fresh, and cream-smooth as a peach.

And he was smiling down at the two boys he now saw locked limb in limb on the grass.

Then, swiftly, he darted in. He must have run upstairs, scrabbled about, and hurtled down again, for suddenly as the two boys outthrashed, outgripped, outraged each other, there was a rain of tinkling, rattling glitter on the lawn.

The nephew leaped the porch rail and landed panther-soft, imbedded in his shadow, on the grass. His hands were delicious with stars. These he liberally sprinkled. They thudded, slithered, winked at Jim's side. Both boys lay stricken by the rain of gold and diamond fire that pelted them.

"Help, police!" cried Robert.

Will was so shocked he let go Jim.

Jim was so shocked he let go of Will.

Both reached at the same time for the cold strewn ice.

"Good grief, a bracelet!"

"A ring! A necklace!"

Robert kicked. Two trash cans at the curb fell thundering.

A bedroom light, above, flicked on.

"Police!" Robert threw one last spray of glitter at their feet, shut up his fresh-peach smile like locking an explosion away in a box, and shot away down the street.

"Wait!" Jim jumped. "We won't hurt you!"

Will tripped him, Jim fell.

The window upstairs opened. Miss Foley leaned out. Jim, on his knees, held a woman's wrist watch. Will blinked at a necklace in his hands.

"Who's there!" she cried. "Jim? Will? What's *that* you got?!"

But Jim was running. Will stopped only long enough to see the window empty itself with a wail as Miss Foley pulled in to see her room. When he heard her full scream, he knew she had discovered the burglary.

Running, Will knew he was doing just what the nephew wanted. He should turn back, pick up the jewels, tell Miss Foley what happened. But he must save Jim!

Far back, he heard Miss Foley's new cries turn on more lights! Will Halloway! Jim Nightshade! Night runners! Thieves! That's us, thought Will, oh my Lord! That's us! No one'll believe *any-thing* we say from now on! Not about carnivals, not about carousels, not about mirrors or evil nephews, not about nothing!

And so they ran, three animals in starlight. A black otter. A tomcat. A rabbit.

Me, thought Will, I'm the rabbit.

And he was white, and much afraid.

chapter twenty-three

They hit the carnival grounds at a good twenty miles an hour, give or take a mile, the nephew in the lead, Jim close behind, and Will further back, gasping, shotgun blasts of fatigue in his feet, his head, his heart.

The nephew, running scared, looked back, not smiling.

Fooled him, thought Will, he figured I wouldn't follow, figured I'll call the police, get stuck, not be believed, or run hide. Now he's scared I'll beat the tar out of him, and wants to jump on that ride and run around getting older and bigger than me. Oh, Jim, Jim, we got to stop him, keep him young, tear his skin off!

But he knew from Jim's running there'd be no help from Jim. Jim wasn't running after nephews. He was running toward free rides.

The nephew vanished around a tent far ahead. Jim followed. By the time Will reached the midway, the merry-go-round was popping to life. In the pulse, the din, the squeal-around of music the small fresh-faced nephew rode the great platform in a swirl of midnight dust.

Jim, ten feet back, watched the horses leap, his eyes striking fire from the high-jumped stallion's eyes.

The merry-go-round was going *forward!*

Jim *leaned* at it.

"Jim!" cried Will.

The nephew swept from sight borne around by the machine. Drifted back again he stretched out pink fingers urging softly: "...Jim...?"

Jim twitched one foot forward.

"No!" Will plunged.

He knocked, seized, held Jim; they toppled; they fell in a heap.

The nephew, surprised, whisked on in darkness, one year older. One year older, thought Will, on the earth, one year taller, bigger, meaner!

"Oh God, Jim, quick!" He jumped up, ran to the control box, the complex mysteries of brass switch and porcelain covering and sizzling wires. He struck the switch. But Jim, behind, babbling, tore at Will's hands.

"Will, you'll spoil it! No!"

Jim knocked the switch full back.

Will spun and slapped his face. Each clenched the other's elbows, rocked, flailed. They fell against the control box.

Will saw the evil boy, a year older still, glide around into night. Five or six more times around and he'd be bigger than the two of them!

"Jim, he'll kill us!"

"Not me, no!"

Will felt a sting of electricity. He yelled, pulled back, hit the switch handle. The control box spat. Lightning jumped to the sky. Jim and Will, flung by the blast, lay watching the merry-go-round run wild.

The evil boy whistled by, clenched to a brass tree. He cursed. He spat. He wrestled with wind, with centrifuge. He was trying to clutch his way through the horses, the poles, to the outer rim of the carousel. His face came, went, came, went. He clawed. He brayed. The control box erupted blue showers. The carousel jumped and bucked. The nephew slipped. He fell. A black stallion's steel hoof kicked him. Blood printed his brow.

Jim hissed, rolled, thrashed, Will riding him hard, pressing him to grass, trading yell for yell, both fright-pale, heart ramming heart. Electric bolts from the switch flushed up in white stars a gush of fireworks. The carousel spun thirty, spun forty—"Will, let me up!"—spun fifty times. The calliope howled, boiled steam, ran ancient dry, then played nothing, its keys gibbering as only chitterings boiled up through the vents. Lightning unraveled itself over the sweated outflung boys, delivered flame to the silent horse stampede to light their way around, around with the figure lying on the platform no longer a boy but a man no longer a man but more than a man and even more and even more, much more than that, around, around.

"He's, he's, oh he's, oh look, Will, he's—" gasped Jim, and began to sob, because it was the only thing to do, locked down, nailed tight. "Oh God, Will, get up! We *got* to make it run backward!"

Lights flashed on in the tents.

But no one came out.

Why not? Will thought crazily. The explosions? The electric storm? Do the freaks think the whole world's jumping through the midway? Where's Mr. Dark? In town? Up to no good? What, where, why?

He thought he heard the agonized figure sprawled on the carousel platform drum his heart superfast, then slow, fast, slow, very fast, very slow, incredibly fast, then as slow as the moon going down the sky on a white night in winter.

Someone, something, on the carousel wailed faintly.

Thank God it's dark, thought Will. Thank God, I can't see. There goes someone. Here comes something. There, whatever it is, goes again. There . . . there . . .

A bleak shadow on the shuddering machine tried to stagger up, but it was late, late, later still, very late, latest of all, oh, very late. The shadow crumbled. The carousel, like the earth spinning, whipped away air, sunlight, sense and sensibility, leaving only dark, cold, and age.

In a final vomit, the switch box blew itself completely apart.

All the carnival lights blinked out.

The carousel slowed itself through the cold night wind.

Will let Jim go.

How many times, thought Will, did it go around? Sixty, eighty . . . ninety . . . ?

How many times? said Jim's face, all nightmare, watching the dead carousel shiver and halt in the dead grass, a stopped world now which nothing, not their hearts, hands or heads, could send back anywhere.

They walked slowly to the merry-go-round, their shoes whispering.

The shadowy figure lay on the near side, on the plank floor, its face turned away.

One hand hung off the platform.

It did not belong to a boy.

It seemed a huge wax hand shriveled by fire.

The man's hair was long, spidery, white. It blew like milkweed in the breathing dark.

They bent to see the face.

The eyes were mummified shut. The nose was collapsed upon gristle. The mouth was a ruined white flower, the petals twisted into a thin wax sheath over the clenched teeth through which faint bubblings sighed. The man was small inside his clothes, small as a child, but tall, strung out, and old, so old, very old, not ninety, not one hundred, no, not one hundred ten, but one hundred twenty or one hundred thirty impossible years old.

Will touched.

The man was cold as an albino frog.

He smelled of moon swamps and old Egyptian bandages. He was something found in museums, wrapped in nicotine linens, sealed in glass.

But he was alive, puling like a babe, and shriveling unto death, fast, very fast, before their eyes.

Will was sick over the side of the carousel.

Then, falling against each other, Jim and Will sledge-hammered the insane leaves, the unbelievable grass, the insubstantial earth with their numbed shoes, fleeing off down the midway. . . .

chapter twenty-four

Moths ticked off the high tin-shaded arc light which swung abandoned above the crossroads. Below, in a deserted gas station in the midst of country wilderness there was another ticking. In a coffin-sized phone booth speaking to people lost somewhere across night hills, two white-faced boys were crammed, holding to each other at every flit of bat, each sliding of cloud across the stars.

Will hung up the phone. The police and an ambulance were coming.

At first he and Jim had shout-whispered-wheezed at each other, pumping along, stumbling: they should go home, sleep, forget—no! they should take a freight train west!—no! for Mr. Cooger, if he survived what they'd done to him, that old man, that old old old man, would follow them over the world until he found and tore them apart! Arguing, shivering, they ended up in a phone booth, and now saw the police car bouncing along the road, its siren moaning, with the ambulance behind. All the men looked out at the two boys whose teeth chattered in the moth-flicked light.

Three minutes later they all advanced down the dark midway, Jim leading the way, talking, gibbering.

"He's alive. He's *got* to be alive. We didn't mean to do it! We're sorry!" He stared at the black tents. "You hear? We're sorry!"

"Take it easy, boy," said one of the policemen. "Go on."

The two policemen in midnight blue, the two internes like ghosts, the two boys, made the last turn past the ferris wheel and reached the merry-go-round.

Jim groaned.

The horses trampled the night air, in midplunge. Starlight glittered on the brass poles. That was all.

"He's *gone* . . ."

"He was here, we swear!" said Jim. "One hundred fifty, two hundred years old, and *dying* of it!"

"Jim," said Will.

The four men stirred uneasily.

"They must've taken him in a tent." Will started off. A policeman took his elbow.

"Did you say one hundred fifty years old?" he asked Jim. "Why not *three* hundred?"

"Maybe he was! Oh God." Jim turned, yelling. "Mr. Cooger! We brought *help!*"

Lights blinked on in the Freak Tent. The huge banners out front rumbled and lashed as arc lights flushed over them. The police glanced up. MR. SKELETON, THE DUST WITCH, THE CRUSHER, VESUVIO THE LAVA SIPPER! danced soft, big, painted each on its separate flag.

Jim paused by the rustling freak show entry.

"Mr. Cooger?" he pleaded. "You . . . *there?*"

The tent flaps mouthed out a warm lion air.

"What?" asked a policeman.

Jim read the moving flaps.

"They said 'Yes.' They said, 'Come in.'"

Jim stepped through. The others followed.

Inside they squinted through crisscrossed tent pole shadows to the high freak platforms and all the world-wandered aliens, crippled of face, of bone, of mind, waiting there.

At a rickety card table nearby four men sat playing orange, lime-green, sun-yellow cards printed with moon beasts and winged sun-symboled men. Here the akimbo Skeleton one might play like a piccolo; here the Blimp who could be punctured every night, pumped up at dawn; here the midget known as The Wart who could be mailed parcel post dirt-cheap; and next to him an even littler accident of cell and time, a Dwarf so small and perched in such a way you could not see his face behind the cards clenched before him in arthritic and tremulous oak-gnarled fingers.

The Dwarf! Will started. Something about those hands! Familiar, familiar. Where? Who? What? But his eyes snapped on.

There stood Monsieur Guillotine, black tights, black long stockings, black hood over head, arms crossed over his chest, stiff straight by his chopping machine, the blade high in the tent sky, a hungry knife all flashes and meteor shine, much desiring to cleave space. Below, in the head cradle, a dummy sprawled waiting quick doom.

There stood the Crusher, all ropes and tendons, all steel and iron, all bone-monger, jaw-cruncher, horseshoe-taffy-puller.

And there the Lava Sipper, Vesuvio of the chafed tongue, of the scalded teeth, who spun scores of fireballs up, hissing in a ferris of flame which streaked shadows along the tent roof.

Nearby, in booths, another thirty freaks watched the fires fly until the Lava Sipper glanced, saw intruders, and let his universe fall. The suns drowned in a water tub.

Steam billowed. All froze in a tableau.

An insect stopped buzzing.

Will glanced swiftly.

There, on the biggest stage, a tattoo needle poised like a blowgun dart in his rose-crusted hand, stood Mr. Dark, the Illustrated Man.

His picture crowds flooded raw upon his flesh. Stripped bare to the navel, he had been stinging himself, adding a picture to his left palm with this dragonfly contraption. Now with the insect droned dead in his hand, he wheeled. But Will, staring beyond him, cried:

"There he is! There's Mr. Cooger!"

The police, the internes, quickened.

Behind Mr. Dark sat the Electric Chair.

In this chair sat a ruined man, last seen strewn wheezing in a collapse of bones and albino wax on the broken carousel. Now he was erected, propped, strapped in this device full of lightning power.

"That's him! He was ... *dying.*"

The Blimp *ascended* to his feet.

The Skeleton spun about, tall.

The Wart flea-hopped to the sawdust.

The Dwarf let fall his cards and flirted his now mad, now idiot eyes ahead, around, over.

I *know* him, thought Will. Oh, God, what they've *done* to him!

The lightning-rod salesman!

That's who it was. Squeezed tight, smashed small, convulsed by some terrible nature into a clenched fist of humanity ...

The seller of lightning rods.

But now two things happened with beautiful promptitude.

Monsieur Guillotine cleared his throat.

And the blade, above, in the canvas sky, like a homing hawk scythed down. Whisper-whisk-slither-thunder-rush—wham!

The dummy head, chop-cut, fell.

And falling, looked like Will's own head, own face, destroyed.

He wanted, he did not want, to run lift the head, turn it to see if it held his own profile. But how could you ever dare do that? Never, never in a billion years, could one empty that wicker basket.

The second thing happened.

A mechanic, working at the back of an upright glass-fronted coffin booth, released a trip wire. This made a last cog click within the machinery under the sign, MLLE TAROT, THE DUST WITCH. The wax woman's figure within the glass box nodded her head and fixed the boys with her pointing nose as the boys passed, leading the men. Her cold wax hand brushed the Dust of Destiny on a ledge within the coffin. Her eyes did not see; they were sewn shut with laced black-widow web, dark threads. A waxworks fright, good and proper, she was, and the policemen beamed, viewing her, and strolled on, and beamed at Monsieur Guillotine for his act, too, and moving, the police were relaxing now, and seemed not to mind being called late on a jolly venture into a rehearsing world of acrobats and seedy magicians.

"Gentlemen!" Mr. Dark and his mob of illustrations surged forward on the pine platform, a jungle beneath each arm, an Egyptian viper scrolled on each bicep. "Welcome! You're just in time! We're rehearsing all our new acts!" Mr. Dark waved, and strange monsters gaped their fangs from his chest, a Cyclops with a navel for a squinted moron eye twitched on his stomach as he strode.

Lord, thought Will, is he bringing that crowd with him or is the crowd pulling him along by his skin?

From all the creaked platforms, from the muffled sawdust, Will felt the freaks wheel and fix their eyes, enchanted, as were internes and police, by this illustrated throng of humanity that in one agglomerative move dominated and filled the immediate air and tent sky with silent shoutings for attention.

Now part of the wasp-needle tattooed population spoke. It was Mr. Dark's mouth over and above this calligraphic explosion, this railroad accident of monsters in tumult upon his sweating skin. Mr. Dark chanted forth the organ tones from his chest. His personal electric blue-green populations trembled, even as the real freaks on the sawdust tent floor trembled, even as, hearing in their most secret marrow, Jim and Will trembled and felt more freak than the freaks themselves.

"Gentlemen! Boys! We've just perfected the new act! You'll be the first to see!" cried Mr. Dark.

The first policeman, his hand casually nestled to his pistol holster, squinted up at that vast corral of beasts and beings. "This boy said—"

"*Said?!*" The Illustrated Man barked a laugh. The freaks leaped in a frolic of shock, then calmed as the carnival owner continued with great ease, patting and soothing his own illustrations, which somehow patted and soothed the freaks. "Said? But what did he *see?* Boys always scare themselves at side shows, eh? Run like rabbits when the freaks pop out. But tonight, especially tonight!"

The policemen glanced beyond to the Erector-set-papier-mâché relic constricted in the Electric Chair.

"Who's he?"

"Him?" Will saw fire lick up through Mr. Dark's smoke-clouded eyes, saw him just as quickly snuff it out. "The new act. Mr. Electrico."

"No! Look at the old man! Look!" Will yelled. The police turned to appraise his demon cry.

"Don't you see!" said Will. "He's dead! Only thing holds him up is the straps!"

The internes gazed up at the great flake of winter flung into and held by the black chair.

Oh gosh, thought Will, we thought it would all be simple. The old man, Mr. Cooger, dying, so we bring doctors to save him, so he forgives us, maybe, maybe the carnival doesn't hurt us, lets us go. But now this, what's next? He's dead! It's too late! Everyone hates us!

And Will stood among the others feeling the cold air waft down from the unearthed mummy, from the cold mouth and cold eyes locked up in frozen eyelids. Inside the frozen nostrils not a white hair stirred. Mr. Cooger's ribs under his collapsed shirt were stone-rigid and his teeth under his clay lips were dry-ice cold. Put him out at noon and fog would steam off him.

The internes glanced at each other. They nodded.

The policemen, at this, took one step forward.

"Gentlemen!"

Mr. Dark scuttled a tarantula hand up an electric brass switch-board.

"One hundred thousand volts will now burn Mr. Electrico's body!"

"No, don't let him!" Will cried.

The policemen took another step. The internes opened their mouths to speak. Mr. Dark flicked a swift demanding glance at Jim. Jim cried:

"No! It's all right!"

"Jim!"

"Will, yes, it's okay!"

"Stand back!" The spider clutched the switch handle. "This man is in a trance! As part of our new act, I have hypnotized him! He could suffer injury if you shocked him from his spell!"

The internes shut their mouths. The police stopped moving.

"One hundred thousand volts! Yet he will come forth alive, whole in sound mind and body!"

"No!"

A policeman grabbed Will.

The Illustrated Man and all the men and beasts asprawl in frenzies on him now snatched and banged the switch.

The tent lights snuffed out.

Policemen, internes, boys jumped up their flesh in cobbles and boils.

But now in the swift midnight shuttering, the Electric Chair was a hearth and on it the old man blazed like a blue autumn tree.

The police flinched back, the internes leaned ahead, as did the freaks, blue fire in their eyes.

The Illustrated Man, hand glued to switch, looked upon the old old old man.

The old man was flintrock dead, yes, but electricity alive sheathed over him. It swarmed on his cold shell ears, it flickered in his deep-as-an-abandoned-stone-well nostrils. It crept blue eels of power on his praying-mantis fingers and his grasshopper knees.

The Illustrated Man's lips thrust wide, perhaps he yelled, but no one heard against the immense fry, blast, the slam and sizzle of power which prowled in around over under about man and prisoning chair. Come alive! cried the hum! Come alive! cried the storming color and light. Come alive! yelled Mr. Dark's mouth, which no one heard but Jim, reading lips, read thunderous loud in his mind, and Will the same, Come alive! willing the old man to live, start up, tick, hum, work juice, summon spit, ungum spirit, melt wax soul. . . .

"He's dead!" But no one heard Will, either, no matter how he pushed against the lightning clamor.

Alive! Mr. Dark's lips licked and savored. Alive. Come alive. He racheted the switch to the last notch. Live, live! Somewhere, dynamos protested, skirled, shrilled, moaned a bestial energy. The light turned bottle-green. Dead, dead, thought Will. But live alive! cried machines, cried flame and fire, cried mouths of crowds of livid beasts on illustrated flesh.

So the old man's hair stood up in prickling fumes. Sparks, bled from his fingernails, dripped seething spatters on pine planks. Green simmerings wove shuttles through dead eyelids.

The Illustrated Man bent violently above the old old dead dead thing, his prides of beasts drowned deep in sweat, his right hand thrust in hammering demand upon the air: Live, live.

And the old man came alive.

Will yelled himself hoarse.

And no one heard.

For now, very slowly, as if roused by thunder, as if the electric fire were new dawn, one dead eyelid peeled itself slowly open.

The freaks gaped.

A long way off in the storm, Jim was yelling, too, for Will had his elbow tight and felt the yell pouring out through the bones, as the old man's lips fell apart and frightful sizzles zigzagged between lips and threaded teeth.

The Illustrated Man cut the power to a whine. Then, turning, he fell to his knees, and put out his hand.

Away off up there on the platform, there was the faintest stir as of an autumn leaf beneath the old man's shirt.

The freaks exhaled.

The old old man sighed.

Yes, Will thought, they're breathing for him, helping him, making him to live.

Inhale, exhale, inhale, exhale—yet it looked like an act. What could he say, or do?

"... lungs so ... so ... so ..." someone whispered.

The Dust Witch, back in her glass box?

Inhale. The freaks breathed. Exhale. Their shoulders slumped.

The old old man's lips trembled.

" ... heart beat ... one ... two ... so ... so ..."

The Witch again? Will feared to look.

A vein ticked a small watch in the old man's throat.

Very slowly now that right eye of the old man opened full wide, fixed, stared like a broken camera. It was like looking through a hole in space, with no bottom forever. He grew warmer.

The boys, below, grew colder.

Now the old and terribly-wise-with-nightmare eye was so wide and so deep and so alive all to itself in that smashed porcelain face that there at the bottom of the eye somewhere the evil nephew peered along and out at the freaks, internes, police, and ...

Will.

Will saw himself, saw Jim, two little pictures posed in reflection on that single eye. If the old man blinked, the two images would be *crushed* by his lid!

The Illustrated Man, on his knees, turned at last and gentled all with his smile.

"Gentlemen, boys, here *indeed* is the man who lives with lightning!"

The second policeman laughed; this motion shook his hand off his holster.

Will shuffled to the right.

The old spittle-eye followed, sucking at him with its emptiness.

Will squirmed left.

As did the phlegm that was the old man's gaze, while his chill lips peeled wide to shape, reshape an echoed gasp, a flutter. From deep below the old man bounced his voice ricocheting off the dank stone walls of his body until it fell out his mouth:

" . . . welcome . . . mmmmmm . . ."

The word fell back in.

"well . . . cummm . . . mmmm . . ."

The policemen nudged each other with identical smiles.

"No!" cried Will, suddenly. "That's no act! He was dead! He'd die again if you cut the power—!"

Will slapped his own hand to his mouth.

Oh Lord, he thought, what am I doing? I want him alive, so he'll forgive us, let us be! But, oh Lord, even more I want him dead, I want them all dead, they scare me so much I got hairballs big as cats in my stomach!

"I'm sorry. . . ." he whispered.

"Don't be!" cried Mr. Dark.

The freaks made a commotion of blinks and glares. What next from the statue in the cold sizzling chair? The old old man's one eye gummed itself. The mouth collapsed, a bubble of yellow mud in a sulphur bath.

The Illustrated Man banged the switch a notch, grinning wildly at no one. He thrust a steel sword in the old man's empty glove-like hand.

A drench of electricity prickled from the sere music-box tines of the ancient stubbled cheeks. That deep eye showed swift as a bullet hole. Hungry for Will, it found and ate of his image. The lips steamed:

"I . . . sssaw . . . the . . . boysssssss . . . sssssneak into . . . thee . . . tent . . . tttttt. . . ."

The desiccated bellows refilled, then pin-punctured the swamp air out in faint wails:

" . . . We . . . rehearsing . . . sssso I thought . . . play . . . thissss trick . . . pretend to be . . . dead."

Again the pause to drink oxygen like ale, electricity like wine.

" . . . let myself fall . . . like . . . I . . . wasssss . . . dying. . . . The . . . boysssssssss . . . ssscreaming . . . *ran!*"

The old man husked out syllable on syllable.

"Ha." Pause. "Ha." Pause. "Ha."

Electricity hemstitched the whistling lips.

The Illustrated Man coughed gently. "This act, it *tires* Mr. Electrico. . . ."

"Oh, sure." One of the policemen started. "Sorry." He touched his cap. "Fine show."

"Fine," said one of the internes.

Will glanced swiftly to see the interne's mouth, what it looked like saying this, but Jim stood in the way.

"Boys! A dozen free passes!" Mr. Dark held them out. "Here!"

Jim and Will didn't move.

"Well?" said one policeman.

Sheepishly, Will reached up for the flame-colored tickets, but stopped as Mr. Dark said, "Your names?"

The officers winked at each other.

"Tell him, boys."

Silence. The freaks watched.

"Simon," said Jim. "Simon Smith."

Mr. Dark's hand, holding the tickets, constricted.

"Oliver," said Will. "Oliver Brown."

The Illustrated Man sucked in a mighty breath. The freaks *inhaled!* The vast ingasped sigh might have, seemed to, stir Mr. Electrico. His sword twitched. Its tip leaped to spark-sting Will's shoulder, then sizzle over in blue-green explosions at Jim. Lightning shot Jim's shoulder.

The policemen laughed.

The old old man's one wide eye blazed.

"I dub thee . . . asses and foolssssss . . . I dub . . . thee . . . Mr. Sickly . . . and . . . Mr. Pale . . . !"

Mr. Electrico finished. The sword tapped them.

"A . . . sssshort . . . sad life . . . for you both!"

Then his mouth slit shut, his raw eye glued over. Containing his cellar breath, he let the simple sparks swarm his blood like dark champagne.

"The tickets," murmured Mr. Dark. "Free rides. Free rides. Come any time. Come back. Come back."

Jim grabbed, Will grabbed the tickets.

They jumped, they bolted from the tent.

The police, smiling and waving all around, followed at their leisure.

The internes, not smiling, like ghosts in their white suits, came after.

They found the boys huddled in the back of the police car.

They looked as though they wanted to go home.

Pursuits

chapter twenty-five

S he could feel the mirrors waiting for her in each room much the same as you felt, without opening your eyes, that the first snow of winter has just fallen outside your window.

Miss Foley had first noticed, some years ago, that her house was crowded with bright shadows of herself. Best, then, to ignore the cold sheets of December ice in the hall, above the bureaus, in the bath. Best skate the thin ice, lightly. Paused, the weight of your attention might crack the shell. Plunged through the crust, you might drown in depths so cold, so remote, that all the Past lay carved in tombstone marbles there. Ice water would syringe your veins. Transfixed at the mirror sill, you would stand forever, unable to lift your gaze from the proofs of Time.

Yet tonight, with the echo of the running feet of the three boys dying away, she kept feeling snow fall in the mirrors of her house. She wanted to thrust through the frames to test their weather. But she was afraid that doing this might cause all the mirrors to somehow assemble in billionfold multiplications of self, an army of women marching away to become girls and girls marching to become infinitely small children. So many people, crammed in one house, would provoke suffocation.

So what must she do about mirrors, Will Halloway, Jim Nightshade, and . . . the nephew?

Strange. Why not say *my* nephew?

Because, she thought, from the first when he came in the door, he didn't belong, his proof was not proof, she kept waiting for . . . what?

Tonight. The carnival. Music, the nephew said, that *must* be heard, rides that *must* be ridden. Stay away from the maze where winter slept. Swim around with the carousel where summer, sweet as clover, honey-grass, and wild mint, kept its lovely time.

She looked out at the night lawn from which she had not yet retrieved the scattered jewels. Somehow she guessed this was a way the nephew had of getting rid of the two boys who might stop her using this ticket she took from the mantel:

CAROUSEL. ADMIT ONE.

She had waited for the nephew to come back. With time passing, she must act on her own. Something must be done not to hurt, no, but slow down interference from such as Jim and Will. No one must stand between her and nephew, her and carousel, her and lovely gliding ride-around summer.

The nephew had said as much, by saying nothing, by just holding her hands, and breathing baked-apple-pie scent from his small pink mouth upon her face.

She lifted the telephone.

Across town she saw the light in the stone library building, as all the town had seen it, over the years. She dialed. A quiet voice answered. She said:

"Library? Mr. Halloway? This is Miss Foley. Will's teacher. In ten minutes, please, meet me in the police station. . . . Mr. Halloway?"

A pause.

"Are you still *there* . . . ?"

chapter twenty-six

I'd have sworn," said one interne. "When we first got there . . . that old man was dead."

The ambulance and the police car had pulled up at the same moment at the crossroads, going back into town. One of the internes had called over. Now one of the policemen called back:

"You're joking!"

The internes sat in their ambulance. They shrugged.

"Yeah. Sure. Joking."

They drove on ahead, their faces as quiet and white as their uniforms.

The police followed, with Jim and Will huddled in back, trying to say more, but the police started talking and laughing, retelling everything that happened to one another, so Will and Jim wound up lying, giving wrong names again, saying they lived around the corner from the police station.

They let the police drop them at two dark houses near the station and they ran up on those porches and grabbed the doorknobs and waited for the prowl car to swing off around the corner into the station, and then they came down and followed and stood looking at the yellow lights of the station all sun-colored at midnight and Will glanced over and saw the whole evening come and go in Jim's face and Jim watching the police station windows as if at any moment darkness might fill every room and put the lights out forever.

On my way back into town, thought Will, I threw away my tickets. But—look . . .

Jim still has his, in his hand.

Will trembled.

What did Jim think, want, plan, now that dead men lived and only lived through the fire of white-hot electric chair machines? Did he still very much love carnivals? Will searched. Faint echoes, yes, they came, they went in Jim's eyes, for Jim, after all, was Jim, even standing here with the calm light of Justice falling on his cheekbones.

"The Chief of Police," Will said. "He'd listen to us—"

"Yeah," said Jim. "He'd wake just long enough to send for the butterfly net. Hell, William, hell, even *I* don't believe what's happened the last twenty-four hours."

"But we got to find someone higher up, keep trying, now we know what the score is."

"Okay, what's the score? What's the carnival done is so bad? Scared a woman with a mirror maze? So, she scared herself, the police'd say. Burgled a house? Okay, where's the burglar? Hiding inside an old man's skin? Who'd believe that? Who'd believe an old old man was ever a boy twelve? What else is the score? Did a lightning-rod salesman disappear? Sure, and left his bag. But he could've left town—"

"That dwarf in the side show—"

"I saw him, you saw him, looks kinda like the lightning-rod man, sure, but again, can you prove he was ever big? No, just like you can't prove Cooger was ever small, so that leaves us right here, Will, on the sidewalk, no proof except what we saw, and us just kids, the carnival's word against ours, and the police had a fine time anyway there. Oh gosh, it's a mess. If only, if only there was *still* some way to apologize to Mr. Cooger—"

"Apologize?" Will yelled. "To a man-eating crocodile? Je-hoshaphat! You still don't see we can't do business with those ulmers and goffs!"

"Ulmers? Goffs?" Jim gazed upon him thoughtfully, for that was how the boys talked of the creatures who dragged and swayed and slumped through their dreams. In the bad dreams of William, the "ulmers" moaned and gibbered and had no faces. In the equally bad dreams of Jim, the "goffs," his peculiar name for them, grew like monster meringue-paste mushrooms, which fed on rats which fed on spiders which fed, in turn, because they were large enough, on cats.

"Ulmers! Goffs!" said Will. "You need a ten-ton safe to fall on you? Look what happened to two folks already, Mr. Electrico, and that terrible crazy dwarf! All kinds of things can go wrong with people on that darn machine. We know, we seen it. Maybe they squashed the lightning-rod man down that way on purpose, or maybe something went wrong. Fact is, he wound up in a wine press anyway, got run over by a steam-roller carousel and's so crazy now he doesn't even *know* us! Ain't that enough to scare the Jesus out of you, Jim? Why, maybe even Mr. Crosetti—"

"Mr. Crosetti's on vacation."

"Maybe yes, maybe no. There's his shop. There's the sign: CLOSED ON ACCOUNT OF ILLNESS. What *kind* of illness, Jim? He eat too much candy out at the show? He get seasick on everybody's favorite ride?"

"Cut it, Will."

"No, sir, I won't cut it. Sure, sure, the merry-go-round sounds keen. You think *I* like being thirteen all the time? Not me! But for cri-yi, Jim, face it, you don't *really* want to be twenty!"

"What *else* we talked about all summer?"

"Talk, sure. But throwing yourself head first in that taffy machine and getting your bones pulled long, Jim, you wouldn't know what to do with your bones then!"

"I'd know," said Jim, in the night. "I'd know."

"Sure. You'd just go away and leave me here, Jim."

"Why," protested the other, "I wouldn't leave you, Will. We'd be together."

"Together? You two feet taller and going around feeling your leg-and-arm-bones? You looking down at me, Jim, and what'd we talk about, me with my pockets full of kite-string and marbles and frog-eyes, and you with clean nice and empty pockets and making fun, is that what we'd talk, and you able to run faster and ditch me—"

"I'd never ditch you, Will—"

"Ditch me in a minute. Well, go on, Jim, just go on leave me because I got my pocket knife and there's nothing wrong with me sitting under a tree playing mumblety-peg while you get yourself plain crazy with the heat of all those horses racing around, but thank God they're not racing any more—"

"And it's your fault!" cried Jim. He stopped.

Will stiffened and made fists. "You mean I should've let young mean-and-terrible get old mean-and-terrible enough to chew our heads off? Just let him ride around and hock his spit in our eye? and maybe you with him, waving good-bye, going around again, waving so long! and all I got to do is wave back, Jim, that what you mean?"

"Sh," said Jim. "Like you say, it's too late. The carousel's broke—"

"And when it's fixed, they ride old horrible Cooger back, make him young enough so he can speak and remember our names, and then they come like cannibals after us, or just me, if you want to get in good with them and go tell them my name and where I live—"

"I wouldn't do that, Will." Jim touched him.

"Oh, Jim, Jim, you *do* see, don't you? Everything in its time, like the preacher said only last month, everything one by one, not two by two, will you remember?"

"Everything," said Jim, "in its time . . ."

And then they heard voices from the police station. In one of the rooms to the right of the entrance, a woman was talking now, and men were talking.

Will nodded to Jim and they ran quietly over to pick their way through bushes and look into the room.

There sat Miss Foley. There sat Will's father.

"I don't understand," said Miss Foley. "To think Will and Jim would break in my house, steal, run off—"

"You saw their faces?" asked Mr. Halloway.

"When I screamed, they looked back under the light."

She's not mentioning the nephew, thought Will. And she won't, of course.

You see, Jim, he wanted to shout, it was a trap! The nephew *waited* for us to come prowling. He wanted to get us in so much trouble, no matter what we said to anybody, police, parents, that nobody'd listen to us about carnivals, late hours, merry-go-rounds, because our word'd be no good!

"I don't want to prosecute," said Miss Foley. "But if they are innocent, where are the boys?"

"Here!" someone cried.

"Will!" said Jim.

Too late.

For Will had jumped high and was scrambling through the window.

"Here," he said, simply, as he touched the floor.

chapter twenty-seven

They walked home quietly on the moon-colored sidewalks, Mr. Halloway between the boys. When they reached home, Will's father sighed.

"Jim, I don't see any reason to tear your mother to bits at this hour. If you promise to tell her this whole thing at breakfast, I'll let you off. Can you get in without waking her up?"

"Sure. Look what we got."

"We?"

Jim nodded and took them over to fumble among the clusters of thick moss and leaves on the side of the house until they found the iron rungs they had secretly nailed and placed to make a hidden ladder up to Jim's room. Mr. Halloway laughed, once, almost with pain, and a strange wild sadness shook his head.

"How long has this gone on? No, don't tell. I did it, too, your age." He looked up the ivy toward Jim's window. "Fun being out late, free as all hell." He caught himself. "You don't stay out too long—?"

"This week was the very first time after midnight."

Dad pondered a moment. "Having permission would spoil everything, I suppose? It's sneaking out to the lake, the graveyard, the rail tracks, the peach orchards summer nights that counts. . . ."

"Gosh, Mr. Halloway, did you once—"

"Yes. But don't let the women know I told you. Up." He motioned. "And don't come out again *any* night for the next month."

"Yes, sir!"

Jim swung monkeywise to the stars, flashed through his window, shut it, drew the shade.

Dad looked up at the hidden rungs coming down out of the starlight to the running-free world of sidewalks that invited the one-thousand-yard dash, and the high hurdles of the dark bushes, and the pole-vault cemetery trellises and walls. . . .

"You know what I hate most of all, Will? Not being able to run any more, like you."

"Yes, sir," said his son.

"Let's have it clear now," said Dad. "Tomorrow, go apologize to Miss Foley again. Check her lawn. We may have missed some of the—stolen property—with matches and flashlights. Then go to the Police Chief to report. You're lucky you turned yourself in. You're lucky Miss Foley won't press charges."

"Yes, sir."

They walked back to the side of their own house. Dad raked his hand in the ivy.

"Our place, too?"

His hand found a rung Will had nailed away among the leaves.

"Our place, too."

He took out his tobacco pouch, filled his pipe as they stood by the ivy, the hidden rungs leading up to warm beds, safe rooms, then lit his pipe and said, "I know you. You're not *acting* guilty. You didn't steal anything."

"No."

"Then why did you say you did, to the police?"

"Because Miss Foley—who knows why?—*wants* us guilty. If she says we are, we are. You saw how surprised she was to see us come in through the window? She never figured we'd confess. Well, we did. We got enough enemies without the law on us, too. I figured if we made a clean breast, they'd go easy. They did. At the same time, boy, Miss Foley's won, too, because now we're criminals. Nobody'll believe what we say."

"I'll believe."

"Will you?" Will searched the shadows on his father's face, saw whiteness of skin, eyeball, and hair.

"Dad, the other night, at three o'clock in the morning—"

"Three in the morning—"

He saw Dad flinch as from a cold wind, as if he smelled and knew the whole thing and simply could not move, reach out, touch and pat Will.

And he knew he could not say it. Tomorrow, yes, some other day, yes, for perhaps with the sun coming up, the tents would be gone, the freaks off over the world, leaving them alone, knowing they were scared enough not to push it, say anything, just to keep their mouths shut. Maybe it would all blow over, maybe . . . maybe. . . .

"Yes, Will?" said his father, with difficulty, the pipe in his hand going dead. "Go on."

No, thought Will, let Jim and me be cannibalized, but no one else. Anyone that knows gets hurt. So no one else must know. Aloud he said:

"In a couple days, Dad, I'll tell you everything. I swear. Mom's honor."

"Mom's honor," said Dad, at last, "is good enough for me."

chapter twenty-eight

The night was sweet with the dust of autumn leaves that smelled as if the fine sands of ancient Egypt were drifting to dunes beyond the town. How come, thought Will, at a time like this, I can even think of four thousand years of dust of ancient people sliding around the world, and me sad because no one notices except me and Dad here maybe, and even us not telling each other.

It was indeed a time between, one second their thoughts all brambled airedale, the next all silken slumbering cat. It was a time to go to bed, yet still they lingered reluctant as boys to give over and wander in wide circles to pillow and night thoughts. It was a time to say much but not all. It was a time after first discoveries but not last ones. It was wanting to know everything and wanting to know nothing. It was the new sweetness of men starting to talk as they must talk. It was the possible bitterness of revelation.

So while they should have gone upstairs, they could not depart this moment that promised others on not so distant nights when man and boy-becoming-man might almost sing. So Will at last said, carefully:

"Dad? Am I a good person?"

"I think so. I *know* so, yes."

"Will—will that help when things get really rough?"

"It'll help."

"Will it save me if I need saving? I mean, if I'm around bad people and there's no one else good around for miles, what then?"

"It'll help."

"That's not good enough, Dad!"

"Good is no guarantee for your body. It's mainly for peace of mind—"

"But sometimes, Dad, aren't you so scared that even—"

"—the mind isn't peaceful?" His father nodded, his face uneasy.

"Dad," said Will, his voice very faint. "Are *you* a good person?"

"To you and your mother, yes, I try. But no man's a hero to himself. I've lived with me a lifetime, Will. I know everything worth knowing about myself—"

"And, adding it all up . . . ?"

"The sum? As they come and go, and I mostly sit very still and tight, yes, I'm all right."

"Then, Dad," asked Will, "why aren't you happy?"

"The front lawn at . . . let's see . . . one-thirty in the morning . . . is no place to start a philosophical . . ."

"I just wanted to know is all."

There was a long moment of silence. Dad sighed.

Dad took his arm, walked him over and sat him down on the porch steps, relit his pipe. Puffing, he said, "All right. Your mother's asleep. She doesn't know we're out here with our tomcat talk. We can go on. Now, look, since when did you think being good meant being happy?"

"Since always."

"Since now learn otherwise. Sometimes the man who looks happiest in town, with the biggest smile, is the one carrying the biggest load of sin. There are smiles and smiles; learn to tell the dark variety from the light. The seal-barker, the laugh-shouter, half the time he's covering up. He's had his fun and he's guilty. And men *do* love sin, Will, oh how they love it, never doubt, in all shapes, sizes, colors, and smells. Times come when troughs, not tables, suit our appetites. Hear a man too loudly praising others, and look to wonder if he didn't just get up from the sty. On the other hand, that unhappy, pale, put-upon man walking by, who looks all guilt and sin, why, often that's your good man with a capital G, Will. For being good *is* a fearful occupation; men strain at it and sometimes break in two. I've known a few. You work twice as hard to be a farmer as to be his hog. I suppose it's thinking about trying to be good makes the crack run up the wall one night. A man with high standards, too, the least hair falls on him sometimes wilts his spine. He can't let himself alone, won't lift himself off the hook if he falls just a breath from grace.

"Oh, it would be lovely if you could just *be* fine, *act* fine, not think of it all the time. But it's hard, right? with the last piece of lemon cake waiting in the icebox, middle of the night, not yours, but you lie awake in a hot sweat for it, eh? do I need tell you? Or, a hot spring day, noon, and there you are chained to your school desk and away off there goes the river, cool and fresh over the rock-fall. Boys can hear clear water like that miles away. So, minute by minute, hour by hour, a lifetime, it never ends, never stops, you got the choice this second, now this next, and the next after that, be good, be bad, that's what the clock ticks, that's what it says in the ticks. Run swim, or stay hot, run eat or lie hungry. So you stay, but once stayed, Will, you know the secret, don't you? don't think of the river again. Or the cake. Because if you do, you'll go crazy. Add up all the rivers never swum in, cakes never eaten, and by the time you get my age, Will, it's a lot missed out on. But then you console yourself, thinking, the more times in, the more times possibly drowned, or choked on lemon frosting. But then, through plain dumb cowardice, I guess, maybe you hold off from too much, wait, play it safe.

"Look at me: married at thirty-nine, Will, thirty-nine! But I was so busy wrestling myself two falls out of three, I figured I couldn't marry until I had licked myself good and forever. Too late, I found you can't wait to become perfect, you got to go out and fall down and get up with everybody else. So at last I looked up from my great self-wrestling match one night when your mother came to the library for a book, and got me, instead. And I saw then and there you take a man half-bad and a woman half-bad and put their two good halves together and you got one human all good to share between. That's you, Will, for my money. And the strange thing is, son, and sad, too, though you're always racing out there on the rim of the lawn, and me on the roof using books for shingles, comparing life to libraries, I soon saw you were wiser, sooner and better, than I will ever be. . . ."

Dad's pipe was dead. He paused to tap it out and reload it.

"No, sir," Will said.

"Yes," said his father, "I'd be a fool not to know I'm a fool. My one wisdom is: you're wise."

"Funny," Will said, after a long pause. "You've told me more, tonight, than I've told you. I'll think some more. Maybe I'll tell you everything, at breakfast. Okay?"

"I'll be ready, if you are."

"Because . . . I want you to be happy, Dad."

He hated the tears that sprang to his eyes.

"I'll be all right, Will."

"Anything I could say or do to make you happy, I would."

"Willy, William." Dad lit his pipe again and watched the smoke blow away in sweet dissolvings. "Just tell me I'll live forever. That would do nicely."

His voice, Will thought, I never noticed. It's the same color as his hair.

"Pa," he said, "don't sound so sad."

"Me? I'm the original sad man. I read a book and it makes me sad. See a film: sad. Plays? they really work me over."

"Is there anything," said Will, "*doesn't* make you sad?"

"One thing. Death."

"Boy!" Will started. "I should think *that* would!"

"No," said the man with the voice to match his hair. "Death makes everything else sad. But death itself only scares. If there wasn't death, all the other things wouldn't get tainted."

And, Will thought, here comes the carnival, Death like a rattle in one hand, Life like candy in the other; shake one to scare you, offer one to make your mouth water. Here comes the side show, both hands *full!*

He jumped to his feet.

"Dad, oh, listen! You'll live forever! Believe me, or you're sunk! Sure, you were sick a few years ago—but that's over. Sure, you're fifty-four, but that's young! And another thing—"

"Yes, Willy?"

His father waited for him. He swayed. He bit his lips, then blurted out:

"Don't go near the carnival."

"Strange," his father said, "that's what I was going to tell you."

"I wouldn't go back to that place for a billion dollars!"

But, Will thought, that won't stop the carnival searching through town to visit *me.*

"Promise, Dad?"

"Why don't you want me to go there, Will?"

"That's one of the things I'll tell tomorrow or next week or next year. You just got to trust me, Dad."

"I do, son." Dad took his hand. "It's a promise."

As if at a signal, both turned to the house. The time was up, the hour was late, enough had been said, they properly sensed they must go.

"The way you came out," said Dad, "is the way you go in."

Will walked silently to touch the iron rungs hidden under the rustling ivy.

"Dad. You won't pull these *off . . . ?*"

Dad probed one with his fingers.

"Some day, when you're tired of them, you'll take them off yourself."

"I'll never be tired of them."

"Is that how it seems? Yes, to someone your age, you figure you'll never get tired of anything. All right, son, up you go."

He saw how his father looked up along the ivy and the hidden path.

"You want to come up this way, too?"

"No, no," his father said, quickly.

"Because," said Will, "you're welcome."

"That's all right. Go on."

But still he looked at the ivy stirring in the dark morning light.

Will sprang up, grabbed the first, the second, the third rungs and looked down.

From just this distance, Dad looked as if he were shrinking, there on the ground. Somehow he didn't want to leave him behind, there in the night, like someone ditched by someone else, one hand up to move, but not moving.

"Dad!" he whispered. "You ain't got the *stuff!*"

Who says!? cried Dad's mouth, silently.

And he jumped.

And laughing without sound, the boy, the man swung up the side of the house, unceasingly, hand over hand, foot after foot.

He heard Dad slip, scrabble, grab.

Hold tight! he thought.

"Ah . . . !"

The man breathed hard.

Eyes tight, Will prayed: hold . . . *there* . . . now . . . !!

The old man gusted out, sucked in, swore in a fierce whisper, then climbed again.

Will opened his eyes and climbed and the rest was smooth, high, higher, fine, sweet, wondrous, done! They swung in and sat upon the sill, same size, same weight, colored same by the stars, and sat embraced once more with grand fine exhaustion, gasping on huge ingulped laughs which swept their bones together, and for fear of waking God, country, wife, Mom, and hell, they snug-clapped hands to each other's mouths, felt the vibrant warm hilarity fountained there, and sat one instant longer, eyes bright with each other and wet with love.

Then, with a last strong clasp, Dad was gone, the bedroom door shut.

Drunk on the long night's doings, lolled away from fear toward better, grander things found in Dad, Will slung off limp-falling clothes with tipsy arms and delightfully aching legs, and like a fall of timber chopped himself to bed....

chapter twenty-nine

He slept for exactly one hour.

And then, as if remembering something he had only half seen, he woke, sat up, and peered out at Jim's rooftop.

"The lightning rod!" he yelped. "It's *gone!*"

Which indeed it was.

Stolen? No. Jim take it down? Yes! Why? For the shucks of it. Smiling, he had climbed to scuttle the iron, dare any storm to strike *his* house! Afraid? No. Fear was a new electric-power suit Jim must try for size.

Jim! Will wanted to smash his confounded window. Go nail the rod back! Before morn, Jim, the blasted carnival'll send someone to find where we live, don't know how they'll come or what they'll look like, but, Lord, your roof's so *empty!* the clouds are moving fast, that storm's rushing at us and . . .

Will stopped.

What sort of noise does a balloon make, adrift?

None.

No, not quite. It noises itself, it soughs, like the wind billowing your curtains all white as breaths of foam. Or it makes a sound like the stars turning over in your sleep. Or it announces itself like moonrise and moonset. That last is best: like the moon sailing the universal deeps, so rides a balloon.

How do you hear it, how are you warned? The ear, does it hear? No. But the hairs on the back of your neck, and the peach-fuzz in your ears, *they* do, and the hair along your arms sings like grasshopper legs frictioned and trembling with strange music. So you know, you feel, you are sure, lying abed, that a balloon is submerging the ocean sky.

Will sensed a stir in Jim's house; Jim, too, with his fine dark antennae, must have felt the waters part high over town to let a Leviathan pass.

Both boys felt a shadow bulk the drive between houses, both flung up their windows, both poked their heads out, both dropped their jaws in surprise at this friendly, this always exquisite timing, this delightful pantomime of intuition, of apprehension, their tandem teamwork over the years. Then, silver-faced, for the moon was rising, both glanced up.

As a balloon wafted over and vanished.

"Holy cow, what's a balloon doing *here!?*" Jim asked, but wished no answer.

For, peering, they both knew the balloon was searching the best search ever; no car-motor racket, no tires whining asphalt, no footstepped street, just the wind clearing a great amazon through the clouds for a solemn voyage of wicker basket and storm sail riding over.

Neither Jim nor Will crashed his window or pulled his shade, they simply *had* to stay motionless waiting, for they *heard* the noise again like a murmur in someone else's dream. . . .

The temperature dropped forty degrees.

Because now the storm-bleached balloon whisper-purled, plummet-sank softly down, its elephant shadow cooling gemmed lawns and sundials as they flaunted their swift gaze high through that shadow.

And what they saw was something akimbo and arustle in the down-hung wicker carriage. Was that head and shoulders? Yes, with the moon like a silver cloak thrown up behind. Mr. Dark! thought Will. The Crusher! thought Jim. The Wart! thought Will. The Skeleton! The Lava Sipper! The Hanging Man! Monsieur Guillotine!

No.

The Dust Witch.

The Witch who might draw skulls and bones in the dust, then sneeze it away.

Jim looked to Will and Will to Jim; both read their lips: *the Witch!*

But why a wax crone flung out in a night balloon to search? thought Will, why none of the others, with their lizard-venom, wolf-fire, snake-spit eyes? Why send a crumbled statue with blind-newt lashes sewn tight with black-widow thread?

And then, looking up, they knew.

For the Witch, though peculiar wax, was peculiarly alive. Blind, yes, but she thrust down rust-splotched fingers which petted, stroked the sluices of air, which cut and splayed the wind, peeled layers of space, blinded stars, which hovered and danced, then fixed and pointed as did her nose.

And the boys knew even more.

They knew that she was blind, but special blind. She could dip down her hands to feel the bumps of the world, touch house roofs, probe attic bins, reap dust, examine draughts that blew through halls and souls that blew through people, draughts vented from bellows to thump-wrist, to pound-temples, to pulse-throat, and back to bellows again. Just as they felt that balloon sift down like an autumn rain, so she could feel their souls disinhabit, reinhabit their tremulous nostrils. Each soul, a vast warm fingerprint, *felt* different, she could roil it in her hand like clay; smelled different, Will could hear her snuffing his life away; *tasted* different, she savored them with her raw-gummed mouth, her puff-adder tongue; *sounded* different, she stuffed their souls in one ear, tissued them out the other!

Her hands played down the air, one for Will, one for Jim.

The balloon shadow washed them with panic, rinsed them with terror.

The Witch exhaled.

The balloon, freed of this small sour ballast, uprose. The shadow passed.

"Oh God!" said Jim. "Now they know where we live!"

Both gasped. Some monstrous baggage brushed and dragged across the shingles of Jim's house.

"Will! She's *got* me!"

"No! I think—"

The drag, brush, rustle scurried from bottom to top of Jim's roof. Then Will saw the balloon whirl up, fly off toward the hills.

"She's gone, there she goes! Jim, she *did* something to your roof. Shove the monkey pole over!"

Jim slid the long slender clothesline pole over, Will fixed it on his sill, then swung out, hand over hand, swung until Jim pulled him through his window and they bare-footed it into Jim's clothes closet and boosted and hoisted each other up inside the attic that smelled like lumber mills, old, dark, and too silent. Perched out on the high roof, shivering, Will cried: "Jim, there it *is*."

And there it was, in the moonlight.

It was a track like a snail paints on a sidewalk. It glistered. It was silver-slick. But this was a path left by a *gigantic* snail that, if it existed at all, weighed a hundred pounds. The silver ribbon was a yard across. Starting down at the leaf-filled rain trough, the silver track shimmered to the rooftop, then tremored down the other side.

"Why?" gasped Jim. "Why?"

"Easier than looking for house numbers or street names. She marked your roof so you can see it for miles around, night *or* day!"

"Ohmigosh." Jim bent to touch the track. A faint evil-smelling glue covered his finger. "Will, what'll we do?"

"I got a hunch," the other whispered, "they won't be back till morning. They can't just start a rumpus. They got some plan. Right now—*there's* what we do!"

Coiled across the lawn below like a vast boa constrictor, waiting for them, was the garden hose.

Will was gone, down, fast, and didn't knock anything over or wake anyone up. Jim, on the roof, was surprised, in no time at all, when Will came scuttling up all panting teeth, the water-fizzing hose in his fist.

"Will, you're a genius!"

"Sure! Quick!"

They dragged the hose to drench the shingles, to wash the silver, flood the evil mercury paint away.

Working, Will glanced off at the pure color of night turning toward morn and saw the balloon trying to make decisions on the wind. Did it sense, would it come back? Would she mark the roof again, and they have to wash it off, and she mark it, and they wash it, until dawn? Yes, if need be.

If only, thought Will, I could stop the Witch for good. They don't know our names or where we live, Mr. Cooger's too near dead to remember or tell. The Dwarf—if he *is* the lightning-rod man—is mad—and, God willing, won't recollect! And they won't dare bother Miss Foley until morning. So, grinding their teeth way out in the meadows, they've sent the Dust Witch to search. . . .

"I'm a fool," grieved Jim, quietly, rinsing the roof where the lightning rod had been. "Why didn't I leave it *up?*"

"Lightning hasn't struck yet," Will said. "And if we jump lively, it won't. Now—over here!"

They showered the roof.

Below, someone put down a window.

"Mom." Jim laughed, bleakly. "She thinks it's raining."

chapter thirty

The rain ceased.

The roof was clean.

They let the hose snake away to thump on the night grass a thousand miles below.

Beyond town, the balloon still paused between unpromising midnight and promised and hoped-for sun.

"Why's she waiting?"

"Maybe she *smells* what we're up to."

They went back down through the attic and soon were in separate rooms and beds after many fevers and chills of talk and now lay quietly separate listening to hearts and clocks beat too quickly toward dawn.

Whatever they do, thought Will, we *must* do it first. He wished the balloon might fly back, the Witch might guess they had washed her mark off and soar down to trace the roof again. Why?

Because.

He found himself staring at his Boy Scout archery set, the big beautiful bow and quiver of arrows arranged on the east wall of his room.

Sorry, Dad, he thought, and sat up, smiling. This time it's me out, alone. I don't want *her* going back to report on us for hours, maybe days.

He grabbed the bow and quiver from the wall, hesitated, thinking, then stealthily ran the window up and leaned out. No need to holler loud and long, no. But just think real hard. *They* can't read thoughts, I know, that's sure, or they wouldn't send her, and *she* can't read thoughts, but she *can* feel body heat and special temperatures and special smells and excitements, and if I jump up and down and let her know just by my feeling good about having tricked her maybe, maybe . . .

Four o'clock in the morning, said a drowsy clock chime, off in another land.

Witch, he thought, *come back.*

Witch, he thought louder and let his blood pound, the roof's clean, hear!? We made our own rain! You got to come back and re-mark it! Witch . . . ?

And the Witch moved.

He felt the earth turn under the balloon.

Okay, Witch, come on, there's just me, the no-name boy, you can't read my mind, but here's me spitting on you! and here's me yelling we tricked you, and the general idea gets through, so come on, come on! dare! double-dare you!

Miles away, there was a gasp of assent rising, coming near.

Holy cow, he thought suddenly, I don't want her back to *this* house! Come on! He thrashed into his clothes.

Clutching his weapons, he aped down the hidden ivy rungs and dogged the wet grass.

Witch! Here! He ran leaving patterns, ran feeling crazy fine, wild as a hare who has chewed some secret, delicious, sweetly poisonous root that now gallops him berserk. Knees striking his chin, shoes crushing wet leaves, he soared over a hedge, his hands full of bristly porcupine weapons, fear and joy a tumble of mixed marbles in his mouth.

He looked back. The balloon swung near! It inhaled, exhaled itself along from tree to tree, from cloud to cloud.

Where am I *going?* he thought. Wait! The Redman house! Not lived in in years! Two blocks more!

There was the swift shush of his feet in the leaves and the big shush of the creature in the sky, while moonlight snowed everything and stars glittered.

He pulled up in front of the Redman house, a torch in each lung, tasting blood, crying out silently: here! this is *my* house!

He felt a great river change its bed in the sky.

Good! he thought.

His hand turned the doorknob of the old house. Oh God, he thought, what if *they* are inside, waiting for me?

He opened a door on darkness.

Dust came and went in that dark, and a harpstring gesticulation of spiders. Nothing else.

Will jumped two at a time up the crumbling stairs, around and out on the roof where he stashed his weapons behind the chimney and stood tall.

The balloon, green as slime, printed with titan pictures of winged scorpions, ancient phoenixes, smokes, fires, clouded weathers, swung its wicker basket wheezing, down.

Witch, he thought, *here!*

The dank shadow struck him like a batwing.

Will toppled. He flung up his hands. The shadow was almost black flesh, striking.

He fell. He clutched the chimney.

The shadow draped him, hushing down.

It was cold as a sea cave in that cloud-dark.

But suddenly the wind, of itself, veered.

The Witch hissed in frustration. The balloon swam a washing circle up around.

The wind! thought the boy wildly, it's on *my* side!

No, don't go! he thought. Come back.

For he feared she had smelled his plan.

She had. She itched for his scheme. She snuffed, she gasped at it. He saw the way her nails filed and scraped the air as if running over grooved wax to seek patterns. She turned her palms out and down as if he were a small stove burning softly somewhere in a nether world and she came to warm her hands at him. As the basket swung in an upglided pendulum he saw her squinched blind-sewn eyes, the ears with moss in them, the pale wrinkled apricot mouth mummifying the air it drew in, trying to taste what was wrong with his act, his thought. He was too good, too rare, too fine, too available to be true! surely she knew that!

And knowing it, she held her breath.

Which made the balloon suspend itself, half between inhale and exhale.

Now, tremulously, experimentally, daring to test, the Witch inhaled. The balloon, so weighted, sank. Exhaled—so freed of vapor—the craft ascended!

Now, now, the waiting, the holding of dank sour breath in the wry tissues of her childlike body.

Will waggled his fingers, thumb to nose.

She sucked air. The weight of this one breath skimmed the balloon down.

Closer! he thought.

But, careful, she circled her craft, scenting the sharp adrenalin wafted from his pores. He wheeled, following as the balloon spun, and him reeling. You! he thought, you want me sick! Spin me, will you? Make me dizzy?

There was one last thing to try.

He stood very still with his back to the balloon.

Witch, he thought, you can't resist.

He felt the sound of the green slime cloud, the kept bag of sour air, the squeal and stir of mouse-wicker on wicker as the shadow cooled his legs, his spine, his neck.

Close!

The Witch took air, weight, night burden, star-and-cold-wind ballast.

Closer!

Elephant shadow stroked his ears.

He nudged his weapons.

The shadow engulfed him.

A spider flicked his hair—her *hand?*

Choking a scream, he spun.

The witch, leaned out, was a mere foot away.

He bent. He snatched.

The Witch tried to scream out breath when she smelled, felt, knew what he held tight.

But, in reaction, horrified, she seized a breath, sucked weight, burdened the balloon. It dragged the roof.

Will pulled the bowstring back, freighted with single destruction.

The bow broke in two pieces. He stared at the unshot arrow in his hands.

The Witch let out her breath in one great sigh of relief and triumph.

The balloon swung up. It struck him with its dry rattle-chuckling heavy-laden basket.

The Witch shouted again with insane happiness.

Clutched to the basket rim, Will with one free hand drew back and with all his strength threw the arrowhead flint up at the balloon flesh.

The Witch gagged. She tore at his face.

Then the arrow, a long hour it seemed in flight, razored a small vent in the balloon. Rapidly the shaft sank as if cutting a vast green cheese. The surface slit itself further in a wide ripping smile across the entire surface of the gigantic pear, as the blind Witch gabbled, moaned, blistered her lips, shrieked in protest, and Will hung fast, hands gripped to wicker, kicking legs, as the balloon wailed, whiffled, guzzled, mourned its own swift gaseous death, as dungeon air raved out, as dragon breath gushed forth and the bag, thus driven, retreated up.

Will let go. Space whistled about him. He turned, hit shingles, fell skidding down the inclined ancient roof, over down to rim, to rainspout where, feet first, he spilled into further emptiness, yelling, clawed at the rain gutter, held, felt it groan, give way, as he swept the sky to see the balloon whistling, wrinkling, flying up like a wounded beast to evacuate its terrified exhalations in the clouds; a gunshot mammoth, not wanting to expire, yet in terrible flux coughing out its stinking winds.

All this in a flash. Then Will flailed into space, with no time to be glad for a tree beneath when it netted him, cut him, but broke his fall with mattress twig, branch and limb. Like a kite he was held face up to the moon where, at his exhausted leisure, he might hear the last Witch lamentations for a wake in progress as the balloon spiraled her away from house, street, town with inhuman mourns.

The balloon smile, the balloon rip was all-encompassing now as it wandered in deliriums to die in the meadows from which it had come, sinking down now beyond all the sleeping, ignorant and unknowing houses.

For a long while Will could not move. Buoyed in the tree branches, afraid he might slip through and kill himself on the black earth below, he waited for the sledge hammer to subside in his head.

The blows of his heart might jar him loose, crash him down, but he was glad to hear them, know himself alive.

But then at last, gone calm, he gathered his limbs, most carefully searched for a prayer, and climbed himself down through the tree.

chapter thirty-one

Nothing much else happened, all the rest of that night.

chapter thirty-two

At dawn, a juggernaut of thunder wheeled over the stony heavens in a spark-throwing tumult. Rain fell softly on town cupolas, chuckled from rainspouts, and spoke in strange subterranean tongues beneath the windows where Jim and Will knew fitful dreams, slipping out of one, trying another for size, but finding all cut from the same dark, mouldered cloth.

In the rustling drumbeat, a second thing occurred:

From the sodden carnival grounds, the carousel suddenly spasmed to life. Its calliope fluted up malodorous steams of music.

Perhaps only one person in town heard and guessed that the carousel was working again.

The door to Miss Foley's house opened and shut; her footsteps hurried away along the street.

Then the rain fell hard as lightning did a crippled dance down the now-totally-revealed, now-vanishing-forever land.

In Jim's house, in Will's house, as the rain nuzzled the breakfast windows, there was a lot of quiet talk, some shouting, and more quiet talk again.

At nine-fifteen, Jim shuffled out into the Sunday weather, wearing his raincoat, cap, and rubbers.

He stood gazing at his roof where the giant snail track was washed away. Then he stared at Will's door to make it open. It did. Will emerged. His father's voice followed: "Want me to come along?" Will shook his head, firmly.

The boys walked solemnly, the sky washing them, toward the police station where they would talk, to Miss Foley's where they would apologize again, but right now they only walked, hands in pockets, thinking of yesterday's fearful puzzles. At last, Jim broke the silence:

"Last night, after we washed off the roof, and I finally got to sleep, I dreamed a funeral. It came right down Main Street, like a visit."

"Or . . . a parade?"

"That's it! A thousand people, all dressed in black coats, black hats, black shoes, and a coffin *forty feet long!*"

"Criminently!"

"Right! What's forty feet long needs to be buried?! I thought. And in the dream I ran up and looked in. Don't laugh."

"I don't feel funny, Jim."

"In the long coffin was a big long wrinkled thing like a prune or a big grape lying in the sun. Like a big skin or a giant's head, drying."

"The *balloon!*"

"Hey." Jim stopped. "You must've had the same dream! But . . . balloons can't die, can they?"

Will was silent.

"And you don't have funerals for them, *do* you?"

"Jim, I . . ."

"Darn balloon laid out like a hippo someone leaked the wind out of—"

"Jim, last night . . ."

"Black plumes waving, band banging on black velvet-muffled drums with black ivory bones, boy, boy! Then on top of it, have to get up this morning and tell Mom, not everything, but enough so she cried and yelled and cried some more, women sure like to cry, don't they? and called me her criminal son but—we *didn't* do anything bad, did we, Will?"

"Someone *almost* took a ride on a merry-go-round."

Jim walked along in the rain. "I don't think I want any more of that."

"You don't *think!?* After all *this!?* Good grief, let me *tell* you! The Witch, Jim, the balloon! Last night, all alone, I—"

But there was no time to tell it.

No time to tell his stabbing the balloon so it gusted away to die in the lonely country sinking the blind woman with it.

No time because walking in the cold rain now, they heard a sad sound.

They were passing an empty lot, deep within which stood a vast oak tree. Under it were rainy shadows, and the sound.

"Jim," said Will, "someone's—*crying*."

"No." Jim moved on.

"There's a little girl in there."

"No." Jim would not look. "What would a girl be doing out under a tree in the rain? Come on."

"Jim! You *hear* her!"

"No! I don't, I don't!"

But then the crying came stronger across the dead grass, flew like a sad bird through the rain, and Jim had to turn, for there was Will marching across the rubble.

"Jim—that voice—I know it!"

"Will, don't go there!"

And Jim did not move, but Will stumbled and walked until he entered the shade of the raining tree where the sky fell and was lost in autumn leaves and crept down at last in shining rivers along the branches and trunk and there was the little girl, crouched, face buried in her hands, weeping as if the town were gone and the people in it and herself lost in terrible woods.

And at last Jim came edging up and stood at the edge of the shadow and said, "Who is it?"

"I don't know." But Will felt tears start to his eyes, as if some part of him guessed.

"It's not Jenny Holdridge, is it . . . ?"

"No."

"Jane Franklin?"

"No." His mouth felt full of novocaine, his tongue merely stirred in his numb lips. " . . . no . . ."

The little girl wept, feeling them near, but not looking up yet.

" . . . me . . . me . . . help me . . . nobody'll help me . . . me . . . I don't *like* this . . ."

Then when she had strength enough and was quieter she turned her face, her eyes almost swollen shut with weeping. She was shocked to see anyone near, then surprised.

"Jim! Will! Oh God, it's you!"

She seized Jim's hand. He writhed back, yelling. "No! I don't know you, let go!"

"Will, help me, Jim, oh don't go, don't leave!" she gasped, brokenly, new tears bursting from her eyes.

"No, no, don't!" screamed Jim, he thrashed, he broke free, fell, leaped to his feet, one fist raised to strike. He stopped, trembling, held it to his side. "Oh, Will, Will, let's get out of here, I'm sorry, oh God, God."

The little girl in the shadow of the tree, flung back, widened her eyes to fix the two in wetness, moaned, clutched herself and rocked back and forth, her own child-baby, comforting her elbows . . . soon she might sing to herself and sing that way, alone beneath the dark tree, forever, no one able to join or stop the song.

" . . . someone must help me . . . someone must help *her* . . ." she mourned as for one dead, "someone must help her . . . nobody will . . . nobody has . . . help her if not me . . . terrible . . . terrible . . ."

"She knows us!" said Will, hopelessly, half bent down to her, half turned to Jim. "I can't leave her!"

"Lies!" said Jim, wildly. "Lies! She don't know us! Never saw her before!"

"She's gone, bring her back, she's gone, bring her back," mourned the girl, eyes shut.

"Find who?" Will got down on one knee, dared to touch her hand. She grabbed him. Almost immediately she knew this was wrong for he tried to tear free, so she let him go, and wept, while he waited near and Jim, far out in the dead grass, called in for them to go, he didn't like it, they must, they must go.

"Oh, she's lost," sobbed the little girl. "She ran off in that place and never came back. Will you find her, please, please . . . ?"

Shivering, Will touched her cheek. "Hey now," he whispered. "You'll be okay. I'll find help," he said, gently. She opened her eyes. "This is Will Halloway, okay? Cross my heart, we'll be back. Ten minutes. But you mustn't go away." She shook her head. "You'll wait here under the tree for us?" She nodded, mutely. He stood up. This simple motion frightened her and she flinched. So he waited and looked at her and said, "I know who you are." He saw the great familiar eyes open gray in the small wounded face. He saw the long rain-washed black hair and the pale cheeks. "I know who you are. But I got to check."

"Who'll believe?" she wailed.

"*I* believe," Will said.

And she lay back against the tree, her hands in her lap, trembling, very thin, very white, very lost, very small.

"Can I go now?" he said.

She nodded.

And he walked away.

At the edge of the lot, Jim stomped his feet in disbelief, almost hysterical with outrage and declamation.

"It can't be!"

"It *is*," said Will. "The eyes. That's how you tell. Like it was with Mr. Cooger and the evil boy—There's one way to be sure. Come on!"

And he took Jim through the town and they stopped at last in front of Miss Foley's house and looked at the unlit windows in the morning gloom and walked up the steps and rang the bell, once, twice, three times.

Silence.

Very slowly, the front door moved whining back on its hinges.

"Miss Foley?" Jim called, softly.

Somewhere off in the house, shadows of rain moved on far windowpanes.

"Miss Foley . . . ?"

They stood in the hall by the bead-rain in the entry door, listening to the great attic beams ashift and astir in the downpour.

"Miss Foley!" Louder.

But only the mice in the walls, warmly nested, made sgraffito sounds in answer.

"She's gone out to shop," said Jim.

"No," said Will. "We know where she is."

"Miss Foley, I know you're here!" shouted Jim suddenly, savagely, dashing upstairs. "Come on out, you!"

Will waited for him to search and drag slowly back down. As Jim reached the bottom of the steps, they both heard the music blowing through the front door with the smell of fresh rain and ancient grass.

The carousel calliope, among the hills, piping the "Funeral March" backwards.

Jim opened the door wider and stood in the music, as one stands in the rain.

"The merry-go-round. They fixed it!"

Will nodded. "She must've heard the music, gone out at sunrise. Something went wrong. Maybe the carousel wasn't fixed right. Maybe accidents happen all the time. Like to the lightning-rod man, him inside-out and crazy. Maybe the carnival *likes* accidents, gets a kick out of them. Or maybe they did something to her on purpose. Maybe they wanted to know more about us, our names, where we live, or wanted her to help them hurt us. Who knows *what?* Maybe she got suspicious or scared. Then they just gave her *more* than she ever wanted or asked for."

"I don't understand—"

But now, in the doorway, in the cold rain, there was time to think of Miss Foley afraid of mirror mazes, Miss Foley alone not so long ago at the carnival, and maybe screaming when they did what they finally did to her, around and around, around and around, too many years, more years than she had ever dreamed of shucked away, rubbing her raw, leaving her naked small, alone, and bewildered because unknown-even-to-herself, around and around, until all the years were gone and the carousel rocked to a halt like a roulette wheel, and nothing gained and all lost and nowhere for her to go, no way to tell the strangeness, and nothing to do but . . . weep under a tree, alone, in the autumn rain. . . .

Will thought this. Jim thought it, and said:

"Oh, the poor . . . the poor . . ."

"We got to help her, Jim. Who else would believe? If she tells anyone, 'I'm Miss Foley!' 'Get away!' they'd say, 'Miss Foley's left town, disappeared! Go on, little girl!' Oh, Jim, I bet she's pounded a dozen doors this morning, wanting help, scared people with her screaming and yelling, then run off, gave up, and hid under that tree. Police are probably looking for her now, but so what? it's just a wild girl crying and they'll lock her away and she'll go crazy. That carnival, boy, do they know how to punish so you can't hit back. They just shake you up and change you so no one ever knows you again and let you run free, it's okay, go ahead, talk, 'cause folks are too scared of you to listen. Only *we* hear, Jim, only you and me, and right now I feel like I just ate a cold snail raw."

They looked back a last time at the shadows of rain crying on the windows inside the parlor where a teacher had often served them cookies and hot chocolate and waved to them from the window and moved tall through the town. Then they stepped out and shut the door and ran back toward the empty lot.

"We got to hide her, until we can help—"

"Help?" panted Jim. "We can't help *ourselves!*"

"There's got to be weapons, right in front of us, we're just too blind—"

They stopped.

Beyond the thump of their own hearts, a greater heart thumped. Brass trumpets wailed. Trombones blared. A herd of tubas made an elephant charge, alarmed for unknown reasons.

"The carnival!" gasped Jim. "We never thought! It can come *right into town.* A parade! Or that funeral I dreamt about, for the balloon?"

"Not a funeral and only what *looks* like a parade but's a search for us, Jim, for us, or Miss Foley, if they want her back! They can march down any old street, fine and dandy, and spy as they go, drum and bugle! Jim, we got to get her before they—"

And breaking off, they flung themselves down an alley, but stopped suddenly, and leaped to hide in some bushes.

At the far end of the alley, the carnival band, animal wagons, clowns, freaks and all, banged and crashed between them and the empty lot and the great oak tree.

It must have taken five minutes for the parade to pass. The rain seemed to move on away, the clouds moving with them. The rain ceased. The strut of drums faded. The boys loped down the alley, across the street, and stopped by the empty lot.

There was no little girl under the tree.

They circled it, looked up in it, not daring to call a name.

Then, very much afraid, they ran to hide themselves somewhere in the town.

chapter thirty-three

The phone rang.

Mr. Halloway picked it up.

"Dad, this is Willy, we can't go to the police station, we may not be home today, tell Mom, tell Jim's mom."

"Willy, where are you?"

"We got to hide. *They're* looking for us."

"*Who*, for God's sake?"

"I don't want you in it, Dad. You got to believe, we'll just hide one day, two, until they go away. If we came home they'd follow and hurt you or Ma or Jim's mom. I got to go."

"Willy, don't!"

"Oh, Dad," said Will. "Wish me luck."

Click.

Mr. Halloway looked out at the trees, the houses, the streets, hearing a faraway music.

"Willy," he said to the dead phone. "Luck."

And he put on his coat and hat and went out into the strange bright rainy sunshine that filled the cold air.

chapter thirty-four

I n front of the United Cigar Store on this before-noon Sunday with the bells of all churches ringing across here, colliding with each other there, showering sound from the sky now that the rain was spent, in front of the cigar store the Cherokee wooden Indian stood, his carved plumes pearled with water, oblivious to Catholic or Baptist bells, oblivious to the steadily approaching sun-bright cymbals, the thumping pagan heart of the carnival band. The flourished drums, the old-womanish shriek of calliope, the shadow drift of creatures far stranger than he, did not witch the Indian's yellow hawk-fierce gaze. Still, the drums did tilt churches and plummet forth mobs of boys curious and eager for any change mild or wild, so, as the church bells stopped up their silver and iron rain, pew-stiffened crowds became relaxed parade crowds as the carnival, a promotion of brass, a flush of velvet, all lion-pacing, mammoth-shuffling, flag-fluttered by.

The shadow of the Indian's wooden tomahawk lay on an iron grille imbedded in the sidewalk in front of the cigar store. Over this grille, with faint metallic reverberations, year after year, people passed, dropping tonnages of mint-gum wrapper, gold cigar band, matchstub, cigarette butt or copper penny which vanished below forever.

Now, with the parade, hundreds of feet rang and, clustered on the grille as the carnival strode by on stilts, roared by in tiger and volcano sounds and colors.

Under the grille, two shapes trembled.

Above, like a great baroque peacock striding the bricks and asphalt, the freaks' eyes opened out, to stare, to search office roofs, church spires, read dentists' and opticians' signs, check dime and dry goods stores as drums shocked plate glass windows and wax dummies quaked in facsimiles of fear. A multitude of hot and incredibly bright fierce eyes, the parade moved, desiring, but not quenching its desire.

For the things it most wanted were hidden in dark.

Jim and Will, under the cigar store sidewalk grille.

Crouch-pressed knee to knee, heads up, eyes alert, they sucked their breaths like iron Popsicles. Above, women's dresses flowered in a cold breeze. Above, men tilted on the sky. The band, in a collision of cymbals, knocked children against their mothers' knees with concussion.

"There!" exclaimed Jim. "The parade! It's right out front the cigar store! What're we *doing* here, Will? Let's go!"

"No!" cried Will, hoarsely, clenching Jim's knee. "It's the most *obvious* place, in front of everybody! They'll never think to check here! Shut up!"

Thrrrummmmm . . .

The grille, above, rang with the touch of a man's shoe, and the worn nails in that shoe.

Dad! Will almost cried.

He rose, sank back, biting his lips.

Jim saw the man above wheel this way, wheel that, searching, so near, yet so far, three feet away.

I could just reach up . . . thought Will.

But Dad, pale, nervous, hurried on.

And Will felt his soul fall over cold and white-jelly quivering inside.

Bang!

The boys jerked.

A chewed lump of pink bubble gum, falling, had hit a pile of old paper near Jim's foot.

A five-year-old boy, above, crouched on the grille, peered down with dismay after his vanished sweet.

Get! thought Will.

The boy knelt, hands to the grille.

Go on! thought Will.

He had a crazy wish to grab the gum and stuff it back up into the little boy's mouth.

A parade-drum thumped one huge time, then—silence.

Jim and Will glanced at each other.

The parade, both thought, it's *halted!*

The small boy stuck one hand half through the grille.

Above, in the street, Mr. Dark, the Illustrated Man, glanced back over his river of freaks, cages, at the sunburst tubas and python brass horns. He nodded.

The parade fell apart.

The freaks hurried half to one sidewalk, half to the other, mingling with the crowd, passing out handbills, eyes fire-crystal, quick, striking like snakes.

The small boy's shadow cooled Will's cheek.

The parade's over, he thought, now the search begins.

"Look, Ma!" The small boy pointed down through the grille. *"There!"*

chapter thirty-five

In Ned's Night Spot, half a block from the cigar store, Charles Halloway, exhausted from no sleep, too much thinking, far too much walking, finished his second coffee and was about to pay when the sharp silence from the street outside made him uneasy. He sensed rather than saw the mild intermingled disturbance as the parade melted among the sidewalk crowds. Not knowing why, Charles Halloway put his money away.

"Warm it up again, Ned?"

Ned was pouring coffee when the door swung wide, someone entered, and splayed his right hand lightly on the counter.

Charles Halloway stared.

The hand stared back at him.

There was a single eye tattooed on the back of each finger.

"Mom! Down there! Look!"

The boy cried, pointing through the grille.

More shadows passed and lingered.

Including—the Skeleton.

Tall as a dead tree in winter, all skull, all scarecrow-stilted bones, the thin man, the Skeleton, Mr. Skull played his xylophone shadow upon hidden things, cold paper rubbish, warm flinching boys, below.

Go! thought Will. Go!

The plump fingers of the child gesticulated through the grille. Go.

Mr. Skull walked away.

Thank God, thought Will, then gasped, "Oh, *no!*"

For the Dwarf as suddenly appeared, waddling along, a fringe of bells on his dirty shirt jingling softly, his toad-shadow tucked under him, his eyes like broken splinters of brown marble now bright-on-the-surface mad, now deeply mournfully forever-lost-and-gone-buried-away mad, looking for something could not be found, a lost self somewhere, lost boys for an instant, then the lost self again, two parts of the little squashed man fought to jerk his flashing eyes here, there, around, up, down, one seeking the past, one the immediate present.

"Mama!" said the child.

The Dwarf stopped and looked at the boy no bigger than himself. Their eyes met.

Will flung himself back, tried to gum his body into the concrete. He felt Jim do the same, not moving but moving his mind, his soul, thrusting it into darkness to hide from the little drama above.

"Come on, Junior!" A woman's voice.

The boy was pulled up and away.

Too late.

For the Dwarf was looking down.

And in his eyes were the lost bits and fitful pieces of a man named Fury who had sold lightning rods how many days how many years ago in the long, the easy, the safe and wondrous time before this fright was born.

Oh, Mr. Fury, thought Will, what they've done to you. Threw you under a pile driver, squashed you in a steel press, squeezed the tears and screams out of you, trapped you in a jack-in-a-box

all pressed down until there's nothing left of you, Mr. Fury . . .
nothing left but this . . .

Dwarf. And the Dwarf's face was less human, more machine
now; in fact, a camera.

The shuttering eyes flexed, sightless, opening upon darkness.
Tick. Two lenses expanded—contracted with liquid swiftness: a
picture-snap of the grille.

A snap, also, of what lay beneath?

Is he staring at the metal, thought Will, or the spaces between
the metal?

For a long moment, the ruined-squashed clay doll Dwarf
squatted while standing tall. His flash-camera eyes were bulbed
wide, perhaps still taking pictures?

Will, Jim, were not seen really at all, only their shape, their
color and size were borrowed by these dwarf camera eyes. They
were clapped away in the box-Brownie skull. Later—how much
later?—the picture would be developed by the wild, the tiny, the
forgetful, the wandering and lost lightning-rod mind. What lay
under the grille would then be really seen. And after that? Revelation! Revenge! Destruction!

Click-snap-tick.

Children ran laughing by.

The Dwarf-child, drawn by their running joy, was swept
along with them. Madly, he skipped off, remembered himself,
and went looking for something, he knew not what.

The cloudy sun poured light through all the sky.

The two boys, boxed in light-slotted pit, hisstled their breath
softly out through gritted teeth.

Jim squeezed Will's hand, tight, tight.

Both waited for more eyes to stride along and rake the steel
grille.

The blue-red-green tattooed eyes, all five of them, fell away
from the counter top.

Charles Halloway, sipping his third coffee, turned slightly on
the revolving stool.

The Illustrated Man was watching him.

Charles Halloway nodded.

The Illustrated Man did not nod or blink, but stared until the janitor wanted to turn away, but did not, and simply *gazed* as calmly as possible at the impertinent intruder.

"What'll it be?" asked the cafe proprietor.

"Nothing." Mr. Dark watched Will's father. "I'm looking for two boys."

Who *isn't*? Charles Halloway rose, paid, walked off. "Thanks, Ned." In passing, he saw the man with the tattoos hold his hands out, palms up toward Ned.

"Boys?" said Ned. "How old?"

The door slammed.

Mr. Dark watched Charles Halloway walk off outside the window.

Ned talked.

But the Illustrated Man did not hear.

Outside, Will's father moved toward the library, stopped, moved toward the courthouse, stopped, waited for some better sense to direct him, felt his pocket, missed his smokes, and turned toward the United Cigar Store.

Jim looked up, saw familiar feet, pale face, salt and pepper hair. "Will! Your dad! Call to him. He'll help us!"

Will could not speak.

"*I'll* call to him!"

Will hit Jim's arm, shook his head, violently, No!

Why not? mouthed Jim.

Because, said Will's lips.

Because . . . he gazed up . . . Dad looked even smaller up there than he had last night, seen from the side of the house. It would be like calling to one more boy passing. They didn't need one more boy, they needed a general, no, a major general! He tried to see Dad's face at the cigar counter window, and discover whether it looked really older, firmer, stronger, than it did last night washed with all the milk colors of the moon. But all he saw was Dad's fingers twitching nervously, his mouth working, as if he didn't dare ask his needs from Mr. Tetley. . . .

"One . . . that is . . . one twenty-five cent cigar."

"My God," said Mr. Tetley, above. "The man's rich!"

Charles Halloway took his time removing the cellophane, waiting for some hint, some move on the part of the universe to show him where he was going, why he had come back this way for a cigar he did not really want. He thought he heard himself called, twice, glanced swiftly at the crowds, saw clowns passing with handbills, then lit the cigar he did not want from the eternal blue-gas flame that burned in a small silver jet pipe on the counter, and, puffing smoke, dropped the cigar band with his free hand, saw the band bounce on the metal grille, and vanish, his eyes following it farther down to where . . .

It lit at the feet of Will Halloway, his son.

Charles Halloway choked on cigar smoke.

Two shadows there, yes! And the eyes, terror gazing up out of the dark well under the street. He almost bent to seize the grate, yelling.

Instead, incredulous, he only blurted softly, with the crowd around, and the weather clearing:

"Jim? Will! What the hell's going on?"

At which moment, one hundred feet away, the Illustrated Man came out of Ned's Night Spot.

"Mr. Halloway—" said Jim.

"Come up out of there," said Charles Halloway.

The Illustrated Man, a crowd among crowds, pivoted slowly, then walked toward the cigar store.

"Dad, we can't! Don't look at us down here!"

The Illustrated Man was some eighty feet away.

"Boys," said Charles Halloway. "The police—"

"Mr. Halloway," said Jim, hoarsely, "we're dead if you don't look up! The Illustrated Man, if he—"

"The *what?*" asked Mr. Halloway.

"The man with the tattoos!"

From the café counter, five electric blue-inked eyes fixed Mr. Halloway's memory.

"Dad, look over at the courthouse clock, while we tell you what happened—"

Mr. Halloway straightened up.

And the Illustrated Man arrived.

He stood studying Charles Halloway.

"Sir," said the Illustrated Man.

"Eleven-fifteen." Charles Halloway judged the courthouse clock, adjusted his wrist watch, cigar in mouth. "One minute slow."

"Sir," said the Illustrated Man.

Will held Jim, Jim held Will fast in the gum-wrapper, tobacco-littered pit, as the four shoes rocked, shuffled, tilted above.

"Sir," said the man named Dark, probing Charles Halloway's face for the bones there to compare to other bones in other half-similar people, "the Cooger-Dark Combined Shows have picked two local boys, two! to be our special guests during our celebratory visit!"

"Well, I—" Will's father tried not to glance at the sidewalk.

"These two boys—"

Will watched the tooth-sharp shoe nails of the Illustrated Man flash, sparking the grille.

"—these boys will ride all rides, see each show, shake hands with every performer, go home with magic kits, baseball bats—"

"Who," interrupted Mr. Halloway, "are these lucky boys?"

"Two selected from photos snapped on our midway yesterday. Identify them, sir, and you will share their fortune. *There* are the boys!"

He *sees* us down here! thought Will. Oh, God!

The Illustrated Man thrust out his hands.

Will's father lurched.

Tattooed in bright blue ink, Will's face gazed up at him from the palm of the right hand.

Ink-sewn to the left palm, Jim's face was indelible and natural as life.

"You know them?" The Illustrated Man saw Mr. Halloway's throat clench, his eyelids squinch, his bones struck vibrant as from a sledge-hammer blow. "Their names?"

Dad, careful! Will thought.

"I don't—" said Will's father.

"You know them."

The Illustrated Man's hands shook, held out to view, asking for the gift of names, making Jim's face on the flesh, Will's face on the flesh, Jim's face hidden beneath the street, Will's face hidden beneath the street, tremble, writhe, pinch.

"Sir, you wouldn't want them to lose out . . . ?"

"No, but—"

"But, but, but?" Mr. Dark loomed closer, magnificent in his picture-gallery flesh, his eyes, the eyes of all his beasts and hapless creatures cutting through his shirt, coat, trousers, fastening the old man tight, biting him with fire, fixing him with thousandfold attentions. Mr. Dark shoved his two palms near. *"But?"*

Mr. Halloway needing something to excruciate, bit his cigar. "I thought for a moment—"

"Thought what?" Grand delight from Mr. Dark.

"One of them looked like—"

"Like *who?*"

Too eager, thought Will. You see that, Dad, don't you?

"Mister," said Will's father. "Why are you so jumpy about two boys?"

"Jumpy . . . ?"

Mr. Dark's smile melted like cotton candy.

Jim scootched himself down into a dwarf, Will crammed himself down into a midget, both looking up, waiting.

"Sir," said Mr. Dark, "is my enthusiasm *that* to you? *Jumpy?*"

Will's father noted the muscles cord along the arms, roping

and unroping themselves with a writhe like the puff adders and sidewinders doubtless inked and venomous there.

"One of those pictures," drawled Mr. Halloway, "looks like Milton Blumquist."

Mr. Dark clenched a fist.

A blinding ache struck Jim's head.

"The other," Will's father was almost bland, "looks like Avery Johnson."

Oh, Dad, thought Will, you're great!

The Illustrated Man clenched his other fist.

Will, his head in a vise, almost screamed.

"Both boys," finished Mr. Halloway, "moved to Milwaukee some weeks ago."

"You," said Mr. Dark, coldly, "lie."

Will's father was truly shocked.

"Me? And spoil the prizewinners' fun?"

"Fact is," said Mr. Dark, "we found the names of the boys ten minutes ago. Just want to double-check."

"So?" said Will's father, disbelieving.

"Jim," said Mr. Dark. "Will."

Jim writhed in the dark. Will sank his head deep in his shoulder blades, eyes tight.

Will's father's face was a pond into which the two dark stone names sank without a ripple.

"First names? Jim? Will? Lots of Jims and Wills, couple hundred, town like this."

Will, crouched and squirming, thought, who told? Miss Foley? But she was gone, her house empty and full of rain shadows. Only one other person . . .

The little girl who looked like Miss Foley weeping under the tree? The little girl who frightened us so bad? he wondered. In the last half hour the parade, going by, found her, and her crying for hours, afraid, and ready to do anything, say anything, if only with music, horses plunging, world racing, they would grow her old again, grow her around again, lift her, shut up her crying, stop up the awful thing and make her as she was. Did the carnival promise, lie to her, when they found her under the tree and ran her off? The little girl crying, but not telling all, because—

"Jim. Will," said Will's father. "First names. What about the last?"

Mr. Dark did not know the last names.

His universe of monsters sweated phosphorus on his hide, soured his armpits, reeked, slammed between his iron-sinewed legs.

"Now," said Will's father, with a strange, and to him almost-delightful-because-new, calm, "I think you're lying. You don't know the last names. Now, why should you, a carnival stranger, lie to me here on a street in some town on the backside of nowhere?"

The Illustrated Man clenched his two calligraphic fists very hard.

Will's father, his face pale, considered these mean, constricted fingers, knuckles, digging nails, inside which two boys' faces, crushed hard in dark vise, tight, very tight in prison flesh, were kept in fury.

Two shadows, below, thrashed in agony.

The Illustrated Man erased his face to serenity.

But a bright drop fell from his right fist.

A bright drop fell from his left fist.

The drops vanished through the steel sidewalk grille.

Will gasped. Wetness had struck his face. He clapped his hand to it, then looked at his palm.

The wetness that had hit his cheek was bright red.

He glanced from it to Jim, who lay still now also, for the scarification, real or imagined, seemed over and both flicked their eyes up to where the Illustrated Man's shoes flint-sparked the grille, grinding steel on steel.

Will's father saw the blood ooze from the clenched fists, but forced himself to look only at the Illustrated Man's face, as he said:

"Sorry I can't be more help."

Beyond the Illustrated Man, rounding the corner, hands

weaving the air, dressed in harlequin Gypsy colors, face waxen, eyes hid behind plum-dark glasses, the Fortune Teller, the Dust Witch came mumbling.

A moment later, looking up, Will saw her. Not dead! he thought. Carried off, bruised, fallen, yes, but now back, and mad! Lord, yes, mad, looking *especially* for *me!*

Will's father saw her. His blood slowed, by instinct alone, to a pudding in his chest.

The crowd opened happily, laughing and commenting on her bright if tattered costume, trying to remember what she rhymed, so as to tell it later. She moved, fingers feeling the town as if it were an immensely complicated and lush tapestry. And she sang:

"Tell you your husbands. Tell you your wives. Tell you your fortunes. Tell you your lives. See me, I know. See me at the show. Tell you the color of his eyes. Tell you the color of her lies. Tell you the color of his goal. Tell you the color of her soul. Come now, don't go. See me, see me at the show."

Children appalled, children impressed, parents delighted, parents in high good humor, and still the Gypsy from the dusts of living sang. Time walked in her murmuring. She made and broke microscopic webs between her fingers wherewith to feel soot fly up, breath fly out. She touched the wings of flies, the souls of invisible bacteria, all specks, mites, and mica-snowings of sunlight filtrated with motion and much more hidden emotion.

Will and Jim cracked their bones, cowered down, hearing:

"Blind, yes, blind. But I see what I see, I see where I be," said the Witch, softly. "There's a man with a straw hat in autumn. Hello. And—why there's Mr. Dark, and . . . an old man . . . an *old* man."

He's not that old! cried Will to himself, blinking up at the three, as the Witch stopped, her shadow falling moist-frog cool on the hidden boys.

" . . . old man . . ."

Mr. Halloway was jolted as by a series of cold knives thrust in his stomach.

" . . . old man . . . old man . . ." said the Witch.

She stopped this. "Ah . . ." The hairs in her nostrils bristled. She gaped her mouth to savor air. "Ah . . ."

The Illustrated Man quickened.

"Wait . . . !" sighed the Gypsy.

Her fingernails scraped down an unseen blackboard of air.

Will felt himself yip, bark, whimper like an aggravated hound.

Slowly her fingers climbed down, feeling the spectrums, weighing the light. In another moment, a forefinger might thrust to the sidewalk grille, implying: there! there!

Dad! thought Will. *Do* something!

The Illustrated Man, gone sweetly patient now that his blind but immensely aware dust lady was here, watched her with love.

"Now . . ." The Witch's fingers itched.

"Now!" said Will's father, loud.

The Witch flinched.

"Now, *this* is a fine cigar!" yelled Will's father, turning with great pomp back to the counter.

"Quiet . . ." said the Illustrated Man.

The boys looked up.

"Now—" The Witch sniffed the wind.

"Got to light it again!" Mr. Halloway stuck the cigar in the eternal blue flame.

"Silence . . ." suggested Mr. Dark.

"Ever smoke, yourself?" asked Dad.

The Witch, from the concussion of his fiercely erupted and overly jovial words, dropped one wounded hand to her side, wiped sweat from it, as one wipes an antenna for better reception, and drifted it up again, her nostrils flared with wind.

"Ah!" Will's father blew a dense cloud of cigar smoke. It made a fine thick cumulus surrounding the woman.

"Gah!" she choked.

"Fool!" The Illustrated Man barked, but whether at man or woman, the boys below could not tell.

"Here, let's buy you one!" Mr. Halloway blew more smoke, handing Mr. Dark a cigar.

The Witch exploded a sneeze, recoiled, staggered away. The Illustrated Man snatched Dad's arm, saw that he had gone too far, let go, and could only follow his Gypsy woman off, in some clumsy and totally unexpected defeat. But then, in going, he heard Will's father say, "A *fine* day to you, sir!"

No, Dad! thought Will.

The Illustrated Man came back.

"Your name, sir?" he asked, directly.

Don't tell him! thought Will.

Will's father debated a moment, took the cigar from his mouth, tapped ash and said, quietly:

"Halloway. Work in the library. Drop by some time."

"You can be sure, Mr. Halloway. I will."

The Witch was waiting near the corner.

Mr. Halloway whetted his forefinger, tested the wind, and sent a cumulus her way.

She flailed back, gone.

The Illustrated Man went rigid, spun about, and strode off, the ink portraits of Jim and Will crushed hard iron tight in his fists.

Silence.

It was so quiet under the grille, Mr. Halloway thought the two boys had died of fright.

And Will, below, gazing up, eyes wet, mouth wide, thought, Oh my gosh, why didn't I see it before?

Dad's tall. Dad's very tall indeed.

Still Charles Halloway did not look down at the grille but only at the small comets of splashed red color left on the sidewalk, trailed around the corner, dropped from the clenched hands of the vanished Mr. Dark. He was also gazing with surprise at himself, accepting the surprise, the new purpose, which was half despair, half serenity, now that the incredible deed was done.

Let no one ask why he had given his true name; even he could not assay and give its real weight. Now he could only read the numerals on the courthouse clock and speak to it, while the boys below listened.

"Oh, Jim, Will, something *is* going on. Can you hide, keep out from under, the rest of the day? We got to have time. With things like this, where do you begin? No law's been broken, none on the books, anyway. But I feel dead and buried a month. My flesh ripples. Hide, Jim, Will, hide. I'll tell your mothers you've got jobs at the carnival, good excuse for you not coming home. Stay hid until dark, then come to the library at seven. Meantime, I'll check police records on carnivals, newspaper files at the library, books, old folios, everything that might fit. God willing, by the time you show up, after dark, I'll have a plan. Walk easy until then. Bless you, Jim. Bless you, Will."

The small father who was very tall now walked slowly away.

His cigar, unnoticed, fell from his hand, dropped in a spark shower through the grate.

It lay in the square pit glowing its single fiery pink eye at Jim and Will, who looked back and at last snatched to blind and put it out.

chapter thirty-six

The dwarf, bearing his demented and wildly lighted eyes, made his way south on Main Street.

Stopping suddenly, he developed a film strip in his head, scanned it, bleated, and blundered back through the forest of legs to reach for and pull the Illustrated Man down where a whisper was as good as a shout. Mr. Dark listened, then fled, leaving the Dwarf far behind.

Reaching the cigar store Indian, the Illustrated Man sank to his knees. Clutching the steel lattice-grille, he peered down in the pit.

Below lay yellow newspapers, wilted candy wrappers, burnt cigars, and gum.

Mr. Dark's cry was muffled fury.

"*Lose* something?"

Mr. Tetley blinked over his counter.

The Illustrated Man clenched the grate, nodding once.

"I clean under the grate once a month for the money," said Mr. Tetley. "How much you lose? Dime? Quarter? Half dollar?"

Bing!

The Illustrated Man glared up.

In the cash-register window a small fire-red sign jumped high: NO SALE.

chapter thirty-seven

The town clock struck seven.

The echoes of the great chime wandered in the unlit halls of the library.

An autumn leaf, very crisp, fell somewhere in the dark.

But it was only the page of a book, turning.

Off in one of the catacombs, bent to a table under a grass-green-shaded lamp, lips pursed, eyes narrowed, sat Charles Halloway, his hands trembling the pages, lifting, rearranging the books. Now and then he hurried off to peer into the autumn night, watchful of the streets. Then again he came back to paper-clip pages, to insert papers, to scribble out quotations, whispering to himself. His voice brought forth quick echoes from the library vaults:

"Look here!"

" . . . here . . . !" said the night passages.

"This picture . . . !"

" . . . picture . . . !" said the halls.

"And *this!*"

" . . . this . . ." The dust settled.

It had been the longest day of all the days he could remember in his life. He had mingled with strange and not-so-strange crowds, he had searched after the searchers, in the wake of the wide-scattering parade. He had resisted telling Jim's mother, Will's mother, more than they needed to know for a happy Sunday, and meantime crossed shadows with Dwarf, traded nods with Pinhead and Fire-eater, kept free of shadowed alleys, and controlled his panic when, doubling back, he saw the basement pit empty under the cigar store grille and knew that the boys were at hide-and-seek somewhere nearby or somewhere, praise God, very far away.

Then, in the crowds, he moved to the carnival ground, stayed out of tents, stayed free of rides, observed, watched the sun go down, and just at twilight, surveyed the cold glass waters of the Mirror Maze and saw just enough on the shore to pull him back before he drowned. Wet all over, cold to the bone, before night caught him he let the crowd protect, warm, and bear him away up into town, to the library, and to most important books . . . which he arranged in a great literary clock on a table, like someone learning to tell a new time. So he paced round and round the huge clock squinting at the yellowed pages as if they were moth-wings pinned dead to the wood.

Here lay a portrait of the Prince of Darkness. Next a series of fantastic sketches of the Temptations of St. Anthony. Next some etchings from the *Bizarie* by Giovanbatista Bracelli, depicting a set of curious toys, humanlike robots engaged in various alchemical rites. At five minutes to twelve stood a copy of *Dr. Faustus,* at two lay an *Occult Iconography;* at six, under Mr. Halloway's trailed fingers now, a history of circuses, carnivals, shadow shows, puppet menageries inhabited by mountebanks, minstrels, stilt-walking sorcerers and their fantoccini. More: *A Manual of the Air Kingdoms* (Things That Fly Down History). At nine sharp: *By Demons Possessed,* lying atop *Egyptian Philtres,* lying atop the *Torments of the Damned,* which in turn crushed flat *The Spell of Mirrors.* Very late up the literary clock one named *Locomotives and Trains, The Mystery of Sleep, Between Midnight and Dawn, The Witches' Sabbath,* and *Pacts With Demons.* It was all laid out. He could see the face.

But there were no hands on this clock.

He could not tell what hour of the night of life it was for himself, the boys, or the unknowing town.

For, in sum, what had he to go by?

A three-o'clock-in-the-morning arrival, a grotesque looking-glass maze, a Sunday parade, a tall man with a swarm of electric-blue pictures itching on his sweaty hide, a few drops of blood falling down through a pavement grille, two frightened boys staring up out of the earth, and himself, alone in mausoleum quiet, nudging the puzzle together.

What was there about the boys that made him believe the simplest word they whispered up through the grille? Fear itself was proof here, and he had seen enough fear in his life to know it, like the smell from a butcher's shop in summer twilight.

What was there about the illustrated carnival owner's silences that spoke thousands of violent, corrupt, and crippling words?

What was there in that old man he had seen through a tent flap late this afternoon, seated in a chair with the words MR. ELECTRICO bannered over him, power webbing and crawling on his flesh like green lizards?

All, all, all of it. And now, these books. This. He touched *Physiognomonie. The secrets of the individual's character as found in his face.*

Were Jim and Will, then, featured all angelic, pure, half-innocent, peering up through the sidewalk at marching terror? Did the boys represent the ideal for your Woman, Man, or Child of Excellent Bearing, Color, Balance, and Summer Disposition?

Conversely . . . Charles Halloway turned a page . . . did the scurrying freaks, the Illustrated Marvel, bear the foreheads of the Irascible, the Cruel, the Covetous, the mouths of the Lewd and Untruthful? the teeth of the Crafty, the Unstable, the Audacious, the Vainglorious, and your Murderous Beast?

No. The book slipped shut. If faces were judged, the freaks were no worse than many he'd seen slipping from the library late nights in his long career.

There was only one thing sure.

Two lines of Shakespeare said it. He should write them in the middle of the clock of books, to fix the heart of his apprehension:

By the pricking of my thumbs,
Something wicked this way comes.

So vague, yet so immense.

He did not want to live with it.

Yet he knew that, during this night, unless he lived with it very well, he might have to live with it all the rest of his life.

At the window he looked out and thought, Jim, Will, are you coming? will you *get* here?

Waiting, his flesh took paleness from his bones.

chapter thirty-eight

The library, then, at seven-fifteen, seven-thirty, seven-forty-five of a Sunday night, cloistered with great drifts of silence and transfixed avalanche of books poised like the cuneiform stones of eternity on shelves, so high the unseen snows of time fell all year there.

Outside, the town breathed back and forth to the carnival, hundreds of people passing near where Jim and Will lay strewn in bushes to one side of the library, now ducking up, now ducking down to nose raw earth.

"Cheezit!"

Both smothered in grass. Across the street there passed what could have been a boy, could have been a dwarf, could have been a boy-with-dwarf-mind, could have been anything blown along like the scuttle-crab leaves on the frost-mica sidewalks. But then whatever it was went away; Jim sat up, Will still lay face buried in good safe dirt.

"Come on, what's wrong?"

"The library," said Will. "I'm even afraid of *it*, now." All the books, he thought, perched there, hundreds of years old, peeling skin, leaning on each other like ten million vultures. Walk along the dark stacks and all the gold titles shine their eyes at you.

Between old carnival, old library and his own father, everything old ... well ...

"I know Dad's in there, but *is* it Dad? I mean, what if *they* came, changed him, made him bad, promised him something they can't give but he thinks they can, and we go in there and some day fifty years from now someone opens a book in there and you and me drop out, like two dry moth wings on the floor, Jim, someone pressed and hid us between pages, and no one ever guessed where we went—"

This was too much for Jim, who had to do something to flog his spirits. Next thing Will knew, Jim was hammering on the library door. Both hammered, frantic to jump from this night to that warmer bookbreathing night inside. Given a choice of darknesses, this one was the better: the oven smell of books, as the door opened and Dad stood with his ghost-colored hair. They tiptoed back through the deserted corridors, Will feeling a crazy urge to whistle as he often did past the graveyard at sundown, Dad asking what made them late, and they trying to remember all the places they hid in one day.

They had hid in old garages, they had hid in old barns, they had hid in the highest trees they could climb and got bored and boredom was worse than fear so they came down and reported in to the Police Chief and had a fine chat which gave them twenty safe minutes right in the station and Will got the idea of touring churches and they climbed all the steeples in town and scared pigeons off the belfries and whether or not it was safer in churches and especially up with the bells or not, no one could claim, but it *felt* safe. But there again they began to get starchy with boredom and fatigued with sameness, and were almost on the point of giving themselves up to the carnival in order to have something to do, when quite fortunately the sun went down. From sundown to now it had taken a wonderful time, creeping upon the library, as if it were a once friendly fort that might now be manned by Arabs.

"So here we are," whispered Jim, and stopped.

"Why am I whispering? It's after hours. Heck!"

He laughed, then stopped.

For he thought he heard a soft tread off in the subterranean vaults.

But it was only his laughter walking back through the deep stacks on panther feet.

So when they talked again, it was still in whispers. Deep forests, dark caves, dim churches, half-lit libraries were all the same, they tuned you down, they dampened your ardor, they brought you to murmurs and soft cries for fear of raising up phantom twins of your voice which might haunt corridors long after your passage.

They reached the small room and circled the table on which Charles Halloway had laid out the books, where he had read many hours, and for the first time looked in each other's faces and saw a dreadful paleness, so did not comment.

"From the beginning." Will's father pulled out chairs. "Please."

So, each taking his part, in their own good time, the boys told of the wandering-by lightning-rod salesman, the predictions of storms to come, the long-after-midnight train, the suddenly inhabited meadow, the moonblown tents, the untouched but full-wept calliope, then the light of noon showering over an ordinary midway with hundreds of Christians wandering through but no lions for them to be tossed to, only the maze where time lost itself backward and forward in waterfall mirrors, only the OUT OF ORDER carousel, the dead supper hour, Mr. Cooger, and the boy with the eyes that had seen all the glistery tripes of the world shaped like hung-and-dripping sins and all the sins tenterhooked and running red and verminous, this boy with the eyes of a man who has lived forever, seen too much, might like to die but doesn't know how. . . .

The boys stopped for breath.

Miss Foley, the carnival again, the carousel run wild, the ancient Cooger mummy gasping moonlight, exhaling silver dust, dead, then resurrected in a chair where green lightning struck his skeleton alight, all of it a storm minus rain, minus thunder, the parade, the cigar store basement, the hiding, and at last them here, finished, done with the telling.

For a long moment, Will's father sat staring blinding into the center of the table. Then, his lips moved.

"Jim. Will," he said. "I believe."

The boys sank in their chairs.

"All of it?"

"All."

Will wiped his eyes. "Boy," he said gruffly. "I'm going to start bawling."

"We got no time for that!" said Jim.

"No time." And Will's father stood up, stuffed his pipe with tobacco, rummaged his pockets for matches, brought out a battered harmonica, a penknife, a cigarette lighter that wouldn't work, and a memo pad he had always meant to write great thoughts down on but never got around to, and lined up these weapons for a pygmy war that could be lost before it even started. Probing this idle refuse, shaking his head, he finally found a tattered matchbox, lit his pipe and began to muse, pacing the room.

"Looks like we're going to do a lot of talking about one particular carnival. Where's it come from, where's it going, what's it up to? We thought it never hit town before. Yet, by God, look here."

He tapped a yellowed newspaper ad dated October 12, 1888, and ran his fingernail along under this:

J. C. COOGER AND G. M. DARK PRESENT THE PANDEMONIUM THEATER CO. COMBINED SIDE SHOWS AND UNNATURAL MUSEUMS, INTERNATIONAL!

"J.C. G.M." said Jim. "Those are the same initials as on the throwaways around town this week. But—it couldn't be the *same* men. . . ."

"No?" Will's father rubbed his elbows. "My goose pimples run counter to that."

He laid forth other old newspapers.

"1860. 1846. Same ad. Same names. Same initials. Dark and

Cooger, Cooger and Dark, they came and went, but only once every twenty, thirty, forty years, so people forgot. Where were they all the other years? Traveling. And *more* than traveling. Always in October: October 1846, October 1860, October 1888, October 1910, and October now, tonight." His voice trailed off. " ... Beware the autumn people. ... "

"What?"

"An old religious tract. Pastor Newgate Phillips, I think. Read it as a boy. How does it go again?"

He tried to remember. He licked his lips. He did remember.

" 'For some, autumn comes early, stays late through life where October follows September and November touches October and then instead of December and Christ's birth, there is no Bethlehem Star, no rejoicing, but September comes again and old October and so on down the years, with no winter, spring, or revivifying summer. For these beings, fall is the ever normal season, the only weather, there be no choice beyond. Where do they come from? The dust. Where do they go? The grave. Does blood stir their veins? No: the night wind. What ticks in their head? The worm. What speaks from their mouth? The toad. What sees from their eye? The snake. What hears with their ear? The abyss between the stars. They sift the human storm for souls, eat flesh of reason, fill tombs with sinners. They frenzy forth. In gusts they beetle-scurry, creep, thread, filter, motion, make all moons sullen, and surely cloud all clear-run waters. The spider-web hears them, trembles—breaks. Such are the autumn people. Beware of them.' "

After a pause, both boys exhaled at once.

"The autumn people," said Jim. "That's them. *Sure!*"

"Then—" Will swallowed—"does that make us ... *summer* people?"

"Not quite." Charles Halloway shook his head. "Oh, you're nearer summer than me. If I was ever a rare fine summer person, that's long ago. Most of us are half-and-half. The August noon in us works to stave off the November chills. We survive by what little Fourth of July wits we've stashed away. But there are times when we're all autumn people."

"Not you, Dad!"

"Not *you*, Mr. Halloway!"

He turned quickly to see both appraising him, paleness next to paleness, hands on knees as if to bolt.

"It's a way of speaking. Easy, boys. I'm after the facts. Will, do you really *know* your Dad? Shouldn't you know me, and me you, if it's going to be us'ns against them'ns?"

"Hey, yeah," breathed Jim. "Who *are* you?"

"We *know* who he is, darn it!" Will protested.

"Do we?" said Will's father. "Let's see. Charles William Halloway. Nothing extraordinary about me except I'm fifty-four, which is always extraordinary to the man inside it. Born in Sweet Water, lived in Chicago, survived in New York, brooded in Detroit, floundered in lots of places, arrived here late, after living in libraries around the country all those years because I liked being alone, liked matching up in books what I'd seen on the roads. Then in the middle of all the running-away, which I called travel, in my thirty-ninth year, your mother fixed me with one glance, been here ever since. Still most comfortable in the library nights, in out of the rain of people. Is this my last stop? Chances are. Why am I here at all? Right now, it seems, to help you."

He paused and looked at the two boys and their fine young faces.

"Yes," he said. "Very late in the game. To help you."

chapter thirty-nine

E very night-blind library window chattered with cold.

The man, the two boys, waited for the wind to pass away.

Then Will said: "Dad. You've always helped."

"Thanks, but it's not true." Charles Halloway examined one very empty hand. "I'm a fool. Always looking over your shoulder to see what's coming instead of right at you to see what's *here*. But then, for what salve it gives me, every man's a fool. Which means you got to pitch in all your life, bail out, board over, tie rope, patch plaster, pat cheeks, kiss brows, laugh, cry, make do, against the day you're the worst fool of all and shout 'Help!' Then all you need is one person's answer. I see it so clear, across the country tonight lie cities, towns and mere jerkwater stops of fools. So the carnival steams by, shakes *any* tree: it rains jackasses. Separate jackasses, I should say, individuals with no one, they think, or no one actual, to answer their 'Help!' Unconnected fools, that's the harvest the carnival comes smiling after with its threshing machine."

"Oh gosh," said Will. "It's hopeless!"

"No. The very fact we're here worrying about the difference between summer and autumn, makes me sure there's a way out. You don't have to *stay* foolish and you don't *have* to be wrong, evil, sinful, whatever you want to call it. There's more than three or four choices. *They,* that Dark fellow and his friends don't hold all the cards, I could tell that today, at the cigar store. I'm afraid of him but, I could see, he was afraid of me. So there's fear on both sides. Now *how* can we use it to advantage?"

"How?"

"First things first. Let's bone up on history. If men had wanted to stay bad forever, they could have, agreed? Agreed. *Did* we stay out in the fields with the beasts? No. In the water with the barracuda? No. Somewhere we let go of the hot gorilla's paw. Somewhere we turned in our carnivore's teeth and started chewing blades of grass. We been working mulch as much as blood, into our philosophy, for quite a few lifetimes. Since then we measure ourselves up the scale from apes, but not half so high as angels. It was a nice new idea and we were afraid we'd lose it, so we put it on paper and built buildings like this one around it. And we been going in and out of these buildings chewing it over, that one new sweet blade of grass, trying to figure how it all started, when we made the move, when we decided to be different. I suppose one night hundreds of thousands of years ago in a cave by a night fire when one of those shaggy men wakened to gaze over the banked coals at his woman, his children, and thought of their being cold, dead, gone forever. Then he must have wept. And he put out his hand in the night to the woman who must die some day and to the children who must follow her. And for a little bit next morning, he treated them somewhat better, for he saw that they, like himself, had the seed of night in them. He felt that seed like slime in his pulse, splitting, making more against the day they would multiply his body into darkness. So that man, the first one, knew what we know now: our hour is short, eternity is long. With this knowledge came pity and mercy, so we spared others for the later, more intricate, more mysterious benefits of love.

"So, in sum, what are we? We are the creatures that know and know too much. That leaves us with such a burden again we have a choice, to laugh or cry. No other animal does either. We do both, depending on the season and the need. Somehow, I feel the carnival watches, to see which we're doing and how and why, and moves in on us when it feels we're ripe."

Charles Halloway stopped, for the boys were watching him so intently he suddenly had to turn, flushing, away.

"Boy, Mr. Halloway," cried Jim, softly. "That's great. Go on!"

"Dad," said Will, amazed. "I never knew you could *talk.*"

"You should hear me here late nights, nothing *but* talk!" Charles Halloway shook his head. "Yes, you should've heard. I should've said more to you any day you name in the past. Hell. Where *was* I? Leading up to love, I think. Yes . . . love."

Will looked bored, Jim looked wary of the word.

And these looks gave Charles Halloway pause.

What could he say that might make sense to them? Could he say love was, above all, common cause, shared experience? That *was* the vital cement, wasn't it? Could he say how he felt about their all being here tonight on this wild world running around a big sun which fell through a bigger space falling through yet vaster immensities of space, maybe toward and maybe away from Something? Could he say: we share this billion-mile-an-hour ride. We have common cause against the night. You start with little common causes. Why love the boy in a March field with his kite braving the sky? Because our fingers burn with the hot string singeing our hands. Why love some girl viewed from a train, bent to a country well? The tongue remembers iron water cool on some long lost noon. Why weep at strangers dead by the road? They resemble friends unseen in forty years. Why laugh when clowns are hit by pies? We taste custard, we taste life. Why love the woman who is your wife? Her nose breathes in the air of a world that I know; therefore I love that nose. Her ears hear music I might sing half the night through; therefore I love her ears. Her eyes delight in seasons of the land; and so I love those eyes. Her tongue knows quince, peach, chokeberry, mint and lime; I love to hear it speaking. Because her flesh knows heat, cold, afflic-tion, I know fire, snow, and pain. Shared and once again shared experience. Billions of prickling textures. Cut one sense away, cut part of life away. Cut two senses; life halves itself on the instant. We love what we know, we love what we are. Common cause, common cause, common cause of mouth, eye, ear, tongue, hand, nose, flesh, heart, and soul.

But . . . how to say it?

"Look," he tried, "put two men in a rail car, one a soldier, the other a farmer. One talks war, the other wheat; and bore each other to sleep. But let one spell long-distance running, and if the other once ran the mile, why, those men will run all night, like boys, sparking a friendship up from memory. So, all men have *one* business in common: women, and can talk that till sunrise and beyond. Hell."

Charles Halloway stopped, flushed, self-conscious again, knowing vaguely there was a target up ahead but not quite how to get there. He chewed his lips.

Dad, don't stop, thought Will. When you talk, it's swell in here. You'll save us. Go on.

The man read his son's eyes, saw the same look in Jim, and walked slowly around the table, touching a night beast here, a clutch of ragged crones there, a star, a crescent moon, an antique sun, an hourglass that told time with bone dust instead of sand.

"Have I said anything I started out to say about being good? God, I don't know. A stranger is shot in the street, you hardly move to help. But if, half an hour before, you spent just ten minutes with the fellow and knew a little about him and his family, you might just jump in front of his killer and try to stop it. Really knowing is good. Not knowing, or refusing to know, is bad, or amoral, at least. You can't act if you don't know. Acting without knowing takes you right off the cliff. God, God, you must think I'm crazy, this talk. Probably think we should be out duck-shooting, elephant-gunning balloons, like you did, Will, but we got to know all there is to know about those freaks and that man heading them up. We can't be good unless we know what bad is, and it's a shame we're working against time. Show'll close and the crowds go home early on a Sunday night. I feel we'll have a visit from the autumn people, then. That gives us maybe two hours."

Jim was at the window now, looking out across the town to the far black tents and the calliope that played by the turning of the world in the night.

"*Is* it bad?" he asked.

"Bad?" cried Will, angrily. "Bad! You ask that!?"

"Calmly," said Will's father. "A good question. Part of that show looks just great. But the old saying really applies: you can't get something for nothing. Fact is, from them, you get nothing for something. They make you empty promises, you stick out your neck and—wham!"

"Where'd they come from?" asked Jim. "Who are they?'

Will went to the window with his father and they both looked out and Charles Halloway said, to those far tents:

"Maybe once it was just one man walking across Europe, jingling his ankle bells, a lute on his shoulder making a hunch-backed shadow, before Columbus. Maybe a man walked around in a monkey skin a million years ago, stuffing himself with other people's unhappiness, chewed their pain all day like spearmint gum, for the sweet savor, and trotted faster, revivified by personal disaster. Maybe his son after him refined his father's dead-falls, mantraps, bone-crunchers, head-achers, flesh-twitchers, soul-skinners. These laid the scum on lonely ponds from which came vinegar gnats to snuff up noses, mosquitoes to ride summer-night flesh and sting forth those bumps that carnival phrenologists dearly love to fondle and prophesy upon. So from one man here, one man there, walking as swift as his oily glances, it became scuttles of dogmen begging gifts of trouble, pandering misery, seeking under carpets for centipede treads, watchful of night sweats, harkening by all bedroom doors to hear men twist basting themselves with remorse and warm-water dreams.

"The stuff of nightmare is their plain bread. They butter it with pain. They set their clocks by death-watch beetles, and thrive the centuries. They were the men with the leather-ribbon whips who sweated up the Pyramids seasoning it with other people's salt and other people's cracked hearts. They coursed Europe on the White Horses of the Plague. They whispered to Caesar that he was mortal, then sold daggers at half-price in the grand March sale. Some must have been lazing clowns, foot props for emperors, princes, and epileptic popes. Then out on the road, Gypsies in time, their populations grew as the world grew, spread, and there was more delicious variety of pain to thrive on. The train put wheels under them and here they run down the long road out of the Gothic and baroque; look at their wagons and coaches, the carving like medieval shrines, all of it stuff once drawn by horses, mules, or, maybe, men."

"All those years." Jim's voice swallowed itself. "The *same* people? You think Mr. Cooger, Mr. Dark are both a couple hundred years old?"

"Riding that merry-go-round they can shave off a year or two, any time they want, right?"

"Why, then—" The abyss opened at Will's feet—"they could live *forever!*"

"And *hurt* people." Jim turned it over, again and again. "But why, why all the hurt?"

"Because," said Mr. Halloway. "You need fuel, gas, something to run a carnival on, don't you? Women live off gossip, and what's gossip but a swap of headaches, sour spit, arthritic bones, ruptured and mended flesh, indiscretions, storms of madness, calms after the storms? If some people didn't have something juicy to chew on, their choppers would prolapse, their souls with them. Multiply *their* pleasure at funerals, their chuckling through breakfast obituaries, add all the cat-fight marriages where folks spend careers ripping skin off each other and patching it back upside around, add quack doctors slicing persons to read their guts like tea leaves, then sewing them tight with fingerprinted thread, square the whole dynamite factory by ten quadrillion, and you got the black candlepower of this one carnival.

"All the meannesses we harbor, they borrow in redoubled

spades. They're a billion times itchier for pain, sorrow, and sickness than the average man. We salt our lives with other people's sins. Our flesh to us tastes sweet. But the carnival doesn't care if it stinks by moonlight instead of sun, so long as it gorges on fear and pain. That's the fuel, the vapor that spins the carousel, the raw stuffs of terror, the excruciating agony of guilt, the scream from real or imagined wounds. The carnival sucks that gas, ignites it, and chugs along its way."

Charles Halloway took a breath, shut his eyes, and said:

"How do I know this? I don't! I *feel* it. I *taste* it. It was like old leaves burning on the wind two nights ago. It was a smell like mortuary flowers. I hear that music. I hear what you tell me, and half what you *don't* tell me. Maybe I've *always* dreamt about such carnivals, and was just waiting for it to come so's to see it once, and nod. Now, that tent show plays my bones like a marimba.

"My skeleton *knows*.

"*It* tells me.

"*I* tell you."

chapter forty

"Can they . . ." said Jim. "I mean . . . do they . . . buy souls?"

"Buy, when they can get them free?" said Mr. Halloway. "Why, most men jump at the chance to give up everything for nothing. There's nothing we're so slapstick with as our own immortal souls. Besides, you're inferring that's the Devil out there. I only say it's a type of creature has learned to live off souls, not the souls themselves. That always worried me in the old myths. I asked myself, why would Mephistopheles want a soul? What does he *do* with it when he gets it, of what use is it? Stand back while I throw my own theory over the plate. Those creatures want the flaming gas off souls who can't sleep nights, that fever by day from old crimes. A dead soul is no kindling. But a live and raving soul, crisped with self-damnation, oh that's a pretty snoutful for such as them.

"How do I know this? I observe. The carnival is like people, only more so. A man, a woman, rather than walk away from, or kill, each other, ride each other a lifetime, pulling hair, extracting fingernails, the pain of each to the other like a narcotic that makes existence worth the day. So the carnival feels ulcerated egos miles off and lopes to toast its hands at that ache. It smells boys ulcerating to be men, paining like great unwise wisdom teeth, twenty

thousand miles away, summer abed in winter's night. It feels the
aggravation of middle-aged men like myself, who gibber after
long-lost August afternoons to no avail. Need, want, desire, we
burn those in our fluids, oxidize those in our souls, which jet
streams out lips, nostrils, eyes, ears, broadcasts from antennae-
fingers, long or short wave, God only knows, but the freak-masters
perceive Itches and come crab-clustering to Scratch. It's traveled
a long way on an easy map, with people handy by every crossroad
to lend it lustful pints of agony to power it on. So maybe the carnival survives, living off the poison of the sins we do each other,
and the ferment of our most terrible regrets."

Charles Halloway snorted.

"Good grief, how much have I said out loud, how much to
myself, the last ten minutes?"

"You," said Jim, "talk a lot."

"In what language, dammit!?" cried Charles Halloway, for
suddenly it seemed he had done no more than other nights
walking exquisitely alone, deliciously propounding his ideas to
halls which echoed them once, then made them vanish forever.
He had written books a lifetime, on the airs of vast rooms in vast
buildings, and had it all fly out the vents. Now it all seemed fireworks, done for color, sound, the high architecture of words, to
dazzle the boys, powder his ego, but with no mark left on retina
or mind after the color and sound faded; a mere exercise in self-
declamation. Sheepishly he accosted himself.

"How much of all this got through? One sentence out of five,
two out of eight?"

"Three in a thousand," said Will.

Charles Halloway could not but laugh and sigh in one.

Then Jim cut across with:

"Is . . . is it . . . Death?"

"The carnival?" The old man lit his pipe, blew smoke, seriously studied the patterns. "No. But I think it uses Death as a
threat. Death doesn't exist. It never did, it never will. But we've
drawn so many pictures of it, so many years, trying to pin it down,

comprehend it, we've got to thinking of it as an entity, strangely alive and greedy. All it is, however, is a stopped watch, a loss, an end, a darkness. Nothing. And the carnival wisely knows we're more afraid of Nothing than we are of Something. You can fight Something. But . . . Nothing? Where do you hit it? Has it a heart, soul, butt-behind, brain? No, no. So the carnival just shakes a great croupier's cupful of Nothing at us, and reaps us as we tumble back head-over-heels in fright. Oh, it shows us Something that might eventually lead to Nothing, all right. That flourish of mirrors out there in the meadow, that's a raw Something, for sure. Enough to knock your soul sideways in the saddle. It's a hit below the belt to see yourself ninety years gone, the vapors of eternity rising from you like breath off dry ice. Then, when it's frozen you stiff, it plays that fine sweet soul-searching music that smells of fresh-washed frocks of women dancing on back-yard lines in May, that sounds like haystacks trampled into wine, all that blue sky and summer night-on-the-lake kind of tune until your head bangs with the drums that look like full moons beating around the calliope. Simplicity. Lord, I do admire their direct approach. Hit an old man with mirrors, watch his pieces fall in jigsaws of ice only the carnival can put together again. How? Waltz around back on the carousel to 'Beautiful Ohio' or 'Merry Widow.' But they're careful not to tell one thing to people who go riding to its music."

"What?" asked Jim.

"Why, that if you're a miserable sinner in one shape, you're a miserable sinner in another. Changing size doesn't change the brain. If I made you twenty-five tomorrow, Jim, your thoughts would still be boy thoughts, and it'd show! Or if they turned *me* into a boy of ten this instant, my brain would still be fifty and that boy would act funnier and older and weirder than any boy ever. Then, too, time's out of joint another way."

"Which way?" asked Will.

"If I became young again, all my friends would still be fifty, sixty, wouldn't they? I'd be cut off from them, forever, for I couldn't tell them what I'd up and done, could I? They'd resent it. They'd hate me. Their interests would no longer be mine, would they? Especially their worries. Sickness and death for them, new life for me. So where's the place in this world for a man who looks twenty but who is older than Methuselah, what man could stand the shock of a change like that? Carnival won't warn you it's equal to postoperative shock, but, by God, I bet it is, and more!

"So, what happens? You get your reward: madness. Change of body, change of personal environment, for one thing. Guilt, for another, guilt at leaving your wife, husband, friends to die the way all men die—Lord, that alone would give a man fits. So more fear, more agony for the carnival to breakfast on. So with the green vapors coming off your stricken conscience you say you want to go back the way you were! The carnival nods and listens. Yes, they promise, if you behave as they say, in a short while they'll give you back your twoscore and ten or whatever. On the promise alone of being returned to normal old age, that train travels with the world, its side show populated with madmen waiting to be released from bondage, meantime servicing the carnival, giving it coke for its ovens."

Will murmured something.

"What?"

"Miss Foley," mourned Will. "Oh, poor Miss Foley, they got her now, just like you say. Once she got what she wanted it scared her, she didn't like it, oh, she was crying so hard, Dad, so hard; now I bet they promise her someday she can be fifty again if she'll mind. I wonder what they're doing with her, right now, oh, Dad, oh, Jim!"

"God help her." Will's father put a heavy hand out to trace the old carnival portraits. "They've probably thrown her in with the freaks. And what are they? Sinners who've traveled so long, hoping for deliverance, they've taken on the shape of their original sins? The Fat Man, what was he once? If I can guess the carnival's sense of irony, the way they like to weight the scales, he was once a ravener after all kinds and varieties of lust. No matter, there he lives now, anyway, collected up in his bursting skin. The Thin Man, Skeleton, or whatever, did he starve his wife's, children's spiritual as well as physical hungers? The Dwarf? Was he or was he not your friend, the lightning-rod salesman, always on the road, never settling, ever-moving, facing no encounters, running ahead of the lightning and selling rods, yes, but leaving others to face the storm, so maybe, through accident, or design, when he fell in with the free rides, he shrank not to a boy but a mean ball of grotesque tripes, all self-involved. The fortune-telling, Gypsy Dust Witch? Maybe someone who lived always tomorrow and let today slide, like myself, and so wound up penalized, having to guess other people's wild sunrises and sad sunsets. You tell me, you've seen her *near*. The Pinhead? The Sheep Boy? The Fire Eater? The Siamese Twins, good God, what were they? twins all bound up in tandem narcissism? We'll never know. They'll never tell. We've guessed, and probably guessed wrong, on ten dozen things the last half hour. Now—some plan. Where do we go from here?"

Charles Halloway placed forth a map of the town and drew in the location of the carnival with a blunt pencil.

"Do we keep hiding out? No. With Miss Foley, and so many others involved, we just can't. Well, then, how do we attack so we won't be picked off first thing? What kind of weapons—"

"Silver bullets!" cried Will, suddenly.

"Heck, no!" snorted Jim. "They're not vampires!"

"If we were Catholic, we could borrow church holy water and—"

"Nuts," said Jim. "Movie stuff. It don't happen that way in real life. Am I wrong, Mr. Halloway?"

"I wish you were, boy."

Will's eyes glowed fiercely. "Okay. Only one thing to do: trot down to the meadow with a couple gallons of kerosene and some matches—"

"That's against the law!" Jim exclaimed.

"Look who's *talking!*"

"Hold on!"

But everyone stopped right then.

Whisper.

A faint tide of wind flowed up along through the library corridors and into this room.

"The front door," Jim whispered. "Someone just opened it."

Far away, a gentle click. The draft that had for a moment
stirred the boys' trouser cuffs and blown the man's hair, ceased.

"Someone just *closed* it."

Silence.

Just the great dark library with its labyrinths and hedgerow
mazes of sleeping books.

"Someone's *inside*."

The boys half rose, bleating in the backs of their mouths.

Charles Halloway waited, then said one word, softly:

"Hide."

"We can't leave you—"

"Hide."

The boys ran and vanished in the dark maze.

Charles Halloway then rigidly, slowly, breathing in, breathing
out, forced himself to sit back down, his eyes on the yellowed
newspapers, to wait, to wait, then again . . . to wait some more.

chapter forty-one

A shadow moved among shadows.

Charles Halloway felt his soul submerge.

It took a long time for the shadow and the man it escorted to come stand in the doorway of the room. The shadow seemed deliberate in its slowness so as to shingle his flesh and cheesegrate his steadily willed calm. And when at last the shadow reached the door it brought not one, not a hundred, but a thousand people with it to look in.

"My name is Dark," said the voice.

Charles Halloway let out two fistfuls of air.

"Better known as the Illustrated Man," said the voice. "Where are the boys?"

"Boys?" Will's father turned at last to appraise the tall man who stood in the door.

The Illustrated Man sniffed the yellow pollen that whiffed up from the ancient books as quite suddenly Will's father saw them laid out in full sight, leaped up, stopped, then began to close them, one by one, as casually as possible.

The Illustrated Man pretended not to notice.

"The boys are not home. The two houses are empty. What a shame, they'll miss those free rides."

"I wish I knew where they were." Charles Halloway started carrying the books to the shelves. "Hell, if they knew you were here with free tickets, they'd shout for joy."

"Would they?" Mr. Dark let his smile melt like a white and pink paraffin candy toy he no longer had appetite for. Softly, he said, "I could kill you."

Charles Halloway nodded, walking slowly.

"Did you hear what I said?" barked the Illustrated Man.

"Yes." Charles Halloway weighed the books, as if they were his judgment. "But you won't kill now. You're too smart. You've kept the show on the road a long time, being smart."

"So you've read a few papers and think you know all about us?"

"No, not all. Just enough to scare me."

"Be more scared, then," said the crowd of nightcrawling illustrations locked under black suiting, speaking through the thin lips. "One of my friends, outside, can fix you so it seems you died of most natural heart failure."

The blood banged at Charles Halloway's heart, knocked at his temples, tapped twice at his wrists.

The Witch, he thought.

His lips must have formed the words.

"The Witch." Mr. Dark nodded.

The other shelved the books, withholding one.

"Well, what have you there?" Mr. Dark squinted. "A Bible? How very charming, how childish and refreshingly old-fashioned."

"Have you ever read it, Mr. Dark?"

"Read it! I've had every page, paragraph, and word read *at* me, sir!" Mr. Dark took time to light a cigarette and blow smoke toward the NO SMOKING sign, then at Will's father. "Do you really imagine that books can harm me? Is naiveté *really* your armor? Here!"

And before Charles Halloway could move, Mr. Dark ran lightly forward and took the Bible. He held it in his two hands.

"Aren't you surprised? See, I touch, hold, even *read* from it."

Mr. Dark blew smoke on the pages as he riffled them.

"Do you expect me to fall away into so many Dead Sea scrolls of flesh before you? Myths, unfortunately, are just that. Life, and by life I could mean so many fascinating things, goes on, makes shift for itself, survives wildly, and I not the least wild among many. Your King James and his literary version of some rather stuffy poetic materials is worth just about *this* much of my time and sweat."

Mr. Dark hurled the Bible into a wastepaper basket and did not look at it again.

"I hear your heart beating rapidly," said Mr. Dark. "My ears are not so finely tuned as the Gypsy's, but they hear. Your eyes jump beyond my shoulder. The boys hide out there in the warrens? Good. I would not wish for their escape. Not that anyone will believe their gibberings, in fact it's good advertisement for our shows, people titillate, night-sweat, then come prowling down to look us over, lick their lips, and wonder about investing in our special securities. You came, you prowled, and it wasn't just for curiosity. How old are you?"

Charles Halloway pressed his lips shut.

"Fifty?" purred Mr. Dark. "Fifty-one?" he murmured. "Fifty-two? Like to be younger?"

"No!"

"No need to yell. Politely, please." Mr. Dark hummed, strolling the room, running his hand over the books as if they were years to be counted. "Oh, it's nice to be young, really. Wouldn't forty be nice, again? Forty's ten years nicer than fifty, and thirty's twenty years nicer by an incredible long shot."

"I won't listen!" Charles Halloway shut his eyes.

Mr. Dark tilted his head, sucked on his cigarette, and observed. "Strange, you shut your eyes, not to listen. Clapping your hands over your ears would be better—"

Will's father clapped his hands to his ears, but the voice came through.

"Tell you what," said Mr. Dark, casually, waving his cigarette. "If you help me within fifteen seconds I'll give you your fortieth birthday. Ten seconds and you can celebrate thirty-five. A rare young age. A stripling, almost, by comparison. I'll start counting by my watch and by God, if you should jump to it, lend a hand, I might just cut thirty years off your life! Bargains galore, as the posters say. Think of it! Starting all over again, everything fine and new and glorious, all the things to be done and thought and savored again. Last chance! Here goes. One. Two. Three. Four—"

Charles Halloway hunched away, half crouched, propped hard against the shelves, grinding his teeth to drown the sound of counting.

"You're losing out, old man, my dear old fellow," said Mr. Dark. "Five. Losing. Six. Losing very much. Seven. Really losing. Eight. Frittering away. Nine. Ten. My God, you fool! Eleven. Halloway! Twelve. Almost gone. Thirteen! Gone! Fourteen! Lost! Fifteen! Lost forever!"

Mr. Dark put down his arm with the watch on it.

Charles Halloway, gasping, had turned away to bury his face in the smell of ancient books, the feel of old and comfortable leather, the taste of funeral dust and pressed flowers.

Mr. Dark stood in the door now, on his way out.

"Stay there," he directed. "Listen to your heart. I'll send someone to fix it. But, first, the boys . . ."

The crowd of unsleeping Creatures, saddled upon tall flesh, strode quietly forth into darkness, borne with and all over upon Mr. Dark. Their cries and whines and utterances of vague but excruciating excitements sounded in his husky summoning:

"Boys? Are you there? Wherever you are . . . answer."

Charles Halloway sprang forward, then felt the room spin and whirl him, as that soft, that easy, that most pleasant voice of Mr. Dark went calling through the dark. Charles Halloway fell against a chair, thought: Listen, my heart! sank down to his knees, he said, Listen to my heart! it explodes! Oh God, it's tearing free!—and could not follow.

The Illustrated Man trod cat-soft in the labyrinths of shelved and darkly waiting books.

"Boys . . . ? Hear me . . . ?"

Silence.

"Boys . . . ?"

chapter forty-two

S omewhere in the recumbent solitudes, the motionless but teeming millions of books, lost in two dozen turns right, three dozen turns left, down aisles, through corridors, toward dead ends, locked doors, half-empty shelves, somewhere in the literary soot of Dickens's London, or Dostoevsky's Moscow or the steppes beyond, somewhere in the vellumed dust of atlas or *Geographic,* sneezes pent but set like traps, the boys crouched, stood, lay sweating a cool and constant brine.

Somewhere hidden, Jim thought: *He's coming!*

Somewhere hidden, Will thought: *He's near!*

"Boys...?"

Mr. Dark came carrying his panoply of friends, his jewel-case assortment of calligraphical reptiles which lay sunning themselves at midnight on his flesh. With him strode the stitch-inked *Tyrannosaurus rex,* which lent to his haunches a machined and ancient wellspring mineral-oil glide. As the thunder lizard strode, all glass-bead pomp, so strode Mr. Dark, armored with vile lightning scribbles of carnivores and sheep blasted by that thunder and arun before storms of juggernaut flesh. It was the pterodactyl kite and scythe which raised his arms almost to fly the marbled vaults. And with the inked and stencilled flashburnt shapes of pistoned or bladed doom came his usual crowd of hangers-on, spectators gripped to each limb, seated on shoulder blades, peering from his jungled chest, hung upside down in microscopic millions in his armpit vaults screaming bat-screams for encounters, ready for the hunt and if need be the kill. Like a black tidal wave upon a bleak shore, a dark tumult infilled with phosphorescent beauties and badly spoiled dreams, Mr. Dark sounded and hissed his feet, his legs, his body, his sharp face forward.

"Boys...?"

Immensely patient, that soft voice, ever the warmest friend to chilly creatures burrowed away, nested amongst dry books; so he scuttered, crept, scurried, stalked, tip-toed, wafted, stood immensely still among the primates, the Egyptian monuments to bestial gods, brushed black histories of dead Africa, stayed awhile in Asia, then sauntered on to newer lands.

"Boys, I know you hear me! The sign reads: SILENCE! So, I'll whisper: one of you still wants what we offer. Eh? *Eh?*"

Jim, thought Will.

Me, thought Jim. No! oh, no! not still! not me!

"Come out." Mr. Dark purred the air through his teeth. "I guarantee rewards! Whoever turns himself in wins it *all!*"

Bangity-bang!

My heart! thought Jim.

Is that me? thought Will, *or Jim!!?*

"I hear you." Mr. Dark's lips quivered. "Closer now. Will? Jim? Isn't it Jim who's the *smart* one? Come along, boy...!"

No! thought Will.

I don't know anything! thought Jim, wildly.

"Jim, yes..." Mr. Dark wheeled in a new direction. "Jim, show me where your friend is." Softly. "We'll shut him up, give you the ride that would have been his if he'd used his head. Right, Jim?" A dove voice, cooing. "Closer. I hear your heart jump!"

Stop! thought Will to his chest.

Stop! Jim clenched his breath. *Stop!!*

"I wonder . . . are you in this alcove . . . ?"

Mr. Dark let the peculiar gravity of a certain group of stacks tug him forward.

"You *here,* Jim . . . ? Or . . . over behind . . . ?"

He shoved a trolley of books mindlessly off on rubber rollers to bump through the night. A long way off, it crashed and spilled its contents to the floor like so many dead black ravens.

"Smart hide-and-seekers, both," said Mr. Dark. "But someone's smarter. Did you hear the carousel calliope tonight? Did you know, someone dear to you was down to the carousel? Will? Willy? William. William Halloway. Where's your mother tonight?"

Silence.

"She was out riding the night wind, Willy-William. Around. We put her on. Around. We left her on. Around. You *hear,* Willy? Around, a year, another year, another, around, around!"

Dad! thought Will. *Where are you!*

In the far room, Charles Halloway, seated, his heart pounding, heard and thought, He won't find them, I won't move unless he does, he can't find them, they won't listen! they won't believe! he'll go away!

"Your mother, Will," called Mr. Dark, softly. "Around and around, can you guess *which* direction, Willy?"

Mr. Dark circled his thin ghost hand in the dark air between the stacks.

"Around, around, and when we let your mother off, boy, and showed her herself in the Mirror Maze, you should have heard the *one single sound* she made. She was like a cat with a hair ball in her so big and sticky there was no way to gag it out, no way to scream around the hair coming out her nostrils and ears and eyes, boy, and her old old old. The last we saw of her, boy Willy, she was running off away from what she saw in the mirrors. She'll bang Jim's house door but when his ma sees a thing two hundred years old slobbering at the keyhole, begging the mercy of gunshot death, boy, Jim's ma will gag the same way, like a hairballed cat sick but can't be sick, and beat her away, send her beggaring the streets, where no one'll believe, Will, such a kettle of bones and spit, no one'll believe this was a rose beauty, your kind relation! So Will, it's up to us to run find, run save her, for we know who she is—right, Will, right, Will, right, right, *right?!*"

The dark man's voice hissed away to silence.

Very faintly now, somewhere in the library, someone was sobbing.

Ah . . .

The Illustrated Man gassed the air pleasantly from his dark lungs.

Yesssssssssss . . .

"Here . . ." he murmured. "What? Filed under B for Boys? A for Adventure? H for Hidden. S for Secret. T for Terrified? Or filed under J for Jim or N for Nightshade, W for William, H for Halloway? Where are my two precious human books, so I may turn their pages, eh?"

He kicked a place for his right foot on the first shelf of a towering stack.

He shoved his right foot in, put his weight there, and swung his left foot free.

"*There.*"

His left foot hit the second shelf, knocked space. He climbed. His right foot kicked a hole on the third shelf, plunged books back, and so up and up he climbed, to fourth shelf, to fifth, to sixth, groping dark library heavens, hands clutching shelfboards, then scrabbling higher to leaf night to find boys, if boys there were, like bookmarks among books.

His right hand, a princely tarantula, garlanded with roses, cracked a book of Bayeaux tapestries aspin down the sightless abyss below. It seemed an age before the tapestries struck, all askew, a ruin of beauty, an avalanche of gold, silver, and sky-blue thread on the floor.

His left hand, reaching the ninth shelf as he panted, grunted, encountered empty space—no books.

"Boys, are you here on Everest?"

Silence. Except for the faint sobbing, nearer now.

"Is it cold here? Colder? Coldest?"

The eyes of the Illustrated Man came abreast of the eleventh shelf.

Like a corpse laid rigid out, face down just three inches away, was Jim Nightshade.

One shelf further up in the catacomb, eyes trembling with tears, lay William Halloway.

"Well," said Mr. Dark.

He reached a hand to pat Will's head.

"Hello," he said.

chapter forty-three

To Will, the palm of the hand that drifted up was like a moon rising.

Upon it was the fiery blue-inked portrait of himself.

Jim, too, saw a hand before his face.

His own picture looked back at him from the palm.

The hand with Will's picture grabbed Will.

The hand with Jim's picture grabbed Jim.

Shrieks and yells.

The Illustrated Man heaved.

Twisting, he fell-jumped to the floor.

The boys, kicking, yelling, fell with him. They landed on their feet, toppled, collapsed, to be held, reared, set right, fistfuls of their shirts in Mr. Dark's fists.

"Jim!" he said. "Will! What were you doing up there, boys? Surely not reading?"

"Dad!"

"Mr. Halloway!"

Will's father stepped from the dark.

The Illustrated Man rearranged the boys tenderly under one arm like kindling, then gazed with genteel curiosity at Charles Halloway and reached for him. Will's father struck one blow before his left hand was seized, held, squeezed. As the boys watched, shouting, they saw Charles Halloway gasp and fall to one knee.

Mr. Dark squeezed that left hand harder and, doing this, slowly, certainly, pressured the boys with his other arm, crushing their ribs so air gushed from their mouths.

Night spiraled in fiery whorls like great thumbprints inside Will's eyes.

Will's father, groaning, sank to both knees, flailing his right arm. "Damn you!"

"But," said the carnival owner quietly, "I am already."

"Damn you, damn you!"

"Not words, old man," said Mr. Dark. "Not words in books or words you say, but real thoughts, real actions, quick thought, quick action, win the day. So!"

He gave one last mighty clench of his fist.

The boys heard Charles Halloway's finger bones crack. He gave a last cry and fell senseless.

In one motion like a solemn pavane, the Illustrated Man rounded the stacks, the boys, kicking books from shelves, under his arms.

Will, feeling walls, books, floors fly by, foolishly thought, pressed close, Why, why, Mr. Dark smells like . . . calliope steam!

Both boys were dropped suddenly. Before they could move or regain their breath, each was gripped by the hair on their head and roused marionettes-wise to face a window, a street.

"Boys, you read Dickens?" Mr. Dark whispered. "Critics hate his coincidences. But we know, don't we? life's *all* coincidence. Turn death and happenstance flakes off him like fleas from a killed ox. Look!"

Both boys writhed in the iron-maiden clutch of hungry saurians and bristly apes.

Will did not know whether to weep with joy or new despair.

Below, across the avenue, passing from church, going home, was his mother and Jim's mother.

Not on the carousel, not old, crazy, dead, in jail, but freshly out in the good October air. She had been not a hundred yards away in church during all the last five minutes!

Mom! screamed Will, against the hand which, anticipating his cry, clamped tight to his mouth.

"Mom," crooned Mr. Dark, mockingly. "Come save me!"

No, thought Will, save *yourself*, run!

But his mother and Jim's mother simply strolled content, from the warm church through town.

Mom! screamed Will again, and some small muffled bleat of it escaped the sweaty paw.

Will's mother, a thousand miles away over on that sidewalk, paused.

She *couldn't* have heard! thought Will. Yet—

She looked over at the library.

"Good," sighed Mr. Dark. "Excellent, fine."

Here! thought Will. See us, Mom! Run call the police!

"Why doesn't she look at this window?" asked Mr. Dark quietly. "And see us three standing as for a portrait. Look over. Then, come running. We'll let her *in*."

Will strangled a sob. No, no.

His mother's gaze trailed from the front entrance to the first-floor windows.

"Here," said Mr. Dark. "Second floor. A proper coincidence, let's make it proper."

Now Jim's mother was talking. Both women stood together at the curb.

No, thought Will, oh, no.

And the women turned and went away into the Sunday-night town.

Will felt the Illustrated Man slump the tiniest bit.

"Not much of a coincidence, no crisis, no one lost or saved. Pity. Well!"

Dragging the boys' feet, he glided down to open the front door.

Someone waited in the shadows.

A lizard hand scurried cold on Will's chin.

"Halloway," husked the Witch's voice.

A chameleon perched on Jim's nose.

"Nightshade," whisked the dry-broom voice.

Behind her stood the Dwarf and the Skeleton, silent, shifting, apprehensive.

Obedient to the occasion, the boys would have given their best stored yells air, but again, on the instant recognizing their need, the Illustrated Man trapped the sound before it could issue forth, then nodded curtly to the old dust woman.

The Witch toppled forward with her seamed black wax sewn-shut iguana eyelids and her great proboscis with the nostrils caked like tobacco-blackened pipe bowls, her fingers tracing, weaving a silent plinth of symbols on the mind.

The boys stared.

Her fingernails fluttered, darted, feathered cold winter-water air. Her pickled green frog's breath crawled their flesh in pimples as she sang softly, mewing, humming, glistering her babes, her boys, her friends of the slick snail-tracked roof, the straight-flung arrow, the stricken and sky-drowned balloon.

"Darning-needle dragonfly, sew up these mouths so they not speak!"

Touch, sew, touch, sew her thumbnail stabbed, punched, drew, stabbed, punched, drew along their lower, upper lips until they were thread-pouch shut with invisible thread.

"Darning-needle dragonfly, sew up these ears, so they not hear!"

Cold sand funneled Will's ears, burying her voice. Muffled, far away, fading, she chanted on with a rustle, tick, tickle, tap, flourish of caliper hands.

Moss grew in Jim's ears, swiftly sealing him deep.

"Darning-needle dragonfly, sew up these eyes so they not see!"

Her white-hot fingerprints rolled back their stricken eyeballs to throw the lids down with bangs like great tin doors slammed shut.

Will saw a billion flashbulbs explode, then suck to darkness while the unseen darning-needle insect out beyond somewhere pranced and fizzed like insect drawn to sun-warmed honeypot, as closeted voice stitched off their senses forever and a day beyond.

"Darning-needle dragonfly, have done with eye, ear, lip and tooth, finish hem, sew dark, mound dust, heap with slumber sleep, now tie all knots ever so neat, pump silence in blood like sand in river deep. So. So."

The Witch, somewhere outside the boys, lowered her hands.

The boys stood silent. The Illustrated Man took his embrace from them and stepped back.

The woman from the Dust sniffed at her twin triumphs, ran her hand a last loving time over her statues.

The Dwarf toddled madly about in the boys' shadows, nibbling daintily at their fingernails, softly calling their names.

The Illustrated Man nodded toward the library.

"The janitor's clock. Stop it."

The Witch, mouth wide, savoring doom, wandered off into the marble quarry.

Mr. Dark said: "Left, right. One, two."

The boys walked down the steps, the Dwarf at Jim's side, the Skeleton at Will's.

Serene as death, the Illustrated Man followed.

chapter forty-four

Somewhere near, Charles Halloway's hand lay in a white-hot furnace, melted to sheer nerve and pain. He opened his eyes. At the same moment he heard a great breath as the front door swung shut and a woman's voice came singing in the hall:

"Old man, old man, old man, old man . . . ?"

Where his left hand should be was this swelled blood pudding which pulsed with such ecstasies of pain it fed forth his life, his will, his whole attention. He tried to sit up, but the pain hammerblowed him down again.

"Old man . . . ?"

Not old! Fifty-four's not old, he thought wildly.

And here she came on the worn stone floors, her moth-fingers tapping, scanning braille book titles, as her nostrils siphoned the shadows.

Charles Halloway hunched and crawled, hunched and crawled, toward the nearest stack, cramming pain back with his tongue. He must climb out of reach, climb where books might be weapons flung down upon any night-crawling pursuer. . . .

"Old man, hear you breathing. . . ."

She drifted on his tide, let her body be summoned by every sibilant hiss of his pain.

"Old man, feel your *hurt*...."

If he could fling the hand, the pain, out the window! where it might lie beating like a heart, summoning her away, tricked, to go seek this awful fire. Bent in the street, he imagined her brisking her palms at this throb, an abandoned chunk of delirium.

But no, the hand stayed, glowed, poisoned the air, hurrying the strange nun-Gypsy's tread as she gasped her avaricious mouth most ardently.

"Damn you!" he cried. "Get it over with! I'm here!"

So the Witch wheeled swift as a black clothes dummy on rubber rollers and swayed over him.

He did not even look at her. Such weights and pressures of despair and exertion fought for his attention, he could only free his eyes to watch the inside of his lids upon which multiple and ever-changing looms of terror jigged and gamboled.

"Very simple." The whisper bent low. "Stop the heart."

Why not, he thought, vaguely.

"Slow," she murmured.

Yes, he thought.

"Slow, very slow."

His heart, once bolting, now fell away to a strange disease, disquiet, then quiet, then ease.

"Much more slow, slow..." she suggested.

Tired, yes, you hear that, heart? he wondered.

His heart heard. Like a tight fist it began to relax, a finger at a time.

"Stop all for good, forget all for good," she whispered.

Well, why not?

"Slower... slowest."

His heart stumbled.

And then for no reason, save perhaps for a last look around, because he *did* want to get rid of the pain, and sleep was the way to do that... Charles Halloway opened his eyes.

He saw the Witch.

He saw her fingers working at the air, his face, his body, the heart within his body, and the soul within the heart. Her swamp breath flooded him while, with immense curiosity, he watched the poisonous drizzle from her lips, counted the folds in her stitch-wrinkled eyes, the Gila monster neck, the mummy-linen ears, the dry-rivulet river-sand brow. Never in his life had he focused so nearly to a person, as if she were a puzzle, which once touched together might show life's greatest secret. The solution was in her, it would all spring clear this moment, no, the next, no, the next, watch her scorpion fingers! hear her chant as she diddled the air, yes, diddled was it, tickling, tickling, "Slow!" she whispered. "Slow!" And his obedient heart pulled rein. Diddle-tickle went her fingers.

Charles Halloway snorted. Faintly, he giggled.

He caught this. Why? Why am I . . . giggling . . . at such a time!?

The Witch pulled back the merest quarter inch as if some strange but hidden electric light socket, touched with wet whorl, gave shock.

Charles Halloway saw but did not see her flinch, sensed but seemed in no way to consider her withdrawal, for almost immediately, seizing the initiative, she flung herself forward, not touching, but mutely gesticulating at his chest as one might try to spell an antique clock pendulum.

"Slow!" she cried.

Senselessly, he permitted an idiot smile to balloon itself up from somewhere to attach itself with careless ease under his nose.

"Slowest!"

Her new fever, her anxiety which changed itself to anger was even more of a toy to him. A part of his attention, secret until now, leaned forward to scan every pore of her Halloween face. Somehow, irresistibly, the prime thing was: nothing mattered. Life in the end seemed a prank of such size you could only stand off at this end of the corridor to note its meaningless length and its quite unnecessary height, a mountain built to such ridiculous immensities you were dwarfed in its shadow and mocking of its pomp. So with death this near he thought numbly but purely upon a billion vanities, arrivals, departures, idiot excursions of boy, boy-man, man and old-man goat. He had gathered and stacked all manner of foibles, devices, playthings of his egotism and now, between all the silly corridors of books, the toys of his life swayed. And none more grotesque than this thing named Witch Gypsy Reader of Dust, tickling, that's what! just *tickling* the air! Fool! Didn't she know what she was *doing!*

He opened his mouth.

Of itself, like a child born of an unsuspecting parent, one single raw laugh broke free.

The Witch swooned back.

Charles Halloway did not see. He was far too busy letting the joke rush through his fingers, letting hilarity spring forth of its own volition along his throat, eyes squeezed shut; there it flew, whipping shrapnel in all directions.

"You!" he cried, to no one, everyone, himself, her, them, it, all. "Funny! You!"

"No," the Witch protested.

"Stop tickling!" he gasped.

"Not!" she lunged back, frantically. "Not! Sleep! Slow! Very slow!"

"No, tickling is all it is, for sure!" he roared. "Oh, ha! Ha, stop!"

"Yes, *stop* heart!" she squealed. "*Stop* blood." Her own heart must have shaken like a tambourine; her hands shook. In mid-gesticulation she froze and became aware of the silly fingers.

"Oh, my God!" He wept beautiful glad tears. "Get off my ribs, oh, ha, go on, my heart!"

"Your *heart*, yesssssss!"

"God!" He popped his eyes wide, gulped air, released more soap and water washing everything clear, incredibly clean. "Toys! The key sticks out your back! Who wound you up!?"

And the largest roar of all, flung at the woman, burnt her hands, seared her face, or so it seemed, for she seized herself as from a blast furnace, wrapped her fried hands in Egyptian rags, gripped her dry dugs, skipped back, gave pause, then started a slow retreat, nudged, pushed, pummeled inch by inch, foot by foot, clattering bookracks, shelves, fumbling for handholds on volumes that thrashed free as she scrambled them down. Her brow knocked dim histories, vain theories, duned-up time, promised but compromised years. Chased, bruised, beaten by his laugh which echoed, rang, swam to fill the marble vaults, she whirled at last, claws razoring the wild air and fled to fall downstairs.

Moments later, she managed to cram herself through the front door, which *slammed!*

Her fall, the door slam, almost broke his frame with laughter.

"Oh God, God, please stop, stop yourself!" he begged of his hilarity.

And thus begged, his humor let be.

In mid-roar, at last, all faded to honest laughter, pleasant chuckling, faint giggling, then softly and with great contentment receiving and giving breath, shaking his happy-weary head, the good ache of action in his throat and ribs, gone from his crumpled hand. He lay against the stacks, head leaned to some dear befriending book, the tears of releaseful mirth salting his cheeks, and suddenly knew her gone.

Why? he wondered. *What did I do?*

With one last bark of mirth, he rose up, slow.

What's happened? Oh, God, let's get it clear! First, the drug store, a half-dozen aspirin to cure this hand for an hour, then, *think.* In the last five minutes you did win something, *didn't* you? What's victory taste like? Think! Try to remember!

And smiling a new smile at the ridiculous dead-animal left hand nested in his right crooked elbow, he hurried down the night corridors, and out into town. . . .

3

Departures

chapter forty-five

The small parade moved, soundless, past the eternally revolving, ending-but-unending candy serpentine of Mr. Crosetti's barber pole, past all the darkening or darkened shops, the emptying streets, for people were home now from the church suppers, or out at the carnival for the last side show or the last high-ladder diver floating like milkweed down the night.

Will's feet, far away below, clubbed the sidewalk. One, two, he thought, someone tells me left, right. Dragonfly whispers: one-two.

Is Jim in the parade?! Will's eyes flicked the briefest to one side. Yes! But who's the other little one? The gone-mad, everything's-interesting-so-touch-it, everything's red-hot, pull-back, Dwarf! Plus the Skeleton. And then behind, who were all those hundreds, no, thousands of people marching along, breathing down his neck?

The Illustrated Man.

Will nodded and whined so high and silently that only dogs, dogs who were no help, dogs who could not speak, might hear.

And sure enough, looking obliquely over, he saw not one, not two, but three dogs who, smelling the occasion, their own parade, now ran ahead, now fell behind, their tails like guidons for the platoon.

Bark! thought Will, like in the movies! Bark, bring the police! But the dogs just smiled and trotted.

Coincidence, please, thought Will. Just a *small* one!

Mr. Tetley! Yes! Will saw-but-did-not-see Mr. Tetley! Rolling the wooden Indian back into his shop, closing for the night!

"Turn heads," murmured the Illustrated Man.

Jim turned his head. Will turned his head.

Mr. Tetley smiled.

"Smile," murmured Mr. Dark.

The two boys smiled.

"Hello!" said Mr. Tetley.

"Say hello," someone whispered.

"Hello," said Jim.

"Hello," said Will.

The dogs barked.

"A free ride at the carnival," murmured Mr. Dark.

"Free ride," said Will.

"At the carnival!" clacked Jim.

Then, like good machines, they shut up their smiles.

"Have fun!" called Mr. Tetley.

The dogs barked joy.

The parade marched on.

"Fun," said Mr. Dark. "Free rides. When the crowds go home, half an hour from now. We'll ride Jim round. You still *want* that, Jim?"

Hearing but not hearing, locked away in himself, Will thought, Jim, don't listen!

Jim's eyes slid: wet or oily, it was hard to tell.

"You'll travel with us, Jim, and if Mr. Cooger doesn't survive (it's a near thing for him, we haven't saved him yet, we'll try again now) but if he doesn't make it, Jim, how would you like to be partners? I'll grow you to a fine strong age, eh? Twenty-two? twenty-five?! Dark and Nightshade, Nightshade and Dark, sweet lovely names for such as we with such as the side shows to run around the world! What say, Jim?"

Jim said nothing, sewn up in the Witch's dream.

Don't listen! wailed his best friend, who heard nothing but heard it all.

"And Will?" said Mr. Dark. "Let's ride *him* back and back, eh? Make him a babe in arms, a babe for the Dwarf to carry like a clown-child, roundabout in parades, every day for the next fifty years, would you like that, Will? to be a babe forever? not able to talk and tell all the lovely things you know? Yes, I think that's best for Will. A plaything, a little wet friend for the Dwarf!"

Will must have screamed.

But not out loud.

For only the dogs barked, in terror; yiping, off they ran, as if pelted with rocks.

A man came around the corner.

A policeman.

"Who's this?" muttered Mr. Dark.

"Mr. Kolb," said Jim.

"Mr. Kolb!" said Will.

"Darning-needle," whispered Mr. Dark. "Dragonfly."

Pain stabbed Will's ears. Moss stuffed his eyes. Gum glued his teeth. He felt a multitudinous tapping, shuttling, weaving, about his face, all numb again.

"Say hello to Mr. Kolb."

"Hello," said Jim.

" . . . Kolb . . ." said the dreaming Will.

"Hello, boys. Gentlemen."

"Turn here," said Mr. Dark.

They turned.

Away toward meadow country, away from warm lights, good town, safe streets, the drumless march progressed.

chapter forty-six

Stretched out over a mile of territory the straggling parade now moved as follows:

At the edge of the carnival midway, stumping the grass with their dead feet, Jim and Will paced friends who constantly retold the wondrous uses of darning-needle dragonflies.

Behind, a good half mile, trying to catch up, walking mysteriously wounded, the Gypsy, who whorl-symboled the dust.

And yet farther back came the janitor-father, now slowing himself with remembrances of age, now pacing swiftly young with thoughts of the brief first encounter and victory, carrying his left hand patted to his chest, chewing medicines as he went.

At the midway rim, Mr. Dark looked back as if an inner voice had named the stragglers in his widely separated maneuver. But the voice failed, he was unsure. He nodded briskly, and Dwarf, Skeleton, Jim, Will thrust through the crowd.

Jim felt the river of bright people wash by all around but not touching. Will heard waterfall laughter here, there, and him walking through the downpour. An explosion of fireflies blossomed on the sky; the Ferris wheel, exultant as a titanic fireworks, dilated above them.

Then they were at the Mirror Maze and sidling, colliding,

bumping, careening through the unfolded ice ponds where stricken spider-stung boys much like themselves appeared, vanished a thousand times over.

That's *me!* thought Jim.

But I can't help me, thought Will, no matter how many of me there are!

And crowd of boys, plus crowd of reflected Mr. Dark's illustrations, for he had taken off his coat and shirt now, crammed and crushed through to the Waxworks at the end of the maze.

"Sit," said Mr. Dark. "Stay."

Among the wax figures of murdered, gunshot, guillotined, garroted men and women the two boys sat like Egyptian cats, unblinked, untwitched, unswallowing.

Some late visitors passed through, laughing. They commented on all the wax figures.

They did not notice the thin line of saliva crept from the corner of one "wax" boy's mouth.

They did not see how bright was the second "wax" boy's stare, which suddenly brimmed and ran clear water down his cheek.

Outside, the Witch limped in through back alleys of rope and peg between the tents.

"Ladies and gentlemen!"

The last crowd of the night, three or four hundred strong, turned as a body.

The Illustrated Man, stripped to the waist, all nightmare viper, sabertooth, libidinous ape, clotted vulture, all salmon-sulphur sky rose up with annunciations:

"The last free event this evening! Come one! Come all!"

The crowd surged toward the main platform outside the freak tent, where stood Dwarf, Skeleton, and Mr. Dark.

"The Most Amazingly Dangerous, ofttimes Fatal—World Famous BULLET TRICK!"

The crowd gasped with pleasure.

"The rifles, if you please!"

The Thin One cracked wide a racked display of bright artillery.

The Witch, hurrying up, froze when Mr. Dark cried: "And here, our death-defier, the bullet-catcher who will stake her life—Mademoiselle Tarot!"

The Witch shook her head, bleated, but Dark's hand swept down to swing her like a child to the platform, still protesting, which gave Dark pause, but, in front of everyone now, he went on:

"A volunteer, please, to fire the rifle!"

The crowd rumbled softly, daring itself to speak up.

Mr. Dark's mouth barely moved. Under his breath he asked, "Is the clock stopped?"

"Not," she whined, "stopped."

"No?" he almost burst out.

He burnt her with his eyes, then turned to the audience and let his mouth finish the spiel, his fingers rapping over the rifles.

"Volunteers, please!"

"Stop the act," the Witch cried softly, wringing her hands.

"It goes on, damn you, *worse* than double-damn you," he whispered, whistled fiercely.

Secretly, Dark gathered a pinch of flesh on his wrist, the illustration of a black-nun blind woman, which he bit with his fingernails.

The Witch spasmed, seized her breast, groaned, ground her teeth. "Mercy!" she hissed, half aloud.

Silence from the crowd.

Mr. Dark nodded swiftly.

"Since there are no volunteers—" He scraped his illustrated wrist. The Witch shuddered. "We will cancel our last act and—"

"Here! A volunteer!"

The crowd turned.

Mr. Dark recoiled, then asked: "Where?"

"Here."

Far out at the edge of the crowd, a hand lifted, a path opened. Mr. Dark could see very clearly the man standing there, alone.

Charles Halloway, citizen, father, introspective husband, night-wanderer, and janitor of the town library.

chapter forty-seven

T he crowd's appreciative clamor faded.

Charles Halloway did not move.

He let the path grow leading down to the platform.

He could not see the expression on the faces of the freaks standing up there. His eyes swept the crowd and found the Mirror Maze, the empty oblivion which beckoned with ten times a thousand million light years of reflections, counterreflections, reversed and double-reversed, plunging deep to nothing, face-falling to nothing, stomach-dropping away to yet more sickening plummets of nothing.

And yet, wasn't there an echo of two boys in the powdered silver at the back of each glass? Did or did he not perceive, with the tremulous tip of eyelash if not the eye, their passage through, their wait beyond, warm wax amongst cold, waiting to be key-wound by terrors, run free in panics?

No, thought Charles Halloway, don't think. Get on with this!

"Coming!" he shouted.

"Go get 'em, Pop!" a man said.

"Yes," said Charles Halloway. "I will."

And he walked down through the crowd.

The Witch spun slowly, magnetized at the night-wandering

volunteer's approach. Her eyelids jerked at their sewn black-wax threads behind dark glasses.

Mr. Dark, the illustration-drenched, superinfested civilization of souls, leaned from the platform, gladly whetting his lips. Thoughts spun fiery Catherine wheels in his eyes, quick, quick, what, what, *what!*

And the aging janitor, fixing a smile to his face like a white celluloid set of teeth from a Cracker Jack box, strode on, and the crowd opened as the sea before Moses and closed behind, and him wondering what to do? why was he here? but on the move, steadily, nevertheless.

Charles Halloway's foot touched the first step of the platform.

The Witch trembled secretly.

Mr. Dark felt this secret, glanced sharply. Swiftly he put his hand out to grab for the good right hand of this fifty-four-year-old man.

But the fifty-four-year-old man shook his head, would not give his hand to be held, touched, or helped up. "Thanks, no."

On the platform, Charles Halloway waved to the crowd.

The people set off a few firecrackers of applause.

"But—" Mr. Dark was amazed—"your left hand, sir, you can't hold and fire a rifle if you have only the use of one hand!"

Charles Halloway paled.

"I'll do it," he said. "With one hand."

"Hoorah!" cried a boy, below.

"Go it, Charlie!" a man called, out beyond.

Mr. Dark flushed as the crowd laughed and applauded even louder now. He lifted his hands to ward off the wave of refreshing sound, like rain that washed in from the people.

"All right, all right! Let's see if he *can* do it!"

Brutally, the Illustrated Man snapped a rifle from its locks, hurled it through the air.

The crowd gasped.

Charles Halloway ducked. He put up his right hand. The rifle slapped his palm. He grabbed. It did not fall. He had it good.

The audience hooted, said things against Mr. Dark's bad manners which made him turn away for a moment, damning himself, silently.

Will's father lifted the rifle, beaming.

The crowd roared.

And while the wave of applause came in, crashed, and went back down the shore, he looked again to the maze, where the sensed but unseen shadow-shapes of Will and Jim were filed among titanic razor blades of revelation and illusion, then back to the Medusa gaze of Mr. Dark, swiftly reckoned with, and on to the stitched and jittering sightless nun of midnight, sidling back still more. Now she was as far as she could sidle, at the far end of the platform, almost pressed to the whorled red-black rifle bull's-eye target.

"Boy!" shouted Charles Halloway.

Mr. Dark stiffened.

"I need a boy volunteer to help me hold the rifle!" shouted Charles Halloway.

"Someone! Anyone!" he shouted.

A few boys in the crowd shifted around on their toes.

"Boy!" shouted Charles Halloway. "Hold on. My son's out there. He'll volunteer, *won't* you, Will?"

The Witch flung one hand up to feel the shape of this audacity which came off the fifty-four-year-old man like a fever. Mr. Dark was spun round as if hit by a fast-traveling gunshot.

"Will!" called his father.

In the Wax Museum, Will sat motionless.

"Will!" called his father. "Come on, boy!"

The crowd looked left, looked right, looked back.

No answer.

Will sat in the Wax Museum.

Mr. Dark observed all of this with some respect, some degree of admiration, some concern; he seemed to be waiting, just as was Will's father.

"Will, come help your old man!" Mr. Halloway cried, jovially.

Will sat in the Wax Museum.

Mr. Dark smiled.

"Will! Willy! Come here!"

No answer.

Mr. Dark smiled more.

"Willy! Don't you hear your old man?"

Mr. Dark stopped smiling.

For this last was the voice of a gentleman in the crowd, speaking up.

The crowd laughed.

"Will!" called a woman.

"Willy!" called another.

"Yoohoo!" A gentleman in a beard.

"Come on, William!" A boy.

The crowd laughed more, jostled elbows.

Charles Halloway called. *They* called. Charles Halloway cried to the hills. *They* cried to the hills.

"Will! Willy! William!"

A shadow shuttled and wove in the mirrors.

The Witch broke out chandeliers of sweat.

"There!"

The crowd stopped calling.

As did Charles Halloway, choked on the name of his son now, and silent.

For Will stood in the entrance of the Maze, like the wax figure that he almost was.

"Will," called his father, softly.

The sound of this chimed the sweat off the Witch.

Will moved, unseeing, through the crowd.

And handing the rifle down like a cane for the boy to grasp, his father drew him up onto the stand.

"*Here's* my good left hand!" announced the father.

Will neither saw nor heard the crowd sound forth a solid and offensive applause.

Mr. Dark had not moved, though Charles Halloway could see

him, during all this, lighting and setting off cannon crackers in his head; but each, one by one, fizzled and died. Mr. Dark could not guess what they were up to. For that matter, Charles Hallo-way did not know or guess. It was as if he had written this play for himself, over the years, in the library, nights, torn up the play after memorizing it, and now forgotten what he had set forth to remember. He was relying on secret discoveries of self, moment by moment, playing by ear, no! heart and soul! And . . . *now?!*

The brightness of his teeth seemed to strike the Witch blinder! Impossible! She flung one hand to her glasses, her sewn eyelids!

"Closer, everyone!" called Will's father.

The crowd gathered in. The platform was an island. The sea was people.

"Watch the bull's-eye targeteer!"

The Witch melted in her rags.

The Illustrated Man looked left, found no pleasure in the Skeleton, who simply looked thinner; found no pleasure looking right to a Dwarf who blandly dwelt in squashed idiot madness.

"The bullet, please!" Will's father said, amiably.

The thousand illustrations on his jerking horseflesh frame did not hear, so why should Mr. Dark?

"If you please," said Charles Halloway. "The bullet? So I may knock that flea off the old Gypsy's wart!"

Will stood motionless.

Mr. Dark hesitated.

Out in the choppy sea, smiles flashed, here, there, a hundred, two hundred, three hundred whitenesses, as if a vast titillation of water had been provoked by a lunar gravity. The tide ebbed.

The Illustrated Man, in slow motion, proffered the bullet. His arm, a long molasses undulation, lazed to offer the bullet to the boy, to see if he would notice; he did not notice.

His father took the missile.

"Mark it with your initials," said Mr. Dark, by rote.

"No, with more!" Charles Halloway raised his son's hand and

made him hold the bullet, so he could take a penknife with his one good hand and carve a strange symbol on the lead.

What's happening? Will thought. I know what's happening. I don't know what's happening? What!?

Mr. Dark saw a crescent moon on the bullet, saw nothing wrong with such a moon, rammed it in the rifle, slapped the rifle back at Will's father, who once more caught it deftly.

"Ready, Will?"

The boy's peach face drowsed in the slightest nod.

Charles Halloway flicked a last glance at the maze, thought, Jim, you there still? Get ready!

Mr. Dark turned to go pat, conjure, calm his dust-crone friend, but cracked to a halt at the crack of the rifle being reopened, the bullet ejected by Will's father, to assure the audience it was there. It seemed real enough, yet he had read long ago that this was a substitute bullet, shaped of a very hard steel-colored crayon wax. Shot through the rifle it would dissolve out the barrel as smoke and vapor. At this very moment, having somehow switched bullets, the Illustrated Man was slipping the real marked bullet into the Witch's jerking fingers. She would hide it in her cheek. At the shot, she would pretend to jolt under the imagined impact, then reveal the bullet caught by her yellow rat teeth. Fanfare! Applause!

The Illustrated Man, glancing up, saw Charles Halloway with the opened rifle, the wax bullet. But instead of revealing what he knew, Mr. Halloway simply said, "Let's cut our mark more clearly, eh, boy?" And with his penknife, the boy holding the bullet in his senseless hand, he marked this fresh new wax unmarked bullet with the same mysterious crescent moon, then snapped it back into the rifle.

"Ready?!"

Mr. Dark looked to the Witch.

Who hesitated, then nodded, once, faintly.

"Ready!" announced Charles Halloway.

And all about lay the tents, the breathing crowd, the anxious freaks, a Witch iced with hysteria, Jim hidden to be found, an ancient mummy still seated glowing with blue fire in his electric chair, and a merry-go-round waiting for the show to cease, the crowd to go, and the carnival to have its way with boys and janitor trapped, if possible, and alone.

"Will," said Charles Halloway conversationally, as he lifted the now suddenly heavy rifle. "Your shoulder here is my brace. Take the middle of the rifle, gently, with one hand. Take it, Will." The boy raised a hand. "That's it, son. When I say 'hold,' hold your breath. Hear me?"

The boy's head tremored with the slightest affirmation. He slept. He dreamed. The dream was nightmare. The nightmare was *this*.

And the next part of this was his father shouting:

"Ladies! Gentlemen!"

The Illustrated Man clenched his fist. Will's picture, lost in it, like a flower, was crushed.

Will twisted.

The rifle fell.

Charles Halloway pretended not to notice.

"Me and Will here will now, together, him being the good left arm I can't use, do the one and only most dangerous, sometimes fatal, Bullet Trick!"

Applause. Laughter.

Quickly the fifty-four-year-old janitor, denying each year, laid the rifle back on the boy's jerking shoulder.

"Hear that, Will? Listen! That's for *us!*"

The boy listened. The boy grew calm.

Mr. Dark tightened his fist.

Will was taken with slight palsy.

"We'll hit 'em bull's-eye on, won't we, boy!" said his father.

More laughter.

And the boy grew very calm indeed, with the rifle on his shoulder, and Mr. Dark squeezed tight on the peach-fuzz face nestled in the flesh of his hand, but the boy was serene in the laughter which still flowed and his father kept the hoop rolling thus:

"Show the lady your teeth, Will!"

Will showed the woman against the target his teeth.

The blood fell away from the Witch's face.

Now Charles Halloway showed her his teeth, too, such as they were.

And winter lived in the Witch.

"Boy," said someone in the audience, "she's great. Acts scared! Look!"

I'm looking, thought Will's father, his left hand useless at his side, his right hand up to the rifle trigger, his face to the sight as his son held the rifle unswervingly pointed at the bull's-eye and the Witch's face superimposed there, and the last moment come, and a wax bullet in the chamber, and what could a wax bullet do? A bullet that dissolved in transit, what use? why were they here, what could they do? silly, silly!

No! thought Will's father. Stop!

He stopped the doubts.

He felt his mouth shape words with no sound.

But, the Witch heard what he said.

Above the dying laughter, before the warm sound was completely gone, he made these words, silently with his lips:

The crescent moon I have marked on the bullet is not a crescent moon.

It is my own smile.

I have put my smile on the bullet in the rifle.

He said it once.

He waited for her to understand.

He said it, silently, again.

And in the moment before the Illustrated Man himself translated the mouthings, quickly, Charles Halloway cried, faintly, "Hold!" Will held his breath. Far back among wax statues, Jim, hid away, dripped saliva from his chin. Strapped in electric chair a dead-alive mummy hummed power in its teeth. Mr. Dark's illustrations writhed with sick sweat as he clenched his fist a final time, but—too late! Serene, Will held breath, held weapon. Serene, his father said, *"Now."*

And fired the rifle.

chapter forty-eight

One shot!

The Witch sucked breath.

Jim, in the Wax Museum, sucked breath.

As did Will, asleep.

As did his father.

As did Mr. Dark.

As did all the freaks.

As did the crowd.

The Witch screamed.

Jim, among the wax dummies, blew all the air from his lungs.

Will shrieked himself awake, on the platform.

The Illustrated Man let the air from his mouth in a great angry bray, whipping up his hands to stop all events. But the Witch fell. She fell off the platform. She fell in the dust.

The smoking rifle in his one good hand, Charles Halloway let his breath go slow, feeling every bit of it move from him. He still stared along the rifle sights at the target where the woman had been.

At the platform rim, Mr. Dark looked down at the screaming crowd and what they were screaming about.

"She's fainted—"

"No, she slipped!"

"She's . . . shot!"

At last Charles Halloway came to stand by the Illustrated Man, looking down. There were many things in his face: surprise, dismay, and some small strange relief and satisfaction.

The woman was lifted and put on the platform. Her mouth was frozen open, almost with a look of recognition.

He knew she was dead. In a moment, the crowd would know. He watched the Illustrated Man's hand move down to touch, trace, feel for life. Then Mr. Dark lifted both her hands, like a doll, in some marionette strategy, to give her motion. But the body refused.

So he gave one of the Witch's arms to the Dwarf, the other to the Skeleton, and they shook and moved them in a ghastly semblance of reawakening as the crowd backed.

" . . . dead . . ."

"But . . . there's no wound."

"Shock, you think?"

Shock, thought Charles Halloway, my God, did *that* kill her? Or the other bullet? When I fired the shot, did she suck the *other* bullet down her throat? Did she . . . choke on my smile! Oh, Christ!

"It's all right! Show's over! Just fainted!" said Mr. Dark. "All an act! All part of the show," he said, not looking at the woman, not looking at the crowd, but looking at Will, who stood blinking around, out of one nightmare and fresh into the next as his father stood with him and Mr. Dark cried: "Everyone home! Show's over! Lights! Lights!"

The carnival lights flickered.

The crowd, herded before the failing illumination, turned like a great carousel, and as the lamps dimmed, hustled toward the few remaining pools of light as if to warm themselves there before braving the wind. One by one, one by one, the lights indeed were going off.

"Lights!" said Mr. Dark.

"Jump!" said Will's father.

Will jumped. Will ran with his father who still carried the weapon that had fired the smile that had killed the Gypsy and put her to dust.

"Is Jim in there?"

They were at the maze. Behind them, on the platform, Mr. Dark bellowed: "Lights! Go home! All over! Done!"

"*Is* Jim in there?" wondered Will. "Yes. Yes, he is!"

Inside the Wax Museum, Jim still had not moved, had not blinked.

"Jim!" The voice came through the maze.

Jim moved. Jim blinked. A rear exit door stood wide. Jim blundered toward it.

"I'm coming for you, Jim!"

"No, Dad!"

Will caught at his father, who stood at the first turn of the mirrors with the pain come back to his hand, racing up along the nerves to strike a fireball near his heart. "Dad, don't go in!" Will grabbed his good arm.

Behind them, the platform was empty, Mr. Dark was running . . . where? Somewhere as the night shut in, the lights went off, went off, went off, the night sucked around, gathering, whistling, simpering, and the crowd, like a shake of leaves from one huge tree, blew off the midway, and Will's father stood facing the glass tides, the waves, the gauntlet of horror he knew waited for him to swim through, stride through to fight the desiccation, the annihilation of one's self that waited there. He had seen enough to know. Eyes shut, you'd be lost. Eyes open, you'd know such utter despair, such gravities of anguish would weight you, you might never drag past the twelfth turn. But Charles Halloway took Will's hands away. "Jim's there. Jim, wait! I'm coming in!"

And Charles Halloway took the next step into the maze.

Ahead flowed sluices of silver light, deep slabs of shadow, polished, wiped, rinsed with images of themselves and others whose souls, passing, scoured the glass with their agony, curried the cold ice with their narcissism, or sweated the angles and flats with their fear.

"Jim!"

He ran. Will ran. They stopped.

For the lights in here were going blind, one by one, going dim, changing color, now blue, now a color like lilac summer lightning which flared in haloes, then a flickerlight like a thousand ancient windblown candles.

And between himself and Jim in need of rescue, stood an army of one million sick-mouthed, frost-haired, white-tine-bearded men.

Them! all of them! he thought. That's *me!*

Dad! thought Will, at his back, don't be afraid. It's only you. All only my father!

But he did not like their look. They were so old, so very old, and got much older the farther away they marched, wildly gesticulating, as Dad threw up his hands to fend off the revelation, this wild image repeated to insanity.

Dad! he thought, it's you!

But, it was more.

And all the lights went out.

And both, squeezed still, in muffle-gasping silence, stood afraid.

chapter forty-nine

A hand dug like a mole in the dark.

Will's hand.

It emptied his pockets, it delved, it rejected, it dug again. For while it was dark he knew those million old men might march, hustle, rush, leap, smash Dad with what they *were!* In this shut-up night, with just four seconds to think of them, they might do *anything* to Dad! If Will didn't hurry, these legions from Time Future, all the alarms of coming life, so mean, raw, and true you couldn't deny that's how Dad'd look tomorrow, next day, the day after the day after that, that cattle run of possible years might sweep Dad under!

So, quick!

Who has more pockets than a magician?

A boy.

Whose pockets contain *more* than a magician's?

A boy's.

Will seized forth kitchen matches!

"Oh God, Dad, here!"

He struck the match.

The stampede was close!

They had come running. Now, fixed by light, they widened

their eyes, as did Dad, amazed their mouths at their own ancient quakes and masquerades. Halt! the match had cried. And
platoons left, squads right, had stilt-muscled themselves to fitful
rest, to baleful glare, itching for the match to whiff out. Then,
given lease to run next time, they'd hit this old, very old, much
older, terribly old man, suffocate him with Fates in one instant.

"No!" said Charles Halloway.

No. A million dead lips moved.

Will thrust the match forward. In the mirrors, a wizened mul-
tiplication of boy-apes did likewise, posing a single rosebud of
blue-yellow flame.

"No!"

Every glass threw javelins of light which invisibly pierced,
sank deep, found heart, soul, lungs, to frost the veins, cut nerves,
send Will to ruin, paralyze and then kick-football heart. Ham-
strung, the old old man foundered to his knees, as did his sup-
pliant images, his congregation of terrified selves one week, one
month, two years, twenty, fifty, seventy, ninety years from now!
every second, minute, and long-after-midnight hour of his possible survival into insanity, there all sank grayer, more yellow as the
mirrors ricocheted him through, bled him lifeless, mouthed him
dry, then threatened to whiff him to skeletal dusts and litter his
moth ashes to the floor.

"No!"

Charles Halloway struck the match from his son's hand.

"Dad, don't!"

For in the new dark, the restive herd of old men shambled
forward, hearts hammering.

"Dad, we gotta see!"

He struck his second and final match.

And in the flare saw Dad sunk down, eyes clenched, fists
tight, and all those other men who would have to shunt, crawl,
scramble on knees once this last light was gone. Will grabbed his
father's shoulder and shook him.

"Oh, Dad, Dad, I don't care how old you are, ever! I don't care what, I don't care anything! Oh, Dad," he cried, weeping. "I love you!"

At which Charles Halloway opened his eyes and saw himself and the others like himself and his son behind holding him, the flame trembling, the tears trembling on his face, and suddenly, as before, the image of the Witch, the memory of the library, defeat for one, victory for another, swam before him, mixed with sound of rifle shot, flight of marked bullet, surge of fleeing crowd.

For only a moment longer he looked at all of himselves, at Will. A small sound escaped his mouth. A little larger sound escaped his mouth.

And then, at last, he gave the maze, the mirrors, and all Time ahead, Beyond, Around, Above, Behind, Beneath or squandered inside himself, the only answer possible.

He opened his mouth very wide, and let the loudest sound of all free.

The Witch, if she were alive, would have known that sound, and died again.

chapter fifty

J im Nightshade, out the back door of the maze, lost on the carnival grounds, running, stopped.

The Illustrated Man, somewhere among the black tents, running, stopped.

The Dwarf froze.

The Skeleton turned.

All had heard.

Not the sound that Charles Halloway made, no.

But the terrific sounds that followed.

One mirror alone, and then a second mirror, followed by a pause, and then a third mirror, and a fourth and another after that and another after that and still another and another after that, in domino fashion, they formed swift spiderwebs over their fierce stares and then with faint tinkles and sharp cracks, fell.

One minute there was this incredible Jacob's ladder of glass, folding, refolding and folding away yet again images pressed in a book of light. The next, all shattered to meteor precipitation.

The Illustrated Man, halted, listening, felt his own eyes, crystal, almost spiderweb and splinter with the sounds.

It was as if Charles Halloway, once more a choir-boy in a strange sub-sub-demon church had sung the most beautiful high note of amiable humor ever in his life which first shook moth-silver from the mirror backs, then shook images from glass faces, then shook glass itself to ruin. A dozen, a hundred, a thousand mirrors, and with them the ancient images of Charles Halloway, sank earthward in delicious moonfalls of snow and sleety water.

All because of the sound he had let come from his lungs through his throat out his mouth.

All because he accepted everything at last, accepted the carnival, the hills beyond, the people in the hills, Jim, Will, and above all himself and all of life, and, accepting, threw back his head for the second time tonight and showed his acceptance with sound.

And lo! like Jericho and the trump, with musical thunders the glass gave up its ghosts, Charles Halloway cried out, released. He took his hands from his face. Fresh starlight and dying carnival glow rushed in to set him free. The reflected dead men were gone, buried under the cymbaled slide, the splash and surfing of glass at his feet.

"Lights . . . lights!"

A far voice cried away more warmth.

The Illustrated Man, unfrozen, vanished among the tents.

The crowd was now gone.

"Dad, what'd you *do?*"

But the match burned Will's fingers, he dropped it, but now there was dim light enough to see Dad shuffle the trash, stir the mess of mirrored glass, heading back through the empty places where the maze had been and was no more.

"Jim?"

A door stood open. Pale carnival illumination, fading, poured through to show them wax figures of murderers and murderees.

Jim did not sit among them.

"Jim!"

They stared at the open door through which Jim had run to be lost in the swarms of night between black canvases.

The last electric light bulb went out.

"We'll *never* find him now," said Will.

"Yes," said his father, standing in the dark. "We'll find him."

Where? Will thought, and stopped.

Far down the midway, the carousel steamed, the calliope tortured itself with musics.

There, thought Will. If Jim's anywhere, it's there, to the music, old funny Jim, the free-ride ticket hid in his pocket still, I bet! Oh, damn Jim, damn him, damn him! he cried, and then thought, no! don't *you*, he's damned already, or near it! So how do we find him in the dark, no matches, no lights, just the two of us, all of them, and us alone in their territory?

"How—" said Will, aloud.

But his father said "There," very softly. With gratitude.

And Will stepped to the door, which was lighter now.

The moon! Thank God.

It was rising from the hills.

"The police . . . ?"

"No time. It's the next few minutes or nothing. Three people we got to worry about—"

"The freaks!"

"Three people, Will. Number one, Jim, number two, Mr. Cooger frying in his Electric Chair. Number three, Mr. Dark and his skinful of souls. Save one, kick the other two to hell and gone. Then I think the freaks go, too. You ready, Will?"

Will eyed the door, the tents, the dark, the sky with new light paling it.

"God bless the moon."

Hands tight together, they stepped out the door.

As if to greet them, the wind flung up and down all the tent canvases in a great prehistoric thunderkite display of leprous wings.

chapter fifty-one

They ran in urine smell of shadow, they ran in clean ice smell of moon.

The calliope steam-throb whispered, tatted, trilled.

The music! thought Will, is it running backward or forward?

"Which way?" Dad whispered.

"Through here!" Will pointed.

A hundred yards off, beyond a foothill of tents, there was a flare of blue light, sparks jumped up and fell away, then dark again.

Mr. Electrico! thought Will. They're trying to move him, sure! Get him to the merry-go-round, kill or cure! And if they cure him, then, oh gosh, then, it's angry him and angry Illustrated Man against just Dad and me! And Jim? Well, where was Jim? This way one day, that way the next, and . . . tonight? Whose side would he wind up on? Ours! Old friend Jim! Ours, of course! But Will trembled. Did friends last forever, then? For eternity, could they be counted to a warm, round, and handsome sum?

Will glanced left.

The Dwarf stood half enfolded by tent flaps, waiting, motionless.

"Dad, look," cried Will, softly. "And there—the Skeleton."

Further over, the tall man, the man all marble bone and Egyptian papyrus stood like a dead tree.

"The freaks—why don't they stop us?"

"Scared."

"Of *us?!*"

Will's father crouched and squinted out from around an empty cage.

"They're walking wounded, anyway. They saw what happened to the Witch. That's the only answer. Look at them."

And there they stood, like uprights, like tent poles spotted all through the meadow grounds, hiding in shadow, waiting. For what? Will swallowed, hard. Maybe not hiding at all, but spread out for the running fight to come. At the right time, Mr. Dark would yell and—they'd just circle in. But the time wasn't right. Mr. Dark was busy. When he'd done what must be done, then he'd give that yell. So? So, thought Will, we got to see he never yells at all.

Will's feet slithered in the grass.

Will's father moved ahead.

The freaks watched with moon-glass eyes as they passed.

The calliope changed. It whistled sadly, sweetly, around a curve of tents, around a riverflow of darkness.

It's going ahead! thought Will. Yes! It *was* going backward. But now it stopped and started again, and this time forward! What's Mr. Dark *up* to?

"Jim!" Will burst out.

"Sh!" Dad shook him.

But the name had tumbled from his mouth only because he heard the calliope summing the golden years ahead, felt Jim isolate somewhere, pulled by warm gravities, swung by sunrise notes, wondering what it could be like to stand sixteen, seventeen, eighteen years tall, and then, oh then, nineteen and, most incredible!—twenty! The great wind of time blew in the brass pipes, a fine, a jolly, a summer tune, promising everything and even Will, hearing, began to run toward the music that grew up like a peach tree full of sun-ripe fruit—

No! he thought.

And instead made his feet step to his own fear, jump to his own tune, a hum cramped back by throat, held fast by lungs, which shook the bones of his head and drowned the calliope away.

"There," said Dad softly.

And between the tents, ahead, in transit, they saw a grotesque parade. Like a dark sultan in a palanquin, a half-familiar figure rode a chair borne on the shoulders of assorted sizes and shapes of darkness.

At Dad's cry, the parade jolted, then broke into a run!

"Mr. Electrico!" said Will.

They're taking him to the carousel!

The parade vanished.

A tent lay between them.

"Around here!" Will jumped, pulling his father.

The calliope played sweet. To pull Jim, to draw Jim.

And when the parade arrived with Electrico?

Back the music would spin, back the carousel run, to shard away his skin, to freshen forth his years!

Will stumbled, fell. Dad picked him up.

And then . . .

There arose a human barking, yapping, baying, whining, as if *all* had fallen. In a long-drawn moan, a gasp, a shuddering sigh, an entire crowd of people with crippled throats made chorus together.

"Jim! They've got Jim!"

"No . . ." murmured Charles Halloway, strangely. "Maybe Jim . . . or us . . . got *them.*"

They stepped around the last tent.

Wind blew dust in their faces.

Will clapped his hand up, squinched his nose. The dust was antique spice, burnt maple leaves, a prickling blue that teemed and sifted to earth. Swarming its own shadows, the dust filtered over the tents.

Charles Halloway sneezed. Figures jumped and scurried

away from an upended, half-tilted object abandoned half-way between one tent and the carousel.

The object was the electric chair, capsized, with straps dangling from wooden arms and legs, and a metal headcap hanging
from its top.

"But," said Will. "Where's Mr. Electrico!? I mean . . . Mr.
Cooger!?"

"*That* must have been him."

"*What* must have been him?"

But the answer was there, sifting down the midway in the
whorling wind devils . . . the burnt spice, the autumn incense that
had floured them when they turned this corner.

Kill or cure, Charles Halloway thought. He imagined them
rushed in the last few seconds, toting the ancient dustsack bone-
heap over starched grasses in his disconnected chair, perhaps
only one in a running series of attempts to foster, encourage, pre-
serve life in what was really nothing but a mortuary junkpile, rust-
flakes and dying coals that no wind could blow alight again. Yet
they must try. How many times in the last twenty-four hours had
they run out on such excursions, only, in panic, to cease activity
because the merest jolt, the slightest breath, threatened to shake
old ancient Cooger down to meal-mush and chaff? Better to leave
him propped in electric-warm chair, a continual exhibit, an ever-
going-on performance for gaping audiences, and try again, but
especially try now, when, lights out, and crowds herded off in the
dark, all threatened by one smile on a bullet, there was need of
Cooger as he once was, tall, flame-headed, and riven with earth-
quake violence. But somewhere, twenty seconds, ten seconds
ago, the last glue crumbled, the last bolt of life fell free, and the
mummy-doll, the Erector-set grotesque disencumbered itself
in smoke puffs and November leaflets, a broadcast of mortality
along the wind. Mr. Cooger, threshed in a final harvest, was now
a billion parchment flecks, tumbled sea-scrolls capered in meadows. A mere dust explosion in a silo of ancient grain: gone.

"Oh, no, no, no, no, no," someone murmured.

Charles Halloway touched Will's arm.

Will stopped saying "Oh, no, no, no." He, too, in the last few moments, had thought the same as his father, of the toted corpse, the strewn bone-meal, the mineral-enriched hills of grass. . . .

Now there was only the empty chair and the last particles of mica, the radiant motes of peculiar dirt crusting the straps. And the freaks, who had been toting the baroque dump, now fled to shadows.

We made them run, thought Will, but something made them drop it!

No, not something. Someone.

Will flexed his eyes.

The carousel, deserted, empty, traveled on its way through its own special time, forward.

But between the fallen chair and the carousel, standing alone, was that a freak? No . . .

"Jim!"

Dad knocked his elbow and Will shut up.

Jim, he thought.

And where, now, was Mr. Dark?

Somewhere. For he had started the carousel, hadn't he? Yes! To draw them, to draw Jim, and—what else? Right now there was no time, for—

Jim turned from the spilled chair, turned and walked slowly toward the free, free ride.

He was going where he had always known he must go. Like a weather vane in wild seasons he had tremored this way, wandered that, hesitated upon bright horizons and warm directions, only at last now to tilt and, half sleepwalking, tremble about in the bright brass pull and summer march of music. He could not look away.

Another step, and then another, toward the merry-go-round, there went Jim.

"Go get him, Will," said his father.

Will went.

Jim raised his right hand.

The brass poles flashed by into the future, pulling the flesh like syrup, stretching the bones like taffy, the sun-metal color burning Jim's cheeks, flinting his eyes.

Jim reached. The brass poles flick-knocked his fingernails, tinkling their own small tune.

"Jim!"

The brass poles chopped by in a yellow sunrise at night.

The music leaped in a clear fountain, high.

Eeeeeeeeeeeeeee.

Jim opened his mouth with the same cry:

"Eeeeeeeeeeeeeee!"

"Jim!" cried Will, running.

Jim's palm slapped one brass pole. The pole whipped on.

He slapped another brass pole. This time, his palm glued itself tight.

Wrist followed fingers, arm followed wrist, shoulder and body followed arm. Jim, sleepwalked, was torn from his roots in the earth.

"Jim!"

Will reached, felt Jim's foot flick from his grasp.

Jim swung round the wailing night in a great dark summer circle, Will racing after.

"Jim, get off! Jim, don't leave me *here!*"

Flung by centrifuge, Jim grasped the pole with one hand, spun, and, as if by some lone lost and final instinct, gestured his other hand free to trail on the wind, the one part of him, the small white separate part that still remembered their friendship.

"Jim, *jump!!*"

Will snatched for that hand, missed, stumbled, almost fell. The first race was lost. Jim must circle once, alone. Will stood waiting the next charge of horses, the fling-about of boy not-so-much boy—

"Jim! Jim!"

Jim awoke! Circle half round, his face showed now July, now December. He seized the pole, bleating out his despair. He wanted, he did not want. He wished, he rejected, he ardently wished again, in flight, in heat-spell river of wind and blaze of metal, in jog of July and August horses whose hoofs thudded the air like thrown fruit, his eyes blazed. Tongue clamped in teeth, he hissed his frustration.

"Jim! Jump! Dad, stop the machine!"

Charles Halloway turned to see where the control box stood, fifty feet off.

"Jim!" Will's side was stabbed with pain. "I need you! Come back!"

And, far over away on the far side of the carousel, traveling, fast-traveling, Jim fought with his own hands, the pole, the empty wind-whipped journey, the growing night, the wheeling stars. He let go the pole. He grabbed it. And still his right hand trailed down and out, begging Will's last full ounce of strength.

"Jim!"

Jim came around. There, below, in the black-night station from which this train pulled away forever in a flurry of ticket-punch confetti, he saw Will—Willy—William Halloway, young pal, young friend who would seem younger still at the end of this journey, and not just young but unknown! vaguely remembered from some other time in some other year . . . but now that boy, that friend, that younger friend, ran along by the train, reached up, asking passage? or demanding he get off? which?!

"Jim! Remember *me?*"

Will lunged his final lunge. Fingers touched fingers, palm touched palm.

Jim's face, white cold, stared down.

Will trot-paced the circling machine.

Where was Dad? Why didn't he shut it *off?*

Jim's hand was a warm hand, a familiar, a good hand. It closed on his. He gripped it yelling.

"Jim, please!"

But still they spun on the journey, Jim borne, Will dragged in a jog-crazy-trot.

"Please!"

Will jerked. Jim jerked. Trapped by Jim, Will's hand was shot with July heat. It went, like a kept animal, held and fondled by Jim, along, around, into older times. So his hand, far-traveling, would be alien to himself, knowing things by night that he himself, abed, might only guess. Fourteen-year boy, fifteen-year hand! Jim had it, yes! cramped it tight, would not let go! And Jim's face, was it older, from the journey round? Was he fifteen now, going on sixteen!?

Will pulled. Jim pulled opposite.

Will fell on the machine.

Both rode the night.

All of Will rode with friend Jim now.

"Jim! Dad!"

How easy it might be to just stand, ride, go round with Jim, if he couldn't pull Jim off, just leave him on and, dear pals, travel! The juices of his body swam, blinding his sight, they drummed his ears, shot electric jolts through his loins. . . .

Jim shouted. Will shouted.

They traveled half a year in slithering orchard-warm dark before Will seized Jim's arm tight and dared to leap from so much promise, so many fine tall-growing years, flail out, off, down, pull Jim with. But Jim could not let go the pole, could not give up the ride.

"Will!"

Jim, half between machine and friend, one hand on each, screamed.

It was like a great tearing of cloth or flesh.

Jim's eyes went blind as a statue's.

The carousel whirled.

Jim screamed, fell, spun crazily, on the air.

Will tried to break his fall, but Jim struck earth rolling. He lay, silent.

Charles Halloway hit the carousel control switch.

Empty, the machine slowed. Its horses paced themselves down from their trot toward some far midsummer night.

Together, Charles Halloway and his son knelt by Jim to touch his wrist, to put ear to his chest. Jim's eyes, skinned white, were fixed on the stars.

"Oh, God," cried Will. "Is he dead?"

chapter fifty-two

D ead ... ?"
        Will's father moved his hand over that cold face,
        the cold chest.
"I don't feel ..."
A long way off, someone cried for help.
They looked up.
A boy came running down the midway, bumping into ticket
booths, falling over tent ropes, looking back over his shoulder.
"Help! He's after me!" the boy cried. "The terrible man! The
terrible man! I want to go home!"
The boy flung himself forward, and grabbed at Will's father.
"Oh, help, I'm lost, I don't like it. Take me home. That man
with the tattoos!"
"Mr. Dark!" gasped Will.
"Yes!" gibbered the boy. "He's down that way! Oh, stop him!"
"Will—" his father rose—"take care of Jim. Artificial respira-
tion. All right, boy."
The boy trotted off. "This way!"
Following, Charles Halloway watched the distraught boy
who led him; observed his head, his frame, the way his pelvis
hung from his spine.

"Boy," he said, by the shadowed merry-go-round, twenty feet around from where Will bent to Jim. "What's your name?"

"No time!" cried the boy. "Jed. Quick, quick!"

Charles Halloway stopped.

"Jed," he said. The boy no longer moved, but turned, chafing his elbows. "How old are you, Jed?"

"Nine!" said the boy. "My gosh, this is no time! We—"

"This is a fine time, Jed," said Charles Halloway. "Only nine? So young. I was *never* that young."

"Holy cow!" shouted the boy, angrily.

"Or unholy something," said the man, and reached out. The boy backed away. "You're only afraid of one man, Jed. Me."

"You?" The boy still backed off. "Cut it out! Why, why?"

"Because, sometimes good has weapons and evil none. Sometimes tricks fail. Sometimes people can't be picked off, led to deadfalls. No divide-and-conquer tonight, Jed. Where were you taking me, Jed? To some lion's cage you got fixed and ready? To some side show, like the mirrors? To someone like the Witch? What, what, Jed, what? Let's just roll up your right shirt sleeve, shall we, Jed?"

The great moonstone eyes flashed at Charles Halloway.

The boy leaped back, but not before the man had leaped with him, seized his arm, grabbed the back of his shirt and instead of simply rolling up the sleeve as first suggested, tore the entire shirt off the boy's body.

"Why, yes, Jed," said Charles Halloway, almost quietly. "Just as I thought."

"You, you, you, you!"

"Yes, Jed, me. But especially you, look at you."

And look he did.

For there, on the back of the small boy's hand, on the fingers, and up along the wrist scrambled blue serpents, blue-venomed snake eyes, blue scorpions scuttling about blue shark maws which gaped eternally hungry to feed upon all the freaks crammed and stung-sewn cheek by jowl, skin to skin, flesh to flesh all up and down the chest, the tiny torso, and tucked in the secret gathering places on this small small very small body, this cold and now shocked and trembling body.

"Why, Jed, that's fine artwork, that is."

"You!" The boy struck.

"Yes, still me." Charles Halloway took the blow in the face and clamped a vise on the boy.

"No!"

"Oh, yes," said Charles Halloway, using just his good right hand, his ruined left hand hanging limp. "Yes, Jed, jump, squirm, go ahead. It was a fine idea. Get me off alone, fix me, then go back and get Will. And when the police come, why, you're just a boy nine or ten and the carnival, oh, no, it's not yours, doesn't belong to you. Stay here, Jed. Why you trying to get out from under my arm? The police look and the owners of the show have vanished, isn't that it, Jed? A fine escape."

"You can't hurt me!" the boy shrieked.

"Funny," said Charles Halloway. "I think I can."

He pressed the boy, almost lovingly, close, very close.

"Murder!" wailed the boy. "Murder."

"I'm not going to murder you, Jed, Mr. Dark, whoever, whatever you are. You're going to murder yourself because you can't stand being near people like me, not this close, *close*, not this *long*."

"Evil!" groaned the boy, writhing. "You're evil!"

"Evil?" Will's father laughed, which made the boy, wasp-stung and brambled by the sound, jerk all the more violently. "Evil?" The man's hands were flypaper fastened to the small bones. "Strange hearing that from you, Jed. So it must seem. Good to evil seems evil. So I will do only good to you, Jed, I will simply hold you and watch you poison yourself. I will do good to you, Jed, Mr. Dark, Mr. Proprietor, boy, until you tell what's wrong with Jim. Wake him up. Let him free. Give him life!"

"Can't . . . can't. . . ." The boy's voice fell down a well inside his body, fading away, away . . . "can't. . . ."

"You mean you won't?"

"... can't ..."

"All right, boy, all right, then here and here and this and this ..."

They looked like father and son long apart, passionately met, embraced, yet more embraced, as the man lifted his wounded hand to gently touch the stricken face as the crowd, the teem, of illustrations shivered and flew now this way and that in microscopic forays quickly abandoned. The boy's eyes swiveled wildly, fixed upon the man's mouth. He saw there the strange and somehow lovely smile once flung as beatification to the Witch.

He gathered the boy somewhat closer and thought, Evil has only the power that we give it. I give you nothing. I take back. Starve. Starve. Starve.

The two matchstick lights in the boy's affrighted eyes blew out.

The boy, and his stricken and bruised conclave of monsters, his felt but half-seen crowd, fell to earth.

There should have been a roar like a mountain slid to ruin.

But there was only a rustle, like a Japanese paper lantern dropped in the dust.

chapter fifty-three

C harles Halloway stood for a long while, breathing deep, lungs aching, looking down at the body. The shadows swooned and fluttered in all the canvas alleys where odd assorted sizes of freaks and people, fleshed in their own terrors and sins, held to poles, moaning in disbelief. Somewhere, the Skeleton moved out in the light. Somewhere else, the Dwarf *almost* knew who he was, and scuttled forth like a crab from a cave to blink and blink again at Will bent working over Jim, at Will's father bent to exhaustion over the still form of the silent boy, while the merry-go-round, at last, slow, slow, came to a stop, rocking like a ferryboat in the watery-blowing grass.

The carnival was a great dark hearth lit with gathered coals, as shadows came to stare and fire their gaze with the tableau by the carousel.

There in the moonlight lay the illustrated boy named Dark.

There lay dragons slaughtered, towers ruined, monsters from dim ages toppled into rusted coinage, pterodactyls smashed like biplanes from old and always meaningless wars, crustacea the color of emeralds abandoned on a white sand shore where the tide of life was going out, all, all the illustrations changing now, shifting, shriveling as the small flesh cooled. There the obscene wink of the navel eye gasped in on itself, there the nipple-iris of a trumpeting mastodon went blind and raved at its blindness; each and every picture remembered from the tall Mr. Dark now rendered down to miniature canvas pronged and forked over a boy's tennis-racket bones.

More freaks, with faces the color of beds where so many had lost the battle of souls, emerged from the shadows to glide in a great and ever more curious carousel motion about Charles Halloway and his dropped burden.

Will paused in his desperate push and relaxation, push and relaxation, trying to shape Jim back to life, unafraid of the watchers in the dark, no time for that! Even if there were time, these freaks, he sensed, were breathing the night as if they had not been fed on such rare fine air in years!

And as Charles Halloway watched, and the foxfire, lobster-moist, phlegm-trapped eyes watched from distances, the boy-who-had-been-Mr.-Dark grew yet colder, as death cut the timbers of nightmares, and the calligraphies, the smoky lightnings of sketch that coiled and crouched and soared like terrible banners of a lost war, began to vanish one by one from the strewn small body.

A score of freaks glanced fearfully round as if the moon had suddenly filled itself full and they could see; they chafed their wrists as if chains had fallen from them, chafed their necks as if weights had crumbled from their bowed shoulders. Stumbled forth after long entombments, they blinked swiftly, disbelieving the packet of their misery sprawled near the spent carousel. If they dared they might have bent to tremble their hands over that suddenly death-sweet mouth, the marbling brow. As it was they watched, benumbed, as their portrait pictures, the vital stuffs of their mortal greed, rancor, and poisonous guilt, the emerald abstracts of their self-blinded eyes, self-wounded mouths, self-trapped bodies melted one by one from this insignificant mound of snow. There melted the Skeleton! there the sidewise-scuttling crayfish Dwarf! Now the Lava Sipper took leave of autumn flesh, followed by the black Executioner from London Dock, there

soared off and gone went the Human Montgolfier, the Balloon
Man, Avoirdupois the Magnificent! deflated to purest air, there!
there fled mobs and bands, as death washed the drawing board
clean!

Now there lay just a plain dead boy, unbruised by pictures,
staring up at the stars with Mr. Dark's empty eyes.

"Ahhhh . . ."

In a chorus of release, the strange people in the shadows
sighed.

Perhaps the calliope gave a last ringmaster's bark. Perhaps
thunder turned, sleeping, in the clouds. Suddenly all wheeled
about. The freaks stampeded. North, south, east, west, free of
tent, master, dark law, free above all of each other, they ran like
albino pigs, tuskless boars, and stricken sloths before storms.

It must have been, it seemed, each yanked a rope, loosed a
tent-peg, running.

For now the sky was shaken with a fatal respiration, the
breathing down, the insunk rattle and pule of collapsing darkness
as the tents gave way.

With hiss of viper, swirl of cobra, the ropes insanely raveled,
slithered, snapped, cut grass with frictioned whips.

The networks of the vast Main Freak Tent convulsed, parted
bones, small from medium, and medium from brontosaur magnificent. All swayed with impending fall.

The menagerie tent shut up like a dark Spanish fan.

Other small tents, caped figures in the meadow, fell down at
the wind's command.

Then at last, the Freak Tent, the great melancholy mothering
reptile bird, after a moment of indecision, sucked in a Niagara
of blizzard air, broke loose three hundred hempen snakes, crack-
rattled its black side-poles so they fell like teeth from a cyclopean
jaw, slammed the air with acres of moldered wing as if trying to
kite away but, earth-tethered, must succumb to plain and most
simple gravity, must be crushed by its own locked bulk.

Now this greatest tent staled out hot raw breaths of earth,

confetti that was ancient when the canals of Venice were not yet staked, and wafts of pink cotton candy like tired feather boas. In rushing downfalls, the tent shed skin; grieved, soughed as flesh fell away until at last the tall museum timbers at the spine of the discarded monster dropped with three cannon roars.

The calliope simmered, moronic with wind.

The train stood, an abandoned toy, in a field.

The freak oil paintings clapped hands high on the last standing pennant poles, then plummeted to earth.

The Skeleton, the only strange one left, bent to pick up the body of the porcelain boy-who-was-Mr.-Dark. He moved away into the fields.

Will, in a swift moment, saw the thin man and his burden go over a hill among all the footprints of the vanished carnival race.

Will's face shadowed this way, then that, pulled by the swift concussions, the tumults, the deaths, the fleeing away of souls. Cooger, Dark, Skeleton, Dwarf-who-was-Lightning-Rod-Salesman, don't run, come back! Miss Foley, where are you? Mr. Crosetti! it's over! Be still! Quiet! It's all right. Come back, come back!

But the wind was blowing their footprints out of the grass and they might run forever now trying to outflee themselves.

So Will turned back astride Jim and pushed the chest and let go, pushed and let go, then, trembling, touched his dear friend's cheek.

"Jim . . . ?"

But Jim was cold as spaded earth.

chapter fifty-four

B eneath the cold was a fugitive warmness, in the white skin lay some small color, but when Will felt Jim's wrist there was nothing and when he put his ear to the chest there was nothing.

"He's *dead!*"

Charles Halloway came to his son and his son's friend and knelt down to touch the quiet throat, the unstirred rib cage.

"No." Puzzled. "Not quite . . ."

"*Dead!*"

The tears burst from Will's eyes. But then, as swiftly, he felt himself knocked, struck, shaken.

"Stop that!" cried his father. "You want to save him?!"

"It's too late, oh, Dad!"

"Shut up! Listen!"

But Will wept.

And again his father hauled off and hit him. Once on the left cheek. Once on the right cheek, hard.

All the tears in him were knocked flying; there were no more.

"Will!" His father savagely jabbed a finger at him and at Jim. "Damn it, Willy, all this, all these, Mr. Dark and his sort, they *like* crying, my God, they *love* tears! Jesus God, the more you bawl, the more they drink the salt off your chin. Wail and they suck your breath like cats. Get up! Get off your knees, damn it! Jump around! Whoop and holler! You hear! Shout, Will, sing, but most of all laugh, you got that, laugh!"

"I can't!"

"You must! It's all we got. I *know!* In the library! The Witch ran, my God, *how* she ran! I shot her dead with it. A single smile, Willy, the night people can't stand it. The sun's there. They hate the sun. We *can't* take them seriously, Will!"

"But—"

"But hell! You saw the mirrors! And the mirrors shoved me half in, half out the grave. Showed me all wrinkles and rot! Blackmailed me! Blackmailed Miss Foley so she joined the grand march Nowhere, joined the fools who wanted everything! Idiot thing to want: everything! Poor damned fools. So wound up with nothing like the dumb dog who dropped his bone to go after the reflection of the bone in the pond. Will, you saw: *every* mirror fell. Like ice in a thaw. With no rock or rifle, no knife, just my teeth, tongue and lungs, I gunshot those mirrors with pure contempt! Knocked down ten million scared fools and let the *real* man get to his feet! Now, on *your* feet, Will!"

"But Jim—" Will faltered.

"Half in, half out. Jim's been that, always. Sore-tempted. Now he went too far and maybe he's lost. But he fought to save himself, right? Put his hand out to you, to fall free of the machine? So we finish that fight *for* him. Move!"

Will sailed up, giddily, yanked.

"Run!"

Will sniffed again. Dad slapped his face. Tears flew like meteors.

"Hop! Jump! Yell!"

He banged Will ahead, shuffled with him, shoved his hand in his pockets, tearing them inside out until he pulled forth a bright object.

The harmonica.

Dad blew a chord.

Will stopped, staring down at Jim.

Dad clouted him on the ear.

"Run! Don't look!"

Will ran a step.

Dad blew another chord, yanked Will's elbow, flung each of his arms.

"Sing!"

"What?"

"God, boy, anything!"

The harmonica tried a bad "Swanee River."

"Dad." Will shuffled, shaking his head, immensely tired. "Silly . . . !"

"Sure! We *want* that! Silly damn fool man! Silly harmonica! Bad off-key tune!"

Dad whooped. He circled like a dancing crane. He was not *in* the silliness yet. He *wanted* to crack through. He had to *break* the moment!

"Will: louder, funnier, as the man said! Oh, hell, don't let them drink your tears and want more! Will! Don't let them take your crying, turn it upside down and use it for their own smile! I'll be damned if death wears *my* sadness for glad rags. Don't feed them one damn thing, Willy, loosen your bones! Breathe! Blow!"

He seized Will's hair, shook him.

"Nothing . . . funny . . ."

"*Sure* there is! Me! You! Jim! All of us! The whole shooting works! Look!"

And Charles Halloway pulled faces, popped his eyes, mashed his nose, winked, cavorted like chimpanzee-ape, waltzed with the wind, tap-danced the dust, threw back his head to bay at the moon, dragging Will with him.

"Death's funny, God damn it! Bend, two, three, Will. Soft-shoe. Way down upon the Swanee River—what's *next*, Will? . . .

Far far away! Will, your God-awful voice! Damn girl soprano. Sparrow in a tin can. Jump, boy!"

Will went up, came down, cheeks hotter, a wincing like lemons in his throat. He felt balloons grow in his chest.

Dad sucked the silver harmonica.

"That's where the old folks—" Will spoke.

"Stay!" bellowed his father.

Shuffle, tap, bounce, jog.

Where was Jim! Jim was forgotten.

Dad jabbed his ribs, tickling.

"De Camptown ladies sing this song!"

"Doo-dah!" yelled Will. "Doo-dah!" he sang it now, with a tune. The balloon grew. His throat tickled.

"Camptown race track, five miles long!"

"Oh, doo-dah day!"

Man and boy did a minuet.

And in midstep *it* happened.

Will felt the balloon grow huge within him.

He smiled.

"What?" Dad was surprised by those teeth.

Will snorted. Will giggled.

"What *say?*" asked Dad.

The force of the exploding warm balloon alone shoved Will's teeth apart, kicked his head back.

"Dad! Dad!"

He bounded. He grabbed his Dad's hand. He raced crazily, hollering, quacking like a duck, clucking like a chicken. His palms hit his throbbing knees. Dust flew off his soles.

"Oh, Susanna!"

"Oh, don't you cry—"

"—for me!"

"For I come from—"

"Alabama with my—"

"Banjo on my—"

Together. "Knee!"

The harmonica knocked teeth, wheezing, Dad hocked forth great chords of squeeze-eyed hilarity, turning in a circle, jumping up to kick his heels.

"Ha!" They collided, half-collapsed, knocked elbows, cracked heads, which blew the air out faster. "Ha! Oh God, ha! Oh God, Will, ha! Weak! Ha!"

In the middle of wild laughter—

A sneeze!

They spun. They stared.

Who lay there on the moonlit earth?

Jim? Jim Nightshade?

Had *he* stirred? *Was* his mouth wider, his eyelids quivering? *Were* his cheeks pinker?

Don't look! Dad swung Will handily round in a further reel. They do-si-do'ed, hands extended, the harmonica seeping and guzzling raw tunes from a father who storked his legs and turkeyed his arms. They hopped Jim one way, hopped back, as if he were but a lump-stone on the grass.

"Someone's in the kitchen with Dinah! Someone's in the kitchen—"

"—I know-oh-oh-*oh!*"

Jim's tongue slid out on his lips.

No one saw this. Or if they saw, ignored it, fearing it might pass.

Jim did the final things himself. His eyes opened. He watched the dancing fools. He could not believe. He had been off on a journey of years. Now, returned, no one said "Hi!" All jigged Sambostyle. Tears might have jumped to his eyes. But before they could start, Jim's mouth curved. He gave up a ghost of laughter. For, after all, there indeed was silly Will and his silly old janitor dad racing like gorillas knuckle-dusting the meadows, their faces a puzzlement. They toppled above him, clapped hands, wiggled ears, bent to wash him all over with their now bright full-river flowing laughter that could not be stopped if the sky fell or the earth rent open, to blend their good mirth with his, to fuse-light and set him off in a detonation which could not stop exploding from lady-fingers to four-inchers to doomsday cannon crackers of delight!

And looking down, jolt-dancing his bones loose and delicious, Will thought: Jim don't remember he was dead, so we won't tell, not now—some day, sure, but not . . . Doo-dah! Doo-dah!

They didn't even say "Hello, Jim" or "Join the dance," they just put out hands as if he had fallen from their swung pandemonium commotion and needed a boost back into the swarm. They yanked Jim. Jim flew. Jim came down dancing.

And Will knew, hand in hand, hot palm to palm, they had truly yelled, sung, gladly shouted the live blood back. They had slung Jim like the newborn, knocked his lungs, slapped his back, shocked joyous breath to where it made room.

Then Dad bent and Will leaped over him and Will bent and Dad jumped him and they both waited, crouched in a line, wheezing songs, deliciously tired, while Jim swallowed spit, and ran full tilt. He got half over Dad when they all fell, rolled in the grass, all hoot-owl and donkey, all brass and cymbal as it must have been the first year of Creation, and Joy not yet thrown from the Garden.

Until at last they drew up their feet, socked each other's shoulders, embraced knees tight, rocking, and looking with swift bright happiness at each other, growing wine-drunkenly quiet.

And when they were done smiling at each other's faces as at burning torches, they looked away across the field.

And the black tent poles lay in elephant boneyards with the dead tents blowing away like the petals of a great black rose.

The only three people in a sleeping world, a rare trio of tomcats, they basked in the moon.

"What happened?" asked Jim, at last.

"What *didn't!*" cried Dad.

And they laughed again, when suddenly Will grabbed Jim, held him tight and wept.

"Hey," Jim said, over and over, quietly. "Hey . . . hey . . ."

"Oh, Jim, Jim," Will said. "We'll be pals forever."

"Sure, hey sure." Jim was very quiet now.

"It's all right," said Dad. "Have a small cry. We're out of the woods. Then we'll laugh some more, going home."

Will let Jim go.

They got to their feet and stood looking at each other. Will examined his father, with fierce pride.

"Oh, Dad, Dad, you *did* it, you did it!"

"No, we did it together."

"But without you it'd all be over. Oh, Dad, I never knew you. I sure know you now."

"Do you, Will?"

"Darn right!"

Each, to the other, shimmered in bright halos of wet light.

"Why then, hello. Reply, son, and curtsey."

Dad held out his hand. Will shook it. Both laughed and wiped their eyes, then looked quickly at the footprints scattered in the dew over the hills.

"Dad, will they ever come back?"

"No. And yes." Dad tucked away his harmonica. "No, not them. But yes, other people like them. Not in a carnival. God knows what shape they'll come in next. But sunrise, noon, or at the latest, sunset tomorrow they'll show. They're on the road."

"Oh, no," said Will.

"Oh, yes," said Dad. "We got to watch out the rest of our lives. The fight's just begun."

They moved around the carousel slowly.

"What will they look like? How will we know them?"

"Why," said Dad, quietly, "maybe they're already here."

Both boys looked around swiftly.

But there was only the meadow, the machine, and themselves.

Will looked at Jim, at his father, and then down at his own body and hands. He glanced up at Dad.

Dad nodded, once, gravely, and then nodded at the carousel, and stepped up on it, and touched a brass pole.

Will stepped up beside him. Jim stepped up beside Will.

Jim stroked a horse's mane. Will patted a horse's shoulders.

The great machine softly tilted in the tides of night.

Just three times around, ahead, thought Will. Hey.

Just four times around, ahead, thought Jim. Boy.

Just ten times around, back, thought Charles Halloway. Lord.

Each read the thoughts in the other's eyes.

How easy, thought Will.

Just this once, thought Jim.

But then, thought Charles Halloway, once you start, you'd always come back. One more ride and one more ride. And, after awhile, you'd offer rides to friends, and more friends until finally...

The thought hit them all in the same quiet moment.

... finally you wind up owner of the carousel, keeper of the freaks ... proprietor for some small part of eternity of the traveling dark carnival shows ...

Maybe, said their eyes, *they're already here.*

Charles Halloway stepped back into the machinery of the merry-go-round, found a wrench, and knocked the flywheels and cogs to pieces. Then he took the boys out and he hit the control box one or two times until it broke and scattered fitful lightnings.

"Maybe this isn't necessary," said Charles Halloway. "Maybe it wouldn't run anyway, without the freaks to give it power. But—"

He hit the box a last time and threw down the wrench.

"It's late. Must be midnight straight up."

Obediently, the City Hall clock, the Baptist church clock, the Methodist, the Episcopalian, the Catholic church, all the clocks, struck twelve. The wind was seeded with Time.

"Last one to the railroad semaphore at Green Crossing is an old lady!"

The boys fired themselves off like pistols.

The father hesitated only a moment. He felt the vague pain in his chest. If I run, he thought, what will happen? Is Death important? No. Everything that happens before Death is what counts. And we've done fine tonight. Even Death can't spoil it. So, there went the boys ... and why not ... *follow?*

He did just that.

And Lord! it was fine printing their life in the dew on the cool fields that new dark suddenly-like-Christmas morning. The boys ran as tandem ponies, knowing that someday one would touch base first, and the other second or not at all, but now this first minute of the new morning was not the minute or the day or morning of ultimate loss. Now was not the time to study faces to see if one was older and the other too much younger. Today was just another day in October in a year suddenly better than anyone supposed it could ever be just a short hour ago, with the moon and the stars moving in a grand rotation toward inevitable dawn, and them loping, and the last of this night's weeping done, and Will laughing and singing and Jim giving answer line by line, as they breasted the waves of dry stubble toward a town where they might live another few years across from each other.

And behind them jogged a middle-aged man with his own now solemn, now amiable, thoughts.

Perhaps the boys slowed. They never knew. Perhaps Charles Halloway quickened his pace. He could not say.

But, running even with the boys, the middle-aged man reached out.

Will slapped, Jim slapped, Dad slapped the semaphore signal base at the same instant.

Exultant, they banged a trio of shouts down the wind.

Then, as the moon watched, the three of them together left the wilderness behind and walked into the town.

a brief afterword

It may seem peculiar to some to find Gene Kelly's name on the dedication page of this book. But his films and his friendship were a catalyst that caused this novel to be born.

Not long after I published *The Martian Chronicles* in 1950, my friend Sy Gomberg took me and my wife, Maggie, over to Gene Kelly's home one evening, and on many evenings after that, when Gene and his friends often performed songs from their films and Broadway musicals with composers like Harold Arlen and Yip Harberg in attendance. Most importantly, during that period, Gene danced and sang in what I consider to be the finest musical in film history, *Singin' in the Rain*. On top of which, it was a science-fiction musical!

How so? you quickly ask.

Well now, didn't it describe how silent films reinvented themselves as a technology of sound? Dreaming a concept and then birthing it? It did! It started with a fiction and ended with a science.

All the more reason then for Gene Kelly to become a friend and inventor in my work.

In 1955, Gene invited Maggie and myself over to MGM Studios for a private screening of his *Invitation to the Dance*, a collection of musical dance numbers with no connecting plot-line, ending with Gene and Jerry, the cartoon-animation mouse, outdancing one another.

Maggie and I walked home from the screening (we still did not own an automobile that year) and on the way I kept saying over and over again how I would give half an arm and part of my soul to work with Gene Kelly.

"Well," Maggie said, "why don't you go through your files; you have dozens of ideas stashed away. Find something that strikes you as absolutely right, do a screenplay-treatment, and send it over to Gene."

Which is exactly what I did. Searching some forty or fifty stories or ideas for stories, I found *The Black Ferris,* no more than ten typewritten pages, the tale of a strange carnival and two small boys and a night with no dawn in sight. I spent the next four or five weeks turning it into an eighty page outline treatment-script and brought it directly to Gene Kelly.

He telephoned me the next day and said, "This is it. This must be the next picture I direct. Do I have your permission to take it to Paris and London next week to try to arrange financing?"

"Take it!" I said.

Gene came back from overseas a month later with the bad news. No one wanted to finance my script.

"I'm sorry," Gene said.

"Sorry?!" I replied. "Good Lord, I'm proud that you even tried!"

I took a long look at the semi-screenplay, which had, at the time, the title *Dark Carnival,* sat down, and spent the next five years turning it into a novel, published in 1962 as *Something Wicked This Way Comes.*

Fifteen years later, the novel turned itself back into a series of screenplays for various producers and directors at Paramount and 20th Century Fox, each time being passed over and forgotten. At one time Sam Peckinpah signed on as director.

"How will you do it, Sam?" I asked.

"Rip the pages out of your book and stuff them in the camera," he replied.

"Correct," I said. For, as you read this novel you can witness the scenes. It cries out to be photographed.

And it finally was, with Jack Clayton directing and Disney producing, almost thirty years after Gene Kelly's *Invitation to the Dance.*

Without his invitation to that screening, this book might never have been born. When it was published in 1962, Gene Kelly got copy Number One.

History,
Context,
and
Criticism

Edited by
Jonathan R. Eller

"We can't be good unless we know what bad is . . ." Gray Foy's dust jacket painting for the 1962 first edition, presenting the title as an eerie dust-devil stirring the dying autumn leaves, became the backdrop for many print advertisements before and after publication.

contents

PART ONE

The Story of *Something Wicked This Way Comes*

I feel lost without SOMETHING WICKED. That final day when you put the page-proofs in the mail is the day we all hear about when the doc cuts the umbilical. You watch your child go off into the world worried, upset, sad, full of wonder and doubt. It is such a strange book, I have more fears for and about it than I have ever had for any other book of mine.

—Ray Bradbury to Don Congdon, June 23, 1962

"My Name Is Dark"

The Story of *Something Wicked This Way Comes*
JONATHAN R. ELLER

In exploring the underlying themes of Ray Bradbury's early stories, fellow writer and critic Damon Knight revealed the intense emotional focus found at the heart of his friend's best supernatural fiction: "Bradbury's strength lies in the fact that he writes about the things that are really important to us . . . not the things we say we are interested in—science, marriage, sports, politics, crime—but the fundamental pre-rational fears and longings and desires: the rage at being born; the will to be loved; the longing to communicate, the hatred of parents and siblings; the fear of things that are not oneself."[1]

This primal emotional focus fueled Bradbury's earliest successes with light horror and tales of terror, but by the late 1940s he was concerned that the fundamental circumstances of modernity had all but quenched the fires of the Gothic literary tradition. In a discarded draft of his 1948 introduction to Theodore Sturgeon's *Without Sorcery*, Bradbury traced the crisis back to "the day of Darwin and the changes that occurred when science marched in the door and religion drifted out the window. . . . We have lost faith not only in God but in God's opposites, the Devil, the apparitions, the werewolves and warlocks."

In these long-lost pages Bradbury went on to define the greatest challenge he felt as a teller of tales in midcentury America: "I cannot help but feel we have lost something essentially vital and stimulating . . . at least there was white Whiteness as well as the dark Dark, while today all is a vast and monotonous plain of unvarying gray."[2] It is little wonder, then, that his first true novel, slowly evolving across sixteen years of his greatest success as a short story writer, would become his most sustained and powerful evocation of the dark fantastic.

Bradbury's initial vision of the dark carnival that would grow into *Something Wicked This Way Comes* first emerged in early 1945, as he planned his first story collection with Arkham House publisher August Derleth:

> The cover jacket might possibly illustrate a small carnival that has set up its merry-go-round and side-show tent and banners in a dark green woodland glade at twilight—the entire atmosphere of the picture would be one of remoteness, of a carnival in the wilderness going full steam, but with no one in sight except one small boy in the foreground, tiny, very alone, staring at the moving carousel and the high banners. And on the banners instead of portraits of Fat Ladies, Thin Men, and Tattooed Freaks would be pictures of strange, nebulous creatures. And on the carousel, instead of horses sliding up and down the gleaming brass poles, would be other impossible, vaguely, disturbingly delineated creatures of such indistinct cast and line that one's imagination could make them anything in the whole universe.[3]

This word picture is markedly surreal, reflecting one of the many possible titles that Bradbury would later suggest for the novel itself: *Between a Dream and a Dream!* By the summer of 1945, this image would veer off from the *Dark Carnival* story collection that he would eventually publish for Arkham House; in fact, the remarkable stories gathered in his 1947 collection had nothing to do with the slowly emerging concept that he most often referred to as *The Dark Carnival* novel. Over the next year, the picture-in-words he had sent to Derleth evolved into thirty typed pages of short vignettes following an opening description of the carnival's arrival. These pages reveal three variations on a mirror maze that casts the viewer into irreversible old age, and several vignettes of husbands who go to the carnival in the prime of life and return to their wives as old men or as children. Here are the origins of the sinister carnival ride that lures Jim Nightshade toward the forbidden secrets and passions of adulthood, and the mirrors of time that nearly destroy young Will Halloway's aging father.

But these enchantments were still waiting, half-formed, in the shadows of his mind. The man-to-boy transformation would be the first to emerge in a full narrative form as Bradbury's May 1948 *Weird Tales* story "The Black Ferris," which he had deliberately held out of his *Dark Carnival* story collection the previous year. This tale introduces two local boys—Pete and Hank—who see Mr. Cooger, the predatory carnival master, regress to childhood by reversing the darkly magical machineries of the Ferris wheel late at night. They track him as he preys on Mrs. Foley,

Lee Brown Coye's title art for "The Black Ferris" (*Weird Tales*, May 1948). Largely self-taught, Coye's extensive knowledge of anatomy and his unmistakable style of horror underlie this caricatured skeleton of Bradbury's carnival master, Mr. Cooger. Over time, the vehicle for Cooger's age transformation would shift from Ferris wheel to carousel.

who has taken him in as an orphan to replace her own lost child; when no one believes their story, the boys follow the child-man back to the carnival and jam the machinery gears full forward in time until only a skeleton remains, holding a bag of money stolen from Mrs. Foley. Some of the character names would carry through the entire arc of creativity from this point, as would the strange off-season arrival of the October carnival, crystalized from the Green Town memories of Bradbury's Waukegan childhood.

The plot of the entire novel would radiate out from this one adventure, but as the 1940s ended Bradbury was beginning to transform his best science-fiction tales and mainstream fantasies into *The Martian Chronicles* (1950), *The Illustrated Man* (1951), *The Golden Apples of the Sun* (1953), and his novella-to-short-novel expansion of *Fahrenheit 451* (1953). The carnival novel project was overshadowed during these breakthrough years, but it never entirely disappeared. His 1952 discovery of the versatile and talented California-based artist Joseph Mugnaini led Bradbury to plan out a wordless novel-in-pictures concept for the book, but his partnership with Mugnaini soon shifted into celebrated cover and interior art for *The Golden Apples of the Sun*, *Fahrenheit 451*, and *The October Country* (1955).[4] Bradbury now had a sustained novel-length structure visualized in his mind, but once again the dark carnival had closed down before its terrors could be fully imagined.

Not surprisingly, his rapidly expanding involvement with film and television ventures led Bradbury to flesh out the entire plot, as we know it today, in the form of a 1955 screenplay. By this time the mechanical enchantments of the Ferris wheel had shifted to the carnival's carousel, and there the magic would remain focused in all further versions of the tale. The catalyst was Gene Kelly, who invited Ray and his wife, Maggie, to the 1955 pre-release screening of Kelly's musical fantasy *Invitation to the Dance*. At Maggie's suggestion he developed his screenplay for Kelly, who thought it was an ideal variation on the kind of departures into fantasy found at the heart of his most successful films. But Kelly's Hollywood was changing, and in spite of earnest efforts he was unable to find backing for production.[5] Bradbury continued to circulate the screenplay version, but he also took the fateful step of bringing the narrative back to its original intended form as a novel. That process would take another seven years.

Bradbury captured the initial excitement of this transformation in an August 1955 letter to his aged friend and mentor, distinguished Renaissance art expert Bernard Berenson:

> Later, perhaps in January of next year, I hope to make another motion picture of a small book I recently finished in manuscript form about a Gothic carnival that arrives one October midnight in a small Illinois town; the carnival having traveled all about the earth, with its alchemists and sorcerers, for hundreds of years, posing the problem of good and evil, and tilting the scales in its own favor—that is, of course, toward evil. I was in a fever, doing the story, for many days, earlier this year, not unlike some I have run with a fine head and chest cold, but without any of the discomforts. After a number of days of absolutely glowing in the dark, and feeling somewhat drunk, the carnival let down its black velvet tents and stole away, leaving me exhausted but happy, at my typewriter . . .[6]

The work on this "small book" continued to focus on the screenplay itself, however; there are many tipped-in pages dated 1956 and 1957, as the revised script continued to circulate with Disney and other studios. The first sustained draft of the novel actually dates from 1958–59, when he began to weave the detailed screenplay plot into a remarkable first-person narrative, *Jamie and Me*.

The boys were now Jamie and Will, and Bradbury aligned his own carnival memories with Will Halloway's direct telling of the tale. This strategy offered a natural way to blend earlier fantasy traditions such as Renaissance carnival with a more modern

"No carnival ever came in October before." Bradbury's 1955 *Dark Carnival* screenplay retained the character names of Peter and Hank from the original 1948 story line of "The Black Ferris." This page from a revised version of the screenplay shows the boys on foot in pursuit of the train, guided by the eerie sound of the dark carnival's calliope. From the Albright Collection; courtesy of Donn Albright and the Bradbury Estate.

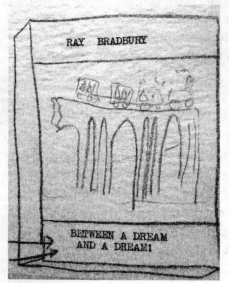

Joseph Mugnaini's "Caravan" (1952), a surreal carnival journey with no beginning and no end, inspired Bradbury to work with Mugnaini on a novel-in-pictures, without text. Only Bradbury's sketch for the cover, provisionally titled *Between a Dream and a Dream!*, is known to survive, but this 1952–53 stage of work represents an important marker on the trail toward *Something Wicked This Way Comes*. Bradbury always maintained that his full sense of the novel's structure began to coalesce here.

carnival tale told from an adolescent point of view, creating a deep and very Bradburyan exploration of the nature and purposes of sentient evil. Will is rapidly approaching his fourteenth birthday, exactly Bradbury's age when he left the world of Midwest carnivals for the last time. Will's story of the dark carnival (and its effect on those around him) probes the undiscovered pleasures and terrors of the adult world—projected as a blend reminiscent of Huckleberry Finn's spontaneous adventures and the more unsettling storytelling of Holden Caulfield in Salinger's *Catcher in the Rye*.

More than one hundred surviving pages of *Jamie and Me* are scattered throughout discards from his later drafts, and the recovered first-person narrative for chapters six, seven, and eight are published for the first time in the selection of prepublication material that follows this essay. But Bradbury soon found that Will's consciousness alone could not convey the full magnitude of terror pursuing the other central characters; during 1960 and throughout 1961, he prepared three successive drafts in the third person. In this way the narrative gains far more immediacy for the reader, as Jamie fully develops into Jim Nightshade and Will's father, Charles Halloway, becomes the insightful protector of both boys, capable of fighting both Cooger and Dark for their souls.

But these changes also required a new title. This search ran parallel to his discovery that he simply had one too many characters in the novel;[7] up to this point, Will seemed to have two fathers—the well-meaning but somewhat superfluous Charles, and the library janitor, Mr. Ellis, an eccentric who knew the town library almost as well as he knew the minds of men. At the suggestion of his friend, writer Jack Guss, Bradbury successfully eliminated Mr. Ellis and gave his role to Charles Halloway, who, in Chapter 37, contemplates the library books he has placed in a great circle, like a clockface, to research the dark traditions that underlie the power of the carnival masters. And here, at last, Bradbury found the novel's title:

There was only one thing sure.

Two lines of Shakespeare said it. He should write them in the middle of the clock of books, to fix the heart of his apprehension:

> By the pricking of my thumbs,
> Something wicked this way comes.

Revision was not an easy process for Bradbury, who in mid-career was feeling his way draft by draft through his first sustained novel. His determination to return to dark fantasy effectively ended his long relationship with Doubleday, where the editors wanted him to expand his mainstream literary footing with more conventional material. Simon & Schuster took up the gambit, and the pressure to bring home this first book for his new house loomed large in the author's mind.[8]

Bradbury encoded tense updates to his agent, Don Congdon, within the metaphor of childbirth, describing his April 1960 submission of the new third-person narrative as an "almost-but-not-quite born state." He had never submitted drafts in such a preliminary form, but in the end he found it best to do just what he had done with his most successful short fiction—he refrained from any degree of critical distance as he wrote and revised, and simply let the novel write and revise itself. He was simply too close to the project, and the resulting explosion of metaphor is perhaps more intense here than anywhere else in the Bradbury canon.

He finally submitted his third complete typescript in late 1961, revising it one final time in the winter of 1962. After reviewing the page proofs, he sent Don Congdon a very revealing assessment of the creative toll:

> I feel lost without SOMETHING WICKED. That final day when you put the page-proofs in the mail is the day we all hear about when the doc cuts the umbilical. You watch

your child go off into the world worried, upset, sad, full of wonder and doubt. It is such a strange book, I have more fears for and about it than I have ever had for any other book of mine.

Simon & Schuster's fall 1962 release of *Something Wicked This Way Comes* went well enough, in spite of a very crowded seasonal book market and October's tense international climate surrounding the Cuban Missile crisis. The critical responses, however, were mixed. Some reviewers, including Orville Prescott, who had highly praised *Fahrenheit 451* in the *New York Times* a decade earlier, wanted a novel that conformed to the formal structural traditions and theme conventions of the horror genre, but that was not what Bradbury intended. Fear of death, not death itself, is what evil feeds on in this novel, and certain critics took Bradbury's final revelation—the restorative power of laughter—far too seriously.

More positive mainstream reviews came from prominent genre critic and editor Anthony Boucher (writing as H. H. Holmes) in the *New York Herald Tribune*, and from popular literary critic Gilbert Highet's endorsement in the *Book-of-the-Month Club News*. Both Boucher and Highet knew Bradbury well, and understood his abiding intent to disregard genre rules and transcend such boundaries altogether. As Neil Gaiman would observe at Bradbury's passing a half century later: "He was a genre on his own, and on his own terms. A young man from Waukegan, Illinois, who went to Los Angeles, educated himself in libraries, and wrote until he got good, then transcended genre and became a genre of one, often emulated, absolutely inimitable."

Bradbury's far-traveling screenplay, with manuscript roots older than the novel itself, evolved through two more decades before the 1983 Disney film adaptation reached theater audiences. But the 1962 novel remains the heart of this creative milestone, and it has never been out of print. Over time, a number of writers and cultural critics offered deeply grounded assessments based on a true understanding of the novel and the genius be-hind it. Russell Kirk, a prominent chronicler of postwar America who also wrote award-winning dark fantasy, felt that Bradbury had revealed the "subterranean, inner reality" of good and evil in *Something Wicked*, and he devoted a chapter to this work in his influential 1969 cultural inquiry, *Enemies of the Permanent Things*. *Danse Macabre*, Stephen King's deep nonfiction examination of the dark fantastic and its American gothic legacy, includes a long chapter on *Something Wicked This Way Comes*.

King rarely fails to include allusions or even overt references to Bradbury's works in his novels. Clive Barker, Peter Straub, Neil Gaiman, and R. L. Stine, to name only a few—writers who, like King, continue to leverage horror into the literary mainstream—have all found inspiration in *Something Wicked* and its precursors in Bradbury's early canon. Award-winning writers such as Michael Dirda, former NEA chair Dana Gioia, and *Shadowlands* author Brian Sibley have recognized the power and endurance of *Something Wicked*; Booker Prize winner Margaret Atwood chronicled how Bradbury engaged and helped shape the American gothic tradition in a retrospective written shortly after Bradbury's pass-ing in 2012. All of these commentaries are significant, and several are included in the "Other Voices" section that follows.

It really didn't take very long for critics and writers to realize that *Something Wicked* represented a capstone for the incredible creativity of Bradbury's first two decades as a writer. With the success of this novel, Bradbury himself realized that he could still enter a creative sanctuary of sorts by returning to the forms of dark fantasy where he had first made his mark on American lit-erature. He had always found great encouragement in historical comparisons to Edgar Allan Poe, and he had already become, in the minds of many readers and critics, the inheritor of Poe's title as "The October Man." But until this point, Bradbury had also been in danger of joining Poe as one of the only American sto-rytellers with an enduring international reputation who had not become a successful novelist. *Something Wicked* broke him free from such a judgment, and extended Bradbury's reputation as a mythmaker, a fabulist, who was not afraid to experiment in new forms of novel-length fiction.

Something Wicked This Way Comes became Ray Bradbury's favorite of all his books, for it illuminated a very personal insight that had simmered beneath the surface throughout his life. Bradbury's father, Leo, had passed away in the fall of 1957, just as his son decided to transform the dark carnival screenplay into novel form. His father was a working-class man who had barely managed to bring his family through the Great Depression. Yet Leo was also a reader; his tastes were not vast or very deep, but he read, and that was a great example. After the novel was published, Ray Bradbury realized that his father was the inspiration for Charles Halloway, a man capable of bridging the profound differences between himself and his son, capable of protecting both Jim and Will from the creature revealed by this chilling proclamation: "My name is Dark."

Jonathan R. Eller is Chancellor's Professor of English and director of the Center for Ray Bradbury Studies in Indiana University's School of Liberal Arts (IUPUI). He also edits *The Collected Stories of Ray Bradbury*, a multivolume series. His most recent books are *Becoming Ray Bradbury* and *Ray Bradbury Unbound*, which together examine the early and middle years of the author's life.

Notes

1   Damon Knight, "Readin' and Writhin'," review of *The Illustrated Man. Science Fiction Quarterly* 1, no. 2 (February 1953): 81 (ellipsis Knight's).

2   Original in the collection of Donn Albright, Professor Emeritus, Pratt Institute; archival copy in the Center for Ray Bradbury Studies, Indiana University School of Liberal Arts. Unless otherwise indicated, Bradbury letters and typescripts cited or quoted in this essay are from the same sources. Permissions courtesy of Donn Albright and the Bradbury Estate.

3   Bradbury to Derleth, March 8, 1945, Wisconsin State Historical Society, Madison. A variant draft also survives in the Albright Collection.

4   Jonathan Eller, *Becoming Ray Bradbury* (Champaign: University of Illinois Press, 2011), 249–56.

5   Jonathan Eller, *Ray Bradbury Unbound* (Champaign: University of Illinois Press, 2014), 57–59; Bradbury, interviews with the author, Los Angeles, October 9, 2005, October 20, 2007, and April 4, 2009.

6   Bradbury to Berenson, August 4, 1955. Original in the Biblioteca Berenson, the Harvard University Center for Italian Renaissance Studies, Florence, Italy; archival copy in the Center for Ray Bradbury Studies, Indiana University.

7   Bradbury, interview with the author, Los Angeles, October 24, 2009.

8   Jonathan Eller and William Touponce, *Ray Bradbury: The Life of Fiction* (Kent, OH: The Kent State University Press, 2004), 265–68.

```
SOMETHING WICKED THIS WAY COMES                          -64-
Bradbury

        Way late at night Will had heard, how often?
                      JETTING        ALONG THE RIM OF      SLEEP,
train whistles ~jumping up~ steam ~through dark~ ~near but~
           /
forlorn, ~and~ alone and far, no matter how near they came.
                       TO FIND
Sometimes he woke ~knowing, found~ tears ~with surprise~
            /
on his cheek, asked why, lay back, listened and ~thought~
thought, ~knowing~ yes! ~trains~ they make me cry, GOING EAST,
~they go~ GOING west, ~leaving going~ the trains so far GONE
                                                        R
~out~ in country deeps they drown in tides of sleep that
escape the towns.

        Those trains and the ~sounds they~ grieved ~were~ SOUNDS WERE
lost forever between stations, not remembering where they
had been, not guessing where they might go, exhaling their
last pale breaths over the horizon, gone. So it was with
all trains, ever.

        Yet this train's whistle!
              WAILS
        ~The~ ~whistles~ of a lifetime were gathered in it
from other NIGHTS in other slumbering years; the howl of
moon-dreamt dogs, the seep of river-cold winter winds through
January porch-screens which stopped the blood ~      ~, a
thousand fire-sirens weeping, or worse! the outgone shreds
of breath, the protests of a billion people dead or dying,
~and~ not wanting to be dead, their groans, their sighs,
burst over the earth!

        Tears jumped to Will's eyes. He lurched, ~            ~
He knelt. He pretended to lace one shoe.
```

"Yet *this* train's whistle!" Bradbury's final revisions to the opening pages of chapter 12 centered on the wailing whistle blast of the dark carnival train and its effect on Will and Jim, sole witnesses to the train's late-night arrival. *From the Albright Collection; courtesy of Donn Albright and the Bradbury Estate.*

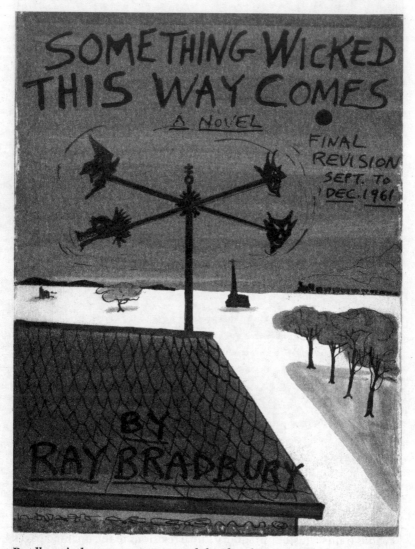

Bradbury's deep engagement with his first long novel led him to paint the lid of the stationery box where he kept the third typescript of the novel. The wind-blown weather vane, with demonic masks representing the points of the compass, dominates the painting as it signals the distant approach of the carnival. A true "final" round of hand revision to this typescript would occupy the middle weeks of February 1962. *From the Albright Collection; courtesy of Donn Albright and the Bradbury Estate.*

*The inconspicuous yellow paper binder containing Ray Bradbury's earliest conception of this novel bears a cover inscription, written in Bradbury's bold hand: "*ORIGINAL MATERIALS 'DARK CARNIVAL' WHICH BECAME 'SOMETHING WICKED T. W. C.' FROM SUMMER 1945 AND 1946—R.B.*" The three opening pages for "Dark Carnival" are scattered among twenty-eight pages of word-pictures, short free-standing paragraphs, and passages revealing small scenes of a mirror maze, a calliope, carnival rides, and the people who venture forth to be changed forever by the carnival's enchantments. This reconstructed opening is the only sustained passage known from the 1945–46 period; it shows how the children of the town, as well as the elderly, hunger the most for the carnival's wonders.*

"*Dark Carnival*"

Original Draft Opening (1945)
RAY BRADBURY

The carnival arrived at supper, a strange hour. There had been a late afternoon thunderstorm, with the sky black, and the rain everywhere. When the rain stopped there was the carnival, three miles from town, in Bodley's forest.

The people in town spoke of it as an affair accomplished in total dark. There was only the creak of winches, a sound of leather and harnessing, a sigh of inflated tent canvas rising; no cursing of men, in fact no sound of voices at all. Now and again shatters of light climbed up the flooded black sky and one hour the space where the carnival had picked for its home was empty and an hour later the dark tents were up and canvases with questionable paintings on them swung like immense flags from moist black poles.

It was just as everyone was at their soup or steak that the news spread through town, and everybody lifted their eyebrows, because why should a carnival arrive at this hour? And how could it expect to coin money if it stayed only one evening? For that, the couriers announced, gasping from their long run, was all the time the carnival was going to stay; just tonight. And it was so damned far out of town, how did they expect to get people to attend the things?

But attend people did.

The poles of the main tent were ebon black and the canvas had the feel and texture of a bat's wing, green and tenuous as it slid upward, tautening and drumming in the summer night wind. In the cages within the tents were strange smells, animals padding and stroking the iron bars, making no other noise.

The rain stopped.

The brass monster stood with its round haunches embedded in the moist weeds. It had huge brass flutes upon it and from these, at a pressure, fumes from hell hissed up, violently, becoming sulfurous clouds. It made a gigantic groaning and trembling and then it began to toot and bang its melody. All through the summer night you could hear its thunder.

Children, in bed early for the night, in their high cupolas of old flinty houses, took their heads off their pillows and listened. The music entered their heads, surrounded their brains, put them in a suspension of brass, steaming symphony in which their little brains bubbled like apples in a water-tub.

The children put their feet into their shoes, drew off their nightclothes, drew on pants and shirts or dresses and set off in precarious balances upon the drainpipes of the porch roofing, slid like rings down poles to plummet onto soft noiseless lawn. Then, across the lawn, along the fragrant street, across meadows, startling their systems with sudden splushings in unexpected creeks, and then the forest, the glade, the calliope, and the Carnival.

By nine thirty all of the young children in the town had left their beds empty and all the old men of the town left tobacco spit drying behind them on the road. It was a thing both incredible and wondrous that only the old men and children danced attendance upon the show, as if they had an interest in it no medium-lifed one could understand.

The children arrived and there were the machines that whirled out great vapors of pink cotton candy for a nickel if you had it. The machine vibrated and shook in sweet centrifuge and the fluff was captured on paper cornucopias and handed over. Huge and wondrous and fat were the ruffles and blooms of sweet pink fuzz and the small boys held them for long moments in their fingers gazing upon the pink wonder before biting into it. Ironic stuff! They bit away and bit away and there was—nothing. There was only a small sweet essence between the teeth, but nothing for the throat, the stomach. Nothing for the tongue. Only the pink vision, the bite, the emptiness—the vast disillusion.

The old men did not even SEE these sweet cotton candy machines. They caned it over to the other tents and canvases, because they knew better than to spend time on those sweet cotton contraptions, long ago they knew that it was nothing in the mouth but a saccharine exhalation. No, with infinite patience born of on-going cane and on-flexed withered legs, they slowly hurried to the places where a dime, a quarter, or sometimes for nothing at all, they were let into places where fine women were in reach and did dances, and where fine gold was in reach and made stacked glitters, and where other things, wines and riches were piled on green-velveted tables where a rattle of dice attained them. And these entertainments were snorted at by the little boys, who somehow knew that the cotton candy and the ladies and the gold and the riches were spun from the same sweet centrifuge and parted and dissolved and were not there if you tried touching too hard.

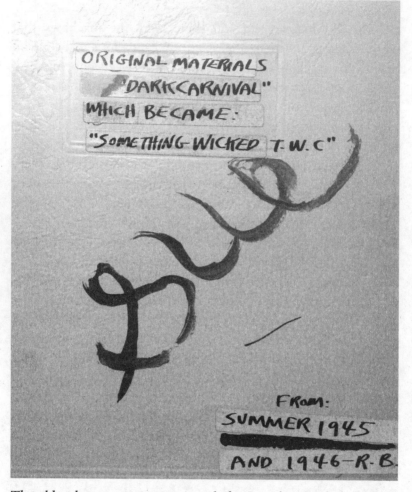

The oldest known surviving materials for *Something Wicked This Way Comes* were later gathered by Bradbury into this three-prong binder for preservation (note the juvenile signature of his oldest daughter, Susan, circa late-1950s). The original draft opening is nested among thirty other narrative fragments describing the enchantments and terrors that would eventually become Cooger & Dark's carnival. *From the Albright Collection; courtesy of Donn Albright and the Bradbury Estate.*

Like the successively rising and falling cities of ancient Troy that fas-
cinated Bradbury all his life, the three surviving 1960–61 drafts of
Something Wicked This Way Comes *obscure the original first-*
person narrative foundations of the novel. More than five hundred
pages of discards from this stage of work include a hundred pages
from Jamie and Me, *Will Halloway's version of the story. The narra-*
tive is preliminary in places; for example, Will's middle name is ini-
tially "Anthony," but becomes "Allan" later on in this excerpt. These
fragments were cast off in no particular order as Bradbury feverishly
worked to revise Will's story into a third-person narrative and give
Jamie a more complex and fully developed identity as "Jim" Night-
shade. The pages recovered here restore the very first layer of chapters
six through eight, where Will relates what he and Jamie encounter as
they walk home from an evening at the library . . .

from Jamie and Me

The earliest draft of *Something Wicked This Way Comes* (1958–59)
RAY BRADBURY

Chapter [Six]

In our running, suddenly Jamie slowed and trotted and then
walked and then almost didn't move.

We had come to the corner of Hickory Street. Jamie looked
down the street and at the books and at me.

"Hey," he said.

"No, Jamie," I said.

"Aw, come on," he said.

"No," I said.

"Why not?" he said.

"Because," I said.

"It's just down that way. The fifth house."

"I know where it is, you told me enough times."

"Just for a minute," he said.

I said nothing but looked down the dark street.

It was the street of the Theatre.

It was a strange street, that street with the Theatre on it, because it wasn't a theatre at all, it was a house with a window, but to Jamie the window was a stage and the room beyond was where the actors played. But I didn't like the play that went on there, what the actors said or did, what they mostly whispered or sighed or what they said out loud at times.

"Come on, Willie."

"No."

"Aw, come on, Willie. Willie, come on."

"I told you a hundred times, I don't want to."

"The play might be on."

"I don't care!"

"You went once, twice."

"Sure I did. But it's not our business."

"Just one more time."

"Not tonight, Jamie."

I thought of the first night Jamie took me there down that dark street to the dark house with the one lighted window, the stage, and our climbing the tree in whispers and staring at the curtains which blew in the wind and Jamie saying every minute or so, "Just wait. Just wait. It won't be long. It won't be long." And then at last. "There. Be quiet now. There."

And me hanging onto that tree looking at the stage, the Theatre, the window and listening to the voices, and after a long time dropping off and running away through the dark.

"Willie," Jamie looked at me, shaking his head. "I give up!"

"No, I give up!"

"You're hopeless!"

"You're another kind of hopeless!" I said, angry and ashamed at the same time.

"Just for a minute, Willie."

"Your minute is my hour," I said. "What's wrong with you, Jamie. We been to the library. We got all these great books. Ain't that enough?"

Jamie thought for a moment. His eyes widened, as if he was surprised at what came out next.

"No," he said, simply. "No."

He handed his books to me.

"Carry these home for me?"

I put the books down on the sidewalk.

"Carry your own books, Jamie," I said.

"Leave them there, then!" he said, and ran off under the shadowy trees. He stopped and looked back at me, hands on his hips.

"Willie, you know what you are?"

"I'm William Anthony Halloway, and I sleep nights!" I said.

"You're a darned old Baptist preacher!"

"Jamie!"

"I didn't say damn I said darn! Baptist!"

I listened to his shoes running away.

Chapter [Seven]

I left the books there where he had put them and walked on half a block. Then, complaining bitterly at my own weakening, I went back to pick them up. [I had just gotten] halfway home, and I heard someone running behind me.

Jamie caught up with me and we walked in silence, him trying to get his breath, looking [back]. I wouldn't look at him. I handed him his books. We walked on.

"Theatre closed for the year?"

"Nobody home."

"Swell," I said.

"Darn dirty Baptist," he said.

"No sir, just a plain old Protestant," I said. "And not pushing nobody."

"Yes, you are! You—"

But just then, around the corner in the wind a tumbleweed slithered, no not a tumbleweed, but a big cotton boll of pale paper skipping along, stopping, floating down, then turning over again. It flew against Jamie's legs and wouldn't go away. It clung shivering there, held by the wind. Jamie turned around but couldn't get free of it. I bent down and grabbed the paper. I pulled it off and let it kite away on the wind. I laughed. I stopped laughing.

Jamie and me, watching the pale throwaway blow off in the trees, were suddenly very cold. We couldn't take our eyes off that pale thing dancing through the branches, coming down and skidding on the sidewalk again, fifty yards away.

"Wait a minute," Jamie said slowly.

We started walking at once after it.

Then we looked at each other and began to run. We didn't know why. All we knew is that something told us to run catch it and look-see. Maybe we had glimpsed something on the paper, out of the corner of our eyes, and it had just hit home maybe lots of things, but all of a sudden we were running, yelling, and grabbing at the paper and at last we had it and held it up. "Don't tear it!" "Careful!"

And it fluttered in our hands, it rat-tatted like a snare drum whipping in the wind under the raw street light.

"COMING!" it said.

"OCTOBER 24th!" it said.

Jamie's lips moved, spelling out the rococo type.

"Cooger and Dark's—"

"Carnival!" he said.

"Cooger and Dark's Carnival!" Jamie smiled wildly at the news. "October 24th. That's tomorrow!"

"Sure! Or is it? Maybe it was last year!"

"Since when was any carnival here last year in October, or any year? No, this bill's new fresh, look the ink comes off on my hand, Willy!"

"Tomorrow," I said, stunned. "It can't be! All carnivals stop coming after Labor Day!"

"I don't care. Look at this. Boy! 1001 WONDERS! MEN SHOT FROM CANNONS. HIGH-WIRE WALKERS! SEE: THE TERRIBLE GIANT! SEE: THE MONTGOLFIER! What's a Montgolfier?

"A balloon."

"A balloon! That so, that's great, I don't believe it. SEE: THE ILLUSTRATED MAN. That's just an old guy with tattoos."

"No," I said, impressed and quiet now. "It isn't. It's a man with illustrations on his skin. That makes it different. Or they wouldn't have spelled it out that way. Him, I just got to see."

"Sure, look, here's his picture! Boy, he's covered with monsters! There's your dinosaur you, Willie! He's a regular menagerie! What's this: SEE the SKELETON! That's a Thin Man, I know them."

"Sounds better called Skeleton," I said.

"Sure does! See, the Human Balloon! That must be a Fat Man! See THE DUST WITCH! What's a Dust Witch?"

"A witch that was born in the Dust, raised in the Dust and some say winds up back in the Dust," I said, as if I were reading it off the bill.

"You made that up," said Jamie.

"Sure," I laughed. "And I got to see a Dust Witch! What else they got here, let's see."

We turned the pale paper in our fingers. It jerked like it wanted to fly away.

"PRESTIDIGITATORS! NECROMANCERS! MEPHIS- TOPHELE THE FIRE-EATER! THE JUGGLER OF FLAM- ING COMETS! MADEMOISELLE TAROT AND THE DANGLING MAN!"

"Boy!" said Jamie.

"Egyptian Mirrors! THE DEMON GUILLOTINE! ST. ANTHONY'S TEMPLE OF TEMPTATION! The most beau- tiful—"

"Woman in the world," finished Jamie.

"CARTOMANCY!" I read.

"Woman in the world," said Jamie. "The most—"

"The Unicorn Carousel!" I read, louder.

"In the world—" said Jamie. "Beautiful." He looked at me. "They mean that? I mean, can a carnival like this have along with it the Most Beautiful Woman in the World?"

"You ever seen carnival women, Jamie?" I said, disgusted.

"Sure."

"You just answered your own question."

"How come they claim it in this handbill, then?"

"They can claim anything in their darned handbill. They can claim they got Moses dancing on the head of a pin, but you don't go down there looking for Moses, do you? And even if you found him there, you'd pull his beard, wouldn't you?"

"Sure."

"Okay, then."

"You mad at me, Willie?"

"No, I'm not, shut up!" I yelled.

The wind tore the handbill from our fingers then.

"Get it!" yelled Jamie. "We didn't see where the carnival was going to set up!"

We ran. But the wind ran faster. It took the handbill end over end, up over the trees and down the street, capering away so we gave up and stood panting, looking after it.

"It can't be true, anyway. No carnival comes this time of year. Weather's bad, who'd go to a carnival like that?"

"Me," said Jamie, standing there beside me.

Me, too, I thought, not saying it, but thinking of the guillotines and Egyptian Mirrors and what have you.

"The calliope," murmured Jamie.

"What?"

"I heard the music, earlier. It must be coming tonight!"

"Carnivals don't come at night, they come at sunrise."

"Licorice," said Jamie, remembering. "We smelled licorice and cotton candy."

"Hey," I said, "that's right."

I thought of Mr. Tetley listening and Mr. Crosetti with tears running down the grooves in his face like rain down the lion's stone muzzle in front of the library. I shivered. I hunched my shoulders.

"Let's get home."

"Home," said Jamie and we turned around.

Outside our houses, we moved silently up our separate walks. On the front porch, Jamie called over to me, "Hey, William. You're not mad at me?"

"No," I whispered.

"What?"

"No!" I said, louder.

"I gave back the purse, Willie!"

"Sure."

"And I won't go near the Theatre again. You hear me?"

"I hear you."

"Good night, Willie."

"Night."

Jamie stared off into the wind, all by himself, small by his front door.

"Licorice," he said. "Calliope, by gosh, calliope."

"I don't smell nothing," I said. "I don't hear nothing!"

"You will," said Jamie. "You will."

We went in and shut our separate doors.

Chapter [Eight]

Parents, like seasons, as the pirates say, be good or bad, too.

Inside my house, I stopped and let the door just tap quietly shut.

The only Theatre I knew or cared about was the one I saw now. Framed through the hall door in a kind of stage was the parlor. The hall door was double and made for sliding into the walls like curtains. And in the parlor now sat my father holding a book but not reading it, looking kind of pale, and in another chair near the fireplace sat my mother, knitting. I didn't say anything. For a moment, I didn't want them to know I was there, watching them like ants in a glass anthill.

There they were and I loved them and hated them, liked them and disliked them, understood and didn't understand them, wanted to be near them, wanted not to be near them, saw them close, saw them far away, all in a moment. I let the thoughts come and go as they wanted. I didn't try to stop my thinking. There it was. I knew it. I didn't fight it.

I was just old enough where they were beginning to look awfully small of a sudden. In that room now they looked as if maybe they couldn't quite be sure they were safe from anything that came in the door nights, including me. I felt sorry for them, which was strange. I never felt sorry for grown people before in my life. I didn't even know why I felt sorry, I just did. More than anything else, at the moment, above any flickers of rebellion or dislike, I knew I loved them and loved them more, suddenly, because they seemed like kids from school, with more exaggerated manners and more on guard, sure, and a few inches taller, but nevertheless, there they were, playing some kind of game I hadn't figured out.

My mother. I looked at her. Her fingers moved, her lips faintly moved counting as the knitting went on. She was the happiest-looking woman I ever saw. You are going through a greenhouse on a winter day and you push aside a green jungle and there, out of nowhere, is a creamy pink hothouse rose. And there she was, nodding and smelling like fresh milk, in her chair, and smiling over some secret thoughts, happy, happy.

And there was my father, not seeing the pages he turned, at last closing the book, staring into the fire, sad, sad.

I looked at the two people, trying to figure out why one was so happy and one was so unhappy, but I couldn't see why. I knew everything was all right, I mean, I knew we were a family, I would have known otherwise if it were so, you know those things without saying. I knew that Dad loved Mom. But nevertheless, there he sat with a worm in him. Now, as I looked at him I saw that he had a piece of paper in his hand, which he turned over and over as he gazed into the fire. The paper looked familiar. It was such a real pale pale color there didn't seem to be any other paper so pale in the world. And when Dad turned the paper, folding and refolding it, unconsciously, in his hands, it fell open and I saw a few letters of type and I knew what it was.

I smiled wildly. "Hey!" I said, making my entrance.

Immediately the Theatre got in order. The actors stopped just doing pantomime, that is, and fixed new faces on and got set with lines they had to make up to fit the son. Mother opened up a smile that was like lighting a second fire in the room. Dad looked startled, almost dismayed, as if I had caught him doing I don't know what.

"Hey!" I said, coming in, looking at the paper in Dad's hand. I was ready to say, "Cooger & Dark's Carnival. Tomorrow 1001 Wonders, what do you say now!"

But before I could open my mouth again, Dad very quietly and casually put away the folded paper, hiding it in the side of the chair upholstery.

That was so unexpected, I just stood there with my mouth open and Cooger and Dark there on my tongue. I shut my mouth. I made myself smile again.

"Dad, Mom!" I said. "Long time no see."

"Hello, William Allan Halloway," said Dad.

"Willy," said Mom.

I kissed Mom on the cheek and shook Dad's hand, gravely.

"Well, all the courtesy and manners," said Dad, cheering up. "What's the reason?"

"The reason is," I said. "Dinosaurs are in the library, *Pithecanthropus erectus* is under my arm—" I showed him my caveman book, "—the wind blew me all the way home, and all's right with the world."

"*Pithecanthropus erectus*," said Mother, laughing. "Did you know words like that when you were a boy, Will?"

Dad nodded sagely. "All boys know big words. All children do. A myth has grown up that they don't. It's only when you get older you get self-conscious about big words and give them up. What a shame. It makes a boy's mouth water to say *Tyrannosaurus rex* and antidisestablishmentarianism, doesn't it, William?"

"Yes, sir," I said, trying not to look at where Dad had hidden the paper. "Boy, what a night. We didn't have to walk, Jamie and me. The wind just *took* us home! Strange things are going on!"

"The boy's a philosopher," said Dad, looking at me with his head cocked.

"Socrates Hemlock Halloway is the name," I said, and waited for them to laugh, which they did. "And I predict avalanches, floods, locust plagues, and Christians being thrown to the lions before morning."

At this last, I saw Dad's eyes open and squinch in. I had to pull my eyes away from the hidden handbill.

I waited for someone to say something about the carnival coming to town, but nobody did, so I knew then that Mother didn't know about it, Dad hadn't told her, and that made me feel funny, too. So I just stood there, rocking on my feet and at last said, "Well, sir, ma'am—" and turned around, heading for the stairs. "I'll take my saber-tooth tigers upstairs, if you don't mind."

"I'll send a Christian up later to tuck you in," said Father, nodding at Mother.

I waved at them and went out of the room.

I walked up the stairs slowly.

Halfway up I heard what I had half expected to hear.

A big fluming whisper as something fresh and new—the handbill?—was tossed on the fire, and went up in a huge burst of light and sound.

I stopped, listening to the loud crackling die away and I could see Dad, in my mind, standing at the hearth looking down at the type as it curled and crinkled and turned black:

"—CARNIVAL—WONDERS—MIRRORS—MOST BEAUTIFUL—IN THE WORLD—"

Somehow, in my mind, Dad looked like Jamie standing there at the fire. I didn't know why. Maybe I didn't want to know.

I hurried upstairs.

I'd hear Mom and Dad talking nights and I'd put my ear over to the wall of the room and listen there and if they talked about things that were all right I listened and if they weren't all right I didn't listen. I got to know, over a long time, when it was all right and when it wasn't, and I held myself to account if I didn't stop right off if it was about things that were crazy and better let alone. But if it was about time and years passing or me or the town or just the way God ran the world, I listened, for it was usually Dad talking, his voice up and down, easy as one hand winging soft on the air like a white bird. It made me go to sleep many a night.

So it was this night going to sleep with my head against the warm plaster and at first Dad's voice like a Congo drum booming real soft way off far away and then getting clearer. And Mother's voice, she sings a clear soprano in the Baptist Church Sundays, not singing but singing back at him. And Dad's voice, him speaking up louder this time. I could see him in my mind, him lying and looking at the ceiling, talking to the empty spaces.

"... man with bills under his arm ..."

I quickened and squinched my eyes.

I looked out in the moonlight. And there like a milkpod plume, I saw white paper blow by in the middle of the street. I knew what it said. But it said nothing to me. I didn't believe a show would come to town in October anyway.

I got under the covers and turned on my flashlight and first thing I saw when I opened my library book was a prehistoric bat flying in a night sky going somewhere off a million years.

CHAPTER _____

Midnight then and the town clock chiming
and shaking the old toys in high attics and shedding
the dust off old mirrors in yet higher attics and
stirring up dreams about clocks in all the beds
where ~~CHILDREN SLEPT~~.T.

With the first stroke of midnight, WILL saw the
dim phantom light over in JIM's bedroom go out and
~~I~~ knew JIM was done staring at brontosaur bones under
his white sheet. At the last stroke of midnight, WILL
~~I~~ clicked off HIS flashlight and the image of a sabre-
tooth with blood ticking off the sword edge of his
teeth snarled quietly in the middle of the ceiling.
WILL looked up and showed HIS teeth back.

HE settled down with the wind from the wide
open window blowing in across THE bed.

The town was dark and all the voices were
silent. HE thought HE heard ~~THE~~ tumbleweed papers
skittering in the alleys and driveways. The trees
held up the stars, and the stars very slowly got away
and moved on.

There was a moment of clear silence.
And then HE heard it.

"And then I heard it." The actual typescript page following the excerpt printed in this volume from *Jamie and Me*, Bradbury's initial first-person narrative draft of *Something Wicked This Way Comes*. On this page, Will relates the moment when he first hears the ominous midnight whistle of the approaching carnival train. Here, as with most of the surviving pages, Bradbury altered the narrative to third-person before typing the entire novel again in that form.

PART TWO

Other Voices

I read Something Wicked *when I was nine, read it again when I was thirteen, again when I was seventeen and I still go back to it. I think it is a tremendous piece of fantastical writing.*

—Clive Barker, 1992

Russell Kirk (1918–1994) *was a cultural critic and scholar who corresponded with T. S. Eliot and wrote regularly for the* National Review. *His influential formulation of postwar American conservatism blended a love of traditional values with a healthy skepticism of those who would manipulate those values. Like Bradbury, Kirk was critical of both the far right and the far left, and he was also an award-winning writer of light horror and ghost stories that ranged from traditional English haunts to American gothic tales. Bradbury and Kirk developed an enduring friendship in the early 1960s; in* Enemies of the Permanent Things *(1969), a widely read study of literature's role in society, Kirk devoted most of his chapter on fantasy to Bradbury. The following excerpt presents Kirk's careful reading of* Something Wicked This Way Comes.

from Enemies of the Permanent Things

RUSSELL KIRK

A carnival comes to a small town; and two boys, thirteen years old, Jim and Will, are fascinated by it. But this particular carnival is not merry. Its master is the Illustrated Man, Mr. Dark, seeking whom he may devour. His captive freaks are sinners whose monstrous bodies are the personifications of their sins. His carousel, running forward or backward at great speed, will give human beings their desire of youth regained or age attained—and send the iron into their souls. His Mirror Maze will entrap the folk who seek what is not in nature, and will convert them into caricatures of themselves. Madame Tarot, the Dust Witch, can murder with a whisper. For centuries, preying upon frailty and folly, this carnival has wandered the world, its proprietors setting their snares for the unwise and the unwary, and often with success.

Only one man in town—Will's father, the library janitor, growing old—recognizes the carnival for what it is. The carnival is not Death. "But I think it uses Death as a threat," says Charles Halloway, the janitor, to the terrified boys. "Death doesn't exist. It never did, it never will. But we've drawn so many pictures of it, so many years, trying to pin it down, comprehend it, we've got to thinking of it as an entity, strangely alive and greedy. All it is, however, is a stopped watch, a loss, an end, a darkness. Nothing. And the carnival wisely knows we're more afraid of Nothing than we are of Something."

This carnival is the evil that men do to one another, and to themselves; it is fed by pain and fear. What Cooger and Dark's Carnival desires is not worthless dead souls, but ulcerated egos, given up to will and appetite. "A dead soul is no kindling. But a live and raving soul, crisped with self-damnation, oh that's a pretty snoutful for such as them." Enslaved to the freak-masters, such souls in agony supply the fuel for the carnival's perpetuity. For every need, want, and desire the carnival proprietors promise a satisfaction beyond the bounds of nature. But their victims fall, instead, into madness and ghastly distortion. There is no need for devils to buy souls, for "most men jump at the chance to give up everything for nothing." This carnival has "traveled a long way on an easy map, with people handy by every crossroad to lend it lustful pints of agony to power it on. So maybe the carnival survives, living off the poison of the sins we do each other, and the ferment of our most terrible regrets."

This carnival's power is mighty, and it converts the lightning-rod salesman into a hideous crumpled dwarf, old Miss Foley into a lost child. Jim, who would grow up too soon, stands on the brink of being whirled by the carousel into monstrosity.

By lusting after the abnormal, by flouting the nature of things, old and young betray themselves into the freak-master's clutch.

Yet one power is stronger than the temptations and threats of the carnival; and that power is laughter. We laugh at the incongruous, at the absurdity of the unnatural. Rediscovering the weapon of humor, Halloway first baffles the Dust Witch, and then shoots her dead with a bullet on which he has imprinted a smile. Evil, after all, is ludicrous; and though God is not mocked, those creatures who batten upon tormented souls are aghast at healthy mockery.

Just when all has seemed lost, Halloway and the boys destroy the carnival by mirth. But other creatures who prey upon warped souls will come to town presently, in some other disguise, and the fools who want everything will become their freaks.

Evil, in essence, is the appetite to undo the natural order of things. It is the glorification of abnormality. And the price one pays for clutching at the unnatural is metamorphosis into a freak, or into a freak-master.

In Bradbury's fables of Mars and of the carnival, fantasy has become what it was in the beginning: the enlightening moral imagination, transcending simple rationality. The everyday world is not the real world, for today's events are merely a film upon the deep well of the past, and they will be swallowed up by the unknowable future. The real world is the world of the permanent things, which often are discerned more clearly in the fictional dead cities of Mars or the fictional carousel of Cooger and Dark than in our own little private slice of evanescent experience. And—what is a wondrous thing in itself—the new generation of Americans are not blind to the truth of the fabulists, for Bradbury is their favorite author.

The second typescript for *Something Wicked This Way Comes* was revised during the summer and again during the fall of 1961 as he worked to complete a third full draft. Bradbury annotated and illustrated this box lid from the ream of Berkshire paper that he used to store the cascading sequence of revisions written on the second draft. *From the Albright Collection; courtesy of Donn Albright and the Bradbury Estate.*

Stephen King (1947–) *is perhaps the most prolific and influential horror writer of our time. He first encountered Ray Bradbury's stories as a boy; he was deeply affected by an early 1950s radio adaptation of "Mars Is Heaven!" and the ultimately terrifying Martian illusion of small-town life and memories, drawn from the collective minds of the doomed expedition from Earth. King considered the urban and small-town terrors of Bradbury's 1947* Dark Carnival *story collection to be "the* Dubliners *of American fantasy fiction," and* Something Wicked This Way Comes *to be his best evocation of the dark fantastic. King's 1981 nonfiction study* Danse Macabre, *which explores the ways that writers, readers, and the media interpret the long horror tradition in literature, includes a chapter on* Something Wicked This Way Comes. *The following excerpt captures the essence of this insightful chapter.*

from Danse Macabre

STEPHEN KING

Something Wicked This Way Comes, a darkly poetic tall tale set in the half-real, half-mythical community of Green Town, Illinois, is probably Bradbury's best work—a shadowy descendant from that tradition that has brought us stories about Paul Bunyan and his blue ox, Babe, Pecos Bill, and Davy Crockett. It is not a perfect book; at times Bradbury lapses into the purple overwriting that has characterized too much of his work in the seventies. Some passages are self-imitative and embarrassingly fulsome. But that is a small part of the total work; in most cases Bradbury carries his story off with guts and beauty and *panache*.

Bradbury has continued to publish fantasy throughout his career, and although the *Christian Science Monitor* called *Something Wicked This Way Comes* a "nightmarish allegory," Bradbury really settles for allegory only in his science fiction. In his fantasy, his preoccupation has been with theme, character, symbol . . . and that fantastic rush that comes to the writer of fantasy when he puts the pedal to the metal, yanks back on the steering wheel, and drives his jalopy straight up into the black night of unreality.

In Bradbury's story an ancient carnival, marvelously named Cooger and Dark's Pandemonium Shadow Show, arrives in Green Town, bringing misery and horror under the guise of pleasure and wonder. Will Halloway and Jim Nightshade—and later, Will's father, Charles, as well—wise up to exactly what this particular carnival is all about. The tale eventually narrows down to the struggle for a single soul, that of Jim Nightshade. To call it an allegory would be wrong, but to call it a moral horror tale—much in the manner of those EC [Entertaining Comics] horror tales which foreran it—would be exactly right. In effect, what happens to Jim and Will is not so much different from Pinocchio's scary encounter on Pleasure Island, where boys who indulge their baser desires (smoking cigars and shooting snooker, for instance) are turned into donkeys. Bradbury is writing here of carnal enticements—not just sexual carnality, but carnality in its broadest forms and manifestations—the pleasures of the flesh run as wild as the tattooed illustrations which cover Mr. Dark's body.

The book asks us to recall and reexamine the facts and myths of our own childhoods, most specifically our small-town American childhoods. Written in a semi-poetic style that seems to suit such concerns perfectly, Bradbury examines these childhood concerns and comes to the conclusion that only children are equipped to deal with childhood's myths and terrors and exhalations. In his mid-fifties story "The Playground," a man who returns magically to childhood is propelled into a world of lunatic horror which is only, after all, the corner playground with its sandboxes and its slippery slide.

In *Something Wicked This Way Comes*, Bradbury interconnects this small-town American boyhood motif with most of the ideas of the new American gothic. Will and Jim are essentially okay, riding easy in their childhoods and used to looking at the world from their shorter height. But when their teacher, Miss Foley, returns to childhood—the first of the carnival's Green Town victims—she enters a world of monotonous, unending horror which is not much different from that experienced by the protagonist of "The Playground." The boys discover Miss Foley—or what remains of her—under a tree.

> . . . and there was the little girl, crouched, face buried in her hands, weeping as if the town were gone and the people in it and herself lost in a terrible woods.
>
> And at last Jim came edging up and stood at the edge of the shadow and said, "Who is it?"
>
> "I don't know." But Will felt tears start to his eyes, as if some part of him guessed.
>
> "It's not Jenny Holdridge, is it?"
>
> "No."
>
> "Jane Franklin?"
>
> "No." His mouth felt full of novocaine, his tongue merely stirred in his numb lips. ". . . no . . ."
>
> The little girl wept feeling them near, but not looking up yet.
>
> ". . . me . . . help me . . . nobody'll help me . . . me . . . me . . . I don't *like* this . . . somebody must help me . . . someone must help *her* . . ." she mourned as for one dead, ". . . someone must help her . . . nobody will . . . nobody has . . . terrible . . . terrible . . ."

The carnival "attraction" which has accomplished this malign trick is one that both Narcissus and Eleanor Vance could relate to: Miss Foley has been trapped in the carnival's mirror maze, imprisoned by her own reflection. Forty or fifty years have been jerked out from under her and she has been tumbled back into her own childhood . . . just what she thought she wanted. She had not considered the possibility of the nameless little girl weeping under the tree.

Jim and Will avoid this fate—barely—and even manage to rescue Miss Foley on her first foray into the mirror maze. One supposes it is not the maze itself but the carousel that has actually accomplished her doubling back in time; the mirrors in the maze show you a time of life you think you'd like to have again, and the carousel actually accomplishes it. The carousel can add a year to your age each time you go around forward or make you a year younger for every circle you make on it going backward. The carousel is Bradbury's interesting and workable metaphor for *all* of life's passages, and the fact that he darkens this ride, which is often associated with the sunniest pleasure we know as children, to fit the motif of this particular black carnival, causes other uneasy associations to come to mind. When we see the innocent merry-go-round ride with its prancing horses in this nether light, it may suggest to us that if time's passages are to be compared to a merry-go-round ride, then we see that each year's revolution is essentially the same as the last; it perhaps causes us to remember how fleeting and ephemeral such a ride is; and most of all it reminds us that the brass ring, which we have all tried so hard and fruitlessly to catch, is kept deliberately, tauntingly, out of reach.

In terms of the new American gothic, we can see that the mirror maze is the catch-trap, the place where too much self-examination and morbid introspection persuades Miss Foley to step over the line into abnormality. In Bradbury's world—the world of Cooger and Dark's Pandemonium Shadow Show—there are no options: first caught in the glass of Narcissus, you then find yourself riding a dangerous carousel charger backwards into an untenable past or forward into an untenable future. Shirley Jackson uses the conventions of the new American gothic to examine character under extreme psychological—or perhaps occult—pressure; Peter Straub uses them to examine the effects of an evil past upon the present; Anne Rivers Siddons uses them to examine social codes and social pressures; Bradbury uses these self-same conventions in order to offer us a moral judgment. In describing Miss Foley's terror and grief in attaining the childhood she so desired, Bradbury goes far toward defusing the potential flood of sticky-sweet romanticism that might have destroyed his tale . . . and I think this defusing reinforces the moral judgments he makes. In spite of imagery that sometimes swamps us instead of uplifting us, he manages to retain his own clear point of view.

This isn't to say Bradbury doesn't make a romantic myth of childhood, because he sure does. Childhood itself is a myth for almost all of us. We think we remember what happened to us when we were kids, but we don't. The reason is simple: we were crazy then. Looking back into this well of sanity as adults who are, if not totally insane, then at least neurotic instead of out-and-out psychotic, we attempt to make sense of things which made no sense, read importance into things which had no importance, and remember motivations which simply didn't exist. This is where the process of mythmaking begins.

Rather than trying to row against this strong current, Bradbury uses it in *Something Wicked This Way Comes*; blending the myth of childhood with the myth of the dream-father, whose part is played here by Will's dad, Charles Halloway . . . and, if Bradbury himself is to be believed, who is also played by that Illinois power-linesman who was Ray Bradbury's dad. Halloway is a librarian who lives his own life of dreams, who is enough boy to understand Will and Jim, but who is also enough adult to provide, in the end, what the boys cannot provide for themselves: simple accountability.

The only effective foil for Bradbury's dream-children is Charles Halloway, the dream-father. In the character of Charles Halloway we find attractions which only fantasy, with its strong mythmaking abilities, can give us. Three points about him are worth mentioning, I think.

First, Charles Halloway understands the myth of childhood the two boys are living; for all of us who grew up and parted with some bitterness from our parents because we felt they didn't understand our youth, Bradbury gives us a portrait of the sort of parent we felt we deserved. His reactions are those which few real parents can ever afford to have. His parenting instincts are apparently supernaturally alert. Early on, he sees the boys running home from watching the carnival set up, and calls their names softly under his breath . . . but does no more. Nor does he mention it to Will later, although the two boys have been out at three o'clock in the morning. He's not worried that they've been out scoring dope or mugging old ladies or *shtupping* their girlfriends. He knows they have been out on boys' business, walking the night as boys sometimes will . . . and he lets it go.

Second, Charles Halloway comes by his understanding legitimately; he is still living the myth himself. Your father cannot be your pal very successfully, the psychology texts tell us, but there are few fathers, I think, who have not longed to be buddies with their sons, and few sons who have not wished for a buddy in their fathers. When Charles Halloway discovers that Jim and Will have nailed rungs under the climbing ivy on their respective houses so they can escape and reenter their bedrooms after bedtime, he does not demand that the rungs be torn down; his response is admiring laughter and an admonition that the boys will not use the rungs until they really have to. When Will tells his father in agony that no one will believe them if they try to explain what really happened in Miss Foley's house, where the evil nephew Robert (who is really Mr. Cooger, looking much younger since he has been reissued) framed them for a robbery, Halloway says simply, "I'll believe." He will believe because he is really just one of the boys and the sense of wonder has not died within him. Much later, when rummaging through his pockets, Charles Halloway almost seems like the world's oldest Tom Sawyer:

> And Will's father stood up, stuffed his pipe with tobacco,
> rummaged his pockets for matches, brought out a battered
> harmonica, a penknife, a cigarette lighter that wouldn't

work, and a memo pad he had always meant to write great thoughts down on but had never got around to. . . .

Almost everything, in fact, except a dead rat and a string to swing it on.

Third, Charles Halloway is the dream-father because he is, in the end, accountable. He can switch hats, in the blink of an eye, from that of the child to that of the adult. He proves his accountability and responsibility by a simple symbolic act: when Mr. Dark asks, Halloway gives him his name.

"A fine day to you, sir!"

No, Dad! thought Will.

The Illustrated Man came back. "Your name, sir?" he asked directly.

Don't tell him! thought Will.

Will's father debated a moment, took the cigar from his mouth, tapped ash and said quietly:

"Halloway. Work in the library. Drop by sometime."

"You can be sure, Mr. Halloway. I will."

. . . [Halloway] was also gazing with surprise at himself, accepting the surprise, the new purpose, which was half despair, half serenity, now that the incredible deed was done. Let no one ask why he had given his true name; even he could not assay and give its real weight. . . .

But isn't it most likely that he has given his true name because the boys cannot? He must front for them—which he does admirably. And when Jim's dark wishes finally lead him into what seems utter ruin, it is Halloway who emerges, first destroying the fearsome Dust Witch, then Mr. Dark himself, and finally leading the fight for Jim's life and soul.

Something Wicked This Way Comes is probably not Bradbury's best work overall—I believe he has always found the novel a difficult form to work in—but its mythic interests are so well suited to Bradbury's dreamy, semi-poetic prose that it succeeds wonderfully and becomes one of those books about childhood (like Hughes's *A High Wind in Jamaica*, Stevenson's *Treasure Island*, Cormier's *The Chocolate War*, and Thomas Williams's *Tsuga's Children*, to name just a few) that adults should take down once in a while . . . not just to give to their own children, but in order to touch base again themselves with childhood's brighter perspectives and darker dreams. Bradbury has introduced his novel with a quotation from Yeats: "Man is in love, and loves what vanishes." He adds others, but we will perhaps agree that the line from Yeats is text enough . . . but let Bradbury himself have the final word, concerning one of Green Town's fascinations for the two dream-children of whom he has written:

As for my gravestone? I would like to borrow that great barber-pole from out front of the town shoppe, and have it run at midnight if you happened to drop by my mound to say hello. And there the old barber-pole would be, lit, its bright ribbons twining up out of mystery, turning, and twining away up into further mysteries, forever. And if you come to visit, leave an apple for the ghosts.

An apple . . . or maybe a dead rat and a string to swing it on.

SOMETHING WICKED ~~THIS WAY COMES~~ -1-
~~Bradbury~~

THIS VERSION INKED AND CUT DURING WEEKS FEB. 12TH TO FEB. 22ND 1962 RAY BRADBURY 2/22/62

PROLOGUE

First of all it was October, a fine month for

boys. Not that all ~~the~~ months ~~altogether~~ aren't fine.

There be bad and good, as the pirates say. ~~September~~

~~you you~~ Take September, a bad month: school begins.

Consider August, a good month: school hasn't begun yet.

July, well, July's really fine: there's no chance in

the world for school. June, no doubting it, June's

best of all, for the school doors spring *WIDE* ~~open~~ and ~~the~~

~~kids pour out yelling lickety-split across the yard and~~

~~down in the ravine swinging on vines and jumping in~~

~~the meadows~~ September's a billion years away.

But you take October now. School's been on a

month and you're riding easier in the reins, ~~not taking~~

~~the bit in your mouth any more, but~~ jogging along. ~~Easy~~

You got time to ~~watch the trees getting ready to let~~

~~down fire, and to~~ think of the garbage you'll dump on

old man Prickett's porch, or the hairy-ape costume you'll

wear to the YMCA the last night of the month. And if

it's around October twentieth and everything smoky-smelling

and the sky orange and ash-grey at twilight, it seems

Bradbury's late-1961 third draft of the novel was revised yet one more
time during mid-February 1962, just prior to submission. His revisions
tighten up the prose at several points, but he has not yet revised his
now-famous opening sentence; October will finally become, "a rare
month for boys." *From the Albright Collection; courtesy of Donn Albright
and the Bradbury Estate.*

Brian Sibley (1949–) *is a prolific author of literary adaptations and documentaries for Britain's BBC Radio, including selections for the 1997 BBC series* Ray Bradbury: Tales of the Bizarre *and a 2014 adaptation of Ray Bradbury's* The Illustrated Man. *He has also written books on J. R. R. Tolkien and C. S. Lewis, who together with Bradbury represent three of the most prominent literary myth-makers of the twentieth century. Sibley's correspondence with Bradbury spanned nearly four decades, revealing fundamental aspects of "the man who took us by the hand and enticed along the carnival midway, lifted the flap of shadow-filled tents and ushered us into the twilight world of freaks and monsters." The following August 2006 reflection on* Something Wicked This Way Comes, *from Sibley's blog,* Ex Libris: Volumes Taken at Idle Moments From My Bookshelves, *examines why this novel endures in the public imagination.*

from Ex Libris

Something Wicked This Way Comes
BRIAN SIBLEY

It all began one August day in a long hot summer month of my youth. I opened a book and read:

"First of all, it was October, a rare month for boys . . ."

I was hooked! Just as I was when I read Charles Dickens's line: "Marley was dead, to begin with . . ." The same cunningly clever opening: something that needs to be understood and explained and the knowledge that it is, first of all, just the beginning . . .

I didn't know then that the author of this story I was about to read revered Dickens's *A Christmas Carol* as one of his favorite books.

Something Wicked This Way Comes—the title, courtesy of one of the witches from Shakespeare's *Macbeth*—is an irresistible beckoning, bony finger.

Resistance is useless ...

It is a dark tale, darkly told, about what happened—or what might have happened, or might yet happen—in the misty, musty, leaf-rustling days of October ...

Will Halloway and Jim Nightshade are the best of friends. They are also opposites. One blond, the other dark-haired, both born on Halloween: Will at one minute to midnight, Jim at one minute after midnight. One is drawn to the light, the other summoned by the dark.

Then, into the sleepy, autumnal atmosphere of their small Midwest American town comes Tom Fury, the seller of lightning rods, with a bag rattling with curiously wrought ironmongery and muttered warnings of storms to come ...

AND COME THEY DO ...

In the early hours of a moonless night, a mournful train whistle heralds the arrival of a carnival that will change the lives of everyone in the town forever.

Cooger and Dark's Pandemonium Shadow Show offers a variety of apparently harmless candyfloss laughs and thrills. But behind the flaps of the great black tent lurk terrifying freaks; and the seemingly innocuous attractions set up along the midway are anything but what they seem: a Mirror Maze that reveals ugly reflections of untrue futures; a Ferris wheel that spins its passengers into oblivion and a Carousel that can ride you backwards to youth or forwards to death ...

Will and Jim discover the secret of the dark carnival and its long, torturous history winding its way across the world and down the years. For them alone: the challenge of confronting and overcoming raw evil; it is their destiny, but it is a task that puts their friendship and their very lives at risk ...

I treasured that book; became the passionate lover of the story: writing and broadcasting about it whenever I got the opportunity, spreading the gospel that this is a tale that everyone should read once before they forget what it is to have been young ...

Why do those who love this book have feelings toward it that are both proprietorial and evangelical?

Like so much of Ray's writings, it is partly to do with the way in which the author luxuriates in language: if you come to Bradbury when you are still young and learning the mystery and mastery of words, then you cannot help but apprentice yourself to someone who is not only a craftsman but also (very probably) a magician!

Bradbury books fizz and sizzle on the eye and the ear: the rich, almost baroque, architecture of the narrative; the startling, metaphor-embellished paragraphs; the lavish, adjective-encrusted sentences; the audacious theatricality of vision and the razor-sharp observation with which the characters are given life and costumed for the beautiful and bizarre dramas they are called on to enact . . .

Ted Gioia (1957–) *is a music historian whose publications range from books and articles on jazz and folk roots to a three-volume study of the social history of music. He is a three-time winner of ASCAP's Deems Taylor Award for his publications, and is also a jazz composer, performer, and recording artist. Gioia's nearly equal passion for literature led him to found a wide range of websites that both document and explode genre boundaries (his alternate-reality Nobel Prize listing for 1987 results in a tie between Ray Bradbury and Robert Heinlein). He shares a love of Ray Bradbury's legacy with his brother, poet and past chair of the National Endowment for the Arts, Dana Gioia. In the following essay from his website,* Conceptual Fiction *(conceptualfiction.com), Ted Gioia revisits* Something Wicked *to consider how Bradbury's determined mid-century departure from traditional horror still resonates with readers today.*

From Conceptual Fiction

"Something Wicked This Way Comes"
TED GIOIA

Ray Bradbury will forever be remembered as a writer of *genre* stories, yet most of his oeuvre reveals a stubborn resistance—that borders on obliviousness—to the accepted formulas of the pulp fiction trade. He has complained about the sci-fi label invariably applied to his work—"I've only done one science fiction book and that's *Fahrenheit 451*, based on reality," is his oft-quoted comeback. And his best-known outer space work, *The Martian Chronicles*, has about as much about the Red Planet as a Mars chocolate bar. In general, the science in his various tales is rarely more than a passing fancy, and sometimes totally absent.

And then we come to his "horror" novel, *Something Wicked*

This Way Comes. How does Bradbury fare when dealing with a terror-inducing tale of the supernatural?

An early warning sign that this book is not your typical scary story arrives even before the opening sentence. The dedication to silver screen idol Gene Kelly will come as a surprise to many readers—even more so, when they learn that Bradbury originally conceived this story as a film feature for the charming song-and-dance man to produce. Even more to the point, I can easily imagine Mr. Kelly residing in the slice-of-Americana, Norman Rockwellish setting (based on Bradbury's hometown of Waukegan, Illinois) where the novel takes place. No, *Nightmare on Elm Street* this is not.

Certainly Bradbury tries to amplify the horror as best he can, which revolves around a sinister carnival coming to town, but his temperament is not suited for dark themes. The supposedly spine-tingling scenes are among the most perfunctory in the book. Meanwhile, the author really hits his stride when waxing nostalgically over issues of youth and aging, life in Middle America, and other familiar Bradbury themes. Two-thirds of the way through the novel, the reader is rewarded with a long monologue on the metaphysics of good and evil, delivered by a janitor at the local library, and this interlude is thought-provoking and powerful, but has taken us so far away from the conventions of the horror story that we wonder whether Bradbury will ever find his way back.

Here is a dose of this speech:

First things first. Let's bone up on history. If men had wanted to stay bad forever they could have, agreed? . . . Somewhere we turned in our carnivore's teeth and started chewing blades of grass. We been working mulch as much as blood, into our philosophy, for quite a few lifetimes. Since then we measure ourselves up the scale from apes, but not half so high as angels. . . . I suppose one night hundreds of thousands of years ago in a cave by a night fire

when one of those shaggy men wakened to gaze over the
banked coals at his woman, his children, and thought of
their being cold, dead, gone forever. Then he must have
wept. And he put out his hand in the night to the woman
who must die some day and to the children who must fol-,
low her. And for a little bit next morning, he treated them
somewhat better, for he saw that they, like himself, had the
seed of night in them. . . .

This goes on, with a few interjections from the youngsters in attendance on the Socratic exercise, for more than ten pages. The
reader can sense Bradbury's excitement, and even get a feeling
that this is the core of the novel from the author's perspective.
What a contrast from horror story maestro H. P. Lovecraft, a key
role model for Bradbury in a book of this sort, or from Stephen
King, who was inspired in turn by this novel, but would never let
his appreciation of metaphysics get in the way of the plot.

The plot, in Bradbury's case, builds on the exploits of two
thirteen-year-old boys, Will Halloway and Jim Nightshade, who
find themselves irresistibly drawn to the strange carnival that has
arrived in town—even as they grow fearful in the face of the mysterious goings-on and odd characters they encounter. One of the
proprietors of the traveling show, Mr. Dark, makes them shudder
with his torso and limbs covered with tattoos. He is sometimes
called the Illustrated Man here, and thus stands as another example of Bradbury's willingness to recycle concepts and character
types, and sometimes entire stories, from his earlier books. But
our young heroes also cross paths with the Dust Witch, the Skeleton, the Dwarf and Mr. Electrico, among other unsavory carnival
characters.

Bradbury tosses in some evil apparatuses for good measure. We have a carousel that can make the rider turn older and
younger, depending on whether it is running forward or reverse.
A house of mirrors beckons people into a frightening labyrinth,
where the reflected images seem to turn on the unwary originals.

We have an electric chair, a predatory hot air balloon, and a guillotine and other instruments of horror. Bradbury is especially skilled at employing these elements as objective correlatives in creating an atmosphere of dread and suspense.

Yet, above all, this is a beautifully written book, perhaps the most poetic horror novel of its time. Not a single page comes across as perfunctory, and even when the plot is moving at its fastest pace, the author measures every phrase, and luxuriates in his imagery and asides. In fact, Bradbury runs the risk of undercutting the scary elements by presenting them in such majestic sentences. In the final analysis, he transforms this novel into a coming-of-age story, in which the darker elements are again and again pushed to the periphery. Yes, you will find more terrifying tales than *Something Wicked This Way Comes*, but few that turn the ingredients of the horror genre into something quite so exquisite.

Seth Grahame-Smith (1976–) *has rapidly become a seminal innovator in early twenty-first-century film and literature. His genre-destroying novels-into-film successes include* Pride and Prejudice and Zombies *and* Abraham Lincoln, Vampire Hunter. *He has written graphic adaptations for Marvel Comics, and the screenplay for Tim Burton's feature film version of the television classic* Dark Shadows. *The title of Grahame-Smith's* How to Survive a Horror Movie: All the Skills to Dodge the Kills, *his entertaining 2007 "guide" through traditional horror tropes, suggests that he is well-equipped to reveal why, so late in time,* Something Wicked This Way Comes *still has the power to simultaneously haunt the imagination and illuminate the darkest corners of the human heart. His commentary first aired on National Public Radio's* All Things Considered *on April 26, 2012, just six weeks before Bradbury's passing.*

Bradbury's Tale: A 'Wicked' Read, A Haunted Book

SETH GRAHAME-SMITH

I know it's strange to be thinking about October right now, but whenever I write, in a way that's always where I am. Growing up in Connecticut, it always held a special place in my heart—"a rare month for boys," as Ray Bradbury begins *Something Wicked This Way Comes.*

It was everything: The way the dying leaves clung to tree branches and crunched underfoot. The first wisps of chimney smoke that wafted in the evening air. The promises of free candy and a good World Series. These were the miniature miracles of my twelve-year-old life.

I worshiped at the altar of Stephen King in those days. (I still do, in a way that's unbecoming a grown man, but I make no apologies for my faith, no sir.) In fact—and this is the hand-on-the-Bible truth—I was holding a paperback copy of *The Shining* when I first laid eyes on a dead body. I was headed to sleep-away camp when our bus came upon the scene of an accident. A car had landed upside down in the water. Despite the panicked orders from our chaperones to "look away, look away," I watched as rescuers pulled one of the bodies out.

It was a year before I found the courage to finish that paperback.

Why am I telling you this?

Because while Stephen King frightened and thrilled me, Ray Bradbury's *Something Wicked* haunted me. Spoke to me. Crawled under my skin and stayed there, like the face of that cold, graying corpse.

I first read *Something Wicked* in middle school. Not for class, but on the advice of my stepfather—a used- and rare-book dealer who kept some five thousand volumes of horror and science fiction in our basement. I'd already tried my hand at Bradbury's other books, but he hadn't yet grabbed a hold of me with the sharp claws I'd hoped. But then, I was twelve, and not quite ready. *Something Wicked*, however, was tailor-made.

I was nearly the same age as its young heroes, Jim Nightshade and Will Halloway. Best friends born just two minutes apart— one a minute before the midnight stroke on Halloween, one a minute after. Darkness and light, baby.

I was part Jim—daring and brash. But I was also the cautious, calculating Will. I recognized some of Will's father, Charles Halloway, in my own stepfather. Charles was a lover of books. A lion in winter who, it turns out, never really was much of a lion at all.

Things get going for Jim and Will when a carnival rolls into their small midwestern town on the heels of a thunderstorm. A carnival led by the aptly named Mr. Dark, who comes bearing promises for the town elders: restored youth, second chances, and fulfilled dreams. These all come for a price, of course. Namely, their souls.

Bradbury's carnival is everything we fear. It's age and death and failure. It's a foreign body, invading the ideal small town the way a virus invades a cell.

But for me, the true horror of the book wasn't the carnival or its soul-swallowing ringmaster. It was a hard truth—the truth that our parents weren't always the heroes we needed them to be.

Bradbury's adults were weak with temptation and worn down by regrets. They were real, and that was the horror of it all.

If *The Shining* terrified me with the possibility that my own father might try to kill me, *Something Wicked* posited something much more frightening and much more likely—that he wouldn't be able to save me if someone else did.

```
THE AUTUMN PEOPLE

      a novel
  by Ray Bradbury



"...for some people autumn
comes early and stays
throughout a lifetime where
October follows September
and November touches October
and then instead of December
and the Birth of Christ, there
is no Star, no Birth, but
September comes again, and
old October and so on and so
forth down the years, with
no winter, no spring, no
revivefying summer. . .for these
people, fall is the norm, the
accepted way, the life, there
is no other. . .these people
are the Autumn People. . .
. .beware of them!. .! . .!
```

This discarded title page survives among Bradbury's late 1959 and early 1960 discards, a time when he was transitioning from *Jamie and Me* to his settled intention to title the book *Something Wicked This Way Comes*. The interim title on this discarded page, *The Autumn People*, is followed by an early draft of Charles Halloway's quotation from "an old religious tract" in Chapter 38, as he reveals the true nature of the carnival masters to Will and Jim. This epigraph was eventually discarded as well, but the final version remains within chapter 38.

Margaret Atwood (1939–) *is a celebrated Canadian novelist and poet whose international honors include the prestigious Booker Prize and a wide range of international literary awards and award nominations. A lifelong Bradbury reader, Atwood was one of the first writers to assess the root metaphors of Bradbury's success as his life closed. The following excerpt is from her feature in the* Guardian, *published June 8, 2012, just three days after Ray Bradbury's passing. Here she examines how he navigated the American gothic legacy that he inherited, and became a writer who worked beyond genre traditions without ever losing his authentic voice as a teller of tales.*

Ray Bradbury: The Tale-Teller Who Tapped into the Gothic Core of America

MARGARET ATWOOD

Any writer who delves as deeply into "horror" writing as Bradbury did has a complex relationship with mortality, and it's not surprising to learn that Ray Bradbury as a child was worried that he would die at any moment, as he tells us in "Take Me Home," a sidebar in this June's *New Yorker* Science Fiction issue. "When I look back now," he says—in what, ironically, was going to be his last published piece—"I realize what a trial I must have been to my friends and relatives. It was one frenzy after one enthusiasm after one hysteria after another. I was always yelling and running somewhere, because I was afraid life was going to be over that very afternoon."

But the flip side of the mortality coin is immortality, and that interested him as well. At the age of twelve—as he tells us on his website—he had a definitive encounter with a stage magician called Mr. Electrico. This was in the age of traveling circuses and the like, and Mr. Electrico had a unique act: he sat in an electrified chair, thus in turn electrifying a sword he held, with which he in turn electrified the spectators, making their hair stand on end and sparks come out of their ears. He electrified young Bradbury in this manner, while shouting, "Live Forever!" The child had to go to a funeral the next day, a close encounter with death that led him to seek out Mr. Electrico once more to find out how this living forever thing was to be done. The old carney showed him around what used to be called the freak show—complete with a tattooed man who was later to morph into the Illustrated Man—and then told him that he, Ray, contained the soul of Mr. Electrico's best friend, who had died in the first world war. You can see how all this would have made an impression. Right after his baptism by electricity at the hands of Mr. Electrico, Bradbury started writing; nor did he stop until his own death.

How do you live forever? Through other people, it seemed: those whose souls turned up in your body. And through other voices, the voices that spoke through you. And through your written words, the code for those voices. At the end of *Fahrenheit 451*, the hero finds—in a world of destroyed books—a group of people who have become the vanished books by memorizing them: a perfect embodiment for the knot of mysteries presented to young Ray by Mr. Electrico.

This evening—in the middle of writing this eulogy, for that is what it is—I had to break off in order to attend a poetry event. At the party afterwards, I told a writer friend that Bradbury had died. "He was the first writer I read all of," he said. "When I was twelve or thirteen. I read every single book—I sought them out. I read them cover to cover." I said I thought that a lot of writers—and a lot of readers—had most likely had the same experience. And that they would be writers and readers of the most diverse kinds—poets and prose writers, all ages, all levels of brow, from low to high.

What accounts for Bradbury's reach—his scope, his influence? And—dreaded question, but one that critics and interviewers are always asking—where would you locate him on the map of literature?

My own view is that, in his best work, Bradbury sinks a tap-root right down into the deep, dark, Gothic core of America. It's no accident that he was descended from Mary Bradbury, convicted as a witch in 1692, during the notorious Salem witchcraft trials, for, among other things, assuming the form of a blue boar. (She was not hanged, as the execution was delayed until the craze was over.) The Salem trials are a seminal trope in American history, one that has repeated itself over and over in various forms—both literary and political—throughout the years. At its heart is the notion of the doubleness of life: you are not who you are, but have a secret and probably evil twin; more importantly, the neighbors are not who you think they are. They might be witches, in the seventeenth century, or people who will falsely accuse you of being a witch; or traitors, in the eighteenth century, at the time of the revolution; or communists, in the twentieth; or people who will stone you to death, in Shirley Jackson's "The Lottery"; or terrorists, in the twenty-first. In the nineteenth century, Nathaniel Hawthorne—himself connected to the Salem trials through his ancestor, a hanging judge—wrote "Young Goodman Brown," a perfect expression of this theme. (Puritan Brown discovers, or perhaps dreams, that his godly neighbors are all members of a satanic coven.) Henry James has his own version: "The Jolly Corner," in which a Europeanized American encounters the ghost of himself as he would have been had he remained in America, a sort of rich monster.

Vladimir Nabokov said, in *Pnin*, that Salvador Dalí "is really Norman Rockwell's twin brother kidnapped by Gypsies in babyhood." But Bradbury was also a twin brother of Rockwell, kidnapped in babyhood by some darker force—Edgar Allan Poe, perhaps, whom he read avidly at the age of eight. Poe's "William Wilson" opposes two twinned selves, and Bradbury can almost be said to have acted them out: the bright self, all sunshine and front porches and lemonade; and the dark one, the one who

could imagine two children luring their own parents to death in
"The Veldt." Two of the *Martian Chronicles* stories twist these
skeins together admirably. In "The Martian," an American family
has moved to Mars to try to create a new life after the death of
their son. But the dead son shows up, just as he used to be, and
father, mother, and son settle into a Rockwell normality. The son
is really a Martian, a shape changer who reflects the desires of
others; and the story spirals down into tragedy, with the equiva-
lent of a mob lynching at the end.

In "The Third Expedition"—called, originally, "Mars Is
Heaven!"—space explorers from Earth find that the mellow,
prewar hometown of their childhood is now on Mars, complete
with old friends and family members, including dead ones. What
a fine reunion they all have, until it turns out that the town and
its inhabitants are mirages, devised by the Martians to lull the
invaders—perceived by the Martians as harmful—so that they
can be exterminated. Who can you trust? Dang near nobody. Or
dang near nobody who claims a Rockwellian normality, which is
bound to be a façade.

But nostalgia for the same Rockwellian normality is very real
in Bradbury's work, the detail lovingly rendered. He was born in
1920 in Waukegan, Illinois, and it is this town and this time—
the '20s and '30s of his youth—that appears again and again in
his work, sometimes on Earth, sometimes on Mars. You can't
go home again, said Thomas Wolfe—another American nostal-
gist—but you can get back the past by writing about it, maybe, as
Wolfe and Bradbury both did. However, the charm lasts only until
midnight strikes and things fall apart. The shadow of the black-
shrouded clock from Poe's "Masque of the Red Death" is never
far from Bradbury's world, even at its sunniest: time is the enemy.

As a writer, Bradbury grew up in the "golden age" of science
fiction—usually thought of as the '30s—and built his career, ini-
tially, on the platform that existed then and for several decades
thereafter: an extensive popular-magazine market for short fiction. Though he would end by publishing in the respected *New*

Yorker, he began in 1938 by publishing in an amateur fan magazine, then his own magazine, *Futuria Fantasia*; then he published in the pulps, including *Super Science Stories* and *Weird Tales*. You could make a living at that, then, if you wrote a lot, and Bradbury did. He wrote every day, and once vowed to write a story a week—a feat he accomplished. His income was helped along by adaptations for the comics, then by screen and TV adaptations. He worked his way up to the glossies, including *Playboy* and *Esquire*. Writing was both his vocation—he was called to it, and wrote intuitively—and his career, by which he supported himself and his family; and he was proud of both of these aspects.

He ducked classification and genre corrals as much as he could: as far as he was concerned he was a tale-teller, a writer of fiction, and as far as he was concerned the tales and the fiction did not need to have labels.

The term "science fiction" made him nervous: he did not want to be shut up in a box. And he, in his turn, made "science fiction" purists nervous, as well he might. Mars in his hands, for instance, is not a place described with scientific accuracy or even much consistency, but a state of mind; he recycles it for whatever he needs at the moment. Spaceships are not miracles of technology, but psychic conveyances, serving the same purpose as Dorothy's whirlwind-borne house in *The Wonderful Wizard of Oz*, or the trance of the traditional shaman: they get you to the Otherworld.

Ray Bradbury saw his writing as a way of living on after his death, and it will certainly perform that service. But then there's Bradbury as a person. All who knew Bradbury testify to his generosity toward others. His imagination had a dark side, and he used that dark twin and its nightmares in his work; but to the waking world he presented a combination of eager, wonder-filled boy and kindly uncle, and that was just as real. In an age of writing classes, he was self-taught; in an age of spin, his was an authentic voice, straight from the heartland; in an age of groomed images, he was a natural.

credits

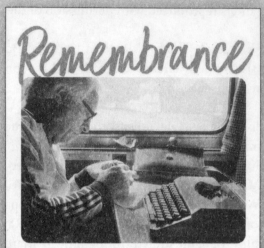